Eleanor of Aquitaine
The Young Life

by Mark Richard Beaulieu

THE ELEANOR CODE : BOOK 1

The Cover for Alienor
Eleanor born as Alienor in 1124, died 1204

Alienor imaged for 1137 was synthetically created in 2011 by a nine-month generative process on a computer called a Macintosh using the software code from a program called Photoshop. An electrical current of 60 hertz powered the computer, display, and digital pen to make the picture and write the novel. The subject is a composite of many women that time gave chance to create.

I shall describe the cover for those unable to see, yet able to hear.

The face is of a Caucasian thirteen-year-old female, although to some, she appears fifteen. Her hair, a mix of vital colors crimson and blonde, starts thickly as a braided crown that runs over her shoulders down her back, uncut since she was born. It runs to her ankles. Dark red waves float wildly in the dark behind. Her temple strands tuck behind her bare listening ears. She wears earrings of pure crystal.* Alienor's right eyelid scar and her genealogical portrait are detailed in the chapter 'Lief and Liege.' For more, listen there.

Her dress is ambiguous, a multi-color stitch-work map on cream-white linen, brought up to her white silk scarfed neck. On her figure are drawn crayon color rivers and castles; some imply tattoos. Two blue serpentine rivers suggest a feminine form; one crosses her vocal cords and stops at her chin. The castle-cities have their legends spelled backward. Her capital city Poitiers spells forward, as does Fontevrault by her right shoulder. Under Poitiers, in a faint mist, runs the rim of a scarlet satin guard for her red-horsehair belt. Rivers and castles come from the style of the ancient William Wey crusader hand map. Gray folds of its separation appear as either an upside-down sword or a crucifix, centered on Poitiers.

Alienor stands before a star field night. Two bright stars align with her eyes and ears, the largest on her heart side. The star spacing is apparently random, derived from deep space telescope images. The sky holes filter the color glass rose cathedral window of Saint-Denis. Up close, they shine intensely as jewels. The unfiltered stained glass skirts along the bottom edge of the cover where a panel runs a stitch-frame of the ivory-tone Bayeux tapestry. Ghostly gray garden shadows fall on her dress-map. These are silhouettes of lavender and rose with leaves that look like flying birds. Large type in small caps reads 'Eleanor of Aquitaine.' Under it, 'The Young Life.' The author line reads 'Mark Richard Beaulieu.'

The top right garden flower bouquet welcomes the reader to open the cover.

---

*Note: The earrings are based on the ancient Merovingian crystal spheres stolen and returned to Saint-Denis in 1974. Vigée Lebrun painted similar gems in her self-portrait at the Kimbell Museum. The painting, remarkable for the dimensionally vivid skin, can only be appreciated, just as a person, in person. The impossible red baby mouth shares with the Alienor portrait: lips parted barely showing teeth; the lower lip thrust and cleft, as if in the act of saying 'live.'

Dedication to The Young Life

To those a thousand years ago, and to those a thousand years from now, whom I hope will possess a colossal dictionary defining only one word. People never tire knowing its many definitions and at every age, often find missing their sense in it, thereby giving further meaning to the spell of love.

———

For Joanna who stirred my heart with her first smile,
attracting me to how accomplished women come to be.

———

Als das Kind Kind war, wußte es nicht, daß es Kind war, alles war ihm beseelt ...

When the child was a child it did not know that it was a child, everything was soulful ...

– Peter Handke
Lied Vom Kindsein / Song of Childhood

The ultimate test of a moral society is the kind of world that it leaves to its children.

– Dietrich Bonhoeffer

Eleanor of Aquitaine - The Young Life

Printed in the United States of America
Set in Adobe Garamond Pro with Times New Roman
First Printing: March 2012, revised October
Second printing: April, September, November 2013
Third printing: March, June, December 2014
Fourth printing: April, May, June, July, November 2015
Fifth printing: January, February, October 2016
Sixth printing: November 2017
Seventh printing: August 2018
Eighth printing: December 2019

ISBN: 978-1480147362

Eleanor of Aquitaine - The Young Life

also known in its first printing as:
Alienor: The Young Life of Eleanor of Aquitaine

Volume One of The Eleanor Code | Alienor
145,398w–312p| v584| 6x9-print-Amazon print

www.eleanorofaquitaine.net
markbrand@me.com

Contents

Eleanor's early family

Eleanor's Family at age 6 in 1130

○ Marriage
◎ Marriage with children
♡ Union with children
◀ Deceased by 1130 (start of *The Young Life*)
◢ Deceased by 1137 (end of *The Young Life*)

ERMENGARDE

AIMERY

DANGEROSSA

WILLIAM 9

PHILLIPA

HUGH

RAUL DE FAYE

ADELAIDE

SYBILLE

HENRI

AENOR

WILLIAM 10

RAYMOND

AGNES

PETRONILLA

ELEANOR

WILLIAM

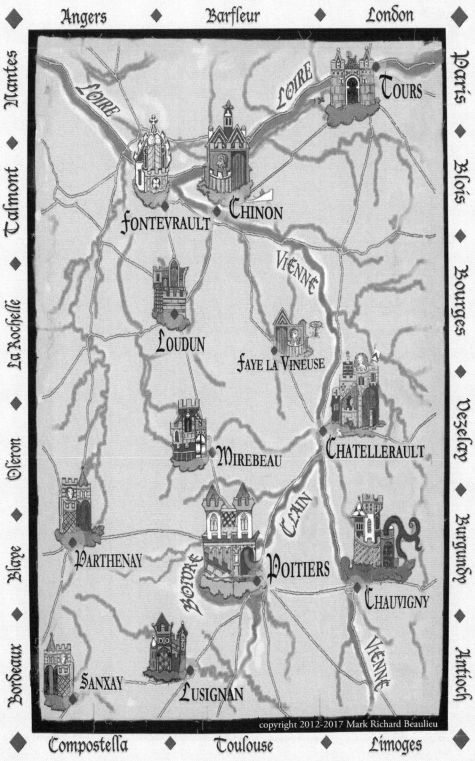

The many-rivered Aquitaine capital Poitiers and nearby castle tribes

Angers ◆ Barfleur ◆ London

Nantes

Paris

Talmont

Blois

LOIRE

LOIRE

TOURS

Bourges

La Rochelle

FONTEVRAULT

CHINON

VIENNE

Oleron

LOUDUN

FAYE LA VINEUSE

Vezelay

Blaye

MIREBEAU

CHATELLERAULT

Burgundy

PARTHENAY

CLAIN

BOIVRE

POITIERS

CHAUVIGNY

Bordeaux

SANXAY

VIENNE

Antioch

LUSIGNAN

copyright 2012-2017 Mark Richard Beaulieu

Compostella ◆ Toulouse ◆ Limoges

7

Prologue

ELEANOR OF AQUITAINE did not know she could change the world. Few caught in her charms could ever guess – her enemies would never believe – that she and her kin court would travel the world, and in time, transform humankind in a fundamental way.

In the twelfth century of the Christian era, when prosperous Aquitaine governed the western region of the Franks, Eleanor was conceived. She could not guess these were medieval times, but then, what person knows into which era they will come into being?

Troubadours set verse to meter while a trove of children twirled through a forest of whirls into bony-kneed youth. The little nobs called themselves hrad; in our time known as rad: a hasty eager elated soul, always ready and quick, as had been its meaning five hundred years prior to her birth. Playing the tongue of the times, hrads were hreds, for the most hrad had tinges of red hair or the full flame itself. The citizens of Poitiers, the capital of the region, hailed the lot 'girls,' including the male. Aquitaines knew that up to the count of years on two hands plus two fingers, a typical female is taller, stronger, and smarter in play. 'Boy' was a title the male earned later on; you'll see. This was the age of troubadours and personal music when water mills drove automatic machines. Rivers, the power of all things, propelled Aquitaine forward, bringing Europa's first light renaissance.

We were all one pink race in the sky blue age. From the milky billow, we unborn angels descended bloody wild – curious and ready to play. Climbing the birdsong trees, we surveyed silvery childhood, unaware how much was brought to luster by our mothers and fathers. Parents afforded that their little ones enjoy, at least briefly, more freedom than they ever had.

Living in such a domain in the year 1130, Amira, a hrad of eight-springs, experienced a day of liberty the same day her father lost his; a day by the waterwheel, the day she broke open the rock and found the fire, the day Amira first discovered Spark.

—◦◦◦—

1130 – 1131
The Summoners

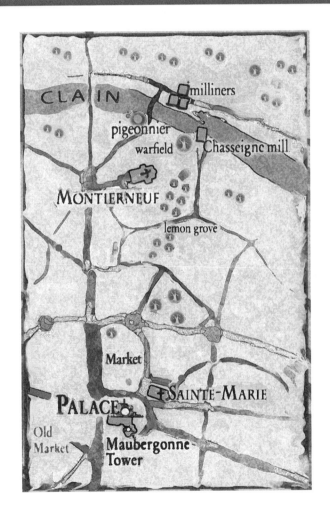

First Readers

The story of 'Alienor' does not begin with her. Only true friends of her age could find her among the rivers and the rocks, hidden in the vital play of curious youth. There, in the wild the causes by which this little girl would become the famous Eleanor of Aquitaine bubbled into her making.

When this princess, long dead, was fairy-high, she was guided from childhood by a chain of being as human's once called their existence. Back then, one forged the curious mettle of self – one's code – as rings wrought to links of chain mail. And so, her truest friends entered the Age of Alienor, for better — or for worse.

Stone and Water

The law, the fear, was coming fast.

It was as if her father whispered in her ear, 'hide the woman.' Amira, a girl of eight springs, pressed the stone fertility figurine she'd been playing with into the soil floor of the workshop. Hastily, she spread the floor reeds between the trestles of her father's alder-wood table and concealed herself. Iron chains echoed down the palace's stone corridor leading to them. Her heart beat in her throat. The blood in her round attentive ears throbbed.

"Heed! You are summoned! Godswoondz-yer-wish't?"

Grinding heels halted. The toes of her father's hunting boots held fast. Amira bravely crawled backward out from under the tracing table, wanting to help. Rising in the dawn-dark room, peeking through long waves of auburn hair, Amira lifted her eyes over the rumpled charts, ready to take in the frightening scene.

Two giant bearded Summoners scowled.

Not at her, but at her father. "Paul Neas!" They pointed. Amira was invisible as most children are to adults. In a verdant mantle, with a clean-shaven face, father glanced down at her, formed his mouth into a shape that said 'wolves,' and pressed a finger to his lips. Ignoring their taunts and iron clamps, he let the Summoners seize his charts. Bending low, the men darkened the archway as they noisily shepherded him out the door, his shoulder-length hair flowing behind.

Into the chill of cocks and crows, Amira would have chased the summoners, but her father had given the forest sign for wolves: be still, be calm, stay invisible. Be confident, show no fear! Summoners shackled a body on the spot, then dragged you off for reasons unknown to a secret court. With anger now greater than fear, Amira found small comfort that her father was not beaten like the other fathers. He did not behave like a victim; he led with his heart, his head held high. His spirit in her soul sent Amira running. "Mother must know!"

~

"Elixirs! Restorers of Youth!"

Helena Neas bartered with the herb peddler in the busy February market, new to the Citadel Poitiers. Leaning forward eye-to-eye, the swarthy-faced man repeated plainly as if it were an answer to her question about his goods, "Elixirs, restorers of youth." The merchant knew that if he knitted his thick brows and said a thing often enough, everyone believes, everyone buys. It was the best thing The Church taught him, and Ian Chaenus embodied the lesson.

"Elixirs, Restorers of Youth!"

Helena watched him entice others. She casually brought her wavy light auburn hair into a knot over her head as she considered a purchase; she wanted to believe the claims of the former sacrist. The deal was no deal when "Mother! Mother!" running up, her panting daughter came, putting worry into words. Helena hid her fear, even when told twice; looking down, her throat tightened. "Dear, there is nothing we can do."

The herb seller gave token sympathy, "Somp-nours..." chewed a bit, "Damisels, ts'way o'the world," and spat. "Live in fear of the Lord."

"In all ways," Helena replied.

Amira gave a hard look to the man eying her mother, giving a zealous look upon her neck.

"To the river now, I have your satchel," Helena minded.

"Wait," Amira said and ran back to her father's workshop. She quickly returned with the buried stone woman hidden up her sleeve. "Thank you, thank you," Helena said, putting it in the satchel, knowing and unable to tell her daughter that if the church found such idols, her husband would be stoned without mercy. This double 'thank you' puzzled Amira. It was said as if her mother owned the figure. Amira owned it; she collected them. Since ancient times, their Pictone tribe venerated female fertility figurines. Though careful to conceal it, Amira did not know why she had to; Father had given it like a gift. This stone figure looked at from say, a bird's point of view, was just a perch-stop gone from a dig by a river. For the arrested Paul Neas, this relic, this quaint doll that meant so much to his curious daughter, had to removed to clear a foundation. He was building the future — one for very special birds.

The two walked north from the market under the Prime sturdy Elm, buoyant Alder, and tall Linden entering a grove of bud-green lemon trees. Helena avoided other passers-by who might overhear them. Swiftly they dashed by nodding confessor priests receiving souls at the Basilica Montierneuf, and head for the watermill.

"What is happening, mother?"

For Helena, the answer to her daughter's question was a thing greater than her husband being taken – the lief of Amira; how to tell her – it was not belief; it was lief, the living root of love and life, her ever-becoming self. She did not want her daughter to know evil; the crazy things adults had made of the world, a belief increasingly shared by Aquitaine parents. Helena and Paul put their life into their three children, but only Amira survived the pox. Helena wanted to protect Amira and yet have her enjoy the entirety of childhood. "It is hard to explain adult ways," she answered.

The River Clain rippled around Poitiers, clean with newly thawed mountain ice. At the grand Oak tree by the pounding water wheel of the mill, they crossed a field and took a breath before crossing the Clain bridge.

Running twenty steps further, Amira said, "Father's tower," and walked around it. Half-built, the white stones were cut of fresh lime-rock. The curves fit as perfect as cathedral quarry stones. The masonry courses reached the height of Amira's shoulders with space left for a doorway. While digging this, her father found the fertility model.

Helena turned right to cross the bridge and halted. She gestured she had something to say. Amira ran and put her hand into her Ma's. Together, they turned away from the castle-city and creaked up the mid of the pontine span. It was Amira's stop, the place where little white rock birds gathered. After watching water flow around branches, Helena voided tremolos in her voice, "Enjoy being a girl. Father will be just fine." Her daughter looked up.

Amira scowled like a Summoner.

"What a horrible face!" Helena thought, *where did her girl learn such a grimace?* "Amira Neas! You give that face a rest! I am going to tickle it off you before it settles in." They played in little darts and jabs until Amira laughed. Helena said words as much to convince herself, "We must accept what we cannot change. The law has taken Paul. Let's not talk of this to anyone now."

"Why?"

"Talk of an arrested family member assumes guilt. Do you want me in a donjon, too?" Amira shook her head no. "These are fearful times to live in. You know how important your childhood is to father – live yours. He'll want to hear every detail when he returns." *Someday, let's hope*, Helena thought but didn't say.

Amira sighed forlorn, helpless as a floating branch taken by the river.

"If it helps, tell me what father did this morning. Quietly," Helena said, gripping the bridge rail. They scanned and double-checked. No one followed. The river's babble would cover their words.

"He gave me the silent wolf sign," Amira reenacted the gesture.

"You know Amira, when you hunt with your father, he sometimes has to stand and fight wild beasts. He gives you the sign, so when too many wolves appear, you will be calm and let them pass." Amira heard the strength return to her mother's voice and stretched up her arms for a hug. Helena knelt, cuddled her daughter, and gave from her heart long, long love.

They turned to study the tower below, cut of fresh limestone, the curves fitting as perfectly as cathedral quarry stones. Helena whispered, mouth to ear: "Your father started that tower by secret agreement with the ruler of Poitiers, the Duke of Aquitaine himself."

Amira was happy to be privy to the truth. This was the place where her father had dug up the stone woman, now in Amira's satchel. "Paul may not have had the Holy blessings of Paris. Chances are he broke some royal rule. There are so many laws we don't know."

"Why can't father do what he wants to do? He's a maker. He only does good."

"He does, doesn't he?" Pushing up Amira's little chin, Helena gave a kiss, and they crossed over to the other side of the river, hand-in-hand.

Like every Friday for the last six months, they crossed the Clain mill bridge, down to the dress-stitcher cottages, where they found fabrics, clothes-mending, weavers, and cooking advice. Amira avoided the porch, where the sewers sat. There she would be passed around like some kissing doll to have her red hair fussed over and rumpled. She was aware of her cuteness, but she was a hrad first.

Helena rejoiced seeing the bank of river-stones, glad the ice had melted. This is where her daughter loved to forage for special stones, and where Amira's mind would be taken off her father. She silently removed the stone goddess, lightening the satchel, to allow more room for her daughter's treasures to be gathered.

"Oh, to be your age, my rock-amour. The wind in your face, the golden sun rising. Look at that big sky! It brings the brightest ideas." Helena bent and handed over the worn leather bag.

Standing on her tip-toes and a quick kiss to her mother, Amira ran to the river bank of fresh rocks. The waterwheel on the other side turned with the power of the river. The satchel was light. *My stone woman, gone? Hmm, more room ... Mother. Nice.* Amira was smart about being a child and smart about rocks. Water became of ice, but stone was forever.

Father, a man who spoke less than she wished, always made her laugh. As she walked, his voice spoke to her vividly: 'Now the great thing about youth is you have no purpose. You are utterly useless to anyone. The gist of youth is to stay that way. Help out, but never show zeal, never become an expert, for others will see. You will be called on. Lay low out of sight, keep your mouth shut. Enjoy your freedom before you must do the purposes of others. A lesson there.' She loved his little secret lessons that always meant something more. Why would father, a hard worker in need of hands, fill her mind with good excuses to dodge his labors? Hmph. For Paul to be recognized as Aquitaine elder meant he had to create natural places for children. 'A lot goes into a playscape. Elders care as much as a Tooty laying out a garden for King Snooty. I'll tell you a secret; I build from memories of my own childhood.'

Satchel in hand, Amira swung forward, looking upon a rocky playscape. No elder had made that, yet for a sparking second, she wondered if a person could. Satchel in hand, she swung forward, humming a tune. She readied to play EXPLORE-FOR-NEW-ROCKS-TO-AMASS-A-FORTUNE. She could picture every rock she'd ever found, as real as the grip of her satchel. Ah, the blessed moment of emptiness before the chances of discovery. She knew it well. Facing the river fates, leather flap open, she closed her eyes.

Young Amira wished hard for a close friend. Her brothers and sisters had left their bodies to be spirits again; parents knew about these things and told Amira their spirits were with her. That was not the same as a real friend to laugh and play with. Wish over, she opened her eyes and surveyed the bank. Her time with father came back in voice. 'Get this, Amira. To make that mill wheel go fast as the river, workers built this dike. See how it forces water to the wheel? To do that, they built towers in the water. How? Board off the Clain, join lumber with pitch, as in our river boat. Masons dug deep to place stone footings for the dike wall. That is a keystone for a watch-gate.' She looked at the metal base plate and the tons of river-stones, ancient rocks hauled-up from the deep earth. The horde of stones lay glittering in the sun, unclaimed, untouched, all hers.

Amira skipped, excited as finding new money. Flat rocks with hairy white threads, one glorious blue, then many green marbles, red-veined slates, half-clears, and mud-coated shell shapes. The primeval secrets of the earth seemed visible only to rock-minded youth. 'Rock-amour,' Amira smiled.

She'd seen the best treasures at school. Cracked open, they revealed gem caves. Amira studied not the colorful insides but their gray outsides - now she could recognize the dull spheres in the field. She'd seen some good rocks in her day, small ones, though. The satchel grew heavy. Lots of noteworthy rocks here, but not one gray stone. Amira wished for one so big it took two to handle. Then she unwished it. Only one wish a day; she'd rather have the friend.

Then, there! A great lode! Amira danced. She squealed. "Uh oh" – down from the cottages, children ran. She darned herself double. She had ignored father's words about youth's sacred lesson: 'Never show glee when having real fun; it attracts others.' Now, a horde of flipping little children was jumping like kid goats, following in her footsteps. *If the tall ones don't get you, the small ones will.*

Fleeting legs footed along the bank, scooting off rock squirrels, flitting away rock pigeons. They bent in chants: "ba-Dump, ba-Dump" like charging horses; "Shoop, Shoop" like bands of archers. Little hands on little rocks clopped and thunked. Amira picked ever quicker. Plenty for all, but only the best for Amira.

The sun climbed higher in the blue sky Amira squinted at a silhouette in the sun, almost her size and red glowing hair bent over a large ochre rock. Let her have that rock, Amira thought. No way would she tell her secret: 'That's junk, not even a gray stone, don't even lift it.' Play dumb.

Amira was eager to see the colors of her harvest. On top of the dike, the water would be clear to wash off her rocks, and then she could really see. Rounding a quiet eddy created by the new dam, she dodged the weedy muck rushes, stepping quickly over the keystone plate. She pulled herself up the half-sized wall. The cut quarry stone smelled sweet as dusty limes. At her spot on the water, she spread the stones.

A big toad caught her eye. As it did some other wee girl on the bank whose game was hit-the-toad-with-a-skipper and THWACK! Amira's dress was wet. The big old frog jumped and SPLASH! Amira's dress was muddy wet. *Toads!*

"Sorry," the blonde tyke said.

More interesting to Amira was the red-haired, taller girl on the hill. *Bretagne or Basque?* Amira skipped back a good rock to the smaller, "thip thap thap." It sunk short. The little one returned a skip with truer aim THOOMP.

"You got me." Amira play-acted The Great Wound. "My name is Amira. What is yours?" With the noisy splash of the watermill wheel, the weak voice sounded like Al-itthh. Alice, Amira surmised. Alice was looking up to the taller.

About to put a rock under water, Amira studied her reflection. *Looking cherub and hrad,* she thought. As she dipped in her hands, cold grains gleamed; variegated purple, silver, red, and gold came alive. Glancing to the water's surface, Amira saw the reflection of the two other girls. Alice rippled, but the taller drew Amira's attention, lugging an ochre clay stone, the size of a cat. The upside-down girls paused to see the dance of their watery other-selves.

The one carrying the heavy rock fussed over it with Alice. *Sisters?* To better hear their words, Amira scooted back to the base of the dike. The rock-girl with red glowing hair had friendly eyes, brows bushy as a Bretagne boy. She seemed to suffer politely, twisting under the rock's weight. Hopping down, Amira came to aid the girl standing on a boulder. *A test to see if I can carry heavy weight,* she thought. A hrad challenge.

Giving Amira the rock to hold, she did not let go.

"It–" Amira began.

"Love it!" the other said.

A gleeful smirk rose on Amira's face. "Right. Love a rock?"

"I can tell you do, as I love water!" Holding the rock together —Amira thought What? The thing was not one bit heavy! The churlish tease needed no help at all! In fact, the rock was light as a ... gray cave stone? A tingle came over Amira. "There is something inside, something big!" The unwritten rules were: show no glee, never pull, never let go.

"What is that expression on your face?" puzzled the new hrad girl. "A smirk," Amira said, sizing her up. "Hmm," the other tried, winking, unable to make one.

Only one way to play it and both knew what to do – up and down. Amira raised the rock, peeping at her toes; the crash might hurt. She scooted her feet back. Up and down they went. The rock-girl peered intensely into Amira and said, "Smirk, you smell sweet as alder wood," looked past her and said firmly, "Watch! I have it!" She possessed the rock, carrying it with one arm. Hopping over the metal plate, she climbed the half wall, ran and skipped over Amira's satchel. At the mid of the dike she stopped.

By then, Amira noticed four things about the runner: definitely younger, longer hair, red and gold, sparkling deep eyes that had seen more of life, but then, socks. No hrad wore socks. The incongruity bothered Amira. What parent had silver for such things? Yet, there she stood, a girl in socks with a rock. As a river runs a mill, a fifth thing emerged. Amira was unable to name it. Her heart beat strongly, the sense of it alien; something of exotic intensity, immaculate, colorful and new. This person had some want about her. A friend to be? One thing for certain, there was no way Amira would fish out of the river any sock-wearing girl.

The great wheel turned the river. The sun was highest. The sock-wearing girl tipped up her heels and ran the dike, humming. Before Amira, with all her might, she threw the ochre-stone down to the metal plate. Strains of sound clapped as a bell. Time stilled. What happened was too rapid to see, too fast to tell. It contained everything possible and impossible in a rock.

<<Spark>>

Cracking a bright flash, the rock exploded in half. Pieces popped into the air, chips whirled into the water, splinters shone with the sun, shards spun to the earth. Silver light scattered in every direction as a blue flame leapt out. The girls gasped. The top sailed up and fell with a good kerchunk into the water, splashing Alice's dress. A flickering firestone sparked out to a far wall. The stone smoked; it smelled. Amazed at the totality, their ears ringing, the rock-thrower jumped down. "Smirk!" she pointed at a dripping splinter of blood below Amira's ear and smoothed it off like a bug bite.

"Spark!" Amira said of the phenomenon, "You are bleeding, too," and guided the rock thrower's fingers to a small gash on her right eyebrow. They clasped their bloody hands and grinned, shaking them.

"Sacred blood sisters, I guess," Amira said and they cleaned off in the stream.

Amira bent over to the rock the other two stepped back. Fascinating was the bottom piece. In the soft ochre layer were strange patterns of shells and fossilized things. Tiny dragon-dogs, maybe dragon-birds, shapes of no living creature ever known.

"See!" Amira turned but the two girls, Spark and Alice, had gone to their minding mothers at the top of the bank and left.

Amira looked over the scatter. Like a broken pot, odd shards were everywhere. The largest piece rippled in the water where Alice had stood. Crystals, long inside! She poured the water out of the helmet-shaped rock and set it to dry. At the edge of her sight smoked a large reddish fragment. Walking to get it, the exotic Spark was fresh on her mind. Amira scanned so as not to miss any odd gem. She picked up the red rock and brought it to her nose - strange odor. Big, it fit her hand.

Striking the longest spindle in the crystal helmet, the red stone flinted, firing sparks, smoking the potent 'broke-open-rock' smell. The struck piece came loose – clear Aquitaine quartz tinted blue, as large as her thumb. In the sun, two pure gold glints sparkled within. She slid the quartz and red fire-rock into her special-sewn pocket, the best place for treasures. Hmm, she pondered, rock globes did not have to be gray; a lesson there.

Helena motioned her up; time to go. Making quick work, Amira gathered the day's horde to her satchel and ran jumping: "Let's do this again." She was too excited to hear, "You're bleeding." Mother wiped her beloved child's cut. Between diligent swipes, Amira scanned the rocks on the river bank. The ochre rock was one of a kind.

· · ·

Reaching the shade of the great Oak at the watermill, Helena cleaned Amira's muddy dress. Off to the market, mother knocked on the mill-house door leaving her girl with the other children. Amira lay along the mill wall; satchel hid behind. The sun-warmed stone rose a pleasant heat through her wet smock. Children shouted. The wheel lifted half-buckets of water to the sky. A harsh sour odor wafted from the mill, a grinding place that usually smelled of toasted wheat.

The mill-house door opened. Out walked Reyna Chasseigne, the miller's daughter, every young male's vision of girlish beauty. Thin with long blonde hair, a girl of eight springs, her bangs reached to the middle of her pretty chestnut eyes; a sweet berry smile glowed from within. Behind Reyna, two knaves followed, older but shorter than the girls. All four wore the same five pieces: a smock, simple belt, under-breeches, and buskins on their feet.

Strong Arno Allant was everyone's friend with his clean husky looks and dark hair. Shorter Calbi Lebeau was from down south; Amira had met him a moon ago. Just as she remembered: thin, light golden curly hair, an impish darling like herself. Amira was sure she could rub both of their noses in the dirt.

Sometimes best friends begin as rude strangers. You might start off on the wrong foot or bump into the one you are fated to know. Arno pushed Calbi into Amira. "Lovebirds!" They both fell over. Amira righted herself. "Well, pleased to meet you again Calbi," as she pushed him off. Calbi huffed at her, and brought himself up, hand on knee whining, "Why'd you do that, Arno?" Amira knew how to deal with this. She sprang up like an Amason woman and stomped her mad foot at Arno. He blinked. She called it: "Flincher!"

Arno spotted a dead thistle-finch and tossed it, leaves and all, "Fincher!" She did not know what the bloody thing was and dodged. This put Amira on the wrong foot. Putting a hrad on the wrong foot was all it took for Amira to shove Reyna into Arno and launch the ritual that other children in the field had fallen into; namely, refighting all the wars of the last four hundred years.

In the grass between mill and Basilica, the tall girls picked up whipping sticks, bark shields, and stones to celebrate famous battles. They ran fast upon the little knaves who gathered the same weapons in retreat. The sides charged and dashed, one bowstick beating high on the other – the towering hrads testing naive bravery.

Losers often threw rocks, a cheat by the rules of bodily war. Stones could be thrown at your feet to make you jump – and knaves did so, inciting devilish dances into the tall girls – but no sharp rocks, no cuts, no crying, because the play would be over, and someone would get a tanning. A code for their rough play: 'Cause no blood – bring no adults.'

Usually, battle escalated for obvious reasons – a jealous stick whacking, an out-shouting, a swearing-dare, but things were different today with the masters of play. Grand wrestling feuds bored the girls, for a girl could lick a knave every time, and there was little honor in hollow victories. These were further unwritten codes of play of their own young chivalry.

Dust danced around the clamor of girls. Every child flew into the whirling caldron of play. Some came to fight the war of their imaginations; more acted out the campfire songs of their warrior clans, a few contended for beautiful Reyna.

Basking in her glory, Reyna surveyed Poitiers from the steps of her mill.

Amira asked, "Men fork heaps of tattered clothes into your mill. What are you milling?"

"We're making paper with a new water machine," Reyna smiled. "You know what paper is." Amira had held parchment, but never soft paper. Like all fine things, paper was made in another land. Reyna led Amira through an open door. The milling-room grindstone sloshed old rags into a mash, the vinegary odor of soiled laundry. A wheel rounded the trough, turned by a spindle-mix of fingers called 'gears,' all driven by water, the power of all things. Shouting over the grind and groan, Reyna's tall mother, taller with a broom, minded the workmen: "No curses! There are young girls!" She looked down to Amira, saying in shouts, "We're! Making! Paper! Trying!"

Amira tugged on the woman's skirt, "The gears are wrong! You need cams!"

The mill woman chittered a laugh, looking down. "I am sure you are right. Well, you two go play with the slimy slough." In all honesty, what could young ones, especially a girl, possibly know about the new machines?

The girls left, closing the noise behind the door. Reyna looked as disappointed as her mother trying to make paper. Amira consoled, "Good always come from bad chances." Reyna molded gray pulpy fibers on a mesh and said, "In a few hours it hardens and turns light." Then she smiled, "More for us to play with?" Amira looked at the shapes drying on the clothesline, thinking *'What can I make on the fun side of trouble?'* The light on Reyna's pretty profile gave her a mischievous idea.

"You sit still in this chair." In minutes, a thick wet sheet of papier-mâché covered the mill daughter's face. While drying, Amira educated her on gears and wood grain. Reyna, smelling like dirty socks, muttered muffled interests. Then off came Reyna's mask with a high nose, pointy chin, and bulgy eyes that Amira poked out. For the mouth, she pried open the jaw and shaped the pulp into dangling teeth. They bloodied up the mouthpiece with weaver stains and hung the head on the line. Amira discovered a strange delight. In dutifully washing Reyna's face and combing her hair, Amira was immensely pleased to bring her beauty back.

The two girls went to the stone porch to view the boys acting out The Hundred Knaves War. SHE was back and with no socks - barefooted Spark pinning down Calbi and Arno, one under each knee, and taking pleasure in the act. Rubbing dirt on one and then the other, she let the knaves up to prove themselves worthy with a bout of bowsticks. Spark lifted her bark shield and on it was drawn a chalk outline of a woman's body, or so it seemed. Spark the Lion fought in the girl tradition, the unwritten code of never being a bully, but firmly putting down a knave, who often left in a huff.

Strong Arno let himself be overpowered by girls, a kind of chivalry to show being in service of girls' power. He was not timid; he just loved girls' edgy spirits. As long as the girls were feisty like Spark the Lion and he was feisted upon, he would leave in a humpf and a grin. Such codes as these made everyone stronger and the games of child-play to go on forever. Well, they might have, except for the tall ones with their infernal bell tolling – loudest thing in all creation. Every child sensed that the rope clapper's pull was almost at hand.

Amira beheld the pathetic sight: knaves gasping for breath from a simple bout of stick and shout. However, they always had enough breath to roll over and gaze upon Reyna and her perfect comb-flowing sunny hair.

On steps under the mill's great Oak tree, Reyna surveyed a field of poor warrior pilgrims, valiantly fallen in front of her castle. She leaned into the sun, radiated her smile, gave regal gestures, and lo, the knights were revived, seeking her approval. She rarely drew a bowstick or got muddy, and everyone liked her that way – Reyna being beautiful.

Amira stumble-kicked her way back to the drying room infuriated that Spark, not she, had wrestled Arno and Calbi down. She unhooked her paper berserking mask to put on, but the stuff was damp. It would serve some other cruel purpose. The rocks! Bounding out, holding the mask she shimmied over the wall and touched her gems. Spark would love to see her discoveries. Amira tipped to her toes and scanned the war field. Running up the hill was red-haired Spark toward the Basilica of Montierneuf – Why did she remember that name or that mill gears were wrong, and why remember cams? Her father's words, his acts, were strong in her mind. Her heart felt bad as she recalled the morning, the summoners.

Amira melted her back to the mill wall. Father once spoke about the meeting at Montierneuf Basilica about water machinists. He took her to the mills and showed how timber was shaped to lumber. Vivid in her mind was his cheerful vigor, the powerful water, and the new machines with cutting gears, levers, and hammering cams that he explained so well.

Watching the great waterwheel scoop and turn, Amira filled with an emptiness she had not felt before. It was not the sadness of knowing it was time to go; it was something deeper. She was angry that Reyna's mother disbelieved her about gears, but that was not causing this feeling. As Amira rooted for causes for her sadness, her legs bore her up.

There in the distance in front of the basilica was sockless, shoeless Spark being preached to by a cackle of mothers. The goings-on were unclear. Followers of sects with no temple often assembled at the Basilica. Maybe Spark was one of those new faiths like Calbi's 'good people.' Montierneuf likely had mass for an old soul, a soul Spark probably knew, judging by the scolding, dress brushings, heart-crossings, and stern faces. Whoa, a stomp, an impish grin, and – was she wagging her little finger at the tall ones? Oh, what a hrad! What lesson was she suffering there? Amira made out the words grinning as if Spark were here hand on heart emoting: 'Fun, love, and trouble. Living is worth more than a mass for the dead!' *Did she really say that?*

Bells struck all over Poitiers. Each loud church chimed its own chain of tones. Amira put on Spark's fire-eating grin that withstood any ordeal. *Let's live!*

It was time to wagon north with Ma.

Home to the orphanage, back home. Soon enough.

•

Wagon wheels rumbled and shifted on well-traveled dirt. Amira sat high as she could, with her mother, looking down the open road. Both gave thanks for Aquitaine's blue sky, a strong horse, working wagon, and a road without thieves.

"Why the smile?" Helena asked. Her daughter confessed, "I might have met a friend today." In dips and rolls, the girl showed off her fiery red stone. Excitedly, she told of hrad Spark, Alice and the toad, the exploding rock, being shoved into Calbi, Arno's Finch, her mill-gear advice, and making pretty Reyna's head into a paper ghoul.

"Amira, more happens to you in half a day then happens to me in a month." It was quite true. Time moved slowly for youth so they could get more done in a day.

Touching the Aquitaine quartz in her pocket, Amira felt some form of warm luck. It was the luck of the few, the luck of making her own chances happen, the luck of having Aquitaine parents. They were fair, loved her, yet stood off to allow a world of unbridled curiosity to grow. Her parents gave Amira a clear sense of childhood, a want of her own to explore and know. She put her hand on her belly to settle a hollow sadness. It was not entirely hunger.

"Father, where is he?"

"I don't know, dear. Let's hope they tell us, maybe in a few weeks."

Until the end of time, she might as well say. Amira understood the present, even pasts, but not futures, not much beyond a day. How could mother give up?

Helena read her daughter's face. "Amira, we cannot change the world. I will petition the abbess. Now, how about a small dinner? No time to stop."

Between rumbles and bumps, Amira broke out apples, cheese, and bread. Hunger satisfied, Amira's head shifted steadily with the bends of the road, resting on her mother's arm. By the time they reached the fortress keep of Mirebeau, she'd fallen to dreams. As the wagon rattled under the massive watchtower, guards whistled catcalls at Helena. She held the reigns, firmly shaking the horses down the open rolling road.

The wagon slowed, and Amira awoke to a cold, cloudy sky. Over her legs was the soft fur blanket tinged with alder smoke that Father had made. She pictured him in his bark-boat, a trapper and furrier before they arrived last fall. Amira remembered exploring forests with him, at every turn always new things to learn. She pulled the warmth to her chest.

Vair, she loved vair– the checkered pattern of an animal's fur coat alternating in gray-blue and pure white. Nature provided rare appearances of this pattern on wolfhound, horse, or large ermine called stoat. Royals often wore its imitation stitched out of squirrel bellies of mini-vair, called miniver. Paul sold stippled miniver to royals, but Amira had a true vair, one of the last of its kind. On a long expedition, her father had found the dead creature, no longer able to take hot summers. The giant stoat was now extinct for future humans to know, but this pelt survived, the size of a prince's full mantle. Father told everyone it had flaws, but none she could see. The hide amply flowed, soft from neck to ankles, in eight rows and columns, smelling musky and giving a pleasant warmth.

Loudun. The letters carved large in stone declared the village they rolled into. The place bothered Amira. She had met girls who ran away from the harsh convent, escaping to Fontevrault orphanage, thankful for the smallest of things. A sign pointed 13 miles ahead to Fontevrault Abbey, their destination; another 31 miles back to Poitiers. Amira longed to be home already.

At the Abbey of Fontevrault, girls and boys were treated equally, unlike the rest of Europa, which only educated males. Why even nuns and monks shared housing under the same roof! Amira liked going to school, and she felt as if one enormous playground had been built for her at the abbey. Her mind filled with orphanage adventure, hospital singing, the open chapel, toys made at the workshops, cottage games.

Just then, Helena snapped her fingers. "This girl you describe as Spark was at the Abbey orphanage with her sister and brother a few days ago. They just moved there. I think she likes to learn, too." Amira could not hide her thrill. , *Fun with new friends? It is going to be a great summer!*

Helena leaned back and let the cart drive itself. The horses, knowing the way to the water trough at the livery stable, trod the cobbles of Loudun. A sad knave clad in white alter cloth took the reins. The stable was closed; they had to liven the horses at the high church. To Amira, the boy looked as unhappy as children on the first day at the orphanage. She gave him a green marble. He returned a smile and guided the wagon to the sluice behind the church. She looked to a high window where a churchman in a red cap and wealthy dress stared down, looking with interest at her and her mother. Amira turned away not wanting to think about any of this now.

Then she saw. "The birds! Look at the birds!" Mother was already smiling. A swirl of small gray and white chirpers fluttered in and out of their high story apartments. They lived in a perfectly finished round tower like the one by the dress-stitcher's mill bridge, her father was building that she'd seen this morning. So father was making a birdhouse. Birds, what was father doing with birds?

The wagon pulled out of Loudun; the abbey a bell-toll ahead. Something troubled the eight-springer, and she was having a devil of a time figuring it out: something about fancy clothes, high clergymen, kings, and titled persons. They made her stomach turn, just like the cross and red velvet of the summoners that took her father this morning; like the wealthy priest now in the high-tower watching her and mother get excited about birds. Royal blib-thee-blab made no sense to a young mind. That could be one of her hrad codes. 'If it made no sense to a child, it was a trick and likely evil.' The high, the holy, the powerful were not common like her. Long-titled wealthy old ladies, the lemon suckers who lived at the end of the orphanage, were visited by dreadful children with even longer titles. Unfriendly, these children never had mud-fun. They lorded their haves over the have-nots, telling how the world works but not as it should. High-nosed heirs, braggers with cruel sneers. All lording titles were evil, thought Amira.

Maybe one exception.

Last moon, 'Chevalier Jofree de Rancon, Lord of Taillebourg arrived. A hill of hay name, yet Amira remembered the name exactly. Perhaps because the man had a gentle side, as good men do. The young lord spoke, arm-on-knee straight to her, like she was a real person. When she told of her deceased siblings, he expressed sorrow and gave comforting advice, the type of advice she would like to give someday. He brought his kinsman, gold-haired Calbi Lebeau, to attend school at the orphanage until harvest-time.

It was dark when they pulled through the gates. Helena let go of the reigns. The cart drove itself, horses pulling hard to the barn knowing where the feed lay. Amira jumped off.

A flicker of candle came from the cottage window, where grandmother Lorraine was waiting up. She had no news of father. Pulling meat bits and vegetable from the pot over the fireplace, Lorraine asked how the city was. Amira replayed the day; dunking buttered pot bread into a savory stew. Pruney skinned Grandma's face lit up as she told stories of her girlhood pranks. Amira's laughs temporarily cured Lorraine's worries for her lost son, Paul. After a face scrubbing, teeth-ragging, and hair-combing, Amira turned to the bed.

After Helena had unsaddled the horses and tended to the farm animals, she came to tuck the blanket up to her daughter's chin. "Imagine father in a safe place. Mind, no talk of him. Arrest brings suspicion. What would father Paul's wish be?"

Amira dragged out a sigh. "I know... Ma. You are like a road-man and me the talking parrot." She pretended her mother's voice. "Enjoy your childhood, brah. Enjoy your childhood, brah." After an approving chuckle Helen said, "You do sound like me," and gave her heart-long love.

Owls hooted into the night. Amira sat up. My Aquitaine gem! Fetching it, she admired the gold flecks sparkling like starlight. From her bed, Amira bent to stand her head to the floor and placed the gem in a cedar box. She plopped her head back to the pillow. This was her room, once filled with a brother and sister. They were gone now, a painful death from the water pox. Rancon and Calbi's people taught her to find the good in things. In a strange way, she felt she had. Amira would live her siblings lives for them. Coming to mind was the sun-lined silhouette of Spark. How would she fit into her pranks? Maybe Spark had her own. Socks? Amira chuckled turning on her belly, flipping over the pillow to its cool side. She threw her arms under and hugged it, hoping her father was sleeping well. Soon after counting the wounds of the day, she found sleep in the joyous place where dreams cross back and forth, between the backroads of yesterdays and the bends of tomorrows.

•

The Birdsong Trees

"Potburns! It is hot today!" Six-springs Spark stood in the fiery sun looking up into a great tree full of chirping birds. She pulled out the back of her smock to cool in a self-made breeze. One long yesterday ago at the river, she played with her sister and now up there, somewhere, climbed a promising new friend.

High in the limbs of an evergreen oak tree, Amira looked off to the Abbey, its black slate roof shining like silver. She incanted to the well-washed girl below: "Woe be to those who suffer the dead quiet heat."

Amira spied Spark cranking her head trying to find her. Spark knew nothing about her imprisoned father or the death of her siblings. It was a hrad's code not to speak of such things, but to play and make crimes. Time to muddy her innocent friend and teach the hrad ways.

"King of the world!" Amira said.

"Don't you mean Queen of the world?"

"King sounds better!"

"Smirk, you don't have a beard."

"Don't be calling me Smirk, I am Amira and I'm the King. Come up and see. We'll be king and queen of the world. Harken to my history of larks."

Spark shouted up. "You know birds?"

"No – pranks, larks. My grandma did them. She threw cats at birds. Say, bring up some stones, we can hit the chirpers easy from up here."

"Why? Birds make song!"

"True, so what? Hot huh? Grandma says February used to be a snow month. She dressed snowmen in under-breaches–"

"That makes no sense. Have you ever seen snow, Amira?"

Amira looked down from her perch. "Not in my life. We live in warmer times. That's good. Mountain melt makes mill-saws run faster. Now don't think of the river, you need to learn to work in the heat. You'll see."

"Time was when..." Spark play-pretended wisdom, pacing around, hand on the trunk, "Grand-mère never knew mill machines, but today my father can't imagine the world without them and their time-saving labor."

"Mine too," said the voice from the high trees, busy climbing.

"Never in history has there been so much music! In my grandfather's time, there were only church songs until he started singing. Now we live in a world of troubadours. Grand-père sounded like this: 'Gaw, harsh to hear men chant-a-moaning. I'd rather sing of love straight from my heart to yours, dear.' "

A great laugh came from the tree. "That was good, Spark."

Footing the crotch of a limb, Amira climbed over her friend on the ground, side-saddled a wide branch, and dangled her feet. Spark puffed the front of her smock to cool herself. Amira's back was wet, too. Pretending to be cool on a hot sticky day, she baited her friend, "No breeze, no mercy, so? I don't want to go to the river; do you?"

Looking up, Spark slapped the high bark of the happy tree. "Course not." Spark liked the simpler talk of her friend and learning the colorful hrad ways. This morning her parents had set her free to play with two-year-older Amira, come what may. If she avoided trouble, they could play more.

"See me wearing socks?" Amira challenged.

Spark squatted fast as a squirrel, yanking them to a ball in her fist. Eyeing the tree-path, she ascended rapidly. Birds flitted away. Laddering up past Amira, tossing the socks to her lap, she grabbed a high limb, swung out, "Higher than the King," then stomped on Amira's branch to unsettle her. *Fast learner*, thought Amira. Riding the high limb, Spark could make out Fontevrault chapel, a place of eternal hammering and chiseling. Men and women left the Abbey refectory, fanning one another, walking into the shade of tall trees.

"Birds don't sing up here when you stand in their bower."

"Spark! Hrads don't talk that way."

"I can say what I want, king. Aye! Look how I bend greenwood branches. They never snap in spring."

"Heed! Talk like a heartless criminal. Today's crime is to scare people to death."

"Really? Where?"

"The King's road."

"No, not the tradeways." Spark peeled bark, decorating her friend below.

"More money in them," Amira assured, brushing the bark-wood off.

"Too much traffic. Might get hurt," Spark cautioned, dusting down tree ants.

Odd point, but true, thought Amira, stepping her foot in a crotch, clutching a limb with one hand and warding off her friend's raining homage with the other. Horse-heavy roads held risk. A hoof could flatten a skull. "Let's start easy and work up."

Spark said distinctly, "I will nod to that," ponying her neck in self-affirmation.

This assured daintiness struck Amira as alien. She shouted to the branch above. "The backroads to the edge of Loudun are best."

The novice shouted down, "That's outside of Fontevrault. Will we be safe?"

"Shoot arrows! What's the point of a venture without thrills? Trust me, we have to go where no one knows us, and we can't get told on. Knave protection is all we need. Let's go get 'em." With that, the hrads banged down the branches, jumped to the ground, and went in search of the knaves.

Calbi and Arno wanted to cool off in the river, but the girls goaded them into their mischief. Hearing of the crime of scaring people to death, the knaves puffed, "That's easy," unsure of what they were talking about.

With four sticks they beat the bushes southwest on the wagon trails from Fontevrault to Loudun. There was some playful butt-cracking – walking, putting an arm-around, then mid-stride, flipping a sudden heel to your neighbor's rump. Some rough shin-digging, too – scraping one's foot on the other's lower calf to put down a walk.

"To be mean and criminal you gotta act like a man." Amira's teeth snarled like a lipless hound. "To scare people to death, act dead on the road. Poor soul comes by and screams in terror! You two Girls, just watch Spark and me. We're going to show you how hrads get things done."

Arno said, "We're not girls." Calbi joined, "We're hrads like you."

"You might be. After you do a crime. First show us your scars, that's half of being hrad." Amira and Spark showed their head scars, the knaves showed knees. Amira rolled her eyes. "You want to be like us? You gotta know how to put people on; scare'm to death, be ready for what happens next; that's the fun: the doings, the chances." Amira meaned-up, showing off her snarling skills. She spat and challenged them. "What're we going to do?"

"Scare'm to death!" the male cohorts cried.

"I shall scare people to death."

The precise, delicate way Spark said this brought roars of laughter. Even Spark laughed at herself. Amira eyed the scrupulous kidder, then continued the drill, demonstrating her best stunt falls: "Do like when you get hit by an ox, when you gut out a stomach-pox, or axe a hard tree – show some misery." Out-acting one another, they pretended at having done this before, although no one had.

Leave it to the tall girls to think of everything – water flasks, a sausage, bread cake, and red goo. Not being the season for blood-red berries, Amira brought rotten beets. But the prize was Spark's - a nasty red pig bladder. Where did she find such a thing? She dangled the big thing in their faces on a hooked pole. They touched it, taking turns as they walked on and on.

Hearing the church bell, Amira said, "We've walked a league, time for drinks."

Calbi said, "A league? What's that?"

"Don't know anything, do you?" Arno replied, giving a what-village-are-you-from look. Amira knew the way of the woods, and that tribes measured the world in different ways. "Calbi, a league is how far a man walks from bell to bell. Bells are struck twelve equal times at daylight. By an equinox hour, that's three miles. An hour is longer in summer, shorter in winter. It requires math."

Calbi was about to argue, like his people did, on the disadvantages of church time and the advantage of ship and travelers time. A rumble deep in the ground almost made them jump. Arno led them to spy from the bushes and behold the awe-inspiring sight.

In an open barley field, men whooped and hallowed riding magnificent horses. Over the drumming of hooves, a concerted shout of "Chevauchée! Ha--Martel! Yah'AOI!" sent thirty knights in armor flying hard on their beasts in two close rows. Long lances first, saber, axe, and mace-hammers second, they ripped everything up in sight and thundered off into the forest.

Spark said, "I'd hate to be their foe having to face that wall."

"My father is the big whooper," Arno said proudly. "And that's Prince Taillebourg, their leader. He makes them practice the chevauchée, the conquering charge of death. My father loves horses. He rides the hair off 'em."

The sight was truly hrad, but the girls weren't letting on that they were in awe. Arno trudged along. "Reyna. Is she a hrad?"

"No way, she's too pretty," Calbi said, "right Amira?" "She's not–"

"Look! Pure water!" Arno pointed to a sparkling rill. Everyone dashed to drink from a rill, the sweetest water that started brooks and streams. Amira filled their leather flask with cold bubbling water. "Calbi drink! No person or animal has peed or duked in it."

"I'm a Cathar. We pray to purity first." He clasped hands.

"O, right. Tell me Spark, yesterday you were hrad! Did you say, 'fun, love and trouble' was worth more than a mass for the dead? You got no spanking?"

"I was quoting my grandfather. That was a mass for his soul. You can't get a spanking for saying the living truth. Not by my family code. Father is strict about the truth."

"Oh, is that all?" Amira said, pretending to know about codes and such. Knaves were present; she would ask later.

After a half-bell, Amira stopped. "This is the scene of the crime."

Arno said, "Oc, Calbi, you ask dumb questions. You hit the road." Sliding a stunt dive, the curly haired knave put a cheek to the hot gravel and stuck out his tongue. Amira tossed her load of rotten beets near his face, stomping them, splattering Calbi.

"Plu-ee!" he spit out the pulp.

"Don't wipe it!" Amira said. "Looks more real, like you were slain."

The red-splattered face smiled up. Spark stressed, "Your head sure looks cracked," then threw down her pig bladder by his belly, giving it a good heel of her leather buskin. "Now you're good and gutted."

Arno awed, "That's Roman!"

Hiding in the bushes, waiting for a victim, the girls whispered, "Arno, what do you mean roman?" He explained, "Roman like the amphitheater in Poitiers. My father says the Romans were enslavers and cruel – pagans who tortured people, not modern like us. Romans were brutes, hardly human. Say it like, 'I am going to get roman on your ass,' means torture. Then there's bizarre pagan rituals, cruel scenes inside the amphitheater, roman antics."

Spark rounded her hands to her mouth and barked loud as a hound.

Calbi lifted his head urgently, rolling over to look behind. Where are the hunting dogs?

"Ha ha, got you, dead man." It was Spark, the jester. She yelled: "Roll the other way!" She was right. Back to face the reeking gunk. Calbi had to look the part, especially with hrad girls on the overwatch.

In the rushes, the companions plaited reeds into woven mats to pass the time. Amira said to Spark. "I had a sister; brothers too. Dead from the pox."

"That's terrible." Spark touched Amira. "Did they suffer?"

"Yeah. I don't like to talk about them. Thought you should know."

Feeling the burn of the sun, Calbi came to his feet. "There's not even a good climbing tree to spy from, let's find a better place." The formidable girls pointed out the hrad advantages. The turn-of-the-road surprise, mysterious shadows, thick rushes to hide in, and gnarled spiky dead trees. The dying swamp set an eery mood. Spark gripped Calbi, "Patience is a virtue."

The trod of distant travelers loudened. "My turn." Spark laid herself out neat against the gore on the sun-dusty road. Amira flipped over the bloody sun-roasted bladder, so the whole mash came fresh out of the victim's head, a markedly better effect. Amira went to her knees and spat on the thing: "Need more, hurry." Calbi knelt, Arno too. They spit, spit, and spit, bobbing up and down five good spittles apiece.

Spark lay still, smelling the foulness of it all.

Jumping to the reeds, the friends envied Spark in the magnificent killing scene. They put their figuring faces on. "She'll get all the fun. Should we come out of the bushes screaming?" In the marsh stink, the dead trunks looked weirder by the minute.

You would think it easy to lie down on a road and be still – the rocks in your back, the dust blowing into your mouth, fleas tickling, blinding white sun on the hottest day in Hades. Then the buzzing of weird winged insects, a rotting pig gut freshly spat on, the aroma of guts inches from your face, all gnaw on your being as you lie upon the cruel self-made road of life.

The dead girl closed her eyes, instinctively turning her head away from the stench to the breathable side of the road, and put on a deep-sleep face.

"Wagon!" Arno warned the friendly corpse.

"Turn your head the other way," Calbi whispered.

How could she forget? The knave was right. She turned back to the horror.

The bush children suffered the unsettling heat. They began seeing things in the gnarls of dead trunks across the road. "Skulls?" Calbi pointed. Sure enough, they looked like heads with black eyes, noses, and maws. The sight inspired weird mouth sounds: warbley yowels, ghosty mmroos. With a part to play now assured, the children whirred grass flutes, blew into hand caves, and generated a vast bestiary of yeowling horses, roaring gulls, and yipping lions.

Heels ground around the bend with voices of women dragging a wagon.

Spark hissed at her friend's bizarre sounds, "Shhiish, be real." The dead girl died again. Wizened, the bush clan barked and meowed, in starts and stops – the animals that gutted the girl!

An elderly woman in a long dusty shift pulled her side of the wagon of house-holdings. Her pregnant daughter pulled the other. Seeing a bloody dead girl on the road might beget struck fear, but the shaking rushes of kitty and puppy sounds meant no danger. They crept to the other side of the road, keeping an eye on the weirdness. No pity would be extracted from these souls.

After they passed, Spark's humiliation could not be quelled. She kicked up a pound of road dust, but Amira spoke for her: "Do you know what we sound like?" Spark finished: "Just be quiet!"

After a short wait came footsteps and whistling.

"Arno! Die!" Spark ordered, giving everyone her dare-me eye.

Arno hesitated. He could not tempt fate by play-acting a glorious death, the kind his chevalier father or even he might face someday; he was superstitious about serious things. Clowning about, he exaggerated a mute beaten agony, stumbling in roman antics, playing the tics of wretched death. Amira, laughing at his foolery, refreshed the hot gut with a good toe mashing. She ran to the reeds where Spark's hand-crab shoulder pinch ensured they were mute as mice.

The tall flour miller and heavy-set fabricator stepped lively. The forgeman sniffed and set his brazen face to Arno, magnificently slain with a bleeding head. "You need real berries there, laddy." Arno opened his eyes to suffer the bane, the words youth hate hearing most: "We used to do that when we were your age."

That was that. The failed caper put them in a terrible mood. They gave each other shin-digs; they gave each other the maw. The day was hot and they would have their crimes; if not on the open road, then upon one another.

Parched Arno accused with a vengeance, "Amira, you are high and mighty. You didn't even fall on the road!"

"I was in charge of guts!" Amira drank a belt of water and hit him with her water sack. He drank with a scowl. It was open season for insults.

"How much comes out of you?" Arno sneered, giving Amira a long hard look. Behind the sweating damisel seemed to rise a wet fartulent sound. She returned, "I belch on thee-yaa-rt!" The four fell into a noisy game of cavernous belches, ratty vomits, rotten pig-bladder wheezes with remarkable skill.

In roman antics of the highest order, Calbi had each play their 'body instruments' of burps and belches. Arno, with only fartist experience, did not stand a candle to a person of imagination who knew the humors of the body. Calbi drew on his special powers and sounded a sniffle'yawn-sneez'n-wheeze'n'cough-hiccup'belch-on'fart'vomit, causing Amira to remind, "You are in the presence of ladies." Oh, the hot serenades on the way home, exhausting every form of bodily explosion. The tall girls let themselves be out-winded.

At the very height of their outrageous musical dunghill skills, the four whiled along paying no mind, when behind came a handful of nuns from Loudun. Startled by this gaggle of muddy, bloody and horrifying children, the nuns fled back in terror to the convent.

Success! Finally, they had scared people!

At a split in the path, Amira watched the hrad knaves leave, realizing lord curly locks had to be invited to her home; such impressive "body-instrument" skills would amaze her father.

Her father.

The two well-sunned girls stopped to cool at a local pond. The suface reflected the Fontevrault bell tower and clouds graying the sky. Spark chased squirrels up a tree and climbed to a limb to swing her heels. Amira squatted near stones by the water, resting her jaw on her hand. Staring into the still surface, Amira fell into a well of sorrow. Seeing her friend below in a dark place, Spark felt her sadness. She hopped down to cheer her up.

"You look fit to cry. Why are you sad?" Spark said to Amira.

"Father. Ma doesn't know where he is. Yesterday, two summoners took him."

"Aww," Spark sympathized. "Were they Canon or Royal?"

"Canon! What's that!" Amira barked. Looking up, she saw her friend's eyes were red with a strong feeling. "Sorry, I didn't mean to be mean."

"It's all right. My father knows laws. Canon is church law. Royal is King law."

"I loath Royals, don't you?" Amira shouted. "With all their blib-thee-blab, stoop-heading names, and fool-head laws. Why can't there be just one law."

"Don't you wish there were none?" Spark said. It was a smart thing to say, and Amira brimmed a smirk. Spark tried to mimic her, showing great difficulty.

"Eyebrow needs to be higher," Amira said.

"Show me."

Amira pushed up her friend's right brow up and her left cheek down. "There."

To see Amira smile was Spark's intent. "I think I've got it. So, who took him?"

"I don't know. Mean-face black-beards. They wore crosses, velvet tunics, and red caps. I guess Canon summoners."

"Father calls them swamp-knowers."

"The potion-maker calls them Sump-knowers." They giggled.

"Shives, Amira, church law is time, trials, and money. So my father says."

"Shives?"

"The off-husks of flax from making linen, you know, crap. I prefer shives."

"Shives!" Amira tested out her friend's better curse. Rock squirrels lifted their heads. Amira spat a gob – a hrad challenge to her friend.

Spark respectfully spit on the spat. "So what did he do?"

"Don't know. Say, you're not a spitting type are you Spark, but I'm honored you tried to make a sump."

"Did you ever see a pretty woman spit?"

"Well, no."

"Women can grow up to be ugly or beautiful. Ugly is not for me. I'll leave the spitting to you."

Amira retorted, "Glad you are hrad and not a woman? Ma can't get anywhere. Hrad girls can do anything. We never give up."

"There's a river of truth. She is not your Ma; she is your Mother."

Somehow this stream of corrections from her younger friend struck Amira as right. I never said Pa. "Father is a good man, Spark. You would love my father."

To Spark, how Amira stressed 'love' and 'father' tugged on her heart. She went about gathering rocks. "You worry about him every night, don't you?"

"Spark, you sound like you worry about your own father." Spark handed over a rock. "Here. It is called empathy – to feel like the other. My father will know what to do. Do not worry, friend." Pooling miseries for a spell, they cocked their arms back and threw. The stones ricocheted off the trunk and splashed loud into the pond. A mass of birds flitted and chirped from their perches. Rock squirrels alerted, tails erect.

"Ssss" snarked Spark at the squirrels, sounding like a crawling king snake. The furry animals raised their heads higher. All at once, the girls leapt up, clawing at the air, sending the furry-tailed rodents scrambling for their holes, all at once.

Spark rolled her eyes to Amira, "Squirrels."

The girls felt immense satisfaction.

•

The Rights of Pigeons and Falcons

Spark, she was the proudest hrad of all, thought Amira as she stacked rocks in front of her cottage. Memories of her last few days came clear as the morning light. They met on Friday at the mill. Saturday they spent on road crimes, but today was Sunday – a no-hammer day at Fontevrault – and Holy Mass would blot out their fun. The good part about Sundays was the tall ones, always building and hammering, were silent. Amira chuckled of mentioning the tall ones. Spark replied, 'all stomachs and knees.' Amira laughed out loud in recall, almost losing the balance placing the top rock. Spark cussed capably in strange words, made sounds like animals. At times, she spoke of changing the world.

Where did she come from? No one would say, partly because her parents wanted it that way, mostly because at an orphanage no one wanted to know the answer to that question.

Just then, Spark came running, pounding the ground on a dead run from the north apartments of the Fontevrault compound. Reaching Amira's timber-man cottage, she shouted, "Amira! Amira!" She panted, catching her breath. "I told my father last night ... about yours ... taken by church summoners!"

"What did he say?"

"After all that ... he tells me to go play."

Amira gave her famous smirk. "Thanks for trying, Spark." Amira added another stone. "You live by the chapel. Does all that hammer-drilling bother you?"

"It's not bad. It is like the world is being made for me. Well it is. The tall ones are making it for all of us, you know."

"Yeah? Maybe. After mass, bring your sister and brother over."

"I will bring my sister to play, but not my brother."

"Is something wrong with him?"

"I don't like him," Spark said. "Besides, he is two years younger."

"Well, I'm two years older than you, and we're friends. I say he can play."

"But he is less than a knave! Aigret gets all my parents' favors. They have purposes for him all the time. Nothing for me."

Amira counseled, "Ah, that leaves more purposes for us!"

"Hmm. I like that answer."

Spark pulled on a frown. "Still, he bothers me to every end. Last Monday, February ten was his birthday. Only boys have them! It makes no sense!"

"Few things make sense when you are angry," Amira said.

Spark ranted, "Birthday-boys are celebrated as if that were the only day that mattered in the world! If anyone achieved anything on a birth day, it is my mother. Celebrate her act. Big hallow and whoop for getting born." To her Aquitaine mind, a birthday-boy was a frivolity. But it was interesting, this birthday puzzle.

Amira overcame her friend's sourness with cheer, "We girls have seasons. The way I figure – if girls count by springs, summers, falls, and winters, we never grow old. That's why on New Year, all women become a year older. Men count their doomsdays. The Pictone chief says, 'The wisdom of aging favors women. Clued into the sense of moon and season, women leave years to men. Best is the general age in which you are born with your friends. Your generation puts you among an era, in a wave of time unfolding.' He's wise."

"How do you remember all that, Amira?"

"Things I like, I don't forget. Calbi's faith says we are born many times in our lives; it is misguided to fix a soul to its first day of innocence. A soul is wiser for celebrating its many births."

Spark puzzled. "I'll have to talk with tooting Calbi. Birthday-brothers, bah!"

"Shives, at least, you have a brother. I miss mine."

Spark looked like a fish that just bit a hook – it would be awful to lose your brother and sister the way Amira did. She felt bad for speaking so thoughtlessly.

The bells rang. Spark said, "I am going now." She ran to the church. Prayers would give her time to think before acting.

Late midday, Spark and her sister skipped with brother Aigret to Amira's cottage. They hid their socks, of course. Straight off, Amira took a liking to the four-year-old knave, and he was smitten with the hrad girl. Amira's fairness charmed him, this dweller of a great playscape.

Aigret smiled to Amira. His sisters had never seen him grin so long. Among shaped stones, timber piles, hollowed logs, and water ditches, Amira showed her backwood curiosities, inviting his play: a field of huge tree stumps her father had pulled, left for her fun before carting them away. The upended shapes conjured strange beasts, the rooted-out holes were giant caves. Aigret felt Amira's sadness for her missing father.

From a plank full of savory pranks, the connoisseurs of childhood whiled their time making clay-crusted mud pies, shimmying up favorite trees, and attempted horse-high rock stacking. In the guise of runaways, outlaws, and summoners, they adventured into the fast hours of twilight.

They played a game of Seek and Sought. This round, Amira was Seeker. She slid her hands on a smooth birch trunk. Hands locked, eyes closed, body swinging side to side, she gave the long count. Letting go, among the chirping crickets she thought, Spark's darling brother, I'll find him last.

Steps came from behind. It would be like big-stomping Spark to creep up and spook her. On her shoulder fell a large hand, familiar and firm. Her feet left the ground. Flying in the air, Amira turned to her father.

She buried her head into the damp, salty smells of a donjon and cried.

Over her father's mantle, Amira peeked. Another father sought his children. He looked like a King or something. Knowing best where his children were, Amira kissed her father and jumped down. Grasses heavy with dew flew by as she probed in purple light. Twigs broke in a ditch. Though she knew the answer, Amira asked playfully:

"Who is in the hidey-hole?"

A male voice boomed: "Children, come out! Wherever are you?"

Amira looked deep into the hole. A ghostly girl came up from wet earth, once the home of a great tree root. Amira turned, "Here is –"

"Hi, Father!" proudly said the girl looking beyond Amira.

The royal man spoke deep, his voice rich, "Alienor!"

Amira blinked in disbelief, Spark? "That's Spark!"

He laughed regally, marveling at his daughter's name. "Spark? Spark!"

"Yes, Father," his girl said. "Looking for Aelith? She's snagged again. Here comes Aigret!" The little knave boosted out of the hole. Grinning in glee, Aigret threw his arms around Amira's waist saying, "I am happy you are happy."

With no time to puzzle, Amira bounded into her father's hardy arms the forty steps to home. Through happy tears, she was perplexed. Friends blurred by – Spark is Alienor? Alice is Aelith? Their royal father let his three huglings drag his silver and gold tunic down. Amira whispered to her father, "Who is that man?"

Paul turned to introduce her. The man came up to greet her.

"Get down Amira and –"

"No." She hugged her father ever tighter, ducking her head.

"It's all right," accepted the well-clad father, respecting shy affection.

"I want you to see," Paul said, twisting her around, "this is Duke William."

Amira reeled in thought, The Duke? She looked at his trusting face and shook his big hand. Alienor is a Princess! And living in lemon-sucker heights?

"Amira Neas!" boomed the Duke. Hearing her name said so richly, and with her father holding her securely, she smiled with great satisfaction.

The Neas cottage filled with contagious noises of reunion. The wood house smelled of Alder smoke. By the hearth-box, the two family-tribes told tales and prepared to give thanks. The hour of meat was upon them. They agreed to supper past the cooing doves, beyond the hooting owls, but before the howling wolves were heard.

Aenor, the Duke's exalted wife, quietly entered the rescued timber worker's cottage with servants and set about epic food and drink. Amira had never seen the likes! Tova, a dark-haired woman of fourteen, took charge, and Helena simply sat. The Duke held everyone spellbound with something unique to the world - he gave his wife, Aenor a long, stylish Aquitaine kiss. Alienor sighed, as always, seeing her parents show affection. Amira took such things for granted though it seemed quite overdone.

This was not a time for mere introductions. There was a rite to be fulfilled by the tribes. For if a Pictone helps a Poitevin, or more simply if any Aquitaine family helps another, that family helps you. In cutthroat times, the bond of aid was treasured and recognized aloud in sacred words, tones, and gestures.

Paul Neas was moved. He bent his knee and rested forth an arm. "Duke William, truly I thank you, my Lord." William opened his arms to Paul as if giving and receiving at the same time. Paul continued, "Lord, hear my blessing on your great wife Aenor, your lovely daughter Alienor whose word reached your ear, your lovely daughter Aelith, and the great Aigret. May the Almighty see your son become the next William of the realm." Amira thought, what a strange night; Alienor seemed used to it.

Duke William opened his arms wider as if to include the world. Only a person who measures up to greater stature could say:

"Know that Aquitaine grows by such heartfelt blessings. After a trial of donjon, and such great service to our timberlands, you, Paul Neas, are my man. Of your great, devoted loving wife Helena, your honest rowdy daughter Amira, and I see a grandmother. Mmm, what's her name?" (Lorraine, my mother), Paul whispered. The room shared the luminous moment. "Of Lorraine, this mother of wise Pictone years, to all here and now; may we live by the love we feel for one another. May we live for greater deeds that our productive families will join to. Make way the future of Aquitaine, we petition Thee." He raised a hand high to heaven. The room answered, "Aye-men," and the two men embraced and gave a cheek kiss. "Long be lief, long be liege, long be love."

Round-eared Amira whispered to Spark, "Your family kisses are many. Long, pucker and vim. Why do they hug and kiss slowly, one cheek to the other?" Alienor explained, "The kiss of peace. Hrad's call it 'the bise.' – a sound between peace and bees. "Aelith, give me the bise. Faster is better, watch." The sisters quickly kissed one lip corner and then the other. Amira commented, "Fast kisses too."

"Before we take meat together," William said, "a blessing on the food of the lands between our tribes we will share." He gestured with his hand to include them all and smiled warmly.

Tova entered. "Zees, I cook!" A feast appeared, and they shared meadow cresses, celtuce, cooked eggs, apples, crispy roast duck, freshly sliced venison, cheese and bread. Alienor and Amira quickly took slices of duck. The fathers mirrored their daughters' exuberant faces for the bird. By the hearth, they supped wine, ate, and spoke of the deeds that made them hungry that day. Spending a rare evening with their fathers brought out an unusual patience in the children, and the daughters did much of the talking.

William asked Amira in his rich, hardy voice, "Tell me of your father before he became a timber lord and what did he teach you? Don't be shy."

"My girl is never shy," Paul said jostling her. They exchanged hugs.

Amira spoke boldly, wanting the Spark in Alienor to know. "Father Paul was both a trapper and furrier, a coureur de bois. He hided fox, ermine, stout, and squirrel. I have a true vair from his longest hunt." William was astonished. "Real vair?" Amira fetched her body-length piece. The Duke examined with great care and admiration. "A vair coat can fetch a prince's ransom." Alienor fondled it lovingly.

"Exuberant Amira, tell about your hunt with Paul," William prompted.

Amira was excited and spoke rapidly, the stories of Father coming all at once. "We boated rivers and passed old Roman river-castles to trap furs. Often there were ducks, like the delicious one served tonight, um, that tasted of Loirian; ugly ducks have the best flavor. Father showed me the ways of animals in the deep forest. Once, a pack of dare-wolves came upon us. I was afraid of the dares, but father was quiet and gave me his wolf sign." Amira showed William the round-mouth shush. "Later, father said he liked trees better than hunting animals. Now he cuts trees and clears land by the code of the forest. One day he'll teach me to hunt deer, but only when there are too many. Some men chop down trees and leave stumps. He digs a hole, jumps in, and roots the trunk out – makes a better field. At the watermill, he turns timber into fast lumber. He finishes Alder wood tables with the new water shaping tools. I know how step-gears work. He fashioned me a box from cedar wood that came from Acre. That's in the Holy lands, the main port to Jerusalem." Self-consciously, she stopped and gulped a breath.

Duke William's voice was deep. "You know, Amira, for a young girl, you have an amazing memory. By taste alone, you can tell a duck out of the Loire River?" Alienor patted Amira's shoulder.

"Yes. It has a clean taste in Spring."

The Duke valued tasters. It was a prized survival skill in the royal household. He lay his arm on Paul saying to Amira, "I imagine you have many of this forester's virtues. There is virtue in digging deep and laying good foundations. He plants baby trees to grow tall beyond our time. Alienor knows of this practice, ask her someday. Tell me Amira, have you felled a tree? To cut down a tree for a home with your father is an Aquitaine tradition."

"Oh yes," Amira knocked on the floor where she was sitting. "Wood floors. Father and I use a red-handled two-person pull saw. On each side we pull, and but I think he pushes, too. He does most of the work."

"Caw," Paul countered, "guiding counts as much. Look what's going on at the mills. Water cuts wood, stamps metal. Judgment and a guiding hand, not brawn." Paul held up a small metal band with a flanged tube. "This is the future."

"And the cause of our troubles," William added.

Paul said, "We are building a pigeonnier, a home for special rock pigeons."

Amira said excitedly to Alienor. "Our own birdhouse of roosts!"

"The first of many." Paul focused on the metal. "With this band on their leg, they carry messages written on thin paper. Birds travel faster than galloping horses and over greater distances. A lesson here." He turned to Amira. "Mother says you saw our work at Chasseigne's mill."

Alienor not wanting to appear dumb said, "We've seen it too, right Aelith?"

Amira said, "I saw a finished tower in Loudun."

Paul said proudly, "Mine will be better." He placed the band into Amira's palm. "For your box." His daughter grinned playing with it.

Alienor observed: "Better? They are just round towers."

"Ah yes, both perfectly round .. when seen from the ground."

The men watched the waterwheels turn in the mill of their daughters' minds. Paul resumed. "To a bird in the sky, mine stands out. It's by a river with a colorful round roof, surrounded by a double circular hedge that deer will not eat."

"Like a target from the sky," Alienor said.

Paul clapped. "Smart girl. By the river. Why? Three good reasons. Bugs are one. Rivers supply worms and insects. The right bushes attract their favorite local bugs." He nibbled a celtuce stalk and winked, "Tastes as good as worms and grubs, here want some?" The girls shriveled away from the offer. "Also, the river limits foxes and cats who eat birds. Finally, like in a mountain view, on the river, banked by trees – easy to see."

The little ones pictured the high ways of birds, imitating flight. Alienor settled on a question. "Sir, how do you tell the birds where to go?"

Like all fathers, Paul enjoyed a child's curiosity.

"Ah, they don't go . . . they come."

"Come?" Alienor said, receiving Amira's bird-band to twiddle.

"The special nature of rock pigeons is this: when they hatch, the first place they see is home. After a full moon, if they feel safe, that is their home forever. Take them fifty leagues away and let them go; they always fly home. That's why you see horse riders carrying cage birds. They exchange carrier doves from pigeonniers at the market. Birds can be kept for months until an urgent message needs sending. We put a message in their leg band and let them fly home with our words for the tower person to pass the message along. Me? I make our flying friends a happy home so they will fly in rain or night."

As Paul took a swallow of wine by the hearth, so did everyone.

"Falcons! We will train them next," Paul said. "The great warbirds fly from your arm. In the sky they gyre – that means turn in circles. From their gyres you can read their bird signs. Looking for prey, they let you know of water or if an enemy is near. With keen eyes, sharp claws, strong beaks, and blazing speed they can kill every form of bird, even enemy messenger pigeons. After they attack, they return to your arm. Castle-kept hawks are trained to defowl the air, keeping the pigeon poop at bay. Oh, you will like this. A Falcon is always female. The male is a Tercel. He is smaller and does not train well."

Helena said, "A lesson there." Everyone in the room laughed.

Alienor thought with delight, Birds returning to your hands. Birds born with love at first sight, flapping their way home. She realized: "They'll trade messages between castle markets. You are not making one pigeonnier but a fleet of them; you'll have a net of working birds."

"Right, Alienor!" Paul was elated. "Messaging will be key to Aquitaine wealth."

"Caw! Dreamer!" Grandma Lorraine shot out. "Don't be fox-fooled by bird talk, heed me. Stick to furring and timbering, honest work."

"Mother!" Helena minded. A civil silence followed.

William jostled Aigret about while asking, "Helena, what busies your day?"

"Family and orphanage. You know we lost our first two to pestilence." Paul drew to her and took her hands contently. "Amira is our only. She and the Abbey orphans fill my day. And my kitchen. I do love to cook. That and my time alone with my tercel, Paul."

William stroked his wife's sleeve grandly saying, "My falcon, Amira calls our eldest Spark." Aenor echoed, "Spark!" The room filled with joyful laughter. The girls liked watching their parents' affections. The tall ones seemed to share some secret. Kissing Aenor's fingers, William gave a serious frown and explained: "The Cistercian order of monks have all the pigeon traveling rights to every house from here to Jerusalem. To free Paul, I had to pay a fee and agree to the terms of dispatch and return."

Aenor said, "Who would have guessed birds were such a serious business."

"What are we going to do about the rights of birds?" William nodded. The men exchanged deeper looks, for the future they knew coming. William chided openly, "The church gets into everything; the trouble is you can't get them to stay in the church."

Amid the tall ones' laughs, Amira broke in, "Father, why didn't you get roman on the summoners?"

Duke William chuckled at her words and gestured warmly, speaking richly, "Dear Amira, your father knows when to fight his battles. Stronger is the man who uses his tongue. Had he laid them low, more would have come in their stead. And here: I have my best timber and bird-man – n'ere e'en a scar." He gentled his knuckle to her cherub cheek. "All it cost was silver for a license, and your great sad worry, of course." Paul would still be in the donjon were it not for Alienor, thought Amira.

Little Aigret, sitting at his mother's feet, grinned as Aenor playfully rolled an apple off her lap and he caught in the air. The fathers cheered. The bit of boy brimmed a smile to Amira, who applauded his catch. He descended into knave-babble that drove the fathers into a fondness. Paul presented a small leather-cased hunting knife to Aigret. The men intoned the rituals of skill and care for swords.

Grandma Lorraine eyed the three girls suspiciously as they slipped off down the hall to Amira's room. When the heavy drapery that made a door was pulled tight, Amira threw out a long sigh. "Alienor, thank you for rescuing my father."

"Sure." It was a mighty sad sure. "Amira, your father is a hunter, an explorer, a timber cutter, and even a bird master. Ours just sits and worries out words for trials, huh, Aelith."

Aelith wiggled her fingers. "He does Dukey things!" They broke into giggles.

Alienor fidgeted and sulked. "My brother laps up all the favors, you saw. He will be the next Duke, and we will be nothing. Now, a real Duke was my grandfather, the Ninth William. He fought the castles of Spain and in the mountains of The Crusade. He was a singer and lived for fun, love, and trouble. Amira! He stole my grandmother right out of her bedroom! The two were already married! My parents? – duller than wayfarer tavern gravy."

"Now that cannot be true!" said Amira. "You father is a great Lord."

Alienor was surprised to hear it. "Amira, you loath Royals. My father even fights the church."

"Who fights the church?" Amira puzzled.

"Why can't my father be adventurous like yours? It's a mad world."

"Now listen to me Alienor, it is not a mad world. It is just you who get mad. I once believed Royals were useless, but I love your father."

"Truly?"

"Yes." Amira picked up a toy horse and played equally with Aelith and Alienor. "He speaks magnificently. You should love him, and your brother. Mine died from a horrible pox. I miss him and my sister every day. I love your father more than you do! Good men deserve love, but you don't know that. I love two fathers now."

"Well, you are two years older, I suppose you know more," Alienor said. Charging the toy horse into a great leap. Amira halted her.

"It is you who are stopping love! Be more openhearted with your family."

Alienor gave a fat lipped-frown. She always thought herself as loving. Like a filly that learns to pick oats over straw, Alienor found herself nodding. Love was a good idea, and Amira's house was filled with it. She put her hand on her heart: "I will this: to be open. I can't say when, but I will." The elder girls traded gallops with their toy horses.

"Alienor, your father is the Duke. Why doesn't he wear a crown?"

"Crown Crabs! I used to wear it around my neck until grandpa warned me."

"Oh, I see."

"You can't see. The bugs are too small to see."

"Your grandfather sounds like he was fun," Amira said, "My grandma? She'll put her wicked eye on you," and imitated the old woman's voice: "'I tell you, they are up to no good!' She is probably out there saying that right now."

Alienor said, "You can make your voice sound just like her. Lorraine may be right; we are troublemakers."

"We!" Aelith pulled forward.

"I was saving this." Amira brought out from under her bed a white mask that spooked the other girls. "A mask of pretty Reyna."

"What is it made out of?" Alienor asked.

"Paper. Let's do a crime with it. Maybe spook Arno if he is worthy." Seeing the curiosity in Alienor's eyes, she handed it over. Alienor turned it over many times. A scheme was forming, against her brother, of course. Amira warned, "Be careful of doing crimes in this house. My grandmother hates wild."

"Wild?" Alienor said primly. "My grandmother is called Dangerossa."

"The one that got stolen by your grandfather?"

"Uh-huh."

Alienor held the mask over her sister's face, who stuck out her tongue.

"Hrad!" Amira admired the name Dangerossa, imagining her character.

Aelith said through the mask, "Wait until you take tea with her!"

Alienor said with glee, "Grand-mère knows the day and the world about trouble!" and put the white mask on herself and muffled: "Jours doesh rook a touch shushpicious." Giggling, she handed it back to Amira. "I think we can handle Lorraine. Maybe we can spend the night?"

"Maybe..." said Amira. Nothing could please her more; families often slept together overnight. From under the bed, she pulled her trove of small stone fertility mothers. The sisters gave reverential awes and promised to keep secret the forbidden naked stone dolls.

"Howling wolves, time to go!" William's deep voice came from outside the room. Amira dropped the bird band into her cedar box and shoved everything under the bed.

The girls pled to spend the night at Amira's. The parents used to wheedle this way when young. Dubiously they granted a sleep-stay in March. For this, the girls would have to do church charity work in Poitiers. "And yes, we girls will watch over Aigret. And yes, we girls promise to help cook." Well, they did not yet know how to cook, but they knew how to stir the pot.

🐦

As alike as two sisters, Alienor and Amira were that close in trust. On their knees, they scrubbed the ancient floor-stones at the Church of Sainte Radegund. The nuns commented on their divine and fervent charity for such an eager effort. Though it was charity, for Alienor and Amira, it was nothing but two hrads, both trying to out-hrad one other, daring ever-harder chores. It was fun to pretend it a penance for having done something wrong. The girls were not good enough sinners yet, so this was for evils to come. For the work being heaped on, you would think they had to set fire to an altar.

The convent was one of the nine local churches in Poitiers that William wanted his daughter to know. The girls' work was holy penance, and it seemed only females were blessed enough to conduct deeds in memory of Sainte Radegund. Such sacred acts: the devout cleaning of the latrines, the holy sweep of the floors, the blessed washing of laundry, and the sacred carry of firewood. Suffering let them better know the Sainte's nature, or so they were told.

They stopped to study Radegund's cloister, a small iron bar cell, fat-oiled so as not to rust, another penitent toil. Here she imprisoned herself in the wall to endure her miserable celibate days until the end. Ever glad these times were over, the girls, coughing on heavy incense, sought the sacred meanings. Through the bars, a priest watched them and took pity.

"Would you girls like to hear one of the miracles of how she got to be a Sainte five hundred years ago? An act of God, right here. Let me recite from the godly monk who wrote down all her miracles. 'Heilige Radegund – she escaped from Germany, invited here by Saint John of Chinon. One day, in that cell, she spun a ball of thread. It hung from the vault of her cell. A mouse chanced to nibble it. Before he broke the thread, he hung there dead in the very act of biting'." The priest looked for the typical awe that miracle stories brought. Instead, the two girls scrunched their noses and went 'eww.' The priest explained, "Don't you see, the mouse died of his greed."

The girls confided their feelings on the short walk to Alienor's home.

"That was a little creepy," Amira said.

"Hungry enough to eat yarn. Poor baby mouse," Alienor sighed. "I would have pet it to be Saintly; a Fontevrist would."

"What kind of miracle was that?"

"Wasn't," Alienor said triumphantly. "The priest who wrote that story was in love with Radegund. Father says anything a lover does, seems like a miracle."

"Radegund sounds hrad. Was she, Alienor?"

"Not hrad, definitely a Saint."

"For all that housework. Then she sleeps in jail?"

Alienor shook her head. "You know Amira, it's like this. First they hook us hrads with mouse stories, then, woom! We are washing floors. Maybe the miracle writer adored her to get his laundry done. Do you think he was that sneaky?"

"Shives Alienor, do you think they make up these saints?"

"I'll have to think on it." Alienor parroted her grandfather, making wise strokes to her chin. As the young girls pondered, they became aware of Ellen, the wise chaperone. The middle-aged, short-haired female steward in boots was always around. She was usually invisible, keeping her distance, as was their parents' order, so that the girls may have their adventures. Ellen mimicked Alienor with long strokes to her chin. The girls laughed out loud, "Women don't have beards." Ellen laughed too.

As the two girls talked out the charity of the day, one memory was vivid. They had poured soup for two wrinkled, feeble ladies. The white-haired, lonely women in tattered gowns waited longingly, holding out their bowls for the girls to bring the pot and ladle.

Alienor remarked, "They were leaning out for love."

Amira added, "They'll be hungry forever, they never lifted their spoons. They watched us and never ate a thing. Probably ate later, though."

"I felt sad seeing the two women at the end of their lives," Alienor said. "They missed being young so much; they saw themselves in us, just two hrad girls." She thought a moment. "Let's say a will! Never say an oath swear, always a will." She led, "I will to never be hungry and always be hrad!"

Amira completed, "I will that too!" They went through the ritual touching right eyebrow scar to left neck scar as their bond, then exchanged a bise. They brooded on the strangeness and being fifty. Alienor chose her words wisely:

"What times do you think we might come to have old friend?"

Walking on, imagining their older ages, they reviewed the day. In spite of an incense so strong they saw things, the girls learned the charity of helping the poor, laundering clothes, and how well the back of a knife gets between the cracks of soap-dirty floors. Amira said, "It sure seems like a man could honor the Saint."

Alienor said, "I don't think we can even persuade knaves to volunteer."

That was pretty much a childhood's end of their Radegund era. And just as well. Given the shroud of saintly myths of what the Church wanted to be remembered of Radegund, her actual life was difficult. As fate would have it, Sainte Radegund's better purposes were taken to a higher level by the new order of Fontevrault, half a day's ride north. Its history and mission would be entirely revealed when the girls matured. Ellen would see to it.

◆

The next morning, Amira was mortified when ornate church clothes arrived at her door, sent by Duke William. She huffed, finding herself inside a barrel of clothes, double-gowned, in socks, hard shoes, and a sash with a bonnet – useless attire to any tree-hanging hrad. Her red hair was buried so she could not even charm anyone. Oh, why had Alienor and she invited the knaves

Arno and Calbi to church to learn about saintly knowledge? If a knave ever saw her in this dress, it would be the end of all hrad respect.

The Aquitaine church on the market square was rich in carvings, was the Holy Roman Church of Saint Marie. What made this the most fun church in Poitiers, besides being able to sit, were its pillars, chalked in patterns of purple, light blue, yellow and red. Then there was the new smell - Frankincense wafted from censers out the door. The pleasant lemony scent came in waves, masking unnamable odors rising from the pews.

As she and Alienor were led down the aisle by their parents, Amira flared snarling lips at the snickering knaves. To her dismay, the parents chose the pew directly in front of the knaves. Amira knew that their hands had to be kept in their laps, or they could be hit by a circuitor priest with a stick. Surely the knaves would be black and blue by the end of the service. Hrads had patience.

Around them now were other girls who went to high church with Alienor, all in this horrid state of dress. Alienor, however, appeared to overcome the humiliation of wearing her slavish clothes. She sat in straight posture, gave polite turns of the head, and other quiet demeanors. She paid no attention to the knaves or snarling Amira. This other side of Alienor surprised Amira. As she stared, open-mouthed and awestruck, Alienor caught Amira's eye and conspiratorially pointed to the unlikely matron who had taught Alienor how to counter this deplorable state.

Lady Bouchard of Châtellerault, better known as Dangerossa, was Alienor's grandmother. In her forties, she had delicate marble-white skin, mannered graces, an incredible smile, and possessed mysterious beauty secrets. From every pew, all the girls turned to watch her. An invitation to have rose tea with Dangerossa was an honor, and said to calm the wildest girl spirit, for the woman was known to be a wild one herself. The priests despised her, and the fact that she could conduct herself with such revered style in church, inspired the hrad spirit. 'Learn by what we desire, not by what we fear.' Calbi framed her dictums in church talk. 'Only by the love of God am I called, not the hate of Satan.' His friends knew what he meant.

Setting the course, Calbi asked, "So what good is a mass?" He was of another Nazarene faith of an older Greek tongue. Amira replied:

"It's a bunch of people in a ritual to watch a priest talk to God."

"What does He say?" Calbi asked.

"God only talks in Latin."

"Not Greek? Can the priests tell us what He is thinking?"

"Um. He thinks in meanings that no one is supposed to know."

"How do they know?" Calbi looked towards the priests.

"We pray devoutly that they know. Mostly, He says we do everything wrong.

"I say we can do everything right, for us to celebrate love and life," Calbi said.

Head spinning from these strange views, Alienor finally said, "The abbot of the says we aren't supposed to enjoy anything, Calbi."

"Alienor, surely you don't believe that? It is a lost faith that does not know the divinity of pleasance. You can't really know your faith because they won't let you read your own bible. Have you tried to?"

"Well, I took a dare. 'Don't Touch a Bible, Ever!' the priest scolded me. I wanted to know what is right. Only clergy can hold one." They quieted as the service began. Catholic Mass had a certain fear and dread. Circuitors, the clergy responsible for discipline, roved the aisles with tall canes meant to thrash sleepers and knaves. They were ready to strike. Calbi, sensing that things were getting a bit dull, exploded a discreet bodily charm. The circuitors searched with a vengeance, but Calbi was too good to be caught.

"Not enough frankincense," Amira whispered. Indeed, the pots had burned out. Since bathing equated with nudity, shameful to all but Calbi's odd faith, pews had their own distinct smells. The girls made up stories for the faces in each row to match their odors: shriveled apple-cheek benches; burning pepper salted pews; hairy shearer sheep seats. Amira held her nose and whispered "pewpeedo." Alienor beheld Amira's countenance 'pew ped Dieu?' Then the meaning came, and Amira exploded a laugh:"Pewpeedo" and quickly covered her mouth The mass broke into low laughter. Down came a cane upon Amira.

Mother Aenor turned in a harsh whisper, "You are six seasons. Shame." The girls fell into a silence, and Alienor fumed. 'Mother, it wasn't me.' What saved the service was chants and responses, but mostly – the end – Amen. The pews emptied. Amira and Alienor looked over at the two knaves.

Confiding to Amira, Alienor spoke loud enough for the knaves. "You know what Calbi told me? He is a 'Good Man,' a Catharic." She knew the knaves liked to be talked about. She encouraged them, making room on the polished pew.

Sliding over to Alienor, Arno said, "What's a Catharic?"

"Well, you know what a Catholic is. Same thing, but different. They both have different ideas about what's not in it. My father says Catharics are Bible worshipers." Calbi swung his feet, delighted when girls talked about him.

"Truth is," Alienor said, "Calbi got me to thinking. Calbi, why don't you tell us about good and evil." Gold-haired Calbi did not want to appear proud. He started softly. "As my people say, there are two sides to things at all times, good and evil, but there is really only pure good. Take light and dark; darkness in a room cannot put out a candle, but light can put out darkness. When good is faint, evil appears; we call it bad. Quest the pure, the good in all things." Calbi was fervent, "When bad happens, find the good in it."

Amira repeated every word back, exactly. Everyone was impressed with her talent to hear and remember things of interest. Aelith dared her to say it again. Leaning in from behind the pew, she put her eyes to Amira's lips, as if she saw each word come out. The last line everyone said out loud, "When bad happens, find the good in it!"

Calbi, seeing his word's effect on the girls, emboldened his sermon from the pew. "Our nature is born in spirit from a light that is always in us. Good Men and Women are different shells of equal spirit. Christ was killed before he could have a family. The 'Unfinished Testament,' that's the New Testament. If Jesus of Nazareth lived on he would have rewritten all the family stories of the Bible, all about love. By the way, there are no miracles."

"No miracles!" Alienor reeled. The thought made her head swim.

Two clergymen stirred at the end of the church, mumbling to one another. "Those are the pew ped Dieu'ers," snickered the younger monk. The elder priest was alarmed by the children's mockery.

"Don't look now, here come the tonsures," Amira whispered harshly.

"Tonsures?" Calbi asked, glancing down the aisle.

"Bald monks with a halo of hair," Amira explained.

In a march of wrath and fire, the two tonsures arrived. The elder flailed sternly.

"Daughter of William! Son who are you?" The men could not attack a princess, but the boy was devil's play. The monk leaned into him with a snarl, scaring everyone. "You dare speak of your Holy Faith in God's house!"

Calbi braved sternly, "Love is in the Bible; we are all Nazarenes."

"Love? Nazarene?" His face was redder than hellfire. "Who is your father?!"

Hearing the ruckus, Duke William darted back through the church door. Saddened to see fear on little faces, he spoke with gravity.

"Is there a problem, Fathers?"

"Sire, this knave is a heretic! He profanes, and before your innocent ones!"

"Youth, youth, you know. Children! Let's be off." The Duke rustled them up. "A donation for your trouble. Let me handle the boy." Coining the priests well, William took Calbi's hand and made for the door.

The priests shouted, "Strike him hard with the hand of God. The sinner must do penance!"

Calbi walked swiftly, apologizing to the Duke all the way.

At a great distance from the church, William said to Calbi, "I am shaking my finger to look mean for the onlooking priests. There is nothing wrong with your ideas. Continue to think them. Heed me, Calbi. Be aware when you speak. Never share words of glory before a man of another religion. This mistake I have made myself. We do not have the spiritual right to be free as birds. Not with zealots who are dangerous like them. All right?"

◆

Apple and Ghost

Amira drew up the day's water for the family stew. The well was not deep. Springs flowed under Fontevrault Abbey and fed outlying grounds. As the early-rising girl bent over the wall, she heard the sound of grinding wheels from the road. She jumped back to see a large coach storm by, horses turning to head to her cottage. Amira ran, sloshing the pail.

Ellen dramatically drove the wagon to thrill the children. Alienor, Aelith, and Aigret bumped along with two guards. March had arrived, and the children had earned their sleep-stay night. As they neared Amira's cottage, the steward put her boots to the footboard and reigned the eight handsome stallions into a jingling trot. She said, "I have wonderful news." The three children looked up. "Next month, you can sleepover again. Girls only, and only if you are good tonight. Is that too tall a wish?" The sisters were delighted. Aigret pouted for not being included.

"I love Amira." Ellen patted his head. He bent away. "No! I love Amira!"

In front of her cottage, Amira greeted them with glee. The little ones leapt off, and Amira's parents boarded. Paul and Helena were invited for their nightstay in Poitiers with William and Aenor. After a pass-around of little bodies and kisses, Helena parted in good cheer, "Tonight, it is just you and the grandparents. Be good." They exchanged the traditional God-be-with-yous. The four children waved as they left, then excitedly ran toward the cottage.

Grandpa Neas, holding a bloody knife, introduced himself "Been away hunting, a week short of a moon." Gladly he showed the young ones how to skin a deer hanging from a tree, flaying off fur, making carving comments as he ripped off the hide. He made a noisy cut-and-bang show as he savagely chopped deer parts into pieces. "To the hearth pot, little serfs." The children raced to the stew pot over the fire, swatting off black flies, and deposited the pieces of meat. They returned to Grandpa, resting at his feet.

Amira whispered to Alienor, "He often goes on long hunts. After running into grandma, you understand why. She's always crabby. She says only two things: 'Be Still,' 'Children Behave'."

"Be still! To a child?" Alienor frowned.

Grandpa seemed to know how to put up with Lorraine. Her frail face hid a hard life. The deep, cross lines came from being a runaway; the worn features from being a woman. In her fifties, all she wanted was peace of mind. When she bent over to pick out a green switch, he kissed her backside to lighten the moment. She ignored his playful gesture and swished the whipping stick in the air to signify that it was not just for show. After soup-supper, she quickened the four little stompers to bed.

As the spring moon filtered through rustling trees, the three guests checked Amira's bedroom over like spies. A tall cabinet dresser with a door, a perfect small table and chair. Alienor grabbed a ball of string and began to play string-figures with it. "I know how we can get out," Amira said, going off into the candlelight rubbing her eyes.

"Can we go to the porch?" They were a restless bunch.

"You go to bed, and be still!" they heard from beyond the door.

The children dove into Amira's large goose-down bed, laying flatter than boards, staging WHO CAN SLEEP THE BEST? Unable to sleep, a snore enactment led to endless snores and rolling turnovers. With tee-hees, they roughed up pillows. Amira gave a lion of a yawn. As yawns are contagious, the whole room stretched wide with too much voice.

"Shush and be still! The four of yous!" came through the door. Grandfather.

"Shush and be-still the four of yous," they imitated, giggling.

"Now Behave And Be Still!" It sounded like a whack on the table.

From the next room, grandfather's voice: "Youth is wasted on the young."

Aelith muttered, "Whatever that means. Must be looking at her wrinkles."

"He is trying to calm her so she won't say 'be still'," Amira enlightened.

"He is saying enjoy being children and not sleep youth away" chimed in Alienor. "Like grandfather said, right Aelith?"

Amira slapped her back, "That's the hrad spirit!" Alienor slapped Amira's her back and soon they were all slapping backs. No sleep for the wicked. Back on the hrad track.

"I am coming with the switch! Be still!" Definitely two whacks to the stool.

"Is she going to say that until we are dead?" Alienor whispered.

Grandpa added a firm, "Heads on beds! Heads I said! Heads on beds!"

The girls giggled. Who rhymes a threat? Hands over their smiles, they whisper-chanted: "Heads on beds! Heads on Heads!" They conked their heads, pretending to pass out.

Off the bed they slid, hands at their sides, wiggling the floor like snakes undulating over one other. Aigret whacked Amira with a pillow. She tickled him silly until he laughed. Uncontrollable giggles rippled through the bedroom.

They heard the footboards creak first; then the door drapery pulled back hard. By the time the eye was upon them, they were straight out, wearing their dead-on-the-side-of-the-road pig-bladder-be-darned faces. The room was quiet as a mouse. The door drape creaked on the rod and closed tight; the steps faded.

The children bolted up wide awake to convene under the bed sheet.

Little Aigret brought out a good-sized green apple. Taking out his little belt knife, he proudly cut slices. "A man always keeps a knife on his person." His small arm reached out and offered a slice to each girl. "Amira first, "he said, shyly smiling at her. He ate his slice last. Amira said, "I compliment your knaveship on your manners." Aigret beamed with pleasure as he ate his apple.

The munching and crunching was a good background for Alienor's goblin-ghost story. Grandpa's art of butchery fresh on their minds and recent play among Roman ruins added the sense of reality. Alienor began:

"In olden times, Romans used to kill and hack up the bodies of Frank slaves. Just for fun, they'd skin them alive, chop them like deer meat into fleshy cubes. Now, a spirit of a dead Frank is strong. At night each rose, each bloody body-part smelling and grabbing another bloody body part to join their pieces together. They made monsters. Imagine the fiends! Two heads on a leg, rear-ends with four arms, torsos of three heads and a hand. How were they going to become whole again? Revenge! The monsters hid in dark caves. On moons like tonight, they came out, Franken-monsters waiting for Roman children to gobble them, take their parts, and form more hideous bodies. White ghostly heads, blood dripping from their mouths! Devil goblins float the air–"

"No more monsters!" cried Aigret, pillowing his head in Amira's gown. She held the boy to her body. "Tell of happier times!"

Alienor recalled white seagulls, the beaches of Bordeaux, the Atlantic ocean, a time before her brother. After a while, he dozed off. Alas, nothing could spare the birthday-boy from the calculating mind of his big sister and what she had in mind with the ball of twine-string.

The moon was high and bright. The house was asleep. Alienor nudged Amira, "Get the mask." Amira unclenched Aigret's hold, and all the girls climbed out of bed. Owls hooted. Alienor unrolled her ball of string, tossed a length over a rafter, and fastened the bed sheet covering the sleeping knave. Eerily the sheet raised and floated down to the floor. Amira held her glowing white paper mask. The teeth dangled from the red mouth. Calmly they tied the skull to the sheet, then stuffed the thing into the cabinet at the foot of the bed. They looped strings through the beams and tested the lines, one for the cover sheet, one for the doors, one for the ghost. They crept past the door curtains.

"Mmmrrrooo, Ai-gret…" sirened Alienor to the sleeping knave. The others mmrooed in chants until their lips tingled in a spookiness that tempted fright. Aigret stirred awake. Strings pulled; his bed sheet floated away; closet doors creaked open. A floating white torso emerged from the shadows. As the spook advanced, staring at him with no eyes and a bloody maw, it hovered high, higher. The head fell off.

The dead of night curdled with a child's scream. Every barking, yowling, and neighing thing answered within half a league. The girls had planned little further than a jump in bed, a fake fall-asleep, but the little lion's roar terrified them to their toes.

The air whipped in master strokes, coming down the hall.

"Where's the bawling-jawer!" When the door drape swooshed open, and the candlelights caught them fully, the devilish girls dramatically wiped sleep from their eyes, and pointed to the window. "A strange demon spirit!"

They were poor actors before the all-seeing eye.

The deed, painfully clear to grandma, brought a fierce switching, but not on the knave's hind as the girls had planned, nor even on Alienor, inventor of the crime, but on Amira. Pathetic Alienor and her sister teared at every lashing, learning the lesson deeper than Amira. What saved Amira from turning into a bloody sack of Frank'n-blood was Aigret. Stomping his feet and crying pleas, he could not bare to see the first love of his life get whipped. Lorraine yielded when Aigret knelt to give her an ankle bite. She could never touch a prince.

Amira's scalded hide made for one memorable night. What burned most were the old lady's curses: no nightstays ever again.

Inside Lorraine's cottage was a place to behave. Outside, however, were opportunities for other mischief.

◆

The whitest of birds flew in the hot April sky. High mountain ice-melt made Aquitaine streams flow full and strong. Water fed the trees, opened the flowers, and pushed up the grasses to make the cows big and buttery.

With her parents and brother gone for many weeks of royal hunt, Alienor curbed her jealousy for not being included. She and her sister spent well-behaved days with the Neas family, who took them to visit the Pictone clans in the forest. The Pictones were great hunters, and they taught Alienor that the purpose of hunting, in fact, the hunter's greatest pride was to bring home enough game to feed the whole clan.

On a chilly morning, Alienor, Amira, and Arno went larking. Calbi was away doing penance in Poitiers for his spiritual showing off. Arno's idea was to cart away a load of some lemon-suckers firewood for a fire of their own. At the small lake in view of Fontevrault Abbey, Amira brought out her red firestone. Soon they had a small smoky fire. Arno showed his new catapult – a leather thong tied between two saplings. They shot splits of burning wood into the water. All those glorious singeing splashes! Soon, a hearth's worth of logs floated on the lake. Searching to shoot off any next thing, Alienor spotted a large dead white bird. The wings reminded her of the great seagulls of her Ombriere family lodge in Bordeaux. Arno readied to make the carcass fly, but Alienor insisted it was too noble to launch. They couldn't roast it, having launched all the fire-logs. They waved off the flies and stuffed the stiff bird into the cart to make a show of their catch. Huntress Alienor would feed the world!

Figuring the bird could satisfy at least the Abbey, they went round to the cookhouse. After musing on the carcass, the cook said bird stew was not on the refectory menu, and to take the honor to their mothers. Arno wished the girls a good feast and went home.

Alienor swelled with hunter's pride as they approached Amira's cottage - she would feed the family! She found Helena sewing and brought the bird in by the neck. "I bring a seagull feast! Do you boil this with feathers on?"

Lorraine came out to see and laughed heartily. "Seagull?"

Alienor said earnestly, "What is funny about providing for a family?"

Helena quietly built a raging bonfire. Then she took the bird and motioned the girls to come close for an inspection. The girls grimaced when shown writhing maggots under the dark wings. With the carcass on the pyre, the women scrubbed the girl's skins with apple vinegar, superstitious about 'evil water.'

While vigorously drying them off, a bit too harshly, they thought, Helena said, "Thieves stole a dear friend's firewood. Have you heard anything about that?" Cringing, the girls gave dark looks to one another, and Amira confessed. Helena gave a reprimand for taking an old lady's firewood, but Alienor knew her father's code of court. "Restitution is a cornerstone of Aquitaine justice. We must be fair. We will replace her property." Surprised at Alienor's maturity, Helena minded, "And apologize, too." Alienor shrunk back a bit, as figuring out words was the hardest part for her.

By midweek, Calbi returned from penance, and the four hrads played at the pond. Alienor and Amira stretched their legs on the waterlogged firewood that had settled onshore. Calbi spoke of his penance, "See? The two-sided nature of things. Good always comes with bad – and here I am." There was much joking debate about whether his presence was a good or bad thing, but in the end, they were quite happy to be together again. The tree catapult creaked as Arno launched a serving plate. "We salute Calbi, our brave martyr!" It sailed wildly toward the other shore.

Unsnagging last year's raft, they pulled it from under the tall trees and tilted it raft into the water. Calbi and Amira bobbed the craft with their feet. Alienor disappeared into the bushes to fetch flowers and stones. Arno sat on the water's edge and pulled his knife to shave moss off last year's push pole.

Whittling away, Arno was startled by commotion and cursing coming from beyond the bushes. He jumped up, brandishing the pole as a spear and shouted, "Alienor is in trouble!"

Amira and Calbi ran like the wind. Arno wielded his staff and headed to charge. Crashing from the bushes, Alienor ran, blood rushing down her face.

"Who did this!" Arno exploded. "His hour of death has come!" Arno steeled himself for the worst, feeling the rage of the world.

Alienor looked up. "Oh Arno, I was just picking my nose, don't tell."

Arno speared the ground. "Grrrr."

Calbi said, "Arno, you keep acting, and you'll believe your own words."

"He's not acting," Amira said. "I've heard. His father talks in knight's curses."

"Chevalier, not knight," Arno insisted. "Honor rules obedience."

Amira leaned her friend back and placed a cool stone on Alienor's forehead. "Are you hurt?"

"Stallions no!" As she replied, Alienor pointed to the vine ropes in the trees. Amira explained how elders twined them for children. "What a grand idea."

The boys were now playing river pirates. Reaching high for the vine ropes, they swung out, flying through the branches to land on the "King's ship". With an "AOI!" and a heave, they ferried the wounded princess out to sea. The forceful spring water bubbled under the raft. Arno pushed out with his pole.

"Look, it's Reyna!" Clearing the distant trees, the blonde miller's daughter hung her head sadly as she rode in a line of horses with her family.

Calbi watched the procession pass the pond. "Her collie just died."

Alienor looked puzzled. "Hmm. Was it a good dog?"

Calbi thought about it. "Who is to say?"

Amira recalled. "My tribe had a new collie litter. You could give her one."

Calbi hopped off the raft with a splash, "I'll tell her!" Happy to have a reason to talk with beautiful Reyna, he gave the raft a shove and waved farewell.

Alienor turned her attention to Arno. Knowing he liked feisty play, Pirate Alienor stomped to teeter him in. "Knave, are you wary of water?"

"Oye! Watch out or we'll all be fish!" Arno evened the boat and gave a spooky eyebrow. "Worry when it's still. Buzzing flies of Beelzebub hover over dead things like they do in a moat! Wrongdoers are punished by evil water-spirits that cast a black sweating-sickness! The devil's death kills with the cruelest pain!"

Alienor bent to see the depth of the lake. The spring was running, but the image of the devil's death terrified her. She calmed, sure that Arno could be trusted. Pushing along into the wobbly deep, Arno poled along happily, until his staff felt no bottom. The boat drifted out. Cooly, he swished his stick.

Amira said, "Aenor minded me to stay out of the water or she will switch us when she gets back. My backside does not want to know another mother. Arno, are you eyeing the waters? You sure are sweating."

"Without wind it's hot, that's all." Arno tried not to desperately pole about.

Alienor revisited a fear. "Arno, we couldn't make Seagull Soup; the bird was dead from pestilence." She changed tone, "I touched a black maggot; the evil spirit Arno! Woo!" She touched his sweaty neck. Arno shrugged off the lame spook.

"Seagull?" Amira said. "That was no seagull, that was an egret."

"Egret?" Alienor angered, "How do you know?"

"The wings. Egret has a long neck, longer legs. Egret feathers are the whitest of them all, didn't you know? They are valuable."

Alienor came right up to her face. "Amira! Egret? Seagull is what I said before Helena and Lorraine. They must think I am a baby or a fool. Never let me call something it is not. Be true, friend. True."

Glad to hear what troubled Alienor, Amira felt better saying, "Friend, true friend, sorry, I will be vigilant." Little was spoken about the art of Aquitaine friendship, but when hrads talked about it, it was how many levels a friendship had. They were at level three – the number of times true or friend were said in one natural breath. Regardless of angry flair-ups, friendship had to be quickly brought back to balance to restore golden trust. Trust yielded greater things.

The sun was hot on the lake. Large puffy clouds rolled by, turning the great light off and on. The trio made bill shadows with their hands searching for a white egret. Shade and light changed places. Arno said, "Plenty of ducks plucking water, but no egrets." He poled steadily, wiping his brow and sang, "Feathers for silver, silver for gold, white bird on a hot summer's day, floating somewhere alone." A good voice for a beautiful day.

Clouds finished with the sun but not with the sky. The three stretched out lazily on the hot deck, heads near. Gigantic clouds let them think every thinkable thing. Amira said, "Biggest sky I've ever seen." The others "Uh-huh," agreeing, she continuing: "Wait until you see the starlings in fall when birds gather like bees."

As the raft drifted to deeper waters, their warm heads together let loose a fever of daydreams. In the white shapes, they herded the clouds of the sky. They imagined names for wild animals mingling with the horse tails curled high. They dared one another to stare until you felt you were falling up into the blue.

Suddenly, shouts of riders from the shore broke the spell.

The three elbowed up to see their fathers, their horses snorting hard. "What are they yelling about?" Alienor looked around; they had drifted to the center of the pond but were in no danger. Frantically, the fathers waved to come ashore. Arno seized the pole and pressed along. What had they done wrong this time?

Footmen yanked the raft to the bank. Across the lapping edge, the stern fathers pulled the others away from Alienor as if she had done some horrible thing. Amira insisted on standing off to wait for her friend. Seeing in her own father's eyes the thing to come, Amira watched the storm.

Duke William, in his narrow hunter cap and shoulder-length hair, went to his knees. He pulled his daughter past his dark blue mantle to his silvery tunic. Feeling her warmth, her life, he hugged, never to let her dearness go. Alienor had never felt the breath taken out of her. Her usually court-minded father now showed deep emotion. He had been crying a miserable lot. Swallowed up in his arms, she felt his dusky chokes.

William pulled her away to see her face. She already felt like crying seeing the rippled stains on his cheeks.

Father's voice wavered, bending from its depth. "How can I tell you?" He pressed a pinch of eyelids to fight tears and steadied a gaze. Alienor knew - whatever words came next, time would freeze for the rest of her life.

"Your mother and your brother, Aenor and Aigret are dead."

Her immediate response was to take control and use her sleeve to wipe away his fountain of tears. Then her face crumpled. The words hit hard. She fell into his dark cloak as her heart dropped. "At the Talmont hunting lodge, the poison pox took them quickly."

"Were they evil?" she sniffled in fright, "the church–" Just then, she saw Amira crying in heaves with her father. Alienor felt her friend's loss of brothers and sisters. Alienor gave new outcries and dove into her father's mantle hearing his muffled tones. "Evil? Of course not dear, they were good," but saying 'were,' brought throat lumps to William. He sobbed upon his sobbing girl. The shore of families cried as long as the well of tears was meant to last.

Alienor comforted her father like Calbi had once calmed her, speaking about the two sides of life. "Father, look for the good when the worst happens. Remind Aelith that good spirits live forever, like pure love."

William felt the light of his daughter's young mind. He need not explain to her the overly complex mechanisms of the official church to properly understand a death. Why confuse her with guilt, sin, and evil when her joy of life was such an obvious cure.

◆

The Character in the Story

A summer of sad silence passed into shorter days of gray. At the first cold snap, the early evening fire crackled. Alienor's candlelit bedroom at the Poitiers Palace smelled of rich Alder wood smoke. Alienor and sister Aelith played ponies and foxes, jumping and flying over each other's nightgown-covered legs, back and forth, singing in duet, "*ooo wah oh wah owe wah, ooh wah ahh wa-oe.*" In tender unconscious harmony, they mixed long runs in endless variations. Unnoticed by the girls, as common patterns are to youth, father William put a log to the fire and the palace staff stood at the half-open door.

The siren song of their pony world filled the halls. Adults treasured to hear the girls' voices months past the family deaths as if they were singing: *we are content, all is well.* Suddenly, the girls stopped their song. They grinned to one another, then looked up at the tall elders. Self-consciously, the staff bowed out.

The door shut quietly. In his fine tunic, William smiled warmly. Pulling a white feather from his cap, he knelt to the floor to take in his even-minded daughters. "We love your songs." His voice was deeper and slower these days. "You know how I talk about family history. It is time to tell you about you. Birth names are first chosen from our tribal words for landforms and creatures. Let's resound your life names, to better match the characters you are becoming."

Their father spoke richly. "Aenor often told me I didn't spend enough time with you. She spoke your Poitevin names when you were born, as is our ancient custom. Let me tell you about them, who you are, and who you will be."

William showed his white feather. "Aigret was named for the pure white Egret that loves the waters of Aquitaine. Elegant white plumes are not worth much - maybe a quill to pen – though swan and crow are best. I wear this in my cap to remember little Aigret." The girls took turns with the feather.

"Aelith of five autumns, your name means 'goodly rock,' the same word for the stones of ancient rituals that stand tall in the overgrown forests. Your name sounds nobler in Greek. Someday you will both meet the First Abbess of Fontevrault, who has a similar name. From now on you are Petronilla, which means 'little rock' – like the colorful soft stones of the river. Alienor, the lithic stone 'li' was placed within your mother's name, Aenor to Alienor, extending the birthmaker's power. I've heard how Alienor has extra meanings: the outsider, the other, the strange one, the alien. To resound your name, I went through many. Mother's wish was to call you Helena, as in Helen of Troy – a legend, said to be so beautiful she launched a thousand ships to war. 'Helienor' is how you will write your name in Latin until a council accepts your name. Al-Nur is Arabic meaning 'the Illuminator.' A royal name has other soundings to consider. From fellow Normans who conquered Angland, Saxons have Elinor. Elanor means life-giver. As you are in the line of Williams, the Saxon sound of the number 'Eleven' would fit to start. Alienora has bounce, Helenor is royal, but the tilted 'Elle' of feminine nature is light, meaning 'she.'" He stretched out on the floor, leaning on one arm; with the other he showed the spelling articulation of her name.

'Eleanor' it would be.

"But I am Alienor." He looked at her patiently. She put her hands on his to show she accepted his reasoning. She simply had to say who she was, to save her thoughts for later. "Where did you learn all of that?"

"You learn meanings over years of travel and speaking with people." Father said excitedly, "There is another way, the Academy. At Sainte Genevieve, a church-college in Paris, you can learn a hundred lifetimes in a season! Every tongue comes there."

"Sainte Genevieve?" Eleanor confirmed.

"A woman, yes, just as Pallas Athena is the Goddess of Wisdom. She could change sexes." Eleanor never heard of such a thing. "The nature of wisdom knows no gender." He gave a strange sign: a knuckle from the brow, the finger wiggling out and travels to the sky: ideas. "The academy is a place where your mind can go places."

"I want to learn all about it!"

"You do? After I put yawny Petronilla to bed, shall I come back?"

Eleanor answered with her happy eyes. He left. She jumped up into her bed. Whiling some time on family names, Alienor found it fascinating to think of a thing called an Academy where her mind could go places.

William did not need to knock, but he did. "Whose room may I enter?"

"I am Eleanor."

Turning logs to their fireside, he spoke deeply. "Mother had me visit Aigret to tell him bedtime stories. Would you like to hear one?"

The girl pushed her legs back and pulled up her pillow. He sat next to her softly, stroking her long, her ruby-gold hair onto the pillow.

"Eleanor, this is a story of two princes. One became a Good ruler, the other Bad." He intoned the two words differently. "I used to tell Aigret of two boys, *Gwehum* and **Gwoetert**; would you rather hear it as two girls, *Hartwilla* and **Horbenda**? Or perhaps the parable of the Wise and Foolish Virgins?" He felt a little childish before his eldest daughter.

Eleanor chuckled and looked up. "Tell me like you told Aigret."

Her father spoke with voice, body, and hands, acting out the roles.

"There was once a wise man called Buskin. In his kingdom, he went on a quest. Buskin searched high; he bent low." Eleanor laughed, seeing her noble father look under her bed, over her head. "Buskin searched for two boys the furthest apart, to know good from bad. Alas, he found them, *Gwehum the Good* and **Gwoetert the Bad**. How did he know which was *good* and which was **bad**? I happen to have Buskin's tests. Would you like to hear?"

Up and down she shook her head, exaggerated like a pony.

"Eleanor don't overdo it. Dear, you have an older mind; act your age with me. Learn this about stories. In court when you judge the law, when you expect someone to tell their story, ask a question for which you already know their answer. This story is built like that."

"Let's hear Buskin's test." He changed his voice, sounding as a sage.

> My hand test! Let me see how these two boys are with their friends. We can tell simply by looking at their hands. Take note: with **his** friends, **Gwoetert** raises his finger, scowls, and bosses them like slaves. With his friends, *Gwehum* opens his hands saying, 'What do you want to do?'

"Would you like to be a **Gwoetert** or a *Gwehum* and why?"

Eleanor replied, "Gwehum because he loves people." They both knew the story was childish, but feeling the telling emotions of her father, Eleanor was catching up with seasons of missed attentions.

"Very Good!" father encouraged.

She nodded quickly. "How do you tell stories so well?"

He tapped his temple. "Rehearsal, you'll learn that at school. Run through the words until you know the stream. Know the story before you speak. Love your story, amend what they care to hear as you look into your listener's eyes."

She opened her eyes wide. William continued:

> Buskin wondered, 'I simply dimply, must make sure who is good, and **who is bad**.' How did he tell the two apart? The test? The bowl of fruit. Buskin placed an apple in each bowl.
>
> **Gwoetert** saw his apple and ate it in front of his friends. When **he** was done, he saw a friend eating a small pie and punched him hard in the face and gobbled it down. 'Mine!' **He** ate it all.
>
> *Gwehum* looked at his apple. With his little knife, he sliced it open, for a man always keeps a knife on his person. *He* reached out to his friends and offered a slice to each one, ladies first. Then *he* ate his share.

Eleanor broke out crying. Before William could speak further, tears filled the cups of her hands. William had no idea what words had triggered such dear pain. Helplessly, he dried his daughter's wet fingers on his tunic. So father would understand, his daughter forced away her fitful cries. Through sniffles, Eleanor urgently explained:

"That sleep-stay night at Amira's, Aigret sliced a big apple with his new knife. He gave us girls our slices, Amira first. He loved her so much, father, and said proudly: 'A man always keeps a knife on his person.' He heard your story and acted it out. Now he is gone." Eleanor shed tears.

Father's eyes became wet. Sharing sad feelings and a burden of sighs, he spoke: "I am glad you told me. Daughter, you may teach the same to your children someday. To know your child's heart puts a parent's heart at ease. That your brother showed manners and showed peaceful knife skill was the point of my story. Look what your brother has taught you already? How noble are my children!"

Slapping her hand to her mouth, Eleanor hid a laugh. That night was anything but noble. She muffled a chortle.

"What?" Father puzzled her secret. "You said your brother loved Amira?"

Eleanor let loose a hard chuckle.

"W-h-a-t," he needled.

Eleanor blushed.

"What is it?"

"Want to hear the story of the spooking of Aigret?"

"Dear, it could not please me more. Leave nothing out."

Eleanor went over every detail of her scheme to get Aigret a tanning at Amira's. The way she animatedly told her goblin story amused her father. "We strung sheets to a ghost mask as he slept, and then hid the spook in the closet. We *mroo'd* Aigret awake and pulled the strings. Out came our ghost that led to a horrid scream. It woke the house! Amira's grandma Lorraine yelled, 'I'm coming with a whip-switch!' The tanning was given to Amira, but Aigret could not stand to see Amira in pain, so he tried to bite Lorraine's ankle!"

Father William, hearing the preciousness of his children's real life, teared up. Then he broke into loud laughter.

"My silvery Eleanor. You conceived this fiendish contraption?"

"Yes."

He sputtered: "Your brother bit Lorraine's ankle? To halt Amira's whipping, and on a scheme meant for him?"

"He didn't bite hard."

It was a terrible thing to laugh about, but neither could stop laughing.

"Poor Amira," he chuckled.

"She moaned all night." Eleanor and William shook and rolled, slapping their knees, chortling hard like two wild horses set free.

Laugh-winded and gasping mercifully for air, they shared a wealth of happy tears, and kissed goodnight. William was amazed that his daughter of six already understood irony. He laughed at the door, feeling his ribs. "That was a good spurring! The story you were in was better than the one I made up."

Outside in the hall, he oathed never to make this mistake again. She did not need juvenile story-lessons, she needed stories that suited a princess of her mind's age. Eleanor had such an intense desire to know things, to feel things, to imagine things, to control things. He would think of something.

◆

William sought to bring joy, not wanting his daughter to feel the sorrows of dark winter. He wondered what to do about stories and songs: she rolled her eyes at simple things; she was not like other children who needed to hear stories repeated. Eleanor understood things the first time.

Help chanced from elsewhere. As the French ruled the Anglish, William received Bleddri of the Welsh dominion to sing winter stories. Crossing the French Channel, he arrived on the shortest day of the year to sing tales of tribal kings, queens, and legends.

His tales of fantasy and legend were good news for Eleanor, who had heard the Bible stories too many times, from nuns whose emotions were masked. Their singular 'moral of the story' replies were as obvious as father's good-boy, bad-boy tales. Eleanor found the honest heart of Bleddri's tales expressive; the colorful superstitions interesting.

"I love troubadours," Eleanor said, catching Bleddri supping.

"I am jongleur not troubadour," he said, putting down his spoon.

Though she knew, Eleanor wanted his view, "What's the difference?"

"Oh, my dear. Takes a foreigner to tell you of your French troubadour? They are the first ever to sing of their own experience. They compose for friends about true feelings and daily happenings. Troubadour song is personal and complex, for older ears. My jongleur stories are common tales, the acts of others, the ancients. They are for everybody. My music is easy and fun for young and old to follow. Listen, hear – a fiddle for feeling, a tweak for humor, a long bow for sorrow, a short tune for merriment."

"Heard about the Lady of the Lake?" Bleddri drew a wavering bow across his fiddle. "If you see something glimmer, dive in." He plucked the strings to make high sounds. "Make a wish." PLINK. "Listen for her voice underwater. She just might grant it." The fiddler finished with a flourish.

In the Poitiers dining hall, after fireside feast when a stormy day prevented play, Bleddri remarked sadly, "Everywhere else comes a hard winter, children slave and starve, Lords are mean, prayer is forced. Your gang's got it good."

Then Bleddri sang his wooly-eyed winter tales. He began with a sign: hands roll over hands, paddling up: 'about to become.' "Arthur," he said. "A tale of a hardy Prince before he became a King." His characters all had hints of mystery or danger. Merlin, a magician, came and went from his stories depending on who was in the room. Church people scared him away; when the crosses left, the magic came back, and so did the rude words Eleanor liked.

"Hear me little fardels, of places in times ago. Eleanor, your gang now hears of Tristan of Yng-land warring against the house of Princess Iseult of Yire-land. To bring peace, Tristan is to deliver Iseult to betroth King Mark, his lord, but potions make them fall in love." Young Eleanor found Bleddri's tale a likable but odd story, not to be believed that enemies could love one another.

Unlike Biblical tales or noble chansons, Bleddri's stories had morals to be taken in many ways. His view, her view, the same view; fascinating that one story could have two sides. As the stories unfolded, they suggested many possibilities.

Welsh stories were full of bloody deeds, deceptions of kings, long speeches, fights of gory glee. Arno, Calbi, and the young males liked these sagas, but girls needed something more. Iseult was King Mark's wife, little more than a gift horse to be gently tended. Eleanor saw, like all hrads, that if a woman just sitting around doe-eyed and pretty could cause such a ruckus, then what would happen if she actually did something? The girls came alive as they made up their own, better endings. The idea of a beautiful Queen making her own realm was plum.

Beyond words was jolly Welsh music that everyone felt. When Bleddri fiddled, Eleanor and her friends would roll their heads, rock their hips, and weave rhythm with song. When story characters danced, he played. The children jumped up to romp and dart. A strange one was this deep-eyed Bleddri. What a bawdy good tribe his must be. Eleanor was glad her Frankish people ruled them. Now they could hear these fun fellows and fables of strange lands and times. Bleddri called them ancient myths; to her they were new experiences.

From Christ's Mass through New Year to Christmastide's end on the twelfth night, the nuns and priests of the Church of Rome read scriptures over and over. They dwelled on the death of The Lord, the suffering of life repeated incessantly. "It's overkill," brooded Eleanor's steward Ellen. After days of helpless sadnesses, Eleanor began to believe that for the nuns, life was a misery. She tried to cheer them up with tales of Bleddri's knights, Iseult's love, and how families help one another in despair. The nuns were horrified. They told her to put these lay-stories out of her mind and dwell on the sorrows of mother Marie and her beloved son. Eleanor said, "Why not tell your story like jongleur Bleddri, to make sense to me? My father has the sorrows of father

Joseph and his beloved daughter, lamenting a dead brother Jesus and a dead wife, Mary." Eleanor had to ask what blasphemy meant.

◆

Eleanor beheld the coming year with far more maturity than most girls of seven. She read letters and added numbers. The books in her library, mostly in Latin that she was forced to read since age five could not compare to the voice of minstrels who sang in the common tongue. Voiced emotions had far more power than mere words.

On an early spring trip to the icy Aquitaine mountains, the Duke invited the famous fable teller, Alberic. He brought his world of classic adventures. At the chalet, the air was crisp in the majestic pines. Eleanor and her friends drew near his fire. White-bearded Alberic told tales of Alexander the Great and the Greek empire. Greater than Caesar's Rome, the earlier Greeks not only conquered the desert lands, they marched all the way to Hindia.

Ever-conquering Alexander was driven by a desire for new worlds. He rode east at the head of 100,000 men. His adventures in the orient were passionate, savage, and strange. To be a successful trader he understood – it was he who was the foreigner in foreign lands. Rather than solely murder and enslave like the brutal Romans, he also arranged marriages and brought trade. To develop trust, he brought love, not fear, and he endured. For his men, he engaged them in marriage and battle. Alexander married exotic Princesses of great tribes. With wives, he acquired far more land for his empire than if he went to war.

Greeks encompassed alien ideas: closets of gifts for visitors of every age and gender; fearless speeches of passionate love; noble minds guided by the Gods.

"The Gods?"

"Goddesses too!"

Alberic told them that ancient religions were forbidden to speak of in the church, and it was unwise to speak of them elsewhere. In the Greek heavens were twelve Olympians – six male, six female, and so on. Therefore, Eleanor and her friends had to learn everything about them. Eleanor knew for months to come that she and her friends would cast about, jesting in togas, and vie for the titles of Zeus and Hera, Ares and Aphrodite, Hestia and Hermes.

Alberic's favorite was the only deity he called by two names. "Eleanor, I shall call you Pallas Athena, do you want to know why?"

Eleanor acted the dumb peasant state of ignorance. Alberic laughed hard. "She is the goddess of wisdom. That is a great virtue to aspire to. She was called Bright-eyed Pallas Athena. Those are your eyes. Funny thing – she had a strange power. She could change genders." Eleanor's father had mentioned that.

"That is a very strange power, Alberic."

"It is how ancient civilization embodied divine wisdom. In stories where a hero needed wisdom, Pallas Athena appealed to the gender she was influencing. It is not so strange? Sometimes you want your father's wisdom, at other times your mother's."

"I don't have a mother."

"That is a terrible thing. Pallas Athena strengthens women, especially."

The enchanting adventures of Alexander in his conquest of the unknown, his exploration of new frontiers, entirely captivated the young minds. There were weird beasts, wonderstones, Amason warrior women, singing trees, trials by sacred bones, moving rocks, and the mysterious powers of passion.

"All," Alberic said, "were once true."

Alberic charmed their imaginations telling of Alexander's court who learned to ride the strange animals of Persia. There were furry snake-necked horses with great hunchbacks called camellas that drank water once a week to fill their humps. They rode beasts in Hindia - enormous round horses of gray leather with long rope noses called olephaunts that dripped white ivory jewels from their mouths. "Such animals still exist," Alberic told his enthralled audience.

To trek in an unknown universe, that a ruler could pursue knowledge of new civilizations, and that Alexander could passionately fall for its exotic women did sound reasonable. The end of his life did not.

> For knowing strange new ways, and reaching life's great end,
>
> Alexander, for ignoring old ways was condemned.
>
> Through this great King Greece grew to its greatest extent
>
> Not sand but ivory, gold, and emeralds were sent.
>
> But the elders were not as wise as you might think
>
> Rumors were they handed poison for his last drink.

"Why would one's country that profited from such bounty, be ungrateful, and cruel?" Eleanor asked sharply.

"A thousand years ago, the powerful church and greedy families were jealous of their King's power and achievements. We live in more enlightened times." Alberic tapped his nose as if it itched.

To blunt the bitter ending and leave on a better note Alberic said, "Let's have a magical hand trick. I have hidden a word, written on my palm in silver ink. If one of you say the secret word, it will speak to you of its magic."

Children shouted out odd words and gleaned for a look at his hands. Eleanor did not want to play games; she was upset about his stories. Bleddri's Lions of Winter and Alberic's Princes of Summer showed only violent male bravery. Men loved men; men loved horses, they kissed killing swords. Eleanor insisted:

"Alberic, my gang of friends and I want a better tale. Tell one of a woman!"

"I must correct you. Not gang, but court. You have a court, Eleanor."

Court of friends did sound better.

"I am curious Eleanor, tell me what you have in mind for a better story."

"You tale-tellers! Your women just sit, groomed like pets. Stallions! You put more words into removing a head than the kissing of one. Knaves like Arno revere Arthur and Alexander, but what does a girl look up to? What does a woman do – just get married and have kissing love?"

<RING>

Alberic had struck a loud bell. Calbi jumped up, his hands on his ears, "Why did you do that!" The eyes of Alberic were closed in a meditating smile, listening to the beauty of the bell ring out. "Love, boy. Love! She said the secret word." He rolled his silver palm for all to see the letters and twinkled his fingers away. "Eleanor, you ask what story has a model woman. She may be you. Live the story you want to be in."

"Well, I can sure be a woman that a man likes better than a horse."

He laughed, and Eleanor found the humor in it herself. She did wonder of brave women, looking at pretty Renee, and if there were truly loving men, and if love was real. She'd figure this out later. Alberic said, "You are a woman yet to be. Maybe the story of you, others will tell. Let it be a good one."

"Oh Alberic, just tell us a good Greek yarn, anything Alexander did."

"Alexander's adventures call many to travel. Yet, why retell old stories when adventures of your own may be richer, truer, deeper. Each one of you! Make people live in your story. Ah. Now, if each of you have your own story, then whose story will you really be in?"

"Mine!" roared the class.

Alberic stroked his fine-bearded chin. "I can tell you only this: to get out of a person's story you don't want to be in, put them in your story." The class stroked their chins pondering possibilities.

"You, Princess Eleanor have a special duty. You must create a landscape of place; a realm, a personal style so attractive that everyone will want to be in it. If you succeed, people will tell stories of life in your great realm. Conjure that, Princess. Love the character in your own story first; it is a strategy; it is the ultimate magic."

By the next moon, everyone around Poitiers told modified versions Alberic's stories, Bleddri's jongleur histories, and singing poems. The youngsters, wrapped in sheets white as marble, played the myths of Greek Gods. Elder servants and priests protested, "Cease your pagan play. You offend our religious beliefs."

At this early age, Eleanor's friends learned secrecy, so they played the Gods away from the church-minded. They privately brought to life lay-stories, myths, and adventures. Amira's memory served well in recreating details. There were not enough of them to play the twelve gods game properly, so Eleanor's court had to grow. Word spread of the rich Aquitaine life with the kind of hope that a young person could believe in, and families head to Poitiers.

William appointed guardian chaperones, knowing his Aquitaine inheritor would travel to meet suitors, strange lords, and cruel teachers. Young Eleanor figured out the game to her advantage by cultivating chaperones. Her favorite, Ellen, was not available. She learned that spinster chaperones became anxious with her range of play. Guardsmen, needed for longer trips to defend against outlaws and ransomers, were short-tempered. Rather than one chaperone, Eleanor requested two, a man and a woman – her first politically useful lesson of balance. Inviting a third, a troubadour to sing, every female servant and guard seemed to become sweet on one another. When the music played, and the couple was 'engaged,' she had time to herself. Ironically, youthful Eleanor was chaperoning them. She received favors for her silence. Yearning couples soon applied for the chaperone position, and young Eleanor earned a certain respect. Managing a better freedom for herself, Eleanor privately learned about tender affections and lasting kisses. She guessed father knew about her arrangement. William never interfered with the improvement of her character. This secretive chaperoning in Eleanor's court, couples oddly came to call courting. *And did courting have anything to do with the court and law?* Eleanor considered it seriously.

Returning from travels, the energetic girl picked up larking with her friends where they had left off: crimes of the roadway, rope swings to oblivion, catapulting of strange things, and the rare exploding of bodily sounds in the most high of places. Of roaming antics and play, Calbi was a born leader.

"How about a new game, Calbi? There could be a court of friendship with rules about kissing. I don't have much to go on, well, more than you."

"Sounds fun, Eleanor. Let me think on it."

It didn't take much. The bell in Calbi's ears still rang about voyaging Alexander in search of exotic mystery brides.

◆

The Quest

Kissing was an idea that no one had any idea about. There was some great mystery about this kissing thing. Until this spring, they had been children playing under the dresses of ten thousand trees. Now full-budded spindles broke open into tender green skies bringing verdant feelings unnoticed before. The natural progress of the greening season compounded curiosities.

When Abbey-school started on a warm spring day of 1131, Vivian, their eager teacher, unknowingly inspired nine-year-old Calbi to uncover the secret of kissing. "Nothing compares to The Quest! To the Frankish peoples, a quest is an almost impossible journey to pursue a worthy thing, and by God's will, attain it. Sixty-five years ago, the Quest meant: The Conquest – of Angland. Thirty years after that, the Quest meant: The Conquest – of the Holy Land. If you took the cross, the quest meant more than conquering, it meant seeking. Nations of pilgrims on a thousand league journey sought Jerusalem. The quest comes to the faithful, to the true seekers who hear The Call."

Such learned guidance. The Quest. THE CALL. PERFECT!

If anything was calling knave Calbi, it was Reyna Chasseigne. One of lesser fortitude might begin a quest with a common girl. Calbi settled for nothing less than to kiss the miller's daughter, the blondest star in heaven.

How noble is the quest for a first kiss. How royal. Especially, if a kissing oath is made before the golden one, in a heroic contest with a gentleman Arno. Calbi asked him to share in the seeking of this fair quest.

The oath began under the prime Oak before the Chasseigne watermill. The waterwheel of her mill house splashed behind Reyna. Around them, the leaves had grown greener; the birds sang sweeter, the flowers swooned with bees. Calbi fawned over Reyna. Arno smiled thinly, going along with it all.

Unsure Arno let skinny, year-younger Calbi explain the rules: "To honor you with a first kiss Reyna, no one will fight over you. This is about love, and love is pure. We will trek through the woods and at the end of our roam, you will freely choose which one of us to kiss." The best part of proposing was the beholding. *Oh Reyna, of the gold blonde ponytail, the sunny front bangs over your dark brows and chestnut brown eyes. Dearest sweet, your cherry smile, you lift our fallen hearts.* Calbi's roman antics had begun.

Poor Reyna. Being asked to take part in, well actually, to be the quest, she felt an odd delight in being yearned for, to be chosen to do the choosing. But did she really want to do this?

"Oc," she said. Calbi wondered; it sounded like okay.

"Oc?"

"Oc!" Reyna insisted. "Are you simple? A likely yes." She wanted to know about this kissing thing, but just not that much.

Calbi bravely pressed on, "Oc. Everyone, Saturday! Let's keep this our secret."

Today it was their secret. By Friday, Reyna had taken her dilemma to Amira; loose-lipped Arno had blabbed it to Amira, and Calbi had intimated the whole of it to Amira.

Amira was a rare soul who kept a secret a secret. That's why everyone came to this formidable hrad of nine springs. She knew when a confidence was coming, and kept your truth your own.

Reyna insisted trustworthy Amira come as referee. So the pact was, all four would take their quest to the nether woods.

Saturday was cold. Each child found errands to run in Poitiers market, but only Amira's purpose was genuine; she wanted to sell her best rocks. Ian Chaenus, the elixir king, figured a girl with a bag of good rocks to stone sinners would draw the faithful. He gave her a corner at his merchant table. His brows raised as she sold basic rocks for silver. A girl after his own heart.

Colorful troubadour Woofan was jesting nearby. Imitating Ian's slogan, 'Elixirs, restorer of youth!' Woofan drew laughs from the crowd, but glares from Ian. Strumming his lute, the troubadour sauntered over to Ian's table, curious about the buyers crowded around Amira. A bearded knight from Paris examined her Aquitaine quartz with flecks of gold. Seeing a mere girl, he swiped it off the table and tossed it to his rough friend. They walked away. Amira gave a shout so frightful that the entire guild of peddlers stepped into their path. "This is a robbery!' Ian boomed with the wrath of God. He needled the knights with his heavy brows. Woofan jumped to stand in their way. One of the soldiers tossed up coins. Ian cursed as only a priest could, "That is a meager donation! Damned be your souls with the finger of a Saint up your ass!" To Amira, the silver was more than she ever dreamed of holding. She beamed and offered the trobar a rock. Woofan selected a soft flat rock with white hairs to play his lute.

The two paramour knaves filled with hope as they caught Reyna's golden glances between aisles of cheese and slaughter. Her contenders raised knowing eyebrows and did impossible things to impress her – Arno pumped his arms and snorted like a horse; Calbi quoted crazy parts of poems and talked to her strangely of good and evil. To Reyna, everything stopped making sense. By the time of the harsh midday sun, Reyna was desperately glad to see the round attentive ears of Amira.

Like everyone, Reyna found that when you spoke to Amira, she rarely gave an opinion. She reflected on the just said, saying little, letting you make up your own mind. Amira listened intently as Reyna anxiously recounted, "I like both of them. They are older knaves. Arno is almost as tall as me, and I feel safe with him. Calbi is smart and funny and bold, but has a weird streak."

Other than a smirk, Amira might just as well have not been there. She only said, "What do you want to do?"

Reyna replied, "I do not want to kiss either! Yet, I have taken their oath. I can't make up my mind which one." It was clear to Amira, however, that she already had.

A quarter bell later, Arno found Amira. He showed off his muscles. "I'll win the kissing contest! Reyna will pick me, don't you think?"

Amira vacantly asked the knave, "Do you know what Reyna wants?"

"That is a stoop-head of an answer, because it is a question, like the one I just asked." Arno thanked Amira anyway and gave her a hard hand-squeeze that nearly made her eyes cross. Calbi was too pensive to seek any council.

When the market closed, the four ventured from the mill bridge into the greening frosty woods. Calbi led, passing lemon groves, seeing a hut roof here, a dunghill there. He drove them past three oaks overlooking Trinity Field into higher hills, in search of the meadowed place of his mind, but that place did not exist until summer. Therefore, they had to settle for bramble and mud. The four faced one another, nodding anxiously at the shape of their breaths.

Amira pointed out their good fortune. "Sacred fairy wands are made of Hawthorne wood. It is said to possess magic." She bounced Reyna into position under the bramble bough, facing the sun, the blonde ponytail bobbing gingerly. Calbi took to her left and stepped high on the surfaced roots. Tallest Amira took the opposite low side. Arno ambled with the sun to his back. He faced Reyna head on. All four eye to eye.

"Choose, Reyna!" Amira said with glee, stroking a honeysuckle vine winding its way up the tree. For good luck, Calbi touched it as well.

Bright sunlight fell on Reyna. Calbi closed his eyes absorbing her radiance, knowing what was to come from the golden-haired one.

"You," came Reyna's soft whisper.

Calbi kept his eyes closed, promising himself he would remember this moment forever — her biscuit-fresh smell, her sunny glow. The blood rushed through his cheeks. His eyes opened softly expecting sweet Reyna's lips. Her finger lay on Arno's chest. Straight in front of Calbi, Amira, eyes sliding side-to-side between the couple smiled her well-known devilish smirk. Calbi slunk back, a sorrowful witness to the quest.

In the golden light, the two winners looked at each other's lips. Reyna opened, closed, then opened her eyes. Horse-wings, who kisses first, and why? Moreover, who wants to appear to be needing a kiss?

Arno dug his fingernails deep into his palms. Was he to kiss strange lips? Had to be like smoking your dad's pipe – take a puff, cough like a fool, never do it again.

Beautiful Reyna tipped her body forward, licking her lips. Stout Arno leaned-to. Amira looked on, her lips forming an involuntary pucker. Calbi closed his eyes, stiff in agony. The four lips stilled to ready in treasured silence.

"KISS! JUST KISS!" a voice blared. A smack-smooch. The deed was done!

Everyone turned to see Eleanor, hands on her hips under barren branches, shaking her head like a jester. It was just like Spark to egg you on, and it was just like Calbi to have told Eleanor of his quest for kisses, and it was just like blabbing Arno to have shared with all creation the secret of the hour.

That evening, Calbi drifted in a strange turmoil. If Reyna would not choose him, he could not choose her. Of her feeble antics with Arno, that was proof; let him win that. Oddly, Calbi found himself thinking of big-eared, fun-smirking Amira. What was it with these girls?

. . .

Next week's Poitiers morning was fair. The River Clain flowed steadily under the miller's bridge. White-sleeved Amira leaned on the rail noting her father's bird-tower, now encircled by freshly planted spring bushes. Sighing deeply, she peered down into the middling waters. The news was Eleanor would be leaving.

Catching a glimpse of Amira on the bridge, Calbi Lebeau strode up the arch. Admiring the white tree blossoms, he stood next to her, saying nothing, sharing her solitude, listening to the chirping birds, both seeing their reflection together in the water below. Amira liked that she could goof with him, even pray with him. Calbi was surprised how much he had lost his reverie for the golden one and how much wavy chestnut red hair and sweet round ears took on greater meaning. Amira turned to share the humor at his silly lost quest and gave her impish smirk, famously etched into his mind. Calbi leaned forward, following his lips.

She saw it coming and did not duck. In a flash, they were lost in one lip-locking kiss. Clumsily embracing, wordless in thought, she just let it be. Time let their lips finish.

It wasn't that bad; neither was medicine if it did some good. The good of it neither could explain. Still, inside, some part of them knew. It made little difference if you were a knave or a hrad, it felt the same. You kissed a young springer, and some unnamed seed was planted.

Calbi skipped north off the bridge, going to the elsewhere place where boys feel like men. Kissing and being kissed well – that was for him.

Amira thought little of it. Wiping her lips, restoring her hrad nature, and returning her resting hand to her jaw, she rejoined the ripple of water to see in her mind. In a few days, she'd watch Eleanor depart with Duke William on a year-long trip. Amira had often thanked her exotic friend for saving her father from the summoners. She recalled the morning a year ago when her mother was buying elixirs, the very morning she met the sock-wearing girl. This girl, Spark, who shared sadness for lost family members, was all things: gifted, alien, possessed of self, yet caring. No creature interested Amira more. It would not be hrad to say, but she would miss her. And that's when it came to Amira. What she wished for that day at the mill, what she felt holding the large rock together, it was a call. One she felt then, one her beating heart felt now. The Call – this was Eleanor! Amira' wanted to become part of Eleanor's journey, an adventure of life!

Amira could almost cry; their lives had kissed one another, and now Eleanor would be gone on some quest. Amira chinned her lips to the press of her palm, looking down at the reflection of the shimmering sky, pondering her future. Just then, the river's surface broke open with a little skipper.

Accompanied by the cooing of white rock pigeons, cheerful Eleanor appeared from the city-side of the bridge. In a white-sleeved, bright yellow gown, she stepped softly up the planks so as not to disturb the gathering doves. Setting a stack of stones on the rail, she pressed her arm alongside Amira's as if to say, look – we're both wearing white sleeves. Amira did not budge. Eleanor sniffed Amira's hair.

"I like how you smell of Alder smoke. Why the dumb glum?"

"Ohh, I don't know."

"Thinking of swamp-knowers?"

"H'yaa. No, elixirs. . . boys and their privileges. One kissed me."

"Did you kiss him back?"

Amira looked to the settled pigeons and smirked briefly.

Eleanor said, "You know, we change knaves. That's how they get to be boys, through us. It's our magic. Wouldn't worry at all . . . It was Calbi, right?"

Amira leaned on the rail in heavy silence. She felt the smooth stones and set her hand by her friend. Beautifully, an entire nation of pigeons lit down about them, whitely alive, all chirping. Some scooted under the miller's bridge. The girls grinned at the magical gathering. With a nod, they quickly tossed out a series of stones, splashing in the river below. Every rock pigeon flew up at once, warbling, wings beating. Wings fluttered hard past their ears; white darts crossed their chests. Blinking, their mouths rounded, "Whoa!" Hands chased, "Bye!" reaching up into the billowing mass. Under the cover of white, they gave their little girl cries, flapping, laughing in flight, leaping up – all little birds, all little white wings.

With barely enough breath and heart pounding, Amira rubbed her left ear. "Why did you say Calbi?"

Eleanor glanced at her, then to the sky. "It's just a call."

"A Call?"

Eleanor saw wet tears rain from her friend's endearing expression. It summoned more than words. In all that Eleanor had heard, of troubadour songs that made chaperones kiss, exotic stories in mountain chalets, hints her father had given of great journeys ahead, Eleanor realized this – she had done something small. She cared enough to rescue a good friend's father which let her see into a family, to behold their love of one another; something Eleanor would never have. Although her mother and brother were taken, what was given was Amira's trove of a family in love. And Eleanor felt it all.

Eyebrow acutely high, cheek rising in glee, giving a steady eye, Eleanor pressed her high–low, angel-devil lips. Amira's smirk, she realized, was now part of her style. Raising her head, she gave a backward salute from her right brow scar. Amira saluted her own left-neck scar. These wounds, scored and shared the first hour they met, were a hrad ritual worth savoring.

With giggling smirks nobly exchanged by the bridge, the girls ribbed one another. When the silence came, and all the spring birds settled, they both knew it was time. After silent jests on silver scars, they mirrored the other's palm, farewell.

1134 -1137
The Aquitaine

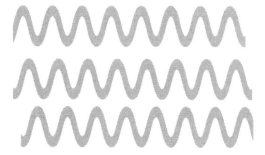

Tower of the Four Winds

Eleanor saw more in the skies, and in the conscience of others than three years ago when her mother and brother lived, when she was just a girl called Alienor and the sky was blue. Since their tragic end, she and her father had drawn closer. Father's hurt, she felt in her heart. Back then she was ignored; stories of princesses had little meaning. Now her father was raising her to become one. Year over year her perception and judgment increased by 'a progress' – a visit to every high-tower castle and town in the vast Aquitaine realm to assess improvements. Every family, hardy and mean; every jousting knight, plow and farmer, watermill and river machine; every way of every court was known to Eleanor. The first-born of William the Tenth learned the merits of the Williams before, along with the stories of generations of Gallic kings and queens who overcame Roman tyranny.

This ordinary Thursday in October 1134 was not much of a day that any youth of ten might remember or forget. Young Eleanor of Aquitaine sat away from an overcast farmhouse window. She could be ordinary or not, it being up to her. After years of travel she had grown. Dim on the wall in a looking glass was the one she must always have been. Hair tied up; she was less round, chin and lips full, body tall. Not sure which face to make, she made them all.

Her sensitivity had grown, since that time long ago, at age six, when she began listening to the feeling songs of troubadours. Being adult songs, they taught her how adults feel. She knew what it meant to lose a wife and son as much as a mother and brother. What William had left undone with his son, his affections unfulfilled, he completed in Eleanor. The princely training for his son he bestowed on his daughter. Father shared the birth of Eleanor's filly named Limona, an ancient word for Poitiers. The two of them had shared the weather and the world on horseback for years. Eleanor got to know both her father's favor and his firmness.

The talk of getting married soon was becoming as bothersome as it was necessary. Father explained life's course: Childhood. Girlhood. Damisel. Married by twelve. Motherhood by fourteen, seeing your children marry while still in your twenties. Grandmother, if you lived as long as your horse, in your thirties. At ten, her childhood ended. Could a quarter of her life be over?

She didn't have to see it; she felt the gray sky overhead looming with clouds.

Father had gone back to Poitiers Palace, leaving her on her tribe's wheat farm that lay at the eastern edge of the realm, on the Fontevrault side of the River Vienne. The land, on the road to Châtellerault, was called Faye-la-Vineuse – the place of fairies on the Vienne. Father had arranged for her to see friends she had not seen for a very long while at Raoul de Faye's farm-estate. There would be someone new in the group.

Her four visitors stomped in from visiting the half-built barn. It was clear the days of youthful smocks had left. Boys wore hose as men do, breachings, a short undergown-shirt, and thigh-length tunics. Girls had long undergowns and 'choices.' For church and show, they wore long laced shirts, free-sleeved gowns, and hard slippers. For country riding days, they wore their tight sleeves, riding hoods, and boots. Friends exchanged brooches for mantles. Males wore belts, as did physical females like Eleanor. Belts had many purposes. On them, travelers had tie-loops for a cup, an eating knife, or they could be used as a binder to carry bundles. Young women also wore flowing sashes about their waists.

Her companions pulled on Eleanor's sashes, trying to get a rise out of her.

"Yike-ah! Leef hur be!" Tova Thizay, the house cook, yelled like a Viking in bad weather. The dark-haired woman of eighteen from Scandinavia, the farm cook pitied her dejected young friend. Aproned, she husked: "Sleet on yuhr face! Don't you ken, she's trafelled the far-sturm. Let hur heff a place of hur own!" The cook was as right as her cooking.

Well-chastised, the friends lay patiently on the old hay flooring, wheeling their heels, awaiting Tova's fine meal. How Tova brought back the tastes of a child's memory! Fish in dill, Loirian duck, hare with wine and lavender, boiled roots of every color, crusty pot bread, fresh thin green beans and rosemary, sweet creamy butter mixed in harvested salt and thyme. Today's meal had been roasted chicken with bread and greens. Here tasted like home to the visitors.

Feeling far outside it all, Eleanor glumly sat by the cold fireplace nursing her mute bundle of concerns. How could they digest what she'd been through in the last three years? Like a morbid nun, Eleanor looked intently at them. "You know, a quarter of your lives are over." Her brusk remark came as little surprise to the group. Few ever tasted her words, and only lifelong friends savored her youthful truths. Her palatable sense of justice was fairer than the mean world they'd come to stomach. The urgency of the world brought upset to Eleanor, so able in mind, but powerless to act. She was unsure that she could swallow living in the upcoming world cooked up by the tall ones.

And it was coming up fast.

Eleanor regarded her old friends, realizing that she must seem as alien to them as they to her. Peculiar Calbi Lebeau had been away for years in the south Frank-lands on his adventures. The boy of twelve spoke his humorous, spiritual mind. His bruises and scars intrigued her, but she would not ask about them. Next to him was chestnut-haired Amira Neas, also twelve. Arno Allant, thirteen, Eleanor's former defender of sorts, had grown a big Adams apple and was moody around Eleanor. He clearly spent more time with men.

New was exotic Maryam Assiri, a girl of eleven-falls from Castile. Born with a smile, the slender dark-haired girl with light bronze skin got along well with everyone. She told fascinating stories and was familiar with every lyric and every troubadour band. She was in tune with the music of her generation. Her Moorish-Spanish family, traders of spices and fabrics, had just moved to ever-wealthier, tolerant Poitiers. Maryam's tribe, besides trading in hard goods, introduced foreign sounds from troubadours and dancers of Lisbon, Aragon, and Castile. A whole new range of performers sang of Iberian nautical themes and played refined Arabic instruments. Composers lived in Spanish exile, banished from Paris, a prosperous city hugely intolerant of anything youthful, passionate, and whatever was deemed unholy.

Maryam's ebullience appealed to withdrawn Eleanor. The almond brown eyes jumped with new experiences. Innocent and alluring, her quick curving shoulder shrug matched the infectious joy of her stories. More so today, for her stories reached new ears. In a warm rolling Castilian accent Maryam appealed with stories or caravans and Moorish lore:

"The Castles of Spain, their markets and customs, spicy foods, perfumes, and therapies enchant! You must travel for exotic fashions, new music, my friends." She shrugged her shoulders as to say, 'well, what do you think?'

Arno, the sad sack, blustered: "Anyone can learn that stuff in school."

School. Eleanor went cold at the sound of the word. She buried her head in her hands. Amira sensed her dismay and stood to take her friends outside, to leave Eleanor to her thoughts, sitting deep in her chair.

"Wait!" said Eleanor. "Do not go. We are old friends, and I will share my stories with you. Then you ken why I detest school."

Her friends tossed out fresh straw to cover the floor. Stretching out, the four lay on the sweet, earthy matting, twiddling wheat shafts in their teeth.

"The purpose of teachers through repetition and beatings is to make young minds old. These last years while visiting castles with Father, I went to their schools. I took the nuns' strappings as well as the next. The leather got your attention, and every student bore the marks. I wanted Father to banish the teachers, but he would not. He said, 'It was the same in my time. Look beyond the meanness of teachers. They have poor personal skills for they never cared to have their own children.' The nuns were also protected by the church. I felt lucky when we visited the courts that forbid girls to learn. Yet this prohibition seemed to trouble Father more than her getting the strap."

She took a breath, "However, I never told him the worst." They drew closer.

"Over trails, riding with Father, we spoke of innocence, the good, justness, willful power, and free action. Father sometimes read aloud the inquisitive writing of ancient Pelagius. His idea of 'free will' was beyond what my friends could understand, but I was burning to know more. I found that these ideas were actually supported by the holy scriptures!" Eleanor was flushed with excitement as she told of her discovery, then she quickly turned dark again.

"One day, in the church-school of Angers at the lunching hour, I was excited to share my newfound knowledge with my fellow students. I declared loudly as they were eating their apples and bread, 'There is no such thing as original sin! We have personal moral choice! It says so in the Bible. Let me show you.'

"The Catholic nun who overheard me was a teacher I adored, more than any I had ever met. Until that moment, we shared prayer and lively wit about life. Before I could open the scroll that I had copied from the Latin Bible to prove the point, the teacher took me to a cell. I was struck for touching a Bible and called the devil for speaking evil. But that was not as painful as seeing my beloved teacher turn into the devil herself! Insanely, her face became a red mask. She screamed, 'We are born evil! Original Sin is essential to Catholic belief! Only the mysteries absolve us from life's never-ending sin!'

"I never told Father about that horrible time. I felt I had betrayed him. He trusted me never to speak of his private knowledge of the People's Faith, saying how dangerous the truth was. Now I understand.

"I told Father that I love learning, but I resent school. He asked me to list some good teachers, and I could not. Arno, I mentioned you and your excitement that at Fontevrault Abbey your two favorite teachers never hit students. They weren't even nuns. They loved teaching and had their own children. As Father had planned, he affirmed I would travel no more. I will reside at Fontevrault through the rest of my learning years. So here I am."

Maryam slid over and motioned with her musical shoulders. "You must come to Castile. Surely, Eleanor, you wish to adventure the outer world."

"Neither Father nor I have ever traveled outside Aquitaine."

"Let's go outside and pretend," Maryam said, with roll of her shoulders.

Eleanor flickered a smile, and reached out and took Maryam's hand.

"To Spain, yes. Take a sister then, lead us away to your foreign land." The wind blew outside. The room darkened from wind-swept clouds.

Amira sang to Arno. "We are leaving. You don't need us."

He rolled his eyes prone on both elbows and warned. "To Spain, with armies of the other side marching everywhere?"

Calbi propped up his head. "We're forbidden to know Moslem ways," he added in a familiar, but deeper voice.

Amira wheeled her heels, "That's why Eleanor is interested."

"You know me too well," Eleanor said.

The once bright cottage went almost black from heavy clouds. "Will the clouds make up their minds?" Still clasping hands, Eleanor looked to Maryam as if she could answer. Sensing the other's pulse, Maryam about to speak—

Blinding whiteness splashed the walls! Faces lit, startling all five. Thunder crashed in a boom! Eleanor jumped, her feet apart. The crack rumbled long across the echoing sky; farm animals brayed. Eleanor ran to the window pointing. "Look! See the dust rise? The lightning struck there! By the tools!" Her friends edged up behind her. "That can kill you," Arno said. She went back and fell to her seat. Hard drops fell. The wet thatch house smelled of souring wood.

Outside came shouting curses, "No more rain! No more rain!" Eleanor mumbled under her breath, "more rain."

"Why would you say that?" Arno asked with concern.

She explained: "People do not understand what is going on. More rain, surely. Empty the clouds first, get it all out."

"Eleanor is right," Calbi cheered. "In my faith it is called catharsis,"

Arno was more of the no more rain camp. He explained, "The hands worry about rain. Harvest is overdue. If the crops rot, they starve."

Stepping to the door, Arno said, "I'm going to see what I can do." Calbi followed. Sizing the safety of the sky, they scuffled out looking for the bolt strike.

Eleanor turned to the girls. "You know I am soon to be a princess?"

"Sure you are." Amira popped her lips, "Spark."

Hearing her hrad name from a fellow hrad, Eleanor cackled, but things had changed for her. She wanted to address them seriously. These were friends who cared for one another. The room settled to an even gray. Imagining the lighter clouds above, she said, "I need to talk to that Calbi."

Amira filled in observant Maryam, "When Eleanor's mother and brother died, she found comfort in Calbi's beliefs. He has a two-sided view of life. Good may come from bad chances–"

"Amira," Eleanor updated firmly, "from my travels, I realize there are not just two, but many sides. During the progress of castles south, I learned all about Calbi's Catharism, the faith of knights who purify themselves, as they say, into a singularity of right action. Transformed, 'manly men' may become chevaliers." Eleanor noted Amira's rising smirk.

"I ken what you need." Amira walked behind Eleanor, untied her bun, letting down her hair. She whispered warmly, "manly men, eh?" The rich red-gold flowed to her elbows.

In her years of travel, Eleanor missed Amira the most. Her friend could read her and keep confidences. Now she could finally share with Amira what the knights said after she won the staring contest – 'return when you can kiss well. Do that, and we will make you a horsehair belt.' The prize of every fair lady. She could also tell of the trobar silvery words that made her lose the ear-tickling contest; the lips that made her want to see the world. She dared not whisper such things in front of Maryam; not until she knew her. They'd talk later. Tapping her belt, Eleanor went to the door and stepped out, fluffing out her hair.

It was the largest cloud she had yet seen. Eleanor had to turn her head and walk about to see it whole. Above the darkened earth a somber hat brimmed a distant circle of cottony white. Straight up in the gloom, a slit of white clouds billowed hard knuckles against a patch of brilliant blue. Nearby, Calbi spoke in foreign tongues excitedly showing Arno various tools. The distant trees were colorful. The storm had gone; the air had a new edge.

Feeling a rising sense to explore the area, Eleanor hurried with her sense of adventure to Tova's kitchen, waving her hands, "Where do we go for a hike—" Brushing a ceramic bottle of milk, it crashed to the stone floor. She apologized as she picked up the pieces. The upset cook wrapped them in a rag. After her Viking rage simmered, Tova motioned, "Zeer is nutheng rong veet playzure. You veel know vut to do at zee veends tooer." Eleanor gave little mind to it and held open her leather belt. Proud to see a girl wear one, Tova packed the bundle and suggested a direction in the nearby woods, getting a promise to return before sunset.

Arno stayed behind to help the farmers, but truth be told, it was the smell of Tova's muffins that resolved his conviction. Arno saw Calbi, Maryam, Amira and Eleanor bend over the animal fencing instead of walking the proper quarter mile to the farm-gate. Concerned, he distracted the farmers with horse talk. As his friends wobbled the posts back up, Eleanor waved a thanks that warmed him.

The four walked over the damp earth changing in trios and couples, stepping over branches, mud works, vines and weeds, the spent growth of autumn.

Maryam asked Eleanor about her travels but wanted to know not of rules, but of things children see: birds flying into a room, catching lovers kissing, how hot was bathwater, spirit stories of animals. Abreast in a grove of yellow Aspen, a distant brown deer sprang away. Maryam counted out the beats of hooves in fours. "It is my hobby," she replied to quizzical Eleanor.

"Calbi, what is this fascination with tools with Arno?" said Eleanor. Maryam added, "We heard Spanish, Italian, and was that Danish or German?"

"Saxon. This summer I skipped school to build walls and gardens for my uncle's vassal, far down south in Puivert. Workers spoke many tongues. Most want to learn Occitan French. They say it is the language of world trade. I learn theirs." He walked gravely, then wistfully as his golden locks blew in the breeze.

"Geb mir thynen Schaufel," Calbi sighed dreamily.

In his tone, Eleanor quickly sensed he had a new girlfriend.

"Oc, what is her name?"

"Daena Hanah."

"Let me guess..." Eleanor twiddled strands of her hair until she found the color, "a blonde?" He had been insufferably drawn to blonde Reyna.

"Oh yes. Daena is a Saxon slave from Angloland. Strong. 'Give me your shovel' was the first thing she said to me, and boy did she show me how to dig." Eleanor delighted in his energetic tone.

"I love her words, say 'rock squirrel.'"

Everyone mouthed 'rock squirrel.' It was hard to speak Anglo-Saxon.

"I have a mouth for her words." They laughed at the suggestion of kissing. "The furry creatures jumped about as we pulled stones and dug. Daena speaks like Bleddri. Remember the jongleur, vivid and lively?"

"Harsh," Eleanor said. "Welsh-Anglish rhythms are harsh."

"Did you kiss her?" Amira asked of Calbi, studying his face.

"And she wanted to be kissed. 'Trueno y lampo, feu et l'eau.'"

Maryam translated, "Thunder and lightning, fire and water."

"She is fifteen," He sighed warmly.

"A real woman!" Amira felt a little set back by Calbi's interest in another.

"That I know. Thanks to you, Amira, I am no longer a knave. Amira was my first kiss, Maryam." Amira took the compliment as they crunched the fall leaves.

"She is my bell," Calbi sang.

"You mean belle – beautiful, not a pair shape," Amira said.

"She is my bell. She rings for me, my belle, and in her bell, I feel my longing."

Amira was not the only female who wished such verse was meant for her. Changing the subject, Amira tossed a stone. "Can you believe we used to belch and gag like devils? Come Calbi, serenade us. Maryam, listen to hoot'n-angel."

He injected, "Amira, that spirit left me a hundred moons ago." In the way of honest Calbi, he said with all sincerity: "My farts have turned to kisses."

Eleanor laughed so hard she split the forked twig she was holding.

"It is true love then," she laughed.

"Must be."

Maryam asked, "Did you feel being struck down like a deer by her arrow?"

"O Yes, it was like that, the first time I saw her. How I wanted to make her smile. She's had a rough life. Daena tells me I kiss sweetly, unlike any male she'd met. I adore her stature . . . I could go on . . . she is a slave and treated badly. I fight for her as need be." He booted odd rocks along.

Amira probed his scars. "Must be worth it. Shouldn't you be with her?"

Calbi halted. He glanced sheepishly at Eleanor, gathering his thoughts.

"How badly is the slave treated?" Eleanor inquired.

"Daena sleeps safely in a good Catharic convent. It's not that bad, once you've made your mind up to fight for whom you love. Your heart blood heels you faster. What happened was, the local hands, having seen the pleasures we shared, made lusty attacks on her almost every day. We figured, if we went to the master and each of us told him in our words of our true love for the other, he would make the other workers lay off. He said, 'That's the way the world works – fend for yourself.' One night they came, drunk, wanting her, you know. She carries a dagger, so she drew first blood. I handled my share. The master realized he'd never finish construction with workers blood being spilled. He whips fairly to keep us in line. Now he sets the dogs out at night. Knowing Daena, she is already back in the field, working on the long wall. She loves building things. Her forefathers built ships. 'Sway of the world. We abide–"

"That's no way to live!" Eleanor said. "The world should work as it should. To any ruler, love matters. Calbi, if you care for her, why are you here?"

Calbi ground his heel through the grit, his eyes moist. "Your father asked me up. Eleanor, I miss you and Amira. It has been years. I miss of our times. I wish we had more of them. "

Eleanor saddened at his gash. "Father could find a new master near Poitiers."

"Oh, could you, Spark?"

"I am Eleanor," she corrected.

"Spark is better, or has the spark gone?" Amira pried.

Eleanor spiced a grin, then looked to Maryam and shivered her musical shrug.

"Like this, an arabesque," Maryam showed them how to roll their shoulders.

With happy music on their lips and hiking spirit engaged, Eleanor looked to the sky. No longer feeling gray, the clouds looked moody as Arno, welcoming as Amira, unpredictable as Calbi, adventurous as Maryam. Ruggedly, they walked on. Calbi said, "We found that lightning strike. Here." He passed the curious shard around, the look of dirty glass. "Keep it, Amira."

"Thank you Calbi. I'll put it my cedar box."

Eleanor spoke with determination, "Calbi, you must come back to school with us. You have a mind."

"Me? Eleanor, Oc. Hmm, I was teaching Arno tool names, he asked what sounded best in any given tongue. Between us four we speak Spanish, Occitan, Roman, Saxon. We went through the words for hammers and axes, flowers and clouds, shields and hearts. A fox darted from the bushes.

"Zorro, Reynard, Volpe, Fox!"

"A sport," Maryam said, "What sounds musically best to your ear?"

"Zorro," Eleanor jumped in with the Spanish word.

"Reynard," chose Amira, stepping over a bramble.

"I like Volpe," Maryam said, just to be different.

"No votes for Fox?" asked Calbi.

"Vulgar sound," Maryam said, having a musical ear. Amira added, "An animal that lies in wait for birds too dumb. Fox-fooled and eaten."

"Maybe bad animals need bad names," Eleanor said. "Zorro sounds like it can go places." She won that round.

Calbi pointed out a rut and led them aside. "Then there are names for things we do not have in our language."

"Like what?" Eleanor bent to fetch a buckle the shape of a 'G.'

"Well, in construction, Daena has big German words. I'll say it when I see it."

Over creeks and stone walls, they scouted higher grounds. The bulby underside of the clouds looked swollen. A boom of thunder traveled the distance. Eleanor chanted, "More rain! More rain!" Everyone joined.

Amira thought, it was just like Spark to bring the devil out in you, and she needed some bringing out herself. "If those farmers hear that chant, they will be chasing us with pitchforks." That was all the challenge required to provoke savage yells at the top of their lungs. The skies darkened.

Amira dared Eleanor, "You're not looking for a storm shelter, are you?"

"Not me." She tapped a right brow two-finger tribute. "I take what comes."

The four looked bravely across the burgeoning sky. An overgrowth sided high to tall trees beyond. Ahead was an odd clearing. Pushing through snags, they shared that common feeling of coming upon a ruins, an eerie sense of once-was. Stepping softly on colorful ground moss, full of about-to-rain smell, the four walked over a rise.

...

A well-weathered site, overgrown with dead vines and tall weeds, concealed eight stone pillars of some ancient Roman temple. Everything seemed going up and coming down at the same time. The structure showed traces of many existences: a roofless cottage burned by housebreakers years ago; built on a tiled Roman villa fountain destroyed by vandals centuries ago; erected over a cave crack sealed off by invader's stones thousands of years before. A skin of black slate scales covered a partial roof, from which a sluice projected, cabled by tree vines to some middle mass.

"What's that in the center?" Maryam noted. They drew close crossing the tile floor of a dwelling; at its edge was a limestone half-wall with a chimney.

"What a place for a hide-out!" Calbi clamored.

Amira and Eleanor probed the center. "Looks like a treasure."

Colorful glass shards were stacked, interlaced with weeds sat in piles made of shattered bottles, mugs, jugs, rusted metal, broken plates, and hollow log pipes. A hundred broken this and thats surrounded rust-eaten shields and crushed suits of armor. Pike lances met to the sky, topped by a vine-trapped wheel. Tendril-covered metal tubes hung from it and rattled of a fore-winding rain.

The site was strangely beautiful. This forgotten temple of refused objects was a mix of chance and unknown purpose. Calbi had the word for it, and therefore, the idea that he would say later. The experience had to come first.

Sometimes a voice says, *do not miss it this time*, for you are in a place that will soon be gone forever. A thing unique leaves itself in eternal wonder, only for you to know. Take heed, this special thing; remember, it is happening now.

A few raindrops hit; beads dotted up blue-violet glass suggesting what was to come. Notes trickled as a tuning began, then stopped altogether. A wild autumn wind ran through the trees.

"Aye!" Maryam shouted, "The Rain!"

Plink, then a 'plank,' then in eights, then in twelves the rain hit in tones alone, metallic, and yet together. The sky let loose uncountable numbers. The natural scale changed with every shift of wind. The center pile of glass, metal, and wood played upon itself. Dull surfaces washed to show true color.

The four walked about the wreckage. They had started nothing; the experience was everything, it was the whole deal, and it called to be listened to. The water-music let up, about to restart. They lived for whatever chanced next.

A tambour symphony beat. Ting tings of rain on metal, plinks pyxs on ceramic bottles, donk danks on cracked plates — myriads of impossible notes swiftly played on instruments. Thin tunes played on –glass –cup – tin – pot – vase –jug. A hundred colors, a rainbow of notes turned into thousands of fine metallic tones. A dripping cascade of notes rang a round. Kablinking rains crashed colored shards, sweeping the scape, playing harps vibrant, resonant, and muted. This lost world of unloved refuse from the summoning past, played freely by nature, as if for nature's own pleasure.

Wet vines in trees bleat in the wind, walloping flights of concord and dissonance. Wind beat across taught ropes – the drums, the drums, the drums, the drums. Gusts blew deep across, the Aeolian jugs piping wooing chords like no music ever heard, the hallows. Zip zith the wind changed direction, and so did they. Zithers and zips whirled overhead, blowing young feelings in a swirl of rainwater webs, going up vine, going down in the watery air. They threw off their hoods, tossed their caps, and opened their collars. It had to be felt on wet skin.

"Alienor?" Maryam spoke, Calbi and Amira clapping.

"That's not my name," said the voice of many names.

Whirling winds in trees rained ka-pingle, pict-pinking in a strange beauty, enchanting the temple. They played a weathered fruit machine of colored cherries, painted apples, stained oranges, purple grapes. Glorious piles of colored glass buzzed with rhythm, a jangle of rods clinked and chinged. The rain dropped heavily, collecting on the tile floor. Surfaces, sluices, splashed blix and blax, pouring deep to stones, echoing in a cellar cave below.

Whistle wind choired, '*wh-oa-oo-oh – oh-wah-we-oh.*'

Hands pressed over cold wet ears, to hear only themselves in the magical rain. Calbi doffed his shirt, imagining Daena as the rain kissed his lips.

Eleanor gyred on the tiles like a hawk, slinging off her slurry-wet gown. In underlinen, she examined the playful clouds.

Maryam rhythmed, *"al la al la – nu-na nu-na,"* pulling Amira. Both freed off clothes to feel the rain. They danced to Maryam's chant: "Only our pounding hearts to know /wild as rain we dance and grow / shout one and shout all, let me go." Stung with rain needles, up they searched, imagining how clouds looked down on rivers and farms. The four winds sent rain seeds frenetically sprinkling thin keys below. Did it hurt a cloud to rain? What inhuman thing knows human rhythm? Turning with the wind – palms pressing temples – thunder drummed within. *It* moved through them, rapid as the tings of the ephemeral. The purified danced through *It*; their cold-tipped ears heard, be the one. *It* is tis-tas, the rhythm-sound you can't yet know. *It* thought as the weather. Do not be known, think what *It* thinks. Drop unalone, we of rain. *It* was not my idea. *It* overjoyed. In cold sheets, *It* poured through the four laughers as composed instruments in a weather of wet feelings. *It* was beyond real. *It* is it, is me, we. *It* was here to sanctify accidents; we felt *It*. The young pure breath of delight in bending weather, free as wind becoming of wind – *'there is nothing wrong with pleasure'* – Eleanor opened her belt finding Tova's bundle of glass, and set it at the base of the tower. Maryam unpacked her poem:

> the offering now, whose idea was this?
> a vessel broken to matter a tower,
> used and useless pieces fated to please,
> evermore in pinking sounds,
> a trip around a rain bottle harp,
> tips and taps and timely drops,
> we walk we walk we walk we walk
> in loops of horns around,
> to again be there that place I choose.
> It makes me feel and feel and feel and I feel it
> like as just so.

Limbs stretched in wind with buzzing pops, whirling bells. Up with ties and off with sop-wet clothes, the four friends danced in the nude, setting Eleanor's shards on top the colored piles in token play to celebrate the temple tower.

Whistling whizzing metal zings, buzzes and bings livened thick the wind, trumpets blowing into being. Drums, forest, wind, water, a symphony. Victorious overjoy, the time had come. It was letting go. It could not happen just one way.

On all fours, they felt the wet tile on their palms and knees. Water pinked their faces, dripping from their chins. Flattening to feel the full music pulsing through the floor, they rolled onto their naked backs. They cyphered the clouds, no longer plump, moving off to the edge of the western sky. In the delight of rain and accident, they were unsure of being children anymore. In the innocent rain, they became aware of their evident genders.

All felt their ice-water skins numb, knowing hardness and cold wetness. Somewhere below, water sloshed to a cave.

"Aye-ho! No more rain." Maryam shouted. They listened to the last chiming drops. The weather was no longer changing – they were. Too many ideas were running, they were numb yet alive.

On top of the tower, a wheel of eight spokes rested on a lance. On its hub were two equal-armed Templar crosses from the arms dangled tins, brass cymbals, and colored shells. Quickly wringing out and donning their clothes, they ripped away wet grasping honeysuckle vines. Within stood broken lances circling the tower high pike; around it were eight stone columns. Calbi gave the last pull of weeds, jumped up, and gave the wheel a shake. Out fell spits of rainfall's end. Mud popped in heavy drops.

Generations had piled up toss-away things to catch the rain and wind. Children of ritualizing tribes, outpost Romans, scavenging Normans, war-spent knights. In some never-to-forget way, they cared for an instrument of chance play.

Maryam and Calbi brought sheltered dry wood to Amira and Eleanor, who organized the hearth. Amira trimmed out kindle-strips with her knife, once Little William's, given to her by the Duke who knew his son adored her. Amira flinted a spark to kindling with her red rock. The colored flame leapt. The four bodies huddled their knees to blow the kindle afire. Smokey flames jumped up the chimney and out the top. Bending close, they looked under the hearth mantel at chiseled words Maryam read aloud:

Who goes out into the rain to hear the music of leaves

Eleanor said, "Sufficient warning for some suffering traveler," not yet familiar with other interpretations. There was no talk, only crackle, drying clothes, and budding sensational thought.

Fondling the old buckle found on the walk, Eleanor examined the familiar shape. "G for 'Guilhèm', as locals spelled William. "My Grandfather's!" Perhaps after years of sun-drying desert war in the Holy Lands, his knights let go their war gear and templed an oath to the rain cooling wind. Eleanor said William's words, "Our unbegun lives, where are we going, when do we start to live, how do we really begin?"

They listened to the subterranean waterfall beneath. A spill-out of heavy rolling pours fell in long splashes. Echoing sounds clapped up from deep in the earth.

Birds chirped to the regained sun. Doves cooed in twos. Black ravens hopped down from the fish-scale slate looking for earth-wet worms. Time to go. The four gathered wood and kindling to replace what they had spent – for future others who might need to find wood dried out as they had.

The smell of woodsmoke increased as they walked in the yellow sun. Rain fell elsewhere, the air felt colorful, the cool earth damp. As any child knows, when sun and rain come together, there is a rainbow. Behind their shiny gold faces, in the distant dark sky a multicolor arch formed – a bridge to treasurable experiences. The tower of winds fell out of sight, distant thunder faded in rains far off, no longer to be heard.

There was no name for the tower grounds in any language except long-worded Germanic Saxon. Calbi said, "When we were building, Daena gave the term as 'einstürzendeneubaten,' don't laugh." They passed the long word around. Its meanings were hilarious. A new building that collapses having been built badly. The richer sense was the breaking down of one structure that provides the base for a newer. This state of coming and going was in all things. Falling apart and coming together at the same time, all being the same event. It was like generations of previous worlds with the next, passing through you.

Another word for their wild experience that left them famished, Calbi called Catharsis. This act, an ecstasy of his Catharic faith, celebrated the release of transformational emotions for a moral purpose., like his bodily love with Daena, or admission of crime. Eleanor looked to the sky, "Like the rain in clouds – getting every drop out." Calbi affirmed. Maryam thought it poetic. "Many things do not yet have names." Eleanor took note in a corner of her mind. Like everyone, she was marching her hungry feet to the farm porch.

The supper table in the thatched farmhouse was full of elbows, bread rolls, and stew-bowls ladled from Tova's herbed hearth pot. Tova saw from the cook-room how Eleanor and her excited friends desperately tried to explain the experience of the rain music dance. The farm laborers disputed the curses of pagan rain-makers. They listened to some to the children tell of bottles in the Tower of the Four Winds. "It sounds like garbage," a boatman said dismissively. "Besides, there are eight winds," Eleanor said. "You don't believe us. Don't you see, we made the clouds go away!" The men grumped.

Maryam invented a fable of Four Dragons. She told it eight beats at a time. The dragons came together breathing a fire that licked up a magic chimney called the tower of the winds. The conflagration sent to the sky made rain clouds vanish. That, they could believe. "Where are you from, girl?"

Eleanor intervened quickly. Having traveled enough, she knew that Maryam Assiri of Moorish blood could never sit at the same table with Catholic Nazarenes.

"This is my new friend, em...uh, Marie of France. She has journeyed everywhere." The men laughed at the fake fairy name and returned to the ordinary worries of reaping-time.

From the kitchen, Tova waved happily to the young explorers. She tossed up from her apron a cloud of utensils that made beautifully random 'ting chingle tang' sounds. In grinning solace, the Nordic cook still remembered the indescribable experiences of her youth. Pink-cheeked Eleanor lifted her wooden bowl in salute, then drank the broth, warming her being. She closed her eyes and smiled for Tova to see the soup was entirely pleasurable.

The farmers would recall this Thursday as the last rain day of 1134. With sharpened scythes and Duke William's share-plow readied, the fields would turn under quickly. Some Lord would be wheat-gladdened, and greater overlords would be happier still.

On that ordinary day, a rainbow adorned the sunset sky over a farmhouse. Wood smoke rose from a hearth. Turning every which way, a rust-spoked tower freed of weeds finally pointed into the long, dry harvest wind.

〰〰

Whitest of Winters

Eleanor of ten-winters and her sister of nine walked close and dear, warm in their lambswool-lined coats. Cold and new was this experience of delicate white fluff falling from the sky. With tongues out to taste the white, they enjoyed their first snowfall. Eleanor imagined snow blankets coating the shapes of the Tower of the four winds.

At the distant Abbey they had left, holy voices restarted their hymn. With every step in the snow, the music faded. The girls had sung their assigned parts in the choir and hour ago. Liturgical music could only be sung one way, whereas their own music could not be sung just one way.

Crunching ever forward in the snow, they counter-hummed a melody, the familiar song of childhood: *"ooh-oooh-ooo-wah-owe · o-wah-o-wah-a-ooh,"* sliding one voice with the other. Girl song just came and flowed; it never restarted and was always right. No notation in human existence would probably ever describe the songs of its children. In their innocent world, they sang a complex musical form, quite beyond the official musics of the earth. Each voice found shrills and lows, harmonies and disharmonizations, softnesses, double edges, overtone warbles, breathiness, bends. Their singing made sacred a youth that could never leave its chain of being. In their song, they loved their lives, sometimes welling an eye for their mother and brother that once lived. Floating notes of wordless intent put them far from the stress and fears of the outer world. Feeling the unconsciousness of freedom, they simply stopped. For they were happy.

Eleanor wiped a brow and politely asked, "Your holy gown, how did it fit?"

"A little big," replied short Petronilla.

"You'll grow into it. I'm burning up. I miss wearing smocks."

"Nothing like smocks," Petronilla agreed.

Eleanor tugged open her collar. "You took your habit off. You're smart."

"I know."

Outmaneuvered by her sister's self-confidence, Eleanor warned, "Well, you should be wearing yours. When you look like them, you get respect."

"Respect?" Petronilla said. "I am not sure I need any of that."

Family supper waited down the village road. Eleanor knew that once home, she had to tell of the emotional events at the Abbey, certainly to Ellen, the steward. In the distance, Amira had left her cottage to join them for supper. She could practice telling the story to her friend.

"Hi Amira," Eleanor greeted, beginning their singsong ritual.

"Hi Amira," greeted her sister.

"Hi, Petronilla, how are you?"

"Fine today, thank you."

"I like your holy gown, Eleanor. How are you?"

Eleanor wiped a brow "I'm burning up, with this fur mantle and layers of clothing. We were just singing for the chapel master."

"Holy songs," Petronilla added.

"Glorious songs?" Amira said, looking around to be safe. She let her notes down in lower pitches. "Odeo lordy lo how low can you go." Not to be outdone, Petronilla and Eleanor stretched their long faces, singing low and woeful until their voices reached scratch bottom. They laughed until the cold air hurt.

"I was telling Petronilla about Berry and Guisana, and their new baby."

"Oh yes?"

It was always good to run things by Amira, she being older, and fair.

"You know the monk with hair coming out his ear, Berry. He had a baby with Guisana, the pretty nun with the pink cheeks, eh, the teaser."

"I heard. We have enough orphans," Petronilla said dismissively. Eleanor glared at her sister.

Amira said, "Tell me, I want to know."

"Before we sang in the choir, I was in the room with the colored horses on the ceiling where we read scriptures forever."

"And ever. You recited almost as well as Amira," Petronilla said.

"Well, I was reading the scriptures so well, all proper in my habit gown," Eleanor lifted her chin. "The nuns asked me to the chapel wing. A lesson in life, I am telling you!"

The cold and thick snow seemed to vanish as the listeners took in the drama of the fast-talking girl. Three columns of breath trailed their hoods.

"Guisana has all kinds of ideas. About how to look lovely for men. She became a nun for loving too many of them. She calls me Elle. I let her." Eleanor flirted her finger, circling from nose to eyebrow to cheeky grin.

"She does have curves." Amira gave her famous smirk.

Eleanor spoke faster, "The head nuns and monks were judging Guisana, Berry, and their baby. Amira, it was like Calbi and Daena who went before their master to tell of their love. Well, it was not going well. A bald monk accused them, 'You did not pass Arbrissel's test!'"

"Slow down, Eleanor." Amira calmed with her hands.

Eleanor drew a breath and said, "Does anyone ken what the test is?" Snow fell on shrugs. "The head monk was angry, trying to make them feel bad about something. Some new abbess with a mean look said, 'We are forbidden to celebrate love,' I think she said. 'You will be whipped and turned to go your separate ways.' Amira, out in the cold! As if love is a sin. I could not bear it."

"What did you do?"

"Stallions, they loved one another, did it matter where they met? I told Guisana, 'Say the things you told me of how you loved Berry.' I told Berry, 'Don't speak holy-like, say as she.' Clear as a bell clap, their hearts rang true."

"Well, what did they do?"

"Oc, they said words didn't matter, then wanted to pat my head. I may look ten-winters, but I ducked them until they gave me a good reason. They said, 'Rome's new edict. Union can no longer be a choice for clergy. For breaking the edict a punishment is fixed.' I said, 'What manner of edict is that? You can't break an edict that you didn't know existed. No one should ever be punished for love!'"

"Eee, Eleanor, did any of that work?"

"I haven't finished. I said, 'Send them to my father to find them a place.' What a moan of commotions. They told me to leave. Guess what chanced?"

"Tell me."

"Grand Abbess Petronille de Chemillé came to the floor. I suppose she was in the back praying or tribulating or something. She shushed everyone. I am talking a serious shush-around. Like "SHUSH!" with her face and hands. "We take no vow of celibacy!" She asked careful questions to make sure, it seemed to me, that the two did love one another. Did they have a trade to practice and all."

"And?"

Eleanor beamed. "They agreed to my plan. I wish you were there Amira, to remember it because I did not get all the words. If you recited it back, I am sure I would understand now. Anyway, when the Grand Abbess left, she patted my head. I let her. I don't care if I was her little lamb, I was right. The couple atoned with words and Abbess de Chemillé granted a wedding blessing."

"That is good news. All in a day?" Amira asked.

"All in the last bell!"

Petronilla said, "The Grand Abbess has powers."

"More than a King!" Eleanor assured.

Amira thought and said, "Did they thank you? You got the deal going."

"Me?" Eleanor said. "It was love speaking. True love is never a sin, it is always right, by every code since Grandfather William."

The girls strode the snowy field into a hard trail of wagon ruts. Eleanor's mind was alive. What was Fontevrault's test? Was it like Buskin's, ferreting out good lovers from bad, turtle toes, what could it be? The three started shivering. Their feet were ice.

In the wee light of winter eve, the heavy door of the townhouse opened to the freezing snowfall. Servants herded the three children to the warmth of the fireplace. Hands on cold cheeks, they laughed as their teeth chattered making a chorus of zzuzzs before the fire. Servants traded wet clothes for blankets and then plopped the children into a grand warm-water tub.

The adults were not yet home. The household staff let the children eat playfully, ambling the thin line of fun and manners. After washing teeth and tongue with white towel-cloth, and combing their hair with fifty strokes, the children went to bed, tired as winter cubs.

From the lulling sleep of her pillow, it sounded like Grand Abbess Petronilla talking with father, but Eleanor was content – it was not her business, she dozed and gradually fell asleep. After a while, the bedroom door opened slowly. Duke William checked on the little ones. He closed it quietly with care, respecting the boundaries of angels in dreamland.

Chinon was another winter experience, new as the rare-fallen snow.

The fire-hearth on the high floor of the Poitiers Palace was not complete. The Aquitaine family court moved temporarily to Chinon, three snowy leagues east of Fontevrault on the other side of the Vienne. Chinon belonged to Anjou, not Aquitaine, so the Dukes made a special arrangement.

Chinon was a high, long castle, a place where the children had to make do with fields, forests, and trails. They explored for new playscapes, saddened to find no new buildings to climb, and every place worn down. Anjou had been generations at war. There were no funds to construct anew as in Aquitaine.

The weak winter sun inched higher into the bright cold blue. The snow mounds about Chinon were peppered with boys and girls. Play was different. Knave chasers of cats and birds became the spearman of lions and dragons. Hrad girls pinned down only one boy at a time. As usual, the boys and girls acted out every war for the last four hundred years. There were far more enemies to pick from now and not just long swordsmen. Now the enemy could be a cruel lord, a villain slave, an outlaw, a taxman. Tribal names from threatening to friendly: Saxon, Vikings, Celts, Danes, Parisii, Norman, Gauls, Angevins, Pictones, and Poitevins.

Romans, Greeks, Egyptians, and Hun hoards were a thing of the past. The new armies of the one and only Great Crusade, of thirty-five years ago, were the Moors of Spain, the Saracens of Turkish land, the Moslems of Arabia, the Shahs of Persia, the Rajas of Hindia. "Glory to God," was the new call.

Young Eleanor talked of her grandfather's Crusade career as noble. High in the Turkish mountains, the Saracens had him outnumbered. He escaped by the skin of his fingertips to Antioch. Like every other child, the girl refought her forefather's battles. She imagined her own courageous victory to lead not 1,000 but 100,000 like Alexander. How real play-dreams seemed to become.

Eleanor was excited. She knew the exact role to play in a mock-crusade battle. "The Duke!"

Everyone welcomed Eleanor's father riding up on a fine stallion.

"Good day! Having fun in your first snow, everyone?"

"Father, we are going to fight the Crusade like grandfather William."

"I see. Well now. Eleanor I am sorry but you must come with me."

"Aww. Do I have to get fit for that stupid gown?"

"You are a Princess. This snow isn't going anywhere! You can play tomorrow. Hop up front now." Eleanor rolled her eyes. Her friends helped her up.

"Amira, will you play my part?"

"Certes!"

Amira agreed to play the enemy, just as Eleanor, as any hrad would. Foes were fun; heroes had to be proper. A foe, by the rules of their 'dark code', got to set the stage and the quest for the challengers. Devious Amira set the sides as Eleanor might – foe upon foe, no obvious heroes, encouraging a challenging sense of play. Saracens and Templars were raring to battle.

High on a Chinon backroad ridge, Amira looked down the slant of the road that turned under a horse bridge. Was it too steep? Squeezing herself into an abandoned cart made into a royal wagon, she was a captured Arabian Sharif Tax Collector hoarding piles of crusade riches. Arno, the corrupt Templar guard escorting her, held the wagon from dashing downhill. Ahead in the high snowy bushes, Saracen horsemen readied, crouching low, peeping for the wagon to descend on and reclaim their treasure. She hid the trove from the bandits, pressing her rocks in her ragged sack under her legs, knees together.

The challenge was this – if they could catch her by ride's end, they got the treasure. If she made it, she could ask them to do anything. They shook spit-hands on the deal.

Arno shoved the gem carry-wagon off. As Amira insisted, he'd greased the axles well with lamb fat. As it rolled, he and his Templar guards kept up, at least at first. The Saracen horde ran down the hillside throwing reed spears, entirely missing the speeding wagon. She did not curse the bump that made the wheels leave the ground. The Sharif shut her eyes, there was nothing to do but soar and keep balance . . . then come down. When the wagon skidded into the sharp turn marking the end of the road, the bag ripped open, scattering her precious collection. The victors snatched silver ingots, rubies, gold, emeralds, marble Venus statues. Amira dusted off, pushing away Arno's pretend escort. Did he even try to slow her down? The chargers took their haul up the snow hill to account in the dry bushes.

The counting voices stilled. Amira climbed the slope to see faces in the shrubs burning with curiosity. From a fine leather valise found in the hedges, they had pulled out yellowed drawings. A tall, very naked woman stood with a tall, very naked man. No part was left undrawn. Sometimes the woman was alone; always the same woman. None had seen a developed woman's sex in such detail. Before anything could be said, out came Amira's fire-flint. "I'm burning these! Give me them." The drawings left their hands. "She has brimstone! Curse the Witch!" the knaves ran down the hill, yelling. "She's going to burn them!" Amira growled, thinking, 'you bet I am.'

Being called a witch was worse than being one. Bad rumors followed, always hard to break. As she gathered sticks to strike sparks and make fire, Amira thought many things. The leather valise with a brass 'G,' looked as noble as the buckle Eleanor had found for her. The drawn eyes of the woman reminded her of Eleanor. The pictures were like Amira's collection of stone mothers, all naked women. The church crushed all mother-stones, the fertility figures of her tribe, once a blessing for crops. Her stone dolls and gem rocks were hers! Now they were in the hands of ignorant boys.

To be called a witch was unfair. She piled twigs and papers imagining the fire in her mind, 'give me my rocks back, or I will curse you.' Set to start a fire, she looked at the paper people. This was the first time she'd seen male anatomy. She felt curiosity, not shame. Maybe the boys never saw a woman. In the midst of her tempest, she had a change of cleverness – the two-sided view of Calbi's belief. Rather than act an accused witch, she would play the opposite. Placing the pictures in the folio, she kicked the sticks, ran down and surprised the huddle of boys.

"Evil Saracens! The Great Mother Neas of Antioch gives you the eye of godly wrath! Sinners of the flesh! You have seen Eve naked like the fertility stones we crush. You must pay for your sins! We spit hands on the deal, right Arno? I made the end of the road, so I get to ask! Saracens, return your ill-gotten treasures!" She shook her new valise open wide. "Come to me on your knees! Repent and see the error of your ways!" Each Saracen hung his head and snaked their way forward on their knees, seeing quite well their errors. In the satchel, every boy carefully placed his gem next to the drawings, so as not to disturb the treasures of the rightful owner.

In the play of the Chinon games, combat fever struck deep. Hrads and knaves naturally wanted to know about real wars, told by an expert. A three-hour walk west of Chinon, on the other side of the Vienne, took the children to Fontevrault to hear of the famous battle of Poitiers in the fall of 732 that entirely changed the world. Knights and men-at-arms came from afar to billet near, to visit this legendary warfield that ran from Poitiers to Tours, pray for souls, and hear the annual telling of this epic event.

At midday, the largest room in Fontevrault Abbey overflowed. Under the ceiling of painted colorful horsemen in woods with shields, swords, and lances, Vivian pulled her hood wide to her shoulders and brushed back her dark hair.

Vivian Burka was an authority on the history of the Battle of Poitiers. Like many of her listeners, she was a descendent of its warriors, although her ancestry was uncontrollably diverse. By teaching on sanctuary grounds, Vivian escaped the dogma of history. Speaking the Frank and not the Roman truth drew a crowd. The teacher used controversy and drama to tell of the sacred battle – that way her story would be remembered. That was her defense; none could deny her ends. Vivian's superiors entered to see what trouble she would cause today.

Pleased by the gathering mass of visiting soldiers, young adults, nuns and monks, Vivian was amused by popular Amira. Boys stopped to talk to the girl with the valise. They let her hold their favorite toy soldier, The Hammer himself.

In walked Duke William with Prince Taillebourg, a proven chevalier. The room came to its feet. Everyone wanted to hear Vivian's story. Without introduction, she barked as the commander of the knowledge she possessed.

"Why do our fathers fight in the Holy Lands today? Did you know a battle as great as The Crusade was fought outside our Abbey? Long before beating the fear of Christ into the Moslem, they were here, beating the fear of Allah into us." The seated Chevaliers used hand gestures to calm the stirring crowd. Vivian walked, pointing to the courtyard. "If through that doorway, you could see through time 400 years ago, you would see the enemy washing his feet in our fountain, right there! Ay you, sitting pretty on the bench! Who is eating your ancestor's harvest? Sisters and brothers, look how the red crescent flies bravely over the chapel! Wait, no, it's a mosque!"

Over the rumblings, Vivian continued, "Now, when the Moslems invaded Europa, they swept through Aquitaine. Our defeats followed on defeats. Every fighting Poitevin, all of your forefathers ran as far as Tours. At the Loire, they lieged to a great overlord to turn the Moslems back." She pointed to the children. "Who was our greatest French general?"

"Charlemagne!" spoke an eager boy.

"Many say that. Sadly, not all stories recited are true. Charles Magnus is officially remembered as the first Holy Roman Emperor, crowned by the Pope of Rome. The famous Chanson de Rollant mentions Charles the Great, but no song remembers Charles the Greater. Who was he?"

"Later I might explain why composers of the Song of Rollant purposely placed Charlemagne too late in the story to make a difference. Most know why. The facts of history were simpler. So, halting the Moslem advance saving the Franks and protected the Church? Right. Out. There! was not Charlemagne, but his grandfather Charles Martel, The Hammer. And I said, Hammer!" Vivian pulled off her shoe, repeatedly banging it on the rostrum.

She made everyone laugh, leading a peasant stoop-heading round: hunching, acting ignorant, throwing head-to-sky. Others jumped about and joined, reached out arms in surrender, slapping their head, mouth gaping open – a masterful custom, well-enjoyed.

Eleanor laughed aloud. "The Hammer?" Vivian's story was nearly grandfather's version. Ever since he met chanson composers, grandfather sang mocking battle songs. There was verse for a Chanson Martel, but the Chanson Rollant was chosen. The writers displaced Charlemagne as far from the song's battle as he was displaced historically from Martel's great battle.

"Outside Poitiers, the Moslem horde was decisively halted. How did Martel do that in 732?" She put on her shoe and lifted a horse stirrup. "Here is the battle stirrup of Charles Martel that gave his army fortitude to stay on their horses." She held it before rows of wondering oooh-ing faces. "Believe that, and I'll trade you a pound of feathers for a pound of silver. In truth, it was battle discipline: never break the line! This is a horse stirrup of our present chevaliers. Stirrups and saddles power the French charge, the chevauchée, today's conquering hammer blow. Back then it was mostly bareback. Martel learned to use stirrups from his foe, in time. So how did he hit the enemy like a hammer?

"Charles the Hammer was feared because no one knew when or where he would strike. Indeed, his weapon was a battle hammer; straight blades were caught in charges. The blow came without warning with swift cavalry concentrated at one point. Martel had a legion of great hunter-scouts who knew the passages of the land, unlike the guessing enemy. These pioneering scouts stealthily destroyed enemy sentinels. This brave counter-scout operation left the enemy blind. Without a word, the Hammer hit in the devastating tactics of lightning surprise and concentration on the battlefield. When enemy cavalry counterattacked, the scouts gave distant warning so that Martel's men-at-arms could set up disciplined shields and phalanxes of long spears.Martel had a legion of great hunter-scouts who knew the passages of the land, unlike the guessing enemy. These pioneering scouts stealthily destroyed enemy sentinels. This brave counter-scout operation left the enemy blind. Without a word, the Hammer hit in the devastating tactics of lightning surprise and concentration on the battlefield. When enemy cavalry counterattacked, the scouts gave distant warning so that Martel's men-at-arms could set up disciplined shields and phalanxes of long spears."

Vivian's winning stories, dreamt of that night, were played out by children in the fresh fallen snow the following day.

Sundays were the best day for war. Adults in mass could not rule their play. Roman ruins were fun, but the best forts were half-built constructions going up.

High on Fontevrault scaffolds, vacated by workers on the holy day of rest, scouts peered at battles below. By unnamed rules, even Reyna could play Charlemagne, but only stripling boys could have title of Le Martel the

Hammer, Dom Rollant the Horn Blower, or El Cid the Sword. Arno's three-year seniority made him King of the Snow Castle.

The battle stratagems of this pure knight were savored.

"Ha-Mar-tellll!" hailed the running boys with an axe-hammer throw, a fist-arm slamming into an open hand. From the snowy woods the charged with sticks and snowballs into greatly imagined fields of carnage. Cavalry charges were numerous. "I'll be your horse, jump up on my shoulders." Girl knights had no issue mounting boys' shoulders, as hrad girls were light and fierce. Teams pushed and pulled to bring riders down and be the last one standing.

With victories every ten minutes, winners piled up waiting to be dubbed.

"A skilled sword fighter becomes a knight by the dub," Arno explained to new ones. "For great deed-doing, a knight is dubbed a Chevalier. To dub, I rest the great stick on your shoulder. Pretend it is a sword and I am going to chop your head off. Don't worry, I won't. You are showing trust. I will tap the sword, halo your head, and tap again. Eleanor, show us." She took the stick and said "Kneel. I dub thee Sir William." She tapped Calbi's shoulder once. That was it. Arno double dubbed him. Eleanor rolled her eyes at the unnecessary work.

Increasingly, Eleanor saw herself being fought over, rather than fighting herself. The role of Queen uninspiring. Remembering Martel's tactics, Eleanor found fulfillment in the role of scout and got to explore and spy. Snow queens like Reyna took her royal place. They adored fluffy lines. "Calbi of the South, a fief I grant if you swear lief to your liege lord Arno. Be his vassal, my champion!"

"What are you talking about?" a boy new to the game asked.

Reyna motioned, "Get the Scout."

Snow queens asked Scout Eleanor to explain fief, vassals, lief and liege. She enjoyed clarifying rules. Questions often gave her new ideas for better play.

"All this snowscape is King Arno's," explained Eleanor. "He granted Calbi a fief, that snow ridge. If attacked, Calbi defends. By himself, he is outnumbered. So Calbi swears his lief to call on others."

"Lief?" frowned the boy.

"One's code of life and the love of it. Swearing your lief to Arno makes him your liege lord. You becomes Arno's vassal. Your snow fief is protected by all vassals showing allegiance to Arno, oc?"

"Oc."

"A final thing. Feuds irk me - they draw out arguments over rules. Do that and you will hear one word you don't want me to call you. Toad. Ugly Toad, if I'm really mad. It is worse than a cheater. A Toad ends the game for all. Have a sense of fair play and don't disappoint everyone."

The boy nodded his understanding to Eleanor.

Sometimes warriors charged a human fortress called a Viking circle defense. It required girls to stand centered within a ring of Viking warriors who were supposedly made valiant by defending their 'women.' Rarely could a young Viking ring be overpowered, not because of valiance – a Viking warrior could go berserk on you.

Calbi played Berserker well. He held his breath until he got red and crazy in the face. Then in wild moves, yelping a fright of nonsense, attacking everything in sight. You never knew what he would do, and that was the fun he had with everyone. Sometimes he went too wild and got thrown in the snow donjon.

Scout Eleanor could be captured and imprisoned like any other. In the snow prison, she met fellow captive Calbi. She was happy to have some time alone with him. She thanked him for sharing his words that guided her when her mother and brother died. They each asked questions about the other's religion and strange holy rituals. Calbi's warm words about honor, directness, knowing your purity – unspoken of in her Catholic faith – entered the church of her heart. Calbi confessed that he missed his Daena, hard at work in Albiga while he took winter school at the Abbey. She was safe. The Catharics 'corrected' the overseer that had treated her so badly. When Calbi said he missed her thin blondness, Eleanor pulled the most gold parts of her elbow-length hair over her shoulder to her front and gave him a joyful hug. Better than a dub.

Then it started. "You are talking about my grandfather! He fought The Crusade!" "Did not!" "I say he did!" "Did not, liar, liar . . ." A hail of snowballs, stick bows and curses filled the air, uglier than a lake of toads. Such feuds never had an end in sight, until the music came, causing the feuders to cease their huffing and shouting, coming to a breath-taking silence.

Music befell the white world. The farmer fiddler was no troubadour, but he plucked at strings, his music making better the cold hours. The fiddler let his tall black-haired daughter of fifteen play as well. She used a horsehair bow and called the instrument a viola. Four years back, no one watched their play. Now, Eleanor made sure extra food and wine came from the Palace for the peaceful peasants and poor farmhands who came to make music and watch the battles. They were accompanied by their children who cared not to play at war.

The elder farm girl bowed songs on her viola as her skinny blonde girlfriend of Eleanor's age skated nimbly on the ice in her own perfect meter. The young dancer gave spirited leaps that sent her gliding like a swan on winter ice. The duo usually hid their unhappy faces behind their long hair, ashamed that they were workers of the field, with no childhood like the others. But for this rare month of winter snow, they became a source of joy for all, entertaining with song and dance. Eleanor had discovered that Calbi was a distant cousin to the farmer fiddler and that the clan had traveled from the beaches south of Aragon. Eleanor gifted the girls privately with her father's agreement, certain they would become masterful troubadour performers. Eleanor's charity was to provide their chance to become more than field workers.

In the music of the romp and stomp, the once feuding knaves whirled wildly on the ice. Farm serfs and villagers danced arm-in-arm, becoming children in snow again. Their raw music brought joy. Dancing in teams, often led by the blonde dancer, they spun in wheels running round in circular trains, harder and harder they pulled to see who would let go. When anyone reeled off, everyone flew to share as one, crashing into the snow.

✳

Fathers played in the snow when they had the time. After a massive snowfall, such a time had come. Snow this deep was rare. The men began a secretive plan for Chinon. They asked their daughters to invite Fontevrault orphans who could behave. Eleanor and Amira offered the tonic of play to the children as a charitable escape from Psalm-singing. The deaf would learn manners, and in return, the girls would learn many hand gestures, some kinder than others.

A good part of the day, fathers William and Paul labored with the children on the forest side of the Chinon castle wall. The daughters could not believe how much muscle the men put into building what looked like a snow tower. In a fury of snow on snow, the fathers heaped the work until it topped their heads. The children watched. The men cut a dozen steps in the back of the main tower, climbed, and added more. At the top, they shaped a throne with arms but no back. Monks in front shoveled and piled up snow, creating a ramp.

At their chatty supper, the men devoted their attention to hear the young. The little storytellers gave their opinions and wished for the world. After hardy eating, fables and much laughter, the children were led off to bed. Duke William held a spike of warm cider and toasted "To the children!" He ran outside into the freezing twilight, followed by the men. Upon the snow ramp, he spilled a libation of cider, "To the children! Aoi!" and the splash turned instantly to ice. Inspired by this happy accident, under torchlight the men poured thin buckets of water to ice down the run.

In the morning sun, the Chinon ice-glide stood, a white tower with a glistening drawbridge and long ramp that run into snow-limbed trees. Paul presented Elmwood sleds he had shaped. William carried a roll of flat rugs for the larger children like himself. The glee of orphans and fathers filled the air with anticipation. Fathers first tested then modified the banks. The bone-shaking sled runners went fast, but rugs were kinder – they did not rut the ice. By unwritten rule, the sleds fell into lesser use, to preserve the rare winter world.

On top of the icy throne, Eleanor climbed over her father's snow-dusted coat. She sat between his legs on his unrolled rug. As she pulled the front up over their feet, William steadied, saying he had done this with his father. A cup of hard cider appeared to imbibe before the ride. With a sip of warm apple nectar from father, she warmed both hands and handed it up for his turn.

She studied the rug patterns in her grandfather's threadbare carpet brought from Antioch long ago. An ornamental garden formed from trellised white gates, red fruit, and yellow flowers. Grape vines and leaves curled in arithmetic patterns of faded gold on deep blue. "Holding tight!" She gripped. His might heaved them off the throne. Buckled legs protected her from side to side danger; he held her hands on her rein of the rug. The wind rushed by as they bumped and slid as fast as galloping horses, so fast the air made tears come from her fast-blinking eyes. Faster went the distant white fields and snow capped trees, ice on the river. Her father was laughing, she imagined wings lifting her.

The flying carpet came to a cold white end. Eleanor's heart beat in her ears, everyone cheering them to rise. They marched back, feet in the snow, catching enough breath to speak. "Go, Eleanor. Glide the white run!" As loud as the lioness could roar, "Go! Go! Go-ooo!"

William said, "Your turn."

Eleanor looked up to the white throne and climbed the icy steps.

"Watch me!"

Looking down the ramp, stunned, she took a sharp breath.

Atop by yourself, looking down the wayward curve, aware of every cold danger, knowing you'll never be this little again, you throw out the rug and run for all its worth, sliding, flying at speeds barely breathable. For it is just you alone, with all the silent confidence of your father. In the savage glee that will so rudely end, a glimmer of a question takes hold. Trudging back up huffing, you realize this is an endless wish. You promise to ask him someday, and you know you never will. He has gone inside. He knows this question and will answer you in another way. Yet, the words escape into clouds, heating the air: "Can the run be made longer?"

Young Eleanor stepped up the stairwell quietly. It was a gray-bound day, weeks past New Year. The Poitiers Palace household had taken a nap. Eleanor softly brought her father's tea to the attic. Chinon had been fun, but it was back to work in Poitiers for him. He had to plan for spring to make an ever-greater harvest. Maidservants reminded relentlessly of mother's dictum. 'Do not bother him – let your father work and rest as he sees fit.' The civil house rules had a sensible rightness. Eleanor reasoned, after all, he did not bother her when she played. Carefully she approached the top of the steps.

William received many visitors in his private office. Here he held the best of courts, better than the throne room. The new attic office with a fresh-cut stone fireplace had two windows. The mid-room desk faced the eastern sunrise view, with the sunset behind. Winter light was good for working on Aquitaine scrolls. Accounting from last year he could maintain the common wealth for

1135. He mused, 'Eleanor is eleven, and I am thirty-five. The snow of their play is melting. Mill streams would soon flow full for production.' Hearing the music of children counting outside gave him the greatest pleasure, and he closed his eyes and leaned back.

At times, his daughter asked polite questions about running the realm. William spoke of judging crimes, family disputes, prior law, keeping the peace, and occasional difficulties with the church and the powerful. In their travels, Eleanor had been upset, seeing favors dispensed rather than justice. He was glad of her sense for fairness. Decisions against a castle lord were sometimes hazardous or even fatal to a ruler who dispensed judgment, yet one must judge property rights. To hear numerous pleas of the realm, one had to group common disputes as single cases and verdicts. That way judgments could be applied in a uniform way, saving time and ensuring fairness. Eleanor never pressed to ask further details about justice, and William worried if she was fearful of such responsibility.

Stepping quietly, Eleanor softly placed the round teacup by her father, then stepped back to the top of the stairs. She thought it impossible that he could read, with all the children outside yapping. Eleanor was tempted to trounce them, but she figured a greater ruckus would disturb him. As quiet as Eleanor could be, she tipped up on her toes to peek. Over his shoulder, the vapor rose from the woodruff bark tea. It had a deep raisiny flavor and was his favorite, fast becoming hers. In the winter light, she found in him something earthy and smart, strong and leathery, smart and willful. Eleanor could not possibly realize she had these same qualities because the servants were so intent on minding them out of her. She rolled down on her toes, being careful, so he did not notice her.

William cleared his throat and sipped the steamy cup as she turned to leave.

"Eleanor, these are the rolls," he said without looking.

Immediately, she raced forward to his front side to show her eager face.

William gave a hopeful look. It comforted him to be with his first-born, creaking the floor, smelling soapy fresh with intent cheer in her eyes. Having shared their whimsical winter sled play, he said in a rich tone, "You sled like a Stoic."

"Stoic?"

"A philosophy from Greece that says pain is irrelevant. You did not let the pain of chill get to you. With no emotion, you did what had to be done, all by yourself." He smiled with a blink.

"The church says philosophy is pagan."

Chuckling, William said, "A way of life knows no bounds. The Fontevrault order believes in Fontevrism the way a Stoic believes in …"

"Stoicism. Is that a good philosophy?"

"Parts are, at times. Choose to be eclectic. Wait until you get to Epicurus, an opposite philosophy that finds good in pleasure." He cleared his throat.

Eleanor wanted to ask, 'And which is better?' She wanted to hug him, everything he said was interesting, but she knew not to ask for more of his time. Probably he answered that question if she thought about it. He was like that. He coughed, ready to speak about what he wanted her for.

William swept his arms over the table. "Ready to take this 'snow run?'"

It was his gaming way to say, let's read together. With both hands, Eleanor took a sip from his round cup, put it down, "mmm, let's go."

He toned deeply, "These are the official rolls of our people and their property. We keep the count of people and property for all Aquitaine taxation and reckoning. Sometimes I am called The Count. These numbers guide how to use the land. The Normans made a census of the English colony called the Domesday Book. The centerpiece of any holding is the plow. There, see dear? We count villagers, free-holders, slaves, and the priests they must house. Priests are required to be boarded, so the church does not have to pay for their keep. Each holding has many priests." Eleanor had surmised it before he said it. She was reading ahead, seeking Fontevrault to ask about the test.

She volunteered, "It looks like five priests per holding on average."

"About. Did you know many owners board more priests than field hands?"

"Do the priests work?"

"H'ah, well, some orders do dear, the worthy do. Bernard's Cistercians are some of the best. Well organized, obedient, but they come at a price. His laws, not ours. Bernard and the Pope of Rome are a pair."

"Why does everyone say Pope of Rome and not Pope? There is only one."

"There are five Popes that the rest of the world calls Patriarchs. They rule from Antioch, Jerusalem, Alexandria, Byzantium, and Rome. Just before the First Crusade, forty years ago, the Pope of Rome split from the others. Your uncle Raymond is to marry the Queen of Antioch." William studied the scroll.

"Then we will have our very own kingdom across the sea."

"Yes in Outremer. I have scrolled past the bishops, their holdings are huge." He put down the parchment.

"The wealth of Aquitaine lies in the mill, my someday Duchess. The plow and workshop count but watermills run every new geared engine. Each has its own industry. I license them and encourage new guilds every spring. Mill saws do the work of four lumbermen, never complaining, working all day long. Mills loom clothing for tailors and bellow fires for foundries. Our neighbors in Toulouse, where I was born, unwisely let Bernard and his beholden Templar knights seize entire rivers of mills. I won't let them."

Eleanor asked, "Templars are knights, not chevaliers." He nodded, tapped on the scroll as if wanting to say something. He looked to his Poitiers window. "When you are older." Eleanor frowned. She wanted to know every adult idea. Father had more on his mind.

"Plows. On a good farm, you want one plow per three workers. That's proper load balancing. Your friend over in Chauvigny, Edeva. Let's look at her property." He scrolled back a bit. "Edeva's land counts two working sisters, three plows, four mares, eight oxen, twenty pigs, ten serfs. Only two priests. Hard work there. No wonder Edeva wanted a new slave. Let me write that in."

"Her name is Daena."

"We don't get personal; slave will do." They looked at one another squarely. Eleanor said, "Since priests don't work, Edeva will need four plows."

"Exactly," William said, surprised at how fast his daughter reasoned. "Ellen can size up the land to see who pulls the weight. If she advises, I will lend a commune plow. The new ones have rounded sides. A good ox team can rip through a furrow."

William talked about land productivity, enlarging the market, and of necessary taxation and proper uses of taxes. The idea was that to have castle wealth, farms must produce enough to be able to sustain their families first. "Many lords are mean to their landowners. You have met the type. 'Mine, mine, mine,' about things they don't properly own. Eleanor, remember this: Avoid greed as you would deadly pestilence. True in wealth, truer in love. The fable of King Midas teaches the reverse to good rulers. The secret of wealth is not taking, but giving. We give silver to make others' efforts greater. There is a fine wisdom to this. We call it investment."

"What was that about love?" she said. They laughed. William took her hands.

"I will tell you about love, is that what you want to hear?" His daughter flashed her eyes. "No one loves unless impelled by the persuasion of love. You felt that in your heart as a potential for those two girl performers that we stipend in Aragon. That, my dear, is a compassionate investment." William proudly kissed her fingers. "Aquitaine fathers, elders, are impelled by this persuasive feeling for our children – only Aquitaine affords to give children a childhood. An investment in a strong foundation allows you to build great things. You improve on a thing; your children will be greater." Eleanor's brows fell into mindfulness.

"Now let's talk about taxation. Due to the King in Paris, the land-fiefs pay in various ways. Mills pay in pack-loads of grain or milled flour; salt-houses pay in pounds of yield. Woodlands are measured in leagues square. Timber-mills use either boardage lengths or weights. Scales are faster and truer than measures." He explained how to use a currency rate in French Sous to value all goods to unify general market barter and the rich world of foreign trade.

To Eleanor, everything seemed obvious. She consumed laws and figures like candy. Father went back to making notes. Reading on, seeing the beginnings of the Fontevrault entry, she rushed questions, "Why is Fontevrault Abbey special? What is Arbrissel's test? No one will tell me."

Without looking up, he answered, "Sweetheart, that will come later. I am busy with accounting today."

Her heart tingled as she tiptoed away – 'Sweetheart.' She wanted to tell him that was her favorite word; perhaps it was the word itself, for it must be said like a floating thing, rich from the soul like a genuine gift. But, manners. She walked to the top steps. He suddenly spoke: "Amira. What do you think of her?"

Eleanor turned with a quick reply, "A friend who can be trusted." That was all he wanted. Down the stairwell, she traveled with his hum.

A week later came amazingly good news. Amira was to live permanently with Eleanor as her maid in training and 'counselor.' William explained, "Amira is two years older, chosen for her, well, generally good sense, and she comes from a trusted family. Ellen and I have seen you two together. Amira has a good ear, a sense for taste, and she knows to stand off to allow your own experiences."

When Amira Neas heard, she exploded with joy. Her parents were happy that she could live some days at home, at least until summer. This station was Amira's wish. A life with Eleanor's strong-willed sense of fairness, adventure, and broad vitality. Household tasks would be many. She learned to be swift and accurate, winning her mother's approval. The prospect of making Eleanor and her court more beautiful made her smile. However, being a counselor, having no idea what that was – well, she could just pretend until she found out and learn on the job.

They started in right away, learning how castle-cities worked, the operations of the forge, mill, and plow. Troubadours were paid for in lord's wealth, mill-rigged tools were paid in common wealth, neither account to be confused. In court practices, judging right from wrong was not as clear as the simple decisions of childhood. Eleanor wished to judge, not to gain favor, but to work out just points of property law. She gave running opinions of the 'morals of the story' from differing views and points in time. Thankfully Amira, the formidable rock collector, loved best the multifaceted ones.

The whitest of winters had brought the Princess closer to her father. It was her first snow and perhaps the last one for years to come. She had glimpsed the secret basis of Aquitaine power and wealth. William saw his angel artfully resolve feuds, play constructively, and grow the size of the court. They had taken a snowy trip to Fontevrault Abbey to hear Vivian, to see a workshop foundry, and to observe men and women living in balance. They also visited a new schoolhouse that was being built for next year.

Amira considered Duke William's charge – add young males to Eleanor's court to bring balance. Amira knew only a few. When the school opened in spring, the court would surely win over male youth; Amira reasoned – after all, Eleanor was the proudest hrad of all. Though womanhood was beginning to visit her soul, the Princess had dexterity, self-aware confidence, bravery, and a strong grip of mind. Such qualities endeared her to males because hers were the same qualities that young men aspired to.

Magicians of the Abbey

In the spring of 1135, during school recess, curious thirteen-springer Amira Neas, maid-in-training, explored the Fontevrault grounds. Its chapel under construction was surrounded by scaffolds, empty of workers. Amira was drawn to the strange sounds of the foundry.

Bing-bangs, wallow-rings, hew-rasps and saws sounded throughout the verdant foliage about the Abbey workshop. Amira approached the entrance and peeked inside. A tall plain-faced apprentice of twelve appeared to be working with an ironsmith.

Eagerly, the lanky dark-haired boy greeted her and explained how both helmets and musical instruments were made on the fabricator's anvil.

Mathieu Nouville liked to talk of tools and ideas from times long ago and lands far away. As he talked, Amira marveled at how tall he was. Strangely tall, because as he engaged you with his fascinations, he instinctively bent to your eye level. You thought of him as your own height. His father had said he would never be a man; he did not have a hulking chest, and he could barely lift a sword with two arms. Now, before this handsome young damisel with wavy auburn hair and round appealing ears, he would overcome his father's jeers with a show of a different sort of manliness.

"I will now lift 750 pounds with one arm!"

Amira thought, *no way, string-bean*. She exclaimed, "My father felled that tree and shaped that beam at the mill! That timber trunk took four fathers to lift."

"Watch this, twenty feet to the sky by my calculations!" The scrawny boy pulled on a hairy plaited rope connected through many pulleys hanging from scaffolds. As he walked along, up rose the beam in gradual amounts. "At its height, it will support the rock-work of the Fontevrault Chapel."

Amira gave the entrancing miracle a cheer.

Mathieu beckoned, "Come here." No one was looking. He had promised the master mason he never would do this, but he let a woman handle a rope! Smooth as silk, Amira gently lowered the beam to the earth, all by herself.

Amira felt powerful! She urged Mathieu to tell her more about this magic. She thrilled at his mathematical explanations of every class of simple machine in the yard: ramps, wheels, levers, wedges, screws, gears, and pulleys. He spoke in terms of machines. Machines made construction possible, and his machines could be driven by watermills. He noted his key principle – use mechanical advantage. "I love the new power of our times," he proclaimed. "I love these machines."

'*Love?*' Amira's ears perked up. Eleanor would have something to say about that. Mathieu would be a perfect friend for Eleanor. She valued people with mindful imagination, the bravery to speak honestly, and ability to use that rare word. He spoke as rapidly as Eleanor's mind worked.

Amira invited him, "Come to class to meet a friend."

"I have never been to a school."

"What?" Amira mystified, "You joke. You know so much. Truly?"

"Truly, I have never been inside a school room."

Walking the first day to class, Amira explained that her friend Eleanor was away for a week. Amira found Mathieu alarmingly truthful. Rather than conceal painful family stories he laid open everything, but then, Amira was not yet aware how her attentive listening brought out honesty in people.

Bending to her level, Mathieu explained how his family had moved up to prosperous Poitiers from the Aquitaine castle of Périgueux. He missed the old town with its Arabian-inspired buildings made with exotic mathematical curves. Such shapes brought to mind what he found most mysterious, the attractive veiled Moorish girls he was getting to know. Because of them, the boy was no longer a knave.

Whether he missed his family or not was complicated. His relatives called him the listless idiot because he took so long to understand things. They did not know that Mathieu saw seven qualities of a thing at once, that his play was a manner of testing. In the argument to commit him to either an orphanage or a monastery, his father made fun of the boy for not being hardhearted and unable to fight to kill. His strong-willed mother prevailed and brought to luster his skill for making things. Fontevrault's workshop provided every opportunity to create anything in the world, and so, the Abbey gained a semi-orphan.

Amira brought Mathieu to the class of numbers. It took him a few minutes to adjust to the wooden school house with benches and shared desks. He seemed to ken as much as the teachers and rattled off everything. "A league is how far a man walks in an hour, three miles per equinox hour. From a watchtower 100 feet tall you can see up to four leagues." He made a habit of measuring all kinds of things and writing them down, reusing an old parchment scroll. This overwriting called a palimpsest, let him overlay many ideas: times and distances between castles for walking, running, rafting, bird flights, horse trots. Many values, all at once.

Arithmetic class thrived with his enthusiasm and the games he made of things. Soon students wanted to add and multiply like him to magically connect numbers to their world. Though he knew the answers, he never showed off. He preferred to see the light shine in his newfound friends. Wisely, he left time so teachers could answer too.

Mathieu followed Amira home to dinner to meet her pioneering father. Whenever he spoke, he was full with every new idea and thing. In her bedroom, they had fun with her white spooking mask and had a good laugh of how Eleanor spooked her brother. Mathieu noticed certain fibers in Amira's mask and had an idea to lighten the costly messaging paper.

Amira showed Mathieu her fire-flinting stone! He rejoiced! He smelled it, put his tooth to it, and wrote of it in his scroll. "Rock-melting is fascinating! When the crucible heats, I get excited. Soot and heat matter not, I love the red run of liquid metal."

At supper, Mathieu dazzled Amira and her father, Paul. "The blacksmith can pour swords and arrowheads, a helmet, or even a helm for a great knight. The same hammer and forge can make instruments of peace – digging tools, cook pots like on your hearth. Heavy metal joints for buildings." Mathieu inhaled the soup and bread. "I have apprenticed forgery enough to mold metal and glass, but no hard hammering for me. I use water machines!"

Paul said, "I saw logs to timber so easily now. Why brawn with an army, when a few smart men can use tools? You are that tall fellow who comes in at night and sets the mill gears when the workers go home?"

"Indeed, I figure out gear wheel sizes, teeth counts, levered tappers, shaft angles, and spacings. That is when I get my best work done. When I first saw water-powered mills, I marveled at how they worked, but I now I love helping make the attached machines – automatic lumber saws, anvil bellows, beating cams, water pumps. I draw machines and sequences of machines operating together. Amira says you are building pigeonniers. I can calculate timetables in every season and bell standard to fly messenger doves to abbeys and castles beyond."

"Stars, Mathieu, you are a magician!" Paul cried. "Moreover, you do not hold onto pet ideas, but rapidly consider all ideas and change your mind when reality becomes clearer." Mathieu had been complimented before, but hearing it from his friend's father really meant something.

He thought about his work with Paul as he walked back to the workshop, something was off. When teachers had presented him his first maps he absorbed them. The French empire ranged from the conquered provinces of England up north to the Holy Land far east. He figured how long birds took to fly to London, Paris, Toulouse, Sicily, Rhodes, Cypress, and Acre – the large port to Jerusalem. He determined how long it took a horse to trot the thousand leagues of The Crusade, a boat to sail to Outremer – the lands over the seas. The computations and the maps were at odds. He'd have to give it more thought.

Monks and masons noticed his mind through his drawings and his sense of time. Whereas children always drew long trunks with little treetops and giant adults with big feet (for that is how a young person has seen the world), the boy sketched realistically as the mature and level eye sees. Everything was sketched in proportion with care for detailed interior composition.

Now, most of Mathieu's time was spent in the workshop – a retreat for the rare men of the era who, rather than destroying, found heart in making things. Some were even good at it. Abbey artisans made everything from pottery and pans to arms and bolts. He was fascinated by the processes of creation and transformation.

. . .

The next morning, as with most mornings, Mathieu eagerly headed to the Abbey. His excitement overwhelmed seeing the scaffolds full – all the workers were back! The magicians of the Abbey were silent men who worked from mid-spring to mid-fall. These masons, builders, carvers, and crane men, who operated the machinery, shaped perfect rock forms that made cathedrals. The Masters of these stone-shaping magicians held the greatest secret – the making of machines! It was a rare intelligence that could grasp the intricacies of machine-making, and the Masters were always on the lookout for gifted apprentices.

Mathieu scuttled under the construction bulwark of the Abbey to fetch sighting strings, plumbs, chisels, nails. He did this work not to please the workers, but to know firsthand how things were made by his own hands. He was fascinated to hold tools that could make and measure things. Respectfully, he heeded masons when they disclosed what they were willing to let a mere boy know. Mathieu was a hive of curiosity, compelled to observe, test, and touch everything until he understood it. Like Amira, he let nothing go by. With nerve and imagination, he considered and explored everything. By combining different ideas without being told of their relationship, he formed wizardly new concepts.

From these mason alchemists, he obtained pure ingredients. Challenged, he made molds of exact angle, dimensional supports, perfect spheres, and whatever shape they desired. Glass was interesting. He'd warp and bead portions to make lenses giving him other worlds to view the very near and the very far. His most challenging shape requiring great expertise was leveling glass – perfectly flat to an evenly thin surface. He could cast a foot of it, the size of a hand mirror.

Once, Mathieu accidentally forged false coins of silver. He was more curious than sinister. The ratio was: in one livre contained one pound of silver. It could be divided into 20 sous or 240 deniers. He replated silver on a base metal. He did not dip, but found a way to haze, saving a fortune. The process made sense to him. Charging a hot bellow on the finest denier dust, he coated molds making silver sous. Fortunately, a lenient friar caught him and understood Mathieu's intentions. The prospect of amputation for such outlawry was terrifying. Turning his attentions to other substances, Mathieu found he could coat a perfectly flat glass surface. A truly perfect optical mirror.

A few days later, an elderly Mason took note.

"How tall is that tree?"

"I guess thirty feet."

"Would you like to know? I can tell you to the inch without climbing."

Mathieu sat at his feet. Strangely, the man fished out a large ring strung from his neck, held it to the sun, kissed it and put it back. The stoneworker whittled a notch on a straight stick and stuck it in the earth. Then he took a rod and showed the notched stick and its shadow were the same length.

"Take me knot-rope. Stake it at the base of the tree. Stretch it out straight, and give me the numbers where the tree shadow falls." Mathieu pulled out a thin rope and counted 43 feet 10 inches. "Minus the radius of the trunk, about 8 inches, that tree is 42 feet 2 inches tall."

Magic. Analogous shadows. In his scroll, The Measure of All Things, he created a geometric entry for the high tree and its shadow. "Now I can measure the height of the Abbey watchtower. What if the time of day were different and the shadow longer?"

"Mathieu, those be ratios. Apprentice with me. Your work be free, and I'll pay you with knowledge. You understand the heavy lifting magic. Do the burrowing, striking, and gathering and I be giving you the methods and measures."

"I happily agree, your honor! What is the ring you kiss?"

"Oh, me Aquitaine shepherd's watch." The mason fished out the silver ring. "See, the sun falls through the pinhole onto slashes, the hours of the day. This is the equipotent hour when the shadows of all things equal their height when love is equal between man and woman."

"That is a superstition."

"One we gladly believe, for she's kissing the same watch I made her right now. It is personal time that lovers share. We osculate at the equipotent hour."

Mathieu chuckled at the word, "Then you kiss twice a day."

"You're catching on. Do you have a girl?"

"Me? Women are but a fantasy."

"Ah, rub the lamp, shape the wish, ring the bell, oc? (Both sexes do it.)"

Mathieu laughed. "Mason, your watch. On a cloudy day, there is no sun."

"Oh, good lad! To ring the hour, the church uses a water clock. Drip, drop."

Soon, Mathieu worked every day. After he was proven and workers left the day's labor, the mason took Mathieu into a room. Then he locked the door.

"Of this, you must not speak to anyone. Agreed? Only a Mason sees this," and he rolled out a great chart. "Mathieu, what do you have in your book for the height of the center watchtower join?"

"66 feet."

"Right, and it says?" The map of the chapel showed 67 feet 9 1/2 inches.

"Why is it longer, you may ask. By the mason's code. This is the height required when we built it. We account for the stone's weight to compresses the earth footings in rain and storm." He flashed a newer chart. "Pointed arches in series. Someday you'll study geometry through time. This is how we build. No secret here, except our instruments. I hear you can make a flat mirror. We could use a few to align stone by light." Mathieu agreed to make some, and never divulge the making.

"Numbers are the real magic, Mathieu. You learn Roman numerals in class, right? We only use them when talking to kings and church authorities. Secretly, we masons use non-Roman thinking. We count numbers a thousand times faster and rarely make a mistake. The Roman Church forbids this knowledge. We use the algebraic math of the Persian and the counting zero of the Hindian. To use the methods of unbelievers is church heresy, punishable by torture. This is why you must swear to keep this a Masonic secret." He made a fast sign of three outer fingers extended, the inner finger and thumb a circle that he brought to his eye. The Mason explained the sign. It was a scout's trick. "This is good for sighting knots at a distance in a pinch, especially for those with poor eyesight. Thumb-fingers to eyes."

Mathieu followed the monk outside wondering, 'Thumb-fingers to eyes.'

"Look a league to the hill tower. Count the crenel notches across the top." The boy squinted at the square openings but was not sure. "You are squinting. Let me know why someday. Now bend your easy finger inside your thumb. See that pin hole by your first knuckle? Hold it to your eye. Wiggle it a bit."

Mathieu saw dimly, but clearly. "Nine crenels, master." 'A lens might–.'

"Right. Now imagine making a mirrored tube that improves on this. One could see the number of bricks. One could send light because we know how to signal in front of a sun mirror. To a distant person who uses thumb-fingers to eyes, no other viewer could see a tube message. Think about it, bright lad."

Mathieu realized, there are some things your friends will never understand. It is your code to ken these things and be true to them yourself. You do not brag. You keep expertise dear. You win others by passionate curiosity. For you have chosen, as others will choose, to be the ones who will expand knowledge further for generations.

Preparing to become that citizen of Poitevin legend – a traveler, a trader, a maker of things – Mathieu of Aquitaine was open to the world. Unlike Roman teaching that demanded everyone use slothful Latin numerals, his adept mind found any system of the world was game enough to know. He was off on a good foot speaking Occitan and Parisian French, the victor's language of world trade.

The rewards of adventurous spirit also made Mathieu bold in love with women. They were mysterious creatures he tried to solve, but then he decided they were most lovely when allowed to be mysterious. He gave his courtesy and humor and loved to see them laugh though few got his better jests. Mostly he preferred the willful to the many sheepish girls. He yearned for a female who was sensible, playful, sensitive, confident of her beauty, a woman of fierce mind, one who could keep up with him; a woman whose default state was happiness. Mathieu increasingly wondered if such a woman could ever be.

After an impressionable week away with Dangerossa, Eleanor traveled the day ride from Poitiers and settled in at Fontevrault to return to school.

Mathieu the strange, as children of the Abbey called him, was on everyone's lips. Eleanor liked strange. It was evident in her fashion. Her changing styles of mood and season unsettled many. The young damisel often wore male belts, two or three at a time; four, even five scarves, just like the troubadours. Once a necklace on the head! Servants complained to her father of wearing inside-seams showing out, stitches and all. Coyly she said she wanted to feel the smoothness. Father let it go, knowing what she'd face in class. It would teach her nerve.

Her current style was to don exotic veils and foreign scarves. How boring were the head shawls of winter. To her, veils were layers of selves worn freely and worn best for no reason at all. They could be rippled alongside the face, cascaded over the eyes, mixed and plaited with vine flowers to extend one's hair. Freely she ran scarves around her waist. She flowed them from her arms tied to her wrists. This spring day, the feeling of whatever she felt to wear, she wore colorfully and playfully. She floated into the class of numbers past someone new.

Mathieu noted this colorfully unsolvable girl sitting in the back at her bench. She answered questions with budding intelligence, and volunteered honest insight, not always right, but true. *'Is she holding back like me?'* he thought. She spoke in rapid curt words, a fury of thought he often felt in his mind, especially with teachers who seemed dim to the obvious.

At recess, green-scarfed Amira introduced multi-scarfed Eleanor to teacher-probing Mathieu. Eleanor stood in front of him looking him over, radiating the rainbow of her mystery. Her multicolored veils drew him like the exotic Moorish maidens of Périgueux; the pangs felt the same too. Eleanor saw wonder in this new boy's strong eyes. He spoke as fast as a river, just like herself. They exchanged lightning quick thoughts about mills and castle works.

On the spot, Eleanor invited him to dine with her father and court of friends two weeks hence. Mathieu spent long sentences thanking her. She told him how she liked dining closely with people unafraid to speak the word love.

Such friends talked more deeply about a world that mattered, but she had never met anyone who 'loved machines,' and grinned eagerly.

Emboldened, and with students and orphans gathering about, Mathieu spoke:

"Time, consider this paradox. Every believer kens hours as bells, but church bells are not the true measure of time. At sunrise we awake at one, sun sets the twelfth hour, a biblical truth, however–"

"Are you a druid?" Blonde Reyna teased. Mathieu melted a smile to the blonde young woman priding her well-developed chest. Eleanor felt a jolt of jealousy.

"No, he is not!" Amira said defensively, "His time calculations to set bell cycles are so fast my father says he is a wizard!"

"I rarely go to school," Reyna said, "but I am glad I came today." Eleanor flared her eyes with the temper of Dangerossa's flirtation, fresh in her mind. Males are drawn to looks, but a woman does not shirk from flaunters. Put them in your story. Show the woman that you are. A good man follows better character.

"Mathieu continue," Amira gave the eye to Reyna, "without interruptions."

Mathieu stood tall and resumed, "Whether a long summer or short winter solstice, we are taught the hours that mark the day shrink and stretch. It challenges bell ringers, but not me. I live by the Equinox hours of sixty minutes. Every day has sixty minutes. Time does not change, the sun does." All along, as he spoke of celestial mechanics, and though he glanced wistfully at blonde Reyna, Mathieu noticed that among the bright eyes, he was drawn to the one woman who understood his every word. Exotic Eleanor stroked her veil and pushed the curve of her scarves back, revealing her demure white skin, the brill of her lashes, eyes that sparkled blue. She teased him by not smiling.

"We know this because the North-South distances of every map are drawn far too short, and the East-West far too long. It is a matter of timing birds flight over long distances. You see, if Aquitaine used noon, the hour of none – the absolute hour of the overhead sun, then by clocking twelve hours on either side of it, we could standardize time. This makes large-scale coordinated work predictable, all year long. Aquitaine time could change the civilized world."

"It is heretical," Eleanor lifted her chin, enchanting with her veiled charm.

"It is simple Math," he said. They chuckled in rejoice of simple wit and great wisdom. It was as if they shared a secret code; as if they were the only two people on Earth who understood the world.

When class resumed, Mathieu turned back to see if she was really there. Whatever Eleanor was thinking, was not of him. Yet, he had been boldly invited to dinner. Why did she choose the word love? Life would do. What young person pretends to know what love is? The teacher asked a question. Eleanor queried back a better one. Mathieu, in one reply, using a mill as a metaphor, answered both. He was rewarded by her widest grin. He could not avoid blonde Reyna, with her smile always for him. It brought back bad memories. A woman like her caused his getting beaten when boyfriends saw his interest. More importantly, Reyna seemed to care nothing about what he was saying. Eleanor had a passion to know.

By the end of class, Eleanor put it together. Knave Mathieu was wonderstruck by her. Obsessed by the new technology of water mill machines, determined to be its master he had said, 'What men brawn to saw, only a guiding hand need do.' How interesting, how feeling, how intelligent, and like any questing wizard, likely a born troublemaker in the eyes of the world. She could see that he oozed in want-to-solve great mysteries. She would leave him with a little something to figure out.

On her way, pushing off the school desk, Eleanor unveiled, walking to Mathieu with her coming smile. Courteously, he stood to let the beautiful creature of eleven-springs pass. Preparing to apprehend her every mysterious feature, he got lost in the strands of her hip-reaching hair. Its vibrant honey-blonde appealed, the crimson-orange excited, her darkest sanguines enchanted. The fiery names of her colors on the tip of his tongue. There she stood in full, holding him with the light of her eyes. Suddenly, blonde Reyna intervened; and getting by, she tagged him with a laugh and a press of her budding breast. Mathieu's eyes opened wide with delight. Eleanor braved her jealousy, stepped forward and took Mathieu's hand and placed it. "This is my heart, something you may never ken." Mathieu fell into a moment that went timeless.

. . .

All the workers had gone, the hour when Mathieu usually lit bright candles to work on his new engines. The boy was in a fever, declaring his good fortune to the stars and the moon. Was the blonde's brush an accident, or was something meant, or was it Eleanor's intelligent boldness that would taunt him for eternity? The mill wheel sloshed in endless turns; the powered engine never failed to engage him, especially tonight. The waters begged for a new invention. His mind alternated between the mystery of wanting to know her and not wanting to know her. Was ever a face and red-gold hair so alluring: her brilliant eyes, her arched brows, her ruddy cheeks. The exotic clothing she wore was as exciting and original as his own ideas. A ready mind as rapid as the river, hair that flowed like fired furnaces, her strands rainbows of reds. It made him crazy to want to see her again, to know the true color of her hair. He kicked rocks and splashed the eddies in the still of the warm night. What machine to make that would make her gift? He would have to apply what little he knew and explore molten metals, perfect glass, and some new process. Yet, what did he want? He wanted to explore her, to see her, to be with her. And yet, his wish was granted. Mathieu was invited! Oh, the hot fates of quick luck. The feel of her, the pressure was how much? He felt his chest. Immeasurable. He muddied his kneel to the night pond. *Forgive me; I do want to know your heart!* The cicadas and crickets beat the pulse of his temples. He saw only reflections. How much he wanted in the calming surface to see ... my dogface, no – hers. Ah, how Eleanor must love to see her beautiful image. A gift of a mirror, the presence of her, her hot, energetic light; it had to go somewhere; it had to be returned to her, to this woman of eleven-springs. He looked long to the silver moon. She was the mystery of his mind. She and only she. He was in another world. Mathieu was in love.

In the coming weeks, Amira took the tall boy aside and told him to clean his muddy tunic and mend his dusty buskins. He was to travel to Poitiers to meet William the Tenth, Duke of Aquitaine. Amira found Mathieu an eager learner of court courtesies like having clean hair combed, showing restraint in eating with one hand, seating a lady, and every detail of grace. He practiced every day until the hour arrived.

Atop the Poitiers Palace steps, richly dressed Amira waited with a bejeweled Eleanor. When their four guests passed the fountain, Eleanor held out her red velvet arm, "Sir Mathieu." He scrambled ahead and held out his, "Lady Eleanor." She slipped hers through his and greeted Arno with Maryam. Calbi stood alone. Eleanor tried to cheer him up, "Rejoice. It is a pleasant spring day; the sun is high, the plaza carpenters hammer a stage for a sunset troubadour performance." Calbi smiled his mind elsewhere. Eleanor led Mathieu, noting a cloth bundle gift under his arm.

Mathieu felt small in the Poitiers reception anteroom. He walked her gait, nervously carrying her arm, carefully matching her steps. The creature from the other plane of existence spoke, "I'm not going to break!" He tried to loosen up.

Duke William complemented their elaborate bows and introductions. Setting formality aside,everyone laughed at how fast Mathieu and Eleanor exchanged words. She drew to his talk of past civilizations, and he drew to her fresh-mindedness. Delighted at being the intrigue of Eleanor's attention, Mathieu presented his amazing gift. "Behold 'Eleanor Glass.' For you to enjoy yourself." He craved to tell her how he used mill double-bellows, an atomizing principle learned from woman's perfume blow-reeds, and the quick flash of a metal better than silver. He bit his tongue, not so much as to keep an inventor's secret, but to enjoy her joy, to see her eyes opened.

Eleanor was thunderstruck. How perfect everything looked in the glass-metaled mirror, an original invention. She knew even then, Mathieu's mirror would stay by her side forever. She adored the pearlescent shell handle carved with flower and fauna figures. She made Mathieu personally show it about the table. The delight on every face seemed magnified, for no human in history had ever seen themselves so clearly. Eleanor said for Mathieu to hear, "Amira, take this to my bedroom. Put it near my pillow."

"No more grinding fine sand on silver. This needs no polishing!" Amira kissed speechless Mathieu's cheek.

The party moved into the sumptuous draped and partitioned family dining hall. Mathieu felt dwarfed by a hall that could hold 500. On a balcony, a handful of Castilian musicians, led by the alluring Portuguese Loira, sang a beautiful carriage of music. Duke William turned his eyes from the blonde singer to watch the young men pull out their ladies' heavy chairs. Calbi seated Amira, moody Arno seated Maryam, yet no one with as much attention as Mathieu carefully placed Eleanor. When William offered his guests wine, Mathieu politely asked it be diluted. Eleanor assured this was not tavern wine for drunkards. The wine was already moderated by her family's method used by all court-supplying vineyards. This appealing ruby-colored wine she called claret, for it had no froth.

The young diners conversed, anticipating the Spanish meal to come. Mathieu and Eleanor politely allowed for others to set conversations that they would finish. Delighted by the Iberian musicians, everyone listened to Maryam translate and expound on their Moorish verse: a tale told in the Toledo markets about King Coya, the conjurer for Mitadolus, known to generations of Williams.

On the long wall in the dining hall hung a tapestry map of Europa. Everyone talked of how as Franks, they had conquered Aenglish-lands and the Holy Land in Outremer. William answered questions about both The Conquest and The Crusade.

Eleanor retold her Aquitaine Progress with William. She colorfully described every castle in poetic pictures. Mathieu joyfully swallowed his claret, becoming lost in her energetic words and delicate fingers that conveyed her journey. Politely, he asked simple points to touch off her response. His questions about tapestry symbologies grew longer as he puzzled estimated hours of travel between cities that did not match his bird calculations. To enjoy the song of her voice and her animated answers, he asked a stemwinder for her orchestration: "Since The Conquest and after the setbacks of the royal ship sinking, can you speculate on the extent of the northern realms of empire across the French channel?"

William took the question, saying whimsically, "Angland is just a Norman colony gone bad! We Aquitaines will fix that." Arno spoke, "The conquest of hardhearted men cannot compare to men with heart. Alexander the Great secured more land through love than by war." Calbi added, "Greathearted women conquer with betrothals." William reiterated the news of the land. "Could be. When King Henri passes, his daughter Mauthild may well settle the English-lands. I met her in Chinon. She was Empress of Germany. She is almost as charming as Lioness Eleanor." Eleanor jested cattish claws.

Dinner was served. The main plate was an earthy spiced lamb. A Persian sitar richly painted the air with Moorish figures. William asked how Mathieu had learned time measures. The boy requested not to divulge what he knew before the uninitiated. The table glared at the boy. No one denied a Duke a request! William appeared tranquil; they would speak privately.

After savoring the Iberian feast, under a late day sun, William took the young man up the Palace balcony past the musician's room. They looked over the busy courtyard to the far Poitiers hilltops. William told Mathieu that Eleanor's court could be trusted and initiated to any mystery. They were to know all truths. Mathieu apologized and said the map tapestry was all wrong and explained why. William was impressed and amazed by the mirror. They talked about the 'thumb-fingers to eyes' scout trick.

William asked, "Have you learned the magic of seeing through walls to look through time?" Mathieu raised a brow. William explained how at Fontevrault, its basements used to be quarters for Roman legions when soil lines were lower. "Study foundations, to see how buildings come through time."

When Eleanor and her guests crossed the windy court below, Mathieu implored William, "Come, Sir! See some real magic!"

Mathieu opened the balcony door for the Duke, and they went inside. Loira's band was playing a gypsy song. Mathieu could not wait to share his recent discovery in studying light in windows. He directed servants to pull the drapes and blacken the small room. He reopened the mid-drape providing the only light, a slit to the court below. He dressed the curtain with a pin to form a natural hole. This oculus, the size of a pea, passed a circular shaft of light.

"On the opposite wall."

When their eyes grew accustomed to the dark, the first apparition was of water pouring up into a fountain on the ceiling. The entire courtyard appeared upside-down, alive, color aglow. The Duke and the magician studied the ghostly wall of dancing light.

William once tried to share the tale of moving images. Priests prayed for his soul warning he had seen demon spirits. It took a young boy to remind him; this was only light. He commemorated the moment, "Musicians of Castile, please compose a music befitting the picture of our court." The players drummed a rolling ocean rhythm with Loira humming along. As if in time to the music, the tableau moved. Horses walking across the wall; a wagon spilling up its people; a child jumping downward to the sky, then falling back up to the street; monks walking on their heads; Maryam brushing her dress up from the wind. Eleanor seemed just as enchanting upside-down, thought Mathieu.

William went out and waved the young party up for the show. The image of upside-down Eleanor and her friends disappeared into a corner of the ceiling. With the rising and falling song of the imaginary island of Cal-Maria, the actual forms navigated the chairs into the room of dim and magical light.

Mathieu seated Eleanor in the illuminated dark. Loira's voice sailed across the room, singing of being lost in the blueness of the sea.

There was something fascinating about ordinary light laid out as a grand painting of color in motion, all on its head. When they got used to seeing the upside-down, right-sided, the couples held hands. In soft rolling Portuguese, *"aea, la la la, aea ea eaa,"* Loira floated liquid song. With new eyes, they watched the simplest things: how horses gaited, how people gestured, how midfield wheat softly waved.

Figures in waves of light unveiled: a battle knight giving courtesy to a smiling prioress; Tova the cook raising her flitting chickens in a cage; poor serfs walking by a high-horsed merchant with a beaver hat; hollow hooded clerks following behind. A manly monk, once a knight's squire, showing friendship in the stables helping his former master leave for a westward pilgrimage to Spanish Compostella. Farmer Edeva and magistrate Ellen, both hands on hips, talking of ox, plow, and harvest. Giving farewell hails, a red-faced sheriff, a summoner, and a pardoning priest illuminated the wall.

They watched as one sits by coals in a fire, glowing waves of people washing by in a tranquil tapestry of moving light. It made William recall an experience and raised his glass of wine as if to love itself. Sensing her father's lonely enjoyment, Eleanor broke Mathieu's hold. She could tell father wished for his long gone Aenor. She sat by him. He whispered softly, "You know that morning you strode into our bedroom and jumped on us. We showed you the moving ceiling pictures; remember the baby ducks waddling? Aenor and I were making love against the upside down world." For Eleanor, the deep memory was of sharing her parents loving warmth. She hugged her father.

When Mathieu seated returning Eleanor, and she said, "You are my moony-eyed duckling," what could he do, but say, "Quack. Quack." His droll exclamation made her laugh, but he inwardly cringed. To a man in first love, the kiss of death is to be compared to baby things.

Eleanor gingerly put his hand back on her velvet sleeve knowing how much it would mean to him. Some boyfriends are strong brutes, some rude with laughter, and others make you feel. This one made her think. She enjoyed Mathieu's compulsion to share his excited humorous mind almost as much as she liked his silent desire for her. Men who mastered nature appealed to Eleanor deeply. Unclouded in their minds, they galloped through life with glee, grasping foreign ideas, ruling the world. Inspired men created a new future, they made things become. He gave a detailed explanation of how to improve the wine's clarity. She poured the mirror-maker a glass of claret in his honor.

Outside on the balcony, William led them to attend troubadours singing below on stage. Eleanor let Mathieu's hold be seen in plain view. A bit cruel, yet trobars said a show of jealousy tested love. The boy knew he was a show pet. He saw it in the Lords' sneers. He was not much more of a fool than the one taking the twilight platform. Cercamon jested of being born in Dogsnobbing or was it Cockingsdown? How fools change moods. Minstrel Cercamon, whose name meant 'search the world,' changed tune. He sang sorrowfully in perfect present rhymes of 'my love for a woman I cannot reach, oh, how I am sick and dying.'

Eleanor's hair was draped over Mathieu's sleeve. "I touch your saffron-gold veil," he said, shaping the air about her head. "I raise a glass to it."

"Saffron?"

"The rarest spice of Outremer." Mathieu breathed in. "You are my spice."

Eleanor scrunched the brill of her eyelashes. '*What a rich thing to say,*' she thought as she smiled. Pulling her hair across the back of his hand, she watched his eyes deepen ever-blacker, calling to her. "Perhaps, sir, we've had too much wine."

Jumping on stage, Audric and his protege Marcabru sang a harsh tenso – a game-song of one against the other. They debated the critical failures of love.

"No imagination," whispered Mathieu, drinking deep the wine.

Eleanor shot back an arrow. "True, but do not disturb a listener of love's songs. You arrest my words posed in thought," and gave a light pinch, "friend."

Mathieu's heart dropped like a stone for disturbing his saffron angel. In mute atonement, he cherished her hold. *Friend*, she said! Downing another claret, he beheld her profile as the music played. He took in the white luster pearls that hung from her bare ears. He studied the elvish shapes of her delicate lobes, her soft canals, guessing round her words that swam through the curves of her beautiful opposing mind. In this swirling space, coming to his head was the fatigue of sleepless nights of labor for her gift. Never having been intoxicated by a woman, wine notwithstanding, the boy rose and wobbled to a back room. Overpowered by his dream, he surrendered. Amira heard the thud. Discreetly she had him placed on her bed. Eleanor took the news in stride.

Chestnut-haired troubadour Garin concluded with his standard advice on love. Be tender, always have something to offer. Be true. Find pleasure in one constant lover rather than behave promiscuously to all. Men, be bold to any woman, even of high rank. Be sturdy in moderate self-measurement. In the applause, Maryam let out: "Eleanor, have a tourney to attract more vibrant singers! Garin is a medicine shelf of love!"

"Classic advice is often the best," Eleanor said, leading them out.

William said, "Be wary, all. As you leave, do not speak of the moving images on the wall. The church says the magic of Lucifer the light bearer is heresy." William looked for Mathieu and wondered where he was.

As the evening ended, Eleanor sensed something wrong. It was a matter of hearts. Calbi's was out of place, for his heart was set on Daena.

"Fare eve, dear Calbi," Eleanor bid at the door. "Love songs have made you forlorn. Next time, you must bring Daena."

Her guests froze, looking fearfully to Duke William. No one expected her to say such a thing, but Eleanor was willful. Calbi spoke with sheepish respect as if apologizing to her father. "Eleanor! She is an English slave!"

Eleanor said with all certainty, "Nothing matters when love is at stake."

The guests left in a silence of bows and curtsies. William secured the door.

"What is wrong with you!" Eleanor could not believe father's nonstop rage. "A slave girl to eat at our table and an Englander? It is not done! Prince-lords pursuing your hand, what would they say?"

Eleanor was quick and sure-eyed. "Sainte Radegund scrubbed floors with slaves. She ate with those poorer than Christ."

Her father shook his head at her cleverness.

"You have not heard my side," she pled.

"Fair enough, by our rule, your side dear." He sat and tapped his elbows.

"Daena has affected everyone. Calbi is in love with her and teaches us her strange Anglo words often in troubadour song. I like friends in love. Father, the truth is no one has ever seen Daena. I am obliging the curiosity of my guests."

"Eleanor, you do see my point."

Reluctantly, she did. Suitors needed high and notable appearances. Even the orphaned Mathieu, whom they wildly enjoyed, tested Court propriety.

"Get used to males who desire your charms. To maintain a court, you must show immediate recognition to any who show great promise, bestow great gifts, or do great deeds. Private favors are best. However, to build a sociable court, Daena cannot come in secret." He anticipated her objection to secrecy. "Tonight I made the exception to let your friends see the forbidden moving light on the walls." He wondered, *where might Mathieu be?*

They came to an understanding. If Daena could prove some meritorious deed, be schooled with a modicum of manners, and if Calbi truly cared for her, then William would allow the slave to a small supper with trusted friends.

William tidied his daughter's fashionable veil. Smiling, he sent her downstairs to socialize with musicians and admirers.

Eleanor rushed to her maid's moonlit room. "You tell Mathieu I did this for his great deeds. Amira, watch." Planting her lovely Eleanor kiss on besotted Mathieu. She wrapped her scarf about the magician's neck. Amira sent him home, asnooze in a wagon. On the patio, Eleanor bid suitors 'good-eve' and waved at father. He leaned on the balcony, looking to the sparkling heavens.

The veil of evil was something William believed in. When childhood passed innocence, it was as if a veil lifted and a young person saw the hell that men had made of the world, the real world in 1135. As did any respectable parent of Aquitaine, he guarded silvery childhood, gradually introducing skills to deal with the inevitable. For when the veil lifted, he could only hope that all his positive wisdom could ground his daughters against the miseries of the world. They would face the corrupt, the insane, and the worst. A large portion of mankind who hated womankind. William would have to explain bigotry, flattery, trickery, deception, meanness, prejudice, misogyny, drunkenness, rape, and murder. In sum: men of short purposes who lacked respect for the mortal property of creatures. Or in Eleanor's simpler view, those absent a code of love.

William had raised his daughter to be self-possessed, confident, and fair, the noble base required to handle the complexity of power. Her virtues would need to handle religion – another problem. There were many Aquitaine faiths, and one branch was unique among Nazarenes. It gave meaning to his tribal warrior line. For honor was part of its creed – character improved through moral choosing and conscience. They came to call themselves the Good Men, an ancient order of Greek-rooted Nazarenes. William favored Calbi for aspiring to be one. They considered women and men equal just as at Fontevrault, where genders lived in balance. To them, evil was an illusion – an absence of rightness, something to mend when good was corrupted. Sins were not pardonable. Wrongdoing required a personal ritual called catharsis – a confrontation of one's wrongful motives to put one's heart right. It needed no priest; one dealt with sin personally, honorably. Such purification was key to chivalry. Because of ritual catharsis, they were called Catharics, or Cathars for short. It was a peculiar religion.

William worried more about the direction of The Church of Rome. They had grown famously intolerant and prosecuted every Nazarene faith that did not worship like them. They put scars on children before they could think. William was fierce about protecting his daughters' minds. He was glad there was a Fontevrault, a middle ground of tolerable beliefs. At its school, he had worked, so the Abbey housed the best teachers to educate blossoming Eleanor and her court of friends. The abbey teachers educated the best magicians – why just look at Mathieu, wherever he was.

〰

Voice Lessons

Invited by Arno to his family feast in the village of Fontevrault, young Eleanor sat at a bare wood table set for dining. Her quiet could easily be taken as shyness; she knew none of the faces, apart from Arno and steward Ellen, who escorted her.

The strangest characters sat at the table. Many had interesting things to say about the world. A well-groomed traveler with regal bearing and fine clothing faced the respectfully frowning, well-mannered Eleanor. They exchanged names, and he engaged her with stories of various ports speaking and gesturing passionately with great understanding of each place. After another sip of un-honeyed wine, he leaned to Eleanor and said, "It has its own honey, you know." Eleanor politely took a mouthful and agreed, 'There is a hint of the ghost of a sweet raisin." She thought of Mathieu's lips, smiling a bit to herself.

The visitor lifted a glass. "You've a hrad smile and a sense for taste! So, what classes do you favor at school?"

"Well, none favor me," she said honestly.

"All that miserable learning. At your age, I'd force myself to take just one course. Ordinary as it is, it is an essential skill for travelers, useful to your generation. Learn Voice and Presence! Gestures make sense to all tongues."

Pearls of wisdom cast before children were easily gathered up by Princess Eleanor, an early lover of jewelry. She figured if life experiences are summed as wisdom felt from the heart – not a repeated adage, mind you – the advice was worth a nod and a go; that the heart bridged all generations and cultures. This code served Eleanor well. She studied her dinner companion; he had sailed seas, yet held on to his chain of being. She would try this one class, at least for a week, just on the merits of his suggestion.

On their first day of class, Eleanor and her friends skirted the dancing shadows of branches. The summer morning wind rustled the trees, leaving half the birds singing. They whistled a tune, along with the bell ringing.

"I was told at Arno's feast," Eleanor said, "in many schools, this class is not even taught. Arno, in all my days, no whippings in class? Surely, a truth half-bent."

"I swear. I am taking the class for a third time."

"Daffy, dofft, and deft. Looking for a senseless thrashing?"

119

"It is not like that.

"Like what, then?"

Arno put on the act. "I seek primordial knowledge; I say fie on astronomy, arithmetic, geometry, music. Nay on philosophy and alchemy—"

Amira cut to the point, "Come on Arno, what we want to know is how in black peat can a teacher profess holier-than-thou wisdoms without rod and belt?"

"It's a mystery to me. None ever show the stripes of lessons beaten into them."

After the yar-sirs and mocking scoffs, moody Arno gladly walked with the one girl showing every sign of belief, although Eleanor smiled for reasons of her own. This course, essential to Aquitaine life, was cultivated by her father, and William's chosen teachers were accountable to him. No troubadour or society could be great without this class; it was the key to all charm and grace. The academies of ancient Greece and Rome called the subject Oratory. Rhetoric, Grammar, and Dialectic were the proper names for the trivium. More simply said in slang as Speech, to Eleanor's friends it was Voice.

•

"Yeah-no how-tu tawk," slanged the bent-over woman. Standing erect with a clear, definite voice she sounded, "Listen! Do you know how to speak?"

Calbi, tying his buskin, rose up looking for the other lady in the room. There was only Patricia Garthomme standing next to a tempting basket of apples on her desk. In her mid-thirties, large in body with long black hair, she wore an elegant, clean, deep-blue dress, a burgundy-red scarf. She smelled of fresh basil.

Walking through the aisles of 'royalty,' knowing they were about to receive the greatest treasure of their lives, the Teacher of Voices could hardly wait. The gems that would make them rich were about to be unveiled. Her fair life of esteem increased with every generation that she taught. Her own children had become moderate successes by her teaching.

Her first of rules was if you ever learned anything from her and wanted to show respect, call her Pat. Otherwise, she wanted to hear 'Lady Patricia Garthomme.' The informality seemed disrespectful yet her best graduates, her hammers, winners of all tourneys, called her Pat.

"Why do we talk?" asked Pat.

Never thought about it, considered Amira.

"Is it to jabber and hum?"

Shives no, it is to say big thoughts.

"Yes, it is to jabber and hum, like we all do with a horse or a pet. We begin with a kind of mindless singing to let our emotions be known. It is not words but how we feel about the world; this is our most important message. Emotion more than thought makes us human. Sapience before sentience, class. Sapience, feeling. Sentience, knowing."

Hadn't thought of that. Sure smiles a lot.

"Why do we speak then?" Pat said with articulation.

Oc, why.

Pat floated about the classroom slowly. She lifted every shy head and defeated every puzzled scowl with her supremely confident smile. She stood tall, holding out her gowned arms as if to embrace the class. Her voice was clear and careful.

"I just told you something without speaking. Can you say what?"

Matter-of-factly, Eleanor said, "Love."

Amira rubbed her ear, uttering a low, "Oh boy."

Pat smiled wider. She looked pointedly at each person as if to ask, what do you think? She waited. Nothing came but the act of frowns. The teacher said every word distinctly, "If by love, you mean I was telling you my state of happiness and that I was caring to listen, then you are right. This is the state necessary to begin any conversation. Good class!" Eleanor felt it was not the class, but she who had answered the question, and crossed her arms in silent protest. Pat's cheeky glance and subtle touch over her heart put Eleanor's arms at rest. They shared the briefest of smiles.

Pat spoke in clear tones, "In our first hum, we reveal the tune of our personal voice. To move beyond that, I will teach you to shape the air and release the hidden spell found in every word. Words form lines that we shoot as sure as arrows. Fletch the feathers to send where you want your meaning to go."

Pat watched the thoughts take roost in their minds.

"We speak to be felt. Achieve that, and then you might be understood. By skill of voice you earn trust. Trusted words cause intended actions to take place. Action in others is your purpose, my fine feathered friends. Speak things into existence."

Pat let her words settle a little longer.

"Haven't you found, try as you might to speak well; you are not understood?"

"My parents!" Reyna blurted; a sentiment quickly shared by the class. Even Pat laughed. The blonde beauty stood and took a bow.

That is how one session went.

Amira appreciated the situation. Eleanor could have had any set of tutors brought to wherever she needed them. However, William insisted educators be appointed to Fontevrault. In this way, Eleanor's knowledge would be shared with her peers, her future court. In dialogs with friends about interpretations, feelings, and meanings, she learned more about people than her privilege. To Eleanor, it was great, the way her friends knew things – feathers of egrets, seagulls, falcons, pigeons; backroads rather than king's highways; workings of mill machines; flower scents; weavers knots; the reading of skies; shared discoveries like the Tower of the four winds. In finding their voices in common, each shared everyone's journey.

"This is the way that water sounds." Pat poured it. "Can you resound it? There are no words for it. Try to write it down." The whole class swished and glugged, scratching feathered quill to parchment. "Listen again." As she poured the remainder, she brought out the sound of each word with exact enunciation. "Drip. Drop. The sound of the water clock."

She wrote letters on her board irregularly and spoke the letters with feeling: "Go! to. The. S-tr-e-a-M. Over. the. RockS. where WateR. FlowSs."

As each student sounded the line, Pat behaved as if she were listening to the voices of angels, although to Amira they showed little of the quality. Eleanor spoke quickly, her mind always ahead. Pat stopped her. "Think of your listeners! Each word has a soul, a spell that makes the word sound like the thing; each animal has a natural call. Call a word and its spell will come from your heart. Care how words feel in the mouth, the nose, the throat, the palate."

Pat enforced her sentence, and set them outside for a word hunt. Giving each child an apple, she challenged, "You got drip, drop. See if you can make out the other tones. Go listen to the murmur of water for the babble of the brook, the jargon of the birds. Tell me what they are saying."

'The voice is all,' Eleanor thought, as she lived by Pat's observations. Few people could read or write the permitted twenty-odd letters to dull out a Latin sentence. Words had confusing spellings. There was deep suspicion about writing. The pen was said to be mightier than the sword, but it never had the power of voice. Lines could be written a few ways; spoken, they could be expressed a hundred more. Speech led directly to action.

A person's voice had its own sound. To speak in the music of one's person, Pat had each student build a dictone, a string of favorite sounds to recite as an anthem of one's self. Often sibilant, the verse improved diction, while signifying character.

Big Boys Bring Bumbling Brooms of Beautiful Bees – Reyna.

Charge a King's Castle Cleverly with Courage – Arno.

Deer Swan Hart Song Dance Two Allure – Maryam.

Round Wheels Gear Chambers of Change – Mathieu.

Ancient Apple Angel Anthems Discover Danes Daily Dreams – Calbi.

Everyone knew Calbi's reference to Daena. The two were occupied every Sunday. Eleanor was reluctant to present her dictone. Amira mocked, "love, love, love, love," in different lilting tones. Feeling put on, out came Eleanor's words:

Silver Signs Through Rolling Palms Touch Forth The Silent Senses

Eleanor never said where her inspiring anthem came from. Her dictone seemed a part of her, perhaps a troubadour whisper in a lover's ear. Calbi's and Reyna's dictones definitely were.

Lastly, Petronilla's was given with a sneer at her sister.

"Hurl a Rock at a Hawk."

Pat had her class learn the interpretive powers of their own voice. They metered their lines, sounded their words, rounded the vowels, enunciated, consonated, verbalized, emphasized, and paused for effect. From chest through throat to nose, they pitched their Occitan voices. The dictones of their personalities became the base for prosody – the new trobar pronunciation of words in meter, and cadence forms appearing everywhere, all at once it seemed.

Everyone loves their voice when they find it. Pat never used a rod or a whip, for her pupils were too busy learning. To Eleanor, when a teacher was head over heels in love with her subject, it proved love's power. Love makes you love.

•

One long day in May, Eleanor brushed back her hip-length hair and faced the uninspiring task before her. In the Poitiers Hall, the trestle tables were pushed to the walls to make room for attendees. The time had come for damisel maidens to converse with suitors.

The art of matching. What a dull business. Sexes gaping at one another. Rude manners. Unfelt words. Eleanor whispered, "Amira, they don't even begin as friends, they presume." Pretty Reyna smiled at kneeling young men who never smiled. Maryam, collector of verse, listened politely to loud talkers. Eleanor counseled, "Obedient boys have no wonder in their eyes, the blustering deceptors. Watch this." Amid a suitor's good bragging roll, Eleanor cleaned out her ear and flicked an imaginary wax. What charming things toads lied about - the glistens of ear. While other damisels were satisfied to know the skills of avoidance, Eleanor learned the interesting art of choosing. To be chosen surely required bringing forth a man's heart and character.

Match-fitting was a show of appearances for the young ones. Fathers met privately, making the real decisions. Thankfully, William was unconventional. He did not like secret meetings and let facts speak for themselves. He refused to consider men who were already fathers. He denied old lords, no matter how wealthy. "Eleanor, rich men want to own you. Greed and adamant possessiveness never lead to happiness." Happiness? What daughter's father considered it? Why, Lords found it insulting! William insisted all suitors provide testimonies of affection. He hinted to the obtuse, 'take a tip from his daughter's love of troubadour song, and if the lad cannot sing, bring the singer along'. The suitors, always older, pretended to listen to what Eleanor enjoyed – songs presenting the poetic sensations, the allures of love. William attended faithfully, as much for his daughter's delight, as to hear words he wished he had spoken to his beloved wife.

There was a grim practicality to the business. Duke William knew that if Eleanor married, his duties would be acquired rather ambitiously by the husband. A timid man would not do. On some level, William wished forever to rule and for his daughter to never marry. She felt much the same. To spare the horrid suitings, he considered that his daughter might become ruler of

Aquitaine outright. She had the prowess of males years older than she. To prepare her way, the Duke amended Aquitaine law, increasing signatory rights of Duchess. He shored up both property and hear-cause rights of women.

This did not go well with the powers that be, especially the older lords wishing to acquire the wealthy realm by marriage. A liege lord from Parthenay, in dispute with the Duke about a law not to his liking, asked the church to investigate William for his unholy concerns for happiness and affection. The Duke knew that any law can be overturned by a clever priest simply by uprooting a fundamental moral premise. The church had many moral premises. To William's dismay, the abbot petitioned to try him was Bernard of Clairvaux, the relentless prosecutor of the family.

Father William did not explain any of this at family supper in the side-hall. He talked with Amira, Petronilla, and Eleanor of their progress in the Abbey-school. After smelling his meal to detect any tainting – a habit acquired after his wife and son died of pox poisoning – he finished three helpings of roasted venison. A big eater of pleasing food, the active man never showed the weight.

"Tell me of that mirror-maker. What became of Mathieu?"

Eleanor said, "He fell ill to some strange fever ... for two weeks." Amira added, "From too much wine," rubbing the side of her nose; an innocent sign indicating there was more to know.

Father probed, "Two weeks? Too much wine?"

"It seems," Eleanor said, a small flush rising in her cheeks.

William said doubtingly, "It seems," knowing lovesickness himself.

Eleanor could not tell her father that Mathieu wore her scarf, after his disbelief in being told how she had kissed him on Amira's bed, after passing out, fatigued from wine. But when Petronilla began to tell this story, she kicked her sister under the table to silence her. Thankfully, a servant presented dessert. Over creamy roasted caramel on fresh apple slices, William listened.

Amira stated, "Mathieu apologizes for confusing wine's taste with his thirst. He vows to be vigilant in Eleanor's presence, and quench thirst with water."

Rather than speak about moderation, father ate another helping. He said richly, "Ladies, your voice, and diction at table – I am amazed by your improvement. Your skills will be greater when you meet Pat's colleague, Genet. Spark, tell me someday how you earned Amira's name someday. I must go."

•

Genet Carrelle, a short youthful, exuberant blonde, and mother of two was unusually dramatic in teaching the art of Presence, though it was as much about hands. She often wore pigtails and smelled like peppermint candy. It was hard to believe that a woman so serious of teaching mind, would pucker her lips and appear to chew words while scrunching her nose, and twirl her hair with a finger like a girl. Genet's wide range of expressive behavior included the youthfulness she saw in her children. Her husband, who seemed milder than she, shared care with them in the Fontevrault Abbey orphanage. Her frenetic concerns about her children was a turmoil she worked to control, sharply increased her teaching of dramatic skills. Genet's teaching, akin to Oratory, was Enacting, or if truth be told, Presence: the sense of always being. Whereas Pat's discipline favored sapient expression, Genet's focus was on sentience, being human.

On her first day, Genet presented three rows of unhearing and unspeaking orphans. Some in her class felt pity, but Genet would have none of that. The orphans began with a sign: fingertips flex on waist drawing up, then graze right and left: *Feeling*. By the next bell, with Genet's guidance, everyone learned their hand-signs. The class had to tell stories this way and practice before the deaf orphans of Fontevrault. The orphans used lyrical gestures for their world: finger-snaps for the paces of animals, hands shaking leaves for trees, aspects of nature Eleanor had not noticed before. Rather than spell the name of the realm, a sign: a finger draws scalloped waves in the air, then shows a flag-like backhand: *Aquitaine*. These were the water-cap patterns of Duke William's blue and silver standard. Putting herself in the shoes of others, sharing orphan's hands with hers, Eleanor increased her empathic skills. With an expressive vocabulary of hand-signs and vocal intonations, in times to come – she could negotiate with tribes and traders of any tongue. Hand signs also let her exchange silent secrets. This gift, her charity gave to her.

Stance. The base for voice and action, as Genet demonstrated, was how your feet are placed and how you stand in posture; "Footing affects voice and action. Slippers are for sleepers, boots for actors When you cross a room, think first where you prefer your feet. Attend. You are always in a dance."

Never calling you girl or boy, she used titles to enroll you into whom you might become. Her reminders were countless. "Manners young lady! Young knight shoulders back! Lords be proud; your chest will speak for you and show respect to elders." Everyone had posture issues, but confidence of chest was a problem with females. She once said: "The Church has female issues." What she meant was unclear. Genet changed tactics often. "Strong angel, your wings are in the way. The world wants to see a direct woman. Set your wings back, breathe in deeply. Good. Now angel, let your seraphim's out, sing your voice erect everyone."

Genet added gesture to Pat's vocal arts. Stance, footing, and facial expression helped create the skill of presence. Presence could be as simple as how to charge or discharge voice on stone walls; how to use the shadows to stand in the sun of a room; and – hard to believe – how you enter a dining hall. How to take a chair, little ways to sip and sup, then bows, little nods. The range from a cross-leg curtsey to a sweeping, authoritative arm in a benevolent arc of influence.

Although she had a collection of plaster masks of every expression, Genet let them study her looks. She gave a profile to reserve emotion, then turned full face to present it. She tilted the underlook of interest from surly hot to remotely cool. Genet made a high nose of false knowledge, a humble brow of truth, a side-look of playfulness, a level head of seriousness, a swooning neck of vulnerable inquiry. Her key point: "Control the visage you want to be seen. Regard. There is a difference in a smile and letting someone see your smile. A smile I feel. If I present it longer, you feel. Present your sapience." To Eleanor, Genet was the Teacher of Presences and in this art, the student found her mastery. Few understood how to engage. "Attend first to what is on the mind of the audience." This came easily to a girl with a skill for reading hearts.

"An enduring lesson of good manners. Great as presence is your absence. With respect, always announce of your going. Never simply walk away. Before nobles we ask to take leave, so be royal to all. Pat, I am going now."

Some are born with it, but all can learn: voice, confidence, and presence. It defined personality. Whomever you were, Pat and Genet brought you to a higher level – this was the teachers' code.

Trials of competition proved the students. Pat's great hammer of past years, a likable model of success, was Paris scholar Bruce Giles, famed for reciting a dictone about roses. Every youngster looked to be Pat's new hammer and sat at the front of their desks to be chosen. Strangely, the students who showed little interest were often selected. Teachers sensed deep talent and hidden skill in Arno and Maryam. Arno was shy to talk; yet when he spoke his voice almost sang. He was chosen. Maryam was like Eleanor, excited to tell stories, speaking quickly in monotone. Chosen. The Princess was not. Tearfully, Eleanor found a sense of justice when her father explained. A Princess had to allow others to grow. How unseemly for her to win every competition like the prancing young lords who lowly showed off their high places. By enabling the powers of her friends, her court could be a mightier force than she alone. Such tears were well spent.

To deepen her articulation and confidence Maryam was taught to speak four, and then eight syllables keeping meter by playing cithara-lyre. Maryam learned this skill doubly by teaching Eleanor.

Arno's fine voice was sloppy with words, his body stiff. He learned to slow his lines, articulate with hands, then speed up to gain dexterity in motion. To him, it was like learning the moves of swordplay or learning to ride a horse.

For tourney readings, the teachers sifted passages of fables, chansons, and poems. Using obscure passages in obvious material, listeners were charmed to hear what they thought they already knew. "More emotion," the teachers challenged, then read with feeling intonation until, in their students, emotion took hold. Rehearsal perfected all. "Practice slowly, and then talent comes quickly."

At market fairs with copied scrolls held like shields, students looked only to the eyes of listeners. They spoke every sentence sentient and every tone sapient. Lines varied emotions, sounded words broke open thoughts. When a phrase had two meanings, a timed pause with an eyebrow or side-touched nose compounded the speaker's intent. Coupled with clever jests, a phrase, and crowds roared. Their practiced words hit every mark. Arno sang, and Maryam told until Pat's hammers found 'victory' their home.

As classes came to end, the teachers brought troubadour poems and odd herald's commerce sayings. The class read them as if by a bishop, a battle commander, or a lady in love. The great imitators Amira and Maryam drew laughs. They could sound like anything, for they listened well.

When Pat heard someone recite poorly, she wrote in chalk "mumble mouth." The offender was asked to repeat. She would frown and say, "Doesn't this sound better?" and put six rocks in her mouth. Out came 'smmbll-smuch.' Humorous lessons of artistry never ended, and the class never wanted them to end. The teachers never made students feel bad. They endowed Eleanor's generation with a confident presence. Every youth spoke with mind, and even the shyest woman or man had a voice.

●

Evening stars rose in the clear twilight sky making the backdrop for Fontevrault's outdoor theater. This early autumn, the students of voice and presence put on a scholar's play from Paris. Eleanor and her actor friends ran the stage around the Abbey courtyard audience. Many were deaf. From the evening heights of 'Abbess De Chemillé's Castle,' the actors showed their hands in lamps, signing while speaking their dramatic pretenses of love and death.

In Greek dress, Eleanor acted a noble lady, a prisoner of the bell-tower. She gave her final lines from a construction scaffold, "A kiss or I die. I am ready. Well it is. Very well." Not knowing whether she would be kissed or executed, all the candles were blown out by orphans. In the darkness, a thousand lightning bugs lit out of jugs ascending in autumn's eve, giving a wonderfully eerie sensation of a soul ascending. Duke William applauded his daughter's performance.

Unlike the plays of fantasy, Calbi lived in a very real world of love, the envy of Eleanor and her court. Troubadour verse seemed meant for him and his mysterious Daena. Thirteen-year-old Calbi sang of the vitality of nature that alluded to her, but no one had seen the slave girl of sixteen. She was as good as a lyric. Yet, she had to be real, Eleanor had seen the slave's purchase stamp by Edeva of Chauvigny in her father's Rolls.

Daena, taken from English-lands, was made a slave by the conquering French. She was the last of a line of Norse ship builders. An able stranger in an alien land she found all men vulgar. The slave dug stone walls alongside Calbi, a free young man, friendly good-natured. Never had she met a male so eager to give a fervent lingering kiss and wish only that. She was charmed by his tender fingertips that worshiped her. His spiritual beliefs were her values: men and women lived in balance, work was more important than prayer, honor was more important than obedience, being good mattered more than priestly words. Then an intriguing notion: you are only really born when you learn to make love. She followed his emerging Catharic faith.

Calbi saw in Daena something deep. He never denied he was attracted by a blonde full-figured women. Daena had a vivid Norse animal nature, a hidden intelligence, and ability to work anything from adze to needle. Calbi found all he ever wanted in a woman. Through his admiration, Daena knew Calbi would release her potential. They shared love poetically, spiritually, bodily, and willingly.

Grateful in saving his lady-love from a hard life down south, Calbi practiced his chansons for Eleanor's circle. Before his Sunday visits to Edeva's farm, he composed regular verses, passionate and humorous like any good troubadour. His songs of desire conjured a woman clever at handling shovels, an anatomy that heaved as if she were the plow itself using a sensual vocabulary of stoop-weeding grunts. His verse turned the lustful imagination. Sharing his wishing-well wishes, he granted the sweating pleasures of hard farming to all. This living, loving woman of farm feats and construction verve lived vividly in colorful verse. Fair Daena, hair of angel floss, made fertile the Aquitaine.

On a beautiful amber Sunday, in the autumn woods south of Châtellerault, Calbi set up his picnic for his rake shaker. In their secret place, he looked at the grasses where he would kneel softly, sing a poem to her belly, lift her dress, and their bodies would make tender love until they breathed as one. He felt all of nature in his breast for his poem's arrival. Humming softly to the rustling trees, he sang an ode to the straight Vienne reeds. After one hour he began to worry. When the evening stars rose, Calbi was desolate. Danae was nowhere to be found.

•   `

Eleanor practiced diction and anxiously walked the rivers Boivre and Clain that surrounded the city. In the Poitiers castle, she bounced her lines off the vaulted stone walls. She stopped rehearsal, upset and confused. Calbi's class bench sat empty, and he could not be found. There was fearful talk of witches in the fields of Chauvigny, and crusade knights seizing Aquitaine land. Ugly side-yard talk came of horrible things happening to women who ran in fear. Eleanor had a vague idea what was meant. Regardless, the peace, the Duke's law, was broken. She had to see father.

Eleanor ascended to the attic, a hint of Alder smoke tinted the air. A graven courier with rolled parchments came down the dark stairwell from Williams' office. At a large table, he read scrolls. Light poured in from two windows. In front of his desk the sun rose; behind him it would set. She did not want to bother him; visitors were frequent, and he was busy. She bit her lip meekly.

"Can I get you something, father?"

"No dear, thanks."

She retreated to the sitting window. Below, people looked frenzied; wheat fields were sunburned. He read for the longest while. Eleanor asked, "What is rape?" Reading along, he answered in his formal legal tone, "A man acting sexually on a woman by force against her will." He wrote, stopped suddenly and motioned her near. "Dangerossa will tell you; rape is the opposite of love."

"Yes, sir," Eleanor said obediently.

"You have heard about this upcoming case. We do not yet know what actually happened. There is much strong talk. This is not going to be easy. Crusaders were involved, so the church has a very strong interest."

Eleanor stood attentively.

"Dear; court is normally where power, justice, and heart rule. In a religious court —which this will be— little of that matters. Only quotes of faith, holy intent, projections of demons, angels, and saints carry weight." He felt her distance. "Eleanor, you are not an ordinary girl. Life is not all fancy dresses, rich parties, troubadour songs, and having only your way. To govern and keep the noble peace, remember: the falcon eyes the whole field. Alert and even about evidence, she strikes with accuracy. Rule with purpose, for the pillars of the earth are our people; majesty rises to *their* cause. In time, you will ken this. This I must do, even speaking against the church." William brushed her head and remarked in a rich tone, "You have such confidence in your voice and manners. I love hearing your rehearsal." He returned to his papers.

She went to the window. The world seemed calmer. Words reassured. "Father, you were right about our teachers. Voice and presence bring things into existence." Without looking up, he spoke, "Yes. Beware, the liar uses the same convincing powers of tone and gesture; the powerful misuse them the most." He looked to her window. "Some Church legates make you believe you are among a family of friends, then rile the mass against you for their own purposes." He looked at her, touching two fingers together. "To them, what is said matters little, but for you and I, what is said must always matter."

Two days passed, little had changed. The talk of the Chauvigny knights and the chastity of women being violated continued. Girls stayed near fathers and elder brothers. Wariness increased. It was becoming a dangerous year.

Well past supper time, the sun had set. Eleanor climbed the warm attic stairs in puzzlement. Father would be busy on the case. He would not talk about it; she just wanted to be near him. She would be still and not ask a thing, not even the rumors. Crusaders were supposed to do good like chevaliers.

She was surprised, arriving at the top step. Father was stretched out in his chair napping. She paced careful steps. His arms were folded across his chest, boots on the desk. She pulled up her hem to rest in the attic window bench to peer into the twilight. What did he see out of his Poitiers window? Finches nesting in branches; end-of-the-day bees hovering in blossoms; church towers. She could hear the river mill's rounding turns. Leaning on the sill, she rested her chin on her arm. The room was sweet with alder wood smoke. Below, people came and went. To the dark horizon, if she could see far enough, she'd see Chauvigny and all the trouble.

"Good evening, Eleanor." The voice made her jump. She had been as silent as a mouse. His eyes were still closed, face to the ceiling.

"Father," she lilted.

"Let's hear," he said to her question forming in her mind.

She spoke as rapid as a river. "What is chivalry, you know, the knight's code?"

No question could be further from his mind. He stretched his arms long. Sitting up, he rolled back his tunic sleeves and motioned her near. Often, his daughter surprised him with a mindfulness that connected to his current problems. She would rule someday; it was rightful she ask about such codes.

William spoke richly, "Chivalry means to be a chevalier not a knight, dear." He pulled her strand of hip-length red gold hair and circled her gown. He sighed for what was on his mind – the codes of ancient Roman laws.

Eleanor liked her hair being played with. In father's caring way he often explained things from his life. They worked right into what was on her mind.

"A knight is just a spearman on a horse. A Chevalier has a battle lance, and a mannered code – his personal law." Her father pulled out another long strand swirling it about her saying, "Your code is what you wrap around yourself so that when time unwraps and life tests you, your code guides your actions. Every person of character lives by a code. To that you must be true, even Eleanor, if you have to stand up to me – not out of anger but because you are yourself, by your own code and have a good reason."

"Tell me more about this personal code."

"Does a church have a code? I am troubling about the role of crusaders."

William laughed. "What a good question. I suppose if they did, it would be confusing to sort out their contradictions in an order to be obeyed. One's code is based on one's lief – strong self-belief. You add to your code as your character grows, Take the Hrad code." His daughter smiled. "Never lose that. In one's code, we are guided by forces of truth, valor, benefit, and compassion."

"Grandfather was a crusader?" Eleanor quested.

William troubled his reply. "A crusader yes, but a Chevalier first. A crusader is an armed pilgrim who serves . . . God. The chevalier serves an inner calling. He takes right action; he does as he says, says as he will do. His word is a bond. Codes are improved by studying better codes. Your grandfather experienced the better ways of his foe. He found heart in their song. He was a chevalier with a code of conscience, not a knight who simply kills for the church."

"Then they have no honor."

"It's easier to take orders than have to think what to do."

Briskly creaking up the steps, administrator Ellen carried an armload of scrolls.

"I have the canons," she said urgently.

Eleanor resigned to end her talk, and helped the steward carry a load of cold metal burnished cylinders ornamented with crowns and small river gems.

Touching them, Eleanor said, "These long metal tubes are canons?"

Ellen drew paper from a copper cylinder and winked.

"Yes, and the scroll inside is Canon Law. That is church law."

"I know that."

"Eleanor . . ." The rising voice of her father meant one thing.

"Candle time?"

"Candle time for me, bedtime for you."

She did not want to go, but there were important things adults had to attend. She hugged father shimmering her best 'I really want to stay' face.

"I will tell you how Amira named me Spark."

He bent close to read her feelings. He kissed her forehead. "Now dear, you know I want to know that more than anything, but it is late."

Using her new dramatic skills, she articulated: "Princess Eleanor recoils in your harsh banishment to bed." She kissed round cheeks. In sighs, she left their stage, acting discouraged, stomping herself downstairs. She thought, *in bad chances find the good.* Seeing herself not being in the room, the good of it struck. She could just listen to what adults actually talked about. On the last step, she rested slowly to avoid its creak.

Her father toned of concern. "How is Edeva?"

"Better. She responds best to you."

Parchments crinkled about the room. "El, it is sad. No evidence is needed. The sermons have already begun. Just say she has the sign of the devil. No wonder womenkind have hard hearts for men. Witchcraft is such an easy-made fear. Undoing that is our trial, but the church may well take her land."

"Will, they want her land for what?" Ellen said.

"If Templar knights chase these rascals off, they'll build a watermill."

"The message checker at Loudun tower confirms legate Flembaugh."

A long silence. Eleanor shifted her seating; the step croaked long! She grimaced, waiting for chastisement to rain. Her father cleared his throat. "Must be cottage crickets." In low tones, his voice continued. "Then they really want something. Legate Flembaugh is too big for this, hmm."

Furniture slid, got picked up and placed down. Father's voice resounded, "El?" The squeal of chairs. "There will be no order in that court without witnesses, evident proofs, reasonings. We must know of the frame of the trial."

"Will, it is going to be a vulgar court of ordeal. We defend gross accusations and plead mercy for every charge leveled on her head."

"Then we must do better, El."

Strikers sounded; the stairwell walls grew bright. A chair settled to rest. His low voice: "To save her life, we deal with the judge, Bishop Rennes. His witchcraft charge will draw the zeal of the crowd. We should meet his honor."

A chair scooted back. Her voice: "His office condemned Blessed Arbrissel. Let's put in motion some of these Roman codes of justice, Will."

"Their purpose is not to render justice, but to spread their power. If he humiliates Edeva and prevails, the Templars will take over her land. El, we will not let him humiliate her; we will not allow him to prevail." Silence.

"You like brave women," she said after a while.

"You will do." Muffled laughs. "El, when Eleanor comes to power, we will have taught her to fix her Holy eyes on the Cross, yet like the all-seeing falcon, see who in Rome holds it. I was talking to her. I told her, pilgrims serve God. I wanted to tell her they serve the Church. She does not yet know God is redefined by every new Pope of Rome. Their reversals of excommunications teach us this. Eleanor is young. She must believe, just like her people, in the fervent word. Later when she is of age, we'll teach her of Arbrissel's mission."

The opening of metal cylinders and scrolls unrolling.

"It will be the word of an English slave woman against crusaders."

"In three weeks?" Ellen sounded concerned.

"The realm will finally see a woman lead this trial. The Church will ignore you. El, speak Edeva's cause! You reason, you are diligent, I've seen you talk the manliest merchant in circles. Should the bishop object, I'll be at your side. Teach Eleanor that a realm is strongest when every advocate is given a chance to be strong. Let us see those words now. Now, if we can find where the wind blasted that slave!"

Eleanor's scalp lifted. *They mean Daena!* She jumped off the steps. *Calbi would know!* The stairs groaned in complaint Eleanor bolted for bed.

As she lay awake on her pillow, there was much to consider. Pulling her hair above her ears, arms stretched out, she alertly followed the warm nightlife: the distant woo-hooting of owls, the near coo of settling doves. Above the thrushing Boivre river, in the branch's turn and stay, the nightingale improved its changing tune, nature felt present with many voices. With wrists to hair, she puzzled out father's words and turned them line by line. Between her germinating thoughts, she chuckled, "cottage crickets." She smiled feeling the warmest sapience of her father's trust. Clearly, he knew she had been sitting on the bottom steps listening all along.

〰〰〰

The Woman Without a Voice

Life came full-force in 1135 to girls in their teens, put to married life by their fathers. Other girls came early to the matters of life because their fathers no longer lived. Such women continued to till their family farmland alone. In Aquitaine some were to become Franklins – frank meant free, and lien meant land – free land owners proven by generations. Whereas Kings awarded titles of land to barons for past bloody deeds, Duke William assigned trusts of land to Franklins to keep future land productive. Title was given for obedience; a Trust was given for family honor. To protect family first was a precept of royalty, but for Duke William, it was an obligation to all. A maintained family brought forth many a glad reaping and fighting hand.

As the Holy Crusade consumed all men, it often left behind loyal families made entirely of women. In Europa, a woman could never own property, but in Aquitaine, family property was conveyed as a trust. Neither church canon nor royal law allowed it – not until rule, case, and order spoke Franklin into existence. Ironically, the church that called The Crusade did not honor the familial wills of the men who died for it. However, the Lords of Aquitaine, by bonds of lief and liege, were compelled to do so. A collision of law over this right of females was unavoidable. As inevitable as Edeva, was her destiny to become the first Franklin of Chauvigny.

Death came swiftly in 1135. Faith itself shortened its coming. Edeva was now thirty-nine. Her mother often spoke of The Crusade that fervently called father, sons, and brothers who left one hard untilled day, never to return. Edeva and her two sisters buried their mother after Sunday mass. There was no looking back as they slapped the soil off their hands.

It had been a good harvest for Edeva and her sisters. As a reward, the lot of farmhands and priests who resided on the farm were granted leave for a six-week pilgrimage. The women themselves would turn under husks to earth by tilling the soil, then sow the winter wheat.

Once was enough to scan the broad fields. The clouds were sparing and time was wasting. Glory be to the new furrowing curve plow! It cleaved earth like the prow of a ship, making a furlong, short work. With the help of a new slave girl, Daena, they hooked up each oxen yoke and horse collar. With a "hey-hey," and spritely "heave-ho," goads in hand, four plows and four women broke the cold earth on this autumn morning in Chauvigny.

. . .

The reputation of bountiful Aquitaine reached far, even to ears that had no sense of its soil. Sensual troubadour songs alluded to its exceptional fertile woman – invitation enough to four young plunderers who rode on to Edeva's farm. Born of great Crusade families, the four men had lost their noble chain of being. Merrily received by the women, their visitors quickly turned on them.

Church heralds cried from town to town, "Witches! Routed by Knights of the Cross in Chauvigny." No other story was going around.

Alone in a Fontevrault sanctuary cell, landowner Edeva was not talking, for she could not – she was a woman without a voice. Duke William and minister Ellen barred any from seeing the woman who lay in great sorrow. Prayer and time's cure were needed so that she could speak again. From her gasping whispers and her sisters' partial words, a story of escape came together. Only farmhand Daena could give the whole account. Assuming she still lived, nothing could bring back a runaway slave, much less a woman, worse yet a foreigner, and never an accused witch.

Upset Eleanor stood on the attic floor before her father's work table. She had overheard father with Ellen and knew they had to find Daena. She did not want to be closed off from truly helping. Calbi's class bench had been empty. His Daena worked Edeva's farm and went missing. Eleanor had some idea where to find her. Eleanor knew not to appear anxious, yet here she was, in front of father.

"Father, the church herald noises on about Chauvigny witches!"

"We are bold today," he said, tapping his papers.

"What are you doing about it?"

"You have Aquitaine blood!" William liked seeing her spirit, but he could not discuss last night. He had dispersed a frantic crowd of men with torches, men whose children Eleanor knew. The men held crosses and tried to force him to give the order to storm Fontevrault and burn witch Edeva.

"Spark, this is my worry. You see I am busy. Don't be rude. I want you to give thought to your temper. Farewell."

Eleanor walked to the Clain. After measuring her temperament, she realized her feelings were founded in truth. She ordered and recited her words.

When William returned from dinner, he read his day list. 'Eleanor.'

Formally at the appointed hour, Eleanor stoutly stated her pleas: "I have three causes. Because we rode all the castle courts of Aquitaine; because you said as a ruler, I must deal with all things; and because of Calbi's love for Daena, I can find her. Tell me your case and let me help."

Eleanor stiffened her confidence.

"No sir! Stallions no. And you know why I won't."

At a certain time in life, one must disobey a parent to uphold one's principles. William judged that his daughter had come to this time in herself. His voice richened as it always did when he discussed things that mattered.

"Very well. A troop of young crusaders appears to have rudely run all the women off Edeva's land and now claim it by occupation. Edeva was assaulted and can no longer speak. Your slave friend Daena witnessed this violence. Her witness could defend Edeva. I am entrusted by Edeva's honorable right to her family land to oppose the crusaders – and that means the Roman church. They do nothing to stop the belief that land-owning women are witches. Ill riots are taking place. You have heard slurred curses spoken against me. Ugly words will fall on you."

Eleanor did want to be the object of jibes and sneers, but for father, the curses would be worse. She had made up her mind.

"I know. By tonight, you will have Daena. Thank you, father."

William took hold of her shoulders and looked at her gravely. Eleanor swallowed a fear. He said as firm as his hold, "This is serious, dear. Remember, though many will call you unholy and think worse, one always stands by one's code, as you are doing now. This coming trial will be as much of Edeva and the crusaders as of yourself."

Eleanor left unshaken and knowing. She had done right, she had earned her father's trust, and she had been a good arguer. Father was not a chair-sitter after all. She pictured the valiant man riding to Edeva's compound, slaying cursed men with his intelligence, like a great chevalier. She had no idea she was actually picturing herself.

Her hunch to send Arno to Tova the cook's farm was right. Calbi and Daena were holed up at the temple tower of the four winds. Tova herself brought the reluctant couple to the sanctuary of Fontevrault. The rules were that no one could see Daena, neither Calbi nor Eleanor until the trial was over.

The week of the trial, further troubles mounted as church heralds fanned the flames of witch-hunters. At the Poitiers castle fountain, the herald on his high horse got out half a line. "Holy Crusaders To Try Witch. Edeva–" Against the angry jeers of the masses, William's summoner pulled the false Chiron down and jailed him for provocation and falsehood. In the upcoming trial by ordeal, the Duke could not have the very people he would plea with be poisoned by wild claims. In the herald's pockets were thin paper wraps, recent messages from planners far away. 'Since the slave has run away, no need to send legate Flembaugh.' The news came as a great relief. He would be spared the monstrous legate. He thought of his daughter. Such a trial would prepare her to deal with such men in years to come. Thankfully she would be absent.

William and Ellen rode to the baron's court of Chauvigny to meet the bishop, who would be the judge. They had to suggest order and process, that is if there were to be any order or process.

"I have traveled far to handle this case," short-necked Bishop Rennes said.

"Decide no cause, until you have heard both sides speak," William pled.

The bishop nodded and pointed to his magistrate who set the sidings. For the church, only two crusaders would appear. William insisted the red-haired crusader be present. For Poitiers, the magistrate allowed Edeva or one of her sisters. In a long argument, in which William reported Daena was found, and that she was so frightened he was not sure he could get her to speak, the bishop allowed her. He had his own reasons. She had to be called Daena the Slave or the Saxon Witch. William consented.

The Duke asked under what lord's flag the knights of the Cross marched. The bishop's magistrate said they were only sons of crusaders. The magistrate presented the Church's claim on Edeva's land, freshly signed by Bishop Rennes. William objected to the judge's direct involvement on a case that benefited the Church. The Duke abided being overruled.

Ellen presented a Ducal land grant, given to Edeva's grandfather, an acknowledged Crusader of Jerusalem. Bishop Rennes refused it, saying ancient customs did not allow women to own land. As for crusaders, Edeva's heritage was protected under canon law. "Show the canon," asked the Bishop. William produced it. "By what right could new crusaders take Edeva's land?" asked the Duke. The bishop said, 'The right was implied by the Pope of Rome's word." William crossed his heart three times to the satisfaction of the bishop.

"Let the land title be settled in Paris by the King," William asked to no avail.

The bishop concluded in passing, "You will release our herald?"

William responded, "Of course, and with my letter of apology."

On their ride back to Poitiers, William told Ellen. "A very long letter of apology. My Latin conjugations must be perfect to be stashed in the church annals. Maybe by trial's end."

Neither side wanted a surprise. William and Ellen had a good idea of what to rehearse for. The bishop ordered more firewood to burn a witch. Eleanor asked her father to visit Daena, a woman she had never seen. He said to wait. Lives were at stake. Soon enough, all would be revealed.

◆

In late October, the trial came. The air was dry and the high sun had not a cloud. The tree-lined road from Poitiers turned into a harsh, dusty trail by the time William and Ellen reached Chauvigny. They first saw a high tower donjon approaching the castle-village. Upon crossing the Vienne River bridge, and passing the wall gates, the stone donjon on the hill joined to the church court of the castle. Along the incline of pebbled streets, horses, farmers, peasant women, ragged children, and vagrants gleefully assembled to partake in a specter of justice. "Where there be crosses and witches, there be fire." Clans came to picnic with extra bundles of wood.

Only men were allowed into the lord's court for the ordeal, the exception being, in a Holy Canon trial, the brides of Christ could attend. Nuns from various orders milled in the bright sun. Men tipped caps innocently. "Hot day, sister!" The nuns were not naive – such interest on this day was to see a woman burn.

Calbi approached one, "Sister, you fit well into your order's gown. I am barred from attending, by your father's order. A blessing on thee." Eleanor smiled back. Behind him, a freelancing scoundrel and his gang eyed her. Eleanor glared at him and stepped back. She patted Calbi's shoulder. "Take heart, dear friend." Calbi did not turn in time to notice Arno thundering by in brilliant armor on his chevalier father's horse.

The double doors, high as a man on a horse, opened from road to courtroom. The nuns passed the bearded church summoners. Into the cool dark room, up the ladder-like steps, they mounted to the second-level benches. Eleanor sat tight with the sisters, overlooking the floor that filled with hard plowmen, serfs, overseers, and ruffians.

Below on a middle table, sturdy Ellen and handsome Father spoke lowly. Before them was a platform with an altar and cross. To their left on the platform, stark Edeva stood with a scarf around her neck. Being accused, she had to stand and face the oncoming crowd of men. To Eleanor, it felt cruel. Further to the left, behind Edeva, sat an elderly bishop and magistrate in red stole and holy garb. To the right by the wall sat two crusaders in mail who looked too young to have ever crusaded. Dressed loosely with dirty hair, they slunk and shifted about in their comfortable chairs. Eleanor searched for Daena, not knowing what she looked like. Ellen and Edeva were the only women below.

The muttering men of the floor burbled "witch," and pointed to Edeva. William held forth his hands in a paternal calming, "Now men." He gave a righteous nod, "Your honors." The magistrate begrudgingly called for less zeal.

The bell rang once. All rose as the bishop gave a long Latin prayer intoning obedience to heaven. He signaled the magistrate to speak the cause of the trial.

"Great Crusaders whose belief fights for the Holy Cross! The Holy Church has granted you the lands discharged of Edeva and her sisters. These lands are for the blessed service to The Crusade. Such is the bond; such is the word of our Holy Father in Rome."

The men looked pleased; the magistrate prodded them to cross their hearts.

"Edeva, the elder. You are deposed of lands given to our Holy warriors. There are charges of witchcraft and temptation, in that you allured these holy warriors. Do you agree to the charges, or, shall we present your shame to all?"

Bedraggled Edeva rested on a rail with a hand. She pulled on her scarf, trying to speak, but her voice failed her. Advocate Ellen caught her whispers and voiced a firm, "No, I do not agree."

"Is that, a woman's voice, I hear?" the decrepit Rennes spoke.

Ellen spoke confidentially, "I am, your honor. I am here to defend the attack by "so-called" crusaders who ran Edeva and her sisters off their land."

A great rolling of guffaws filled the floor. This was not the story the church herald had been repeating. The bishop stood and retook control. "I will not hear a female plead law and justice. There is no place for a woman's voice in this court!"

William was surprised. Nothing was said of Ellen when they met earlier.

"Forgive me, your Honor. I will restore your order." William motioned Ellen to sit, and they shared their anger in silence. Eleanor wanted to shout from the banister. Ellen had worked so hard. Along the row, nuns balled their fists and cringed at one another.

William picked up his chair to seat Edeva. While walking, he said, "My counselor was too eager. You'll hear from her no more." He seated sad Edeva. "This family has farmed the Aquitaine for generations, and now she finds her land contested by these men."

The bishop leaned forward. "The wretch cannot talk. What's the point?"

Eleanor squirmed in the rafters – how could a judge speak of a woman this way. *And why is she the accused?* Her fellow nuns seemed used to it. Looking down, she felt a small swell of pride, seeing her confident father look calmly over the jury crowd of men. She resisted the temptation to wave.

He spoke richly for the bishop's ear. "Your Honor, The Crusade. How noble are men to take the cross? There have been evil rumors that these Knights of the Cross were tempted; that they took Edeva and her ladies by force. Though she is voiceless, I have the very witness who saw it all and can clear these men's honor of these charges. She will completely and entirely save their crusader reputations. If you please, hear the voice of a Daena the Slave, sworn to tell God's truth."

The bishop, tongue to his lips, looked at miserable Edeva. This was his opportunity to put down yet another. A trinity of a slave, woman, and witch. Two for the fire.

"Bring the wretch."

Benches creaked as the light opened into the hall.

Calbi, hoping to find Danae, stood outside Chauvigny court in a field of peasants. Summoners guarded the hall as the portal opened. A man in shining armor swiftly escorted a lady in a bonnet. The Chevalier talked his way past the doormen. Calbi pressed forward, and the guards warned, "Back knave!" When the lady turned, Calbi was transfixed, amazed. The Chevalier was Arno and on his arm was Daena, never clad so finely. Daena winked at her love. When the door closed them inside, Calbi, who never swore oaths, knelt and vowed to become a Chevalier that very hour.

The shadow darkening the door was a young knight presenting the silhouette of a young woman. She let go his arm and walked alone, slowly into the court hall. As the door closed, William cleared her path to make way. On the floor, men shouted. "Saxon! Slave! Woman! Anglo!" William said, "Hold your tongues!" The bishop enforced nothing. They did not say, 'witch'. No, not with this woman's demeanor. Eleanor and the nuns leaned over the banister.

What appeared as a confident bride proceeding with grace to the altar, William announced as, "Daena the Saxon, please stand here by this bar." The woman stepped up to the altar platform. William guided her. The magistrate puzzled her arrival. The bishop measured his victim.

The woman approached the alter carefully in a clean, light, garden-patterned gown with deep sleeves. With a fervent energy, she knelt and crossed her heart. On her knees, back to the room, cool and demure, with a ready handkerchief, she waited patiently, as if she had all the time in the world.

"You may rise," the bishop said. "I remind all to ascript her as The Slave or The Witch. Face the court. Say what you will."

Eleanor leaned forward to see for the first time the face that Calbi desired.

Daena Hanah removed her bonnet properly, turned with poise to face the room, radiating a strange athletic beauty. Sparse of features, most striking, was her shoulder-length, frizzled platinum blonde hair. It was as if The Creator, after making too much perfection, decided to thin out the hair of an angel, then saddened by the loss, set her with full ready lips. Rarely did the woman smile, and she was not smiling now, nor did she have any reason to. The bright blue eyes showed no feeling. Her stark appeal fell across the room, creating a natural want in men to see her smile. Before the altar, she glowed in a thin aura of angel floss. Fresh and immaculate of stature, Daena stood in perfect posture. Eleanor could see she had been scrubbed, dressed, mannered, and rehearsed by the best teachers, Pat and Genet. By the look of her, no one could believe she was a farm slave.

William approached the blonde lady and noticed an edginess in the two Crusaders, especially the one with the dirty red hair. Daena swung her firm shoulders and hips ever so slightly to suggest control of her form.

"Daena the Slave of Edeva?" William asked, bowing to the bishop's rule of address. As would be her style, she waited out a polite count of three, then in perfect Occitan French, voiced clear thoughtful words, a mastery of control.

"My Lord, I affirm Edeva is my mistress."

William paced a slow walk across the creaking floorboards of the platform. He waited in front of the young men's seats, then pulled his hand through his hair, giving the look of a disapproving father, contemning sloven sons. He took two considered steps to Daena. She stood strongly. He spoke roughly, "On the eve of Edeva's exodus, four weeks ago, you were there!"

She eyed him steadily, unafraid of his tone and brought her hand to rest lightly on the wooden bar, as if her skin could only rest on the most comfortable grains.

"I was present, yes," came her clarion voice.

"You were there, with Edeva, her two sisters and these um, these men!"

A count of three. "Yes, with oh, those most noble two. There were two other men as well." Liking their undeserved eloquent depiction, the young men smiled. William enrolled in Daena's tenor as if being dealt a reprimand.

"I beg your pardon for overlooking the esteem you place on these men. You were there, and you would know. As I understand, you women were turned out into the night, yet Edeva had received them a few nights before?"

"Yes."

"You received these fine gentlemen at your house."

"Yes."

"Every night, you entertained these noble men for dinner."

"We are good at that."

The courtroom gave to mixed chuckles.

"You and Edeva spent ten hours a day plowing, as has been the custom of her forebears. What did these men do for their days?" He tapped three fingers.

She counted. "They sat in the barn-shade drinking ale, mostly watching us plow and weed, waiting for us to come home and cook them dinner."

"Oh, we men understand that," William attested. His low familiarity drew out the sentiment of the men on the floor.

"These fine young men did nothing? Seems unmanly not to help. Why keep them?"

"A woman has to have fun after a hard day in the field."

Eleanor was surprised to hear the laughter of nuns. She noticed her father now addressed Daena giving the ascription 'slave' not to her but to the following words.

"You are doing fine, Daena - a slave by God above. On the night of your exodus, tell us all what happened."

Daena nervously asked permission of the magistrate for a drink. A hooded monk quickly brought out a mug. William intercepted it. The witness reached. William teetered it and let it crash, as if by accident. He booted away the chards of swamp-water crawling with tadpoles and worms on the floor. An accolade cleared it off.

"Clumsy me. Ellen?"

The counselor brought a fine glass goblet of clear lemon-honeyed water.

"Thank you, mistress Ellen." Daena looked the picture of a thirsty elegant woman. She drank daintily, assuredly, gratefully, but not completely. She tapped her lips with a kerchief and handed the part-full glass back. "Saints, it is hot today. The Lord bless us all." Without emotion, she composed herself elegantly. All eyes were on her. Edeva leaned forward, lifted by such elegance and testimony. The bishop and magistrate grew uneasy.

William resumed, "By your own true words, by God's high oath, please save the reputations of these fine young holy men. What happened that night?"

Men of the floor pressed forward, nuns in benches creaked as the room took a collective breath. Horse bridles and children's voices sounded outside. Daena in her noble frame spoke clearly, "Truth be to God. That night, our second together, these fine young men finished much wine, and we took to dance a-clapping. Edeva sat with a man and held hands. The two sisters went out with their men to see the stars. I washed the meal dishes. The red-haired gentleman over there came to watch me work. He gave his respect and attention."

"Now Daena, the slave of the stove. With this able man," William flourished, "was there no interest in walking away from the dish pan, especially after such wine."

"Sir William, look at his fine noble face! A cherub by lamplight. I would dearly like to know him better. Yet, as I told him, I've trusted my heart to another, and I could never leave a pledged love." She pressed her lips together.

"Continue."

"Well, I had to push his hot hands off me to finish the pans."

"And . . ."

She saw his three fingers tapping his belt. She took three breaths, folded her hands in her lap, spoke with restrained emotion and honesty.

"The lad with the red hair let me be. I heard shouting in the next room. The two gentlemen complained that they were tired of sleeping in the barn. The captain dictated, 'Edeva, you either take me to your bed and act as my bride, or leave now and never come back. If you run off this land, it will be ours. For our fathers were Crusaders and the church owes us."

The floor filled with the murmurs of men. Eleanor frowned at the two boys. *The church owes them what?* She steamed. The bishop and magistrate were riled.

William was quick. "If it pleases your Honored Highnesses, this is a very important point. To save the honor of these noble men, Daena, the slave of truth, by your oath to God above, please tell everyone in the court, did any of these men hold any woman against her will and force themselves? Were any of you raped?"

William looked over the stone room. Men of the floor edged forward with the devil in their faces, hoping to hear sordid details. He directed their eyes up to the top gallery. "Holy Sisters, forgive my blunt question." He pressed his hands together to his lips as if praying. It was a risky defense, for rape was often allowed and easily sidestepped. Might a renewed sense of honor prevail?

Daena breathed evenly, as taught. She turned to Edeva whose mouth formed a no. "Edeva is saying no, but the captain had his sword drawn."

"Remember these are noble men, and the truth, please. What happened?"

"Hearing the ruckus," Daena composed, "I came out with my fry pan. The red-haired one had his hands around Edeva's throat – beet-red, near death."

"It seemed so," William calmed.

"Yes, it seemed. I threw my pan at him with all my might. I gathered Edeva and ran out in night-fear with the sisters, two on a horse."

William finished, "Which is why, if you lift his hair, you will see the gash he hides on his left temple." He looked to the bishop for permission. The bishop held back his delight. This revelation would lead into his trap. The bishop showed mock wonder and obliged with an open hand.

Lifting the red mop to show a long red gash, William did not see it coming.

"They tempted us! She is a witch! This is the devil's mark!" The lad sprang up as coached, repeating the remembered words. "They tempted us! She is a witch!"

The other lad joined, "They put a spell on us. We, who follow the cross!"

The bishop folded his fingers, about to smile. William prepared to respond. From the back:

A young sister of Christ stood. "Great Crusaders! Where is your just knighthood, your code to honor love? Where is your chivalry?"

The proceeding halted. William wisely pretended not to know the source.

"Is that, a woman's voice, I hear?" the decrepit Rennes squinted at the gallery.

The good nuns of Fontevrault had the sense to hide their disciple. The eldest abbess shouted: "The sister is shushed! Pray Holy justice continue!"

William could not let the sense of the exclaimer's urgency go.

"Noble knights, you rode your horses onto Edeva's property, by her grace. Did you need to escape a woman who looks like Daena? Hardly a witch. Perhaps the heavy wine put a spell on you?"

The men of the floor broke out in riotous laughter.

"Hold there!" The bishop could see the flock slip out of his control. He reconsidered the proofs of witchcraft. Daena was too self-assured. She had no sense of guilt to pounce on, no haze of mind he could confuse, and worst of all, no haggard pain or umbrage expected of a slave or the look of Edeva the suffering soul. He could not burn them. Had they actually been beaten and raped, as the crusaders assured, then they would have acted as good victims, rattled and easy to condemn for temptation. Sadly, there would be no inferno.

The bishop's cause returned – the assignment of land for his purposes. He signaled Daena to step from the bar, then spoke privately to his magistrate.

The magistrate marched about the courtroom straightening his sleeves. "So we see that men are men, women are women. No real harm done. The issue is of land due these Crusaders. The church assigns the deed for following the cross." He looked confident against Edeva's scowl.

"Good! It is righteous to follow the cross!"

William took control walking firmly past the magistrate to the altar. "I bow to Knights of the Cross." He nodded to Edeva and turned to the jury-court. "Let us examine the cross." He tapped over his heart, first sideways, then up and down before the metal crucifix, his hands almost shaking, his countenance holy. His cross examination was fervent.

"To take the cross! To march a thousand leagues to fight for our Lord! This is an awesome responsibility. Bishop Rennes, is this not the noblest thing a man can do? Young men, have you traveled to Antioch or Jerusalem?"

"No, but our fathers did."

"Excellent sons! God be praised! So did Edeva's great father, and every man in her lineage. Ellen, show the commendation from King Baldwin of Jerusalem. This acknowledges her fallen father of The Crusade." Ellen pulled the scroll taught for all to see. "And his brother." She pulled that. "And his sons. These men of Chauvigny left Edeva's family for the Call of the Cross. They died for its cause, yet these young men ride in and claim their land. Land that their wives, mothers and sisters have worked for generations. Edeva pays the King's taxes–"

"Halt!" the magistrate said, pandering to the bishop. "These are real men. She is just a woman, and that one – a foreign slave and a woman. We have signs that they are witches."

"Witches by what signs?" William asked calmly.

"We have testimonies of priests."

"No, I want to see, the people want to see, not with words. Let us put before the jury-court your claiming priest against our lady. Let all see the devil and the angel side by side. Let us all see good and evil!"

The floor echoed William's urging. "Let us see!"

The bishop hammered the dais. "The church recognizes the words of its priests! No exhibition is needed. The eyes deceive, and I see evil. By the Bible, the tempter of Adam cannot own Adam's land. This land reverts to living men."

"Forgive me, your grace, I apologize." William said, then quickly, "May I summarize the case of Edeva, run off her trusted land by false sons?"

"No, you may not." Even though he just had.

"The land is awarded, and this trial is over. Let us pray." The bishop gave a holy Latin text, long enough to cool tempers with repeated calls to obey.

The doors broke open. Into the yards poured noisy talk of the court spectacle. Waiting peasants were disappointed. "No damned witches?"

"Enjoy your bonfire," William offered. "Calbi, there is a woman inside who needs proper escorting to the Palace dining hall."

Aquitaine lost the case, but William and Ellen saved two women from the sure fires of the Church. Eleanor was both heartened and ashamed. To witness her father fight with valiant words was as uplifting as if he wielded a sword.

Yet, it was as if curtains had drawn up revealing the sting of too much light. Edeva lost her land, and Eleanor had seen in too many eyes a contempt for women. She had seen the injustice of crusaders and the wrongfulness of the greater church, forces she had once believed stood for morality. She had seen the false charge of witchcraft, the loveless wish for female torture, the sad plight of Edeva run off her family land. It was all too much. And this was why Eleanor cried.

Not even the Duke of Aquitaine could grant rightful title to a family trust of his realm. Eleanor wished until her palms tingled – *if I had the King's power*. She felt charged in her blood to never to forget this.

The veil over evil had lifted. Weighty lines appeared on young foreheads. Eleanor and her court beheld things they did not want to think about before. On the road, when passing an overseer whipping a child, they halted the strappings with angry beratings. To a young girl sitting abandoned on the roadside, crying with her newborn baby, they offered a charitable Abbey. Priests licking their lips from high windows at women received their glares. The horror of what orphans, nuns, and monks had to run from, so much evil, even from stations of trusted power. Students beaten bloody by teachers, altar boys and choir girls molested by priests, cruel and incestuous parents. In short, the many stories of a loveless world. Eleanor wept for her generation and felt bitter contempt for chosen elders who should have known better, who could change things for the better.

As some consolation for lifting the veil of evil, the young life who impersonated a nun, whose name was officially unknown, was asked by the order of Fontevrault to visit next spring. Ellen said they had something to share with the daughter of William. He consented. His daughter had proven herself. She had stood up to him, not out of spite, but for good reasons. She demanded to help him, and she did. His daughter was writing the code of herself, the best time to know of Fontevrault's mission, and 'the test'.

By his word, William allowed Daena to dine at the Poitiers Palace with Eleanor's friends. He did not attend, not because Daena was a slave, but because he wanted his daughter to have her own world. He visited Edeva at Fontevrault's infirmary and brought her flower-honey to mend her voice. Edeva requested Calbi sing his songs of Danae at the ward, then asked

William to free the slave. William took pen to sign. Writ outside Edeva's hospital door he proclaiming her last name she would be called forevermore: franklin. Even though the powerful Church claimed title to all she once had, she was certain, Edeva Franklin was certain, that her voice and land would one day be hers again.

There was something much larger going on. Echoes of the trial reached beyond Aquitaine. In a candlelit cell at the Abbey of Clairvaux, a tall, gaunt man with burning eyes, Abbot Bernard, the ear of the contesting Pope of Rome, listened. Aquitaine donations and attendance dropped to the lowest point ever. He asked questions. He was saddened to hear of a recent Canon trial, where 'Crusader' had fallen low in esteem. The Abbot's imagination was fired by a nun, the very bride of Christ, who stood up to speak of Crusader nobility. He wondered if there were more like her. Strengthening Templar and Crusader values fit with his reevaluation of women as reformers of the Church.

Bernard listened further. William of Aquitaine, seed of his vile father, troubadour William, appealed Edeva's land title to King Louis Six. Nothing to do there. The French monarch was in poor health, a result of his sinful obesity, for which he was called Louis the 'Large.' Unlikely to rule on the case, it would go into indefinite suspension. In the candle flame, Bernard saw evil in Duke William, a thorn of regular concern – a speaker in canon proceedings against a bishop, an opposer of Bernard's Pope with his Pope, a stifler of Templar claims on mills. Pilgrim deposits could be kept safely at the mills and flowed directly to the church without meddlesome lords. These so-called crusaders of Chauvigny were upstarts, not accountable to Bernard. By messenger pigeon, he sent word for Templars to investigate. Meanwhile, with an invitation from the Lord of Parthenay, the abbot would make Duke William the subject of an Inquisition to ensure the Pope of God.

In Aquitaine thatched houses, over many a harvest wives' bubbling stewpots, hot over the hearth, went the meat of the matron's make, the garnish of her seasonings, the matron's stew art brand. Salt for the Duke, who stood out boldly for the right! Pepper for the nun who called out the truth! Honey for the brave woman of Chauvigny! A ladle more, a bit of beef, came to those who listened to the tale of a frizzle-haired blonde woman slave, whose forthrightness had proven the better match.

Plow peasants over many a bonfire from fall to winter discussed the legendary Daena, the nun who spoke up, and the plight of Edeva's taken land.

Cold came the new year. The land title floated into the hands of the church and was awarded to so-called crusaders who had little farm-skill. No worker within fifty leagues came near the unearned deed.

It was all a terrible mistake. After running the women from their land, the Chauvigny lads could not interest Bernard's Templars in buying the farm to build a watermill. That part of the Vienne River was too shallow. With little farm-skill, the Chauvignists found it easier to sell than lift a heavy plow. A fallow spring faced them. They lived off the women's harvest, consuming the farm stores. Though strong young men, they produced nothing. They had no code to guide them. Spending the last of their inheritance on spirits to carry on idle glories, the sons of crusaders took all they could. They drifted off to find Lusignan, the city south of Poitiers, where men gloried to live by no code.

Only wolves and rats prowled the abandoned Chauvigny farm.

〽

The Abbey

Abbeys were a big business. Ellen knew this well. At twenty-eight, Duke William's steward, an able administrator of Poitiers law and special projects, worked with the Grand Abbess of Fontevrault to enlarge the Abbey franchise. This morning the trusted manager would give a foundation and share a personal view of the Abbey to her spring 'guests.'

Ellen had a great skill in speaking. Beginning from anyone's subject of interest, she brought it to her own concern and, in the end, got business done. Ellen looked respectable in her buckled riding boots, long pine-green breaching tunic, and chestnut horsehair belt. Much as men, she wore her umber hair to the shoulder.

The magistrate beheld her wide-eyed, sharply dressed redheads in their clean gray light-woolen gowns. Fourteen-springs Amira sat patiently with her mistress. Curious Eleanor of twelve rested her arms on her knees, barely showing the bright orange of her under-sleeve. Ellen paced.

"This is Fontevrault, once a forted vault over a fountain. Say *Fonte Ebraudi* when speaking to Latin priests. It was first cut in the woods by men like your grandfather William the Ninth, thirty years ago. Building on the ruins of a Roman fort, the men hollowed out underground vaulted rooms to reclaim their use. Beneath, a natural spring feeds L'Arceau, our river. You are familiar with its school and forge; there are deeper things to know — I will tell you of its mission."

From the wood bench, Eleanor surveyed the square courtyard. It was a very busy place. Spring plantings were in progress; everything was being rebuilt, everything was in flux. Vigorous men and women in highly colored robes stepped over timbers. Some recognized the young damisel who spoke out at the Chauvigny trial, celebrating her in champion hand-signs. Eleanor acknowledged in little nods. She smiled with Amira. What was it like to live here, what did they believe, and what was the test? Robed members swept past in tempered arguments, disappearing to their right into the timber-framed chapel being rebuilt in stone. Chisel-masons pounded away on blocks of sawn limestone.

The chapel formed one side of the square. Along the other three sides were longhouses of wooden work rooms. The first, behind them, was a line of communal rooms for small meetings, congregation, and sewing. To their left was a long row of women's quarters with a refectory, a cookhouse at the end – the place the girls once brought a dead bird in a cart to cook. In front of them, a line of men's quarters and administration offices with a second floor. The stones of the former walled-in Roman legionnaire's barracks were put to new uses. Men on scaffolding reworked an eight-hundred-year-old military watchtower into a chapel bell tower. Outside the Fontevrault complex were orphanages, residences, a forge with workshops, a hospital, and a schoolhouse.

Amira asked Ellen, "Is this a church?"

"It looks like one, doesn't it? Fontevrault Abbey is special. Remember scrubbing the floors at Sainte Radegund's? That was a convent for women. This is a new type of monastery where men and women live together." Robed couples walked the quadrangle wearing what looked like vibrant quilts.

"At times, that chapel is open to outsiders to get to know of and worship with the current order. The chapel is a temple of the order's beliefs."

"What is an order?" asked Eleanor.

"Each class of abbey has its own order. An order explores a unique set of spiritual ideas that followers choose to live by. Here they work out Fontevrist principles. Compared to a church, an abbey has a key difference. The Roman Church provides a common worship plan, a mass for every town and castle. The people's church comprises a set of dogmatic beliefs that have become more complex over time. The abbey has an ordered set of ideas, a constitution that becomes simpler over time. It is practiced only in these walls by those who seek its mission. Fontevrault reorders the priority of church beliefs." Ellen fit the new word. "It re-searches the origins of spiritual values, in spite of church doctrine."

Eleanor puzzled, "To search again? Is something wrong with the church?"

"You must be careful how you ask that question," Ellen warned. "If the Pontiff were right there, would you ask that?"

"Yes." Eleanor had no doubts. The instructor's sardonic grin showed concern.

"Well, then I will answer your question honestly. A word of caution. If standing there were his legate or a cardinal, they would have the power to arrest you, just for asking that question. Do you understand what I am saying?"

The girls nodded with frowns – questions should not be crimes.

"I am going to be as direct and honest as father William. First, give thought to how you will speak with others of what I say. Truth is only to be shared with the truthful. All right? After hundreds of years, church leaders took advantage of their position of power. Some spent large sums of money, bought large estates, lived secretly with women who had their babies. Some arranged murders, and, I am sorry to say this, but you must know, some beat and grope innocent boys and girls. Such priests are abundant. It goes on within the church of Rome in silence."

The girls were upset. Amira emoted, "The church sins!"

Eleanor extended, "The church has no honorable code to purify itself."

"You sound like your father. Everyone is disturbed by church corruption. We must watch our tongues and take care." Eleanor did not care, as only from truth came progress. The trial of Chauvigny gnawed on her. Power was supposed to be used for good.

"Deep Eleanor, no need to pout. In many ways, our Abbey exists because of the church's shortcomings. Scholarly minds examine problems of religion. One of the great researchers of spiritual questions is Peter Abelard. He teaches in Paris at the same college where founder Robert Arbrissel once learned. Because Abelard pursues wisdom freely, he is called a philosopher. You might like this. He wrote a scholar's guide called, Yes and No, Sic et Non in Latin. In it, Peter asks over 150 deep questions to the faith that reveal contradictions in the Bible by the letters of the Saints. He asks, is something true, yes OR no? But in his answer book, Peter concludes yes AND no. He researches both sides and cites spiritual authorities. Logically impossible—well, that is for later. The people's church does not even like the idea of questioning, for it unleashes curious minds."

Yes and no, the two-sided view of life. Eleanor was immediately interested.

"Give us a question," Amira begged.

"Well, is God a single being or is he not? Abelard cites religious authors. Both views are ordained true. You might read his work or meet him someday."

"Abelard is still alive?" Eleanor wondered.

"One of our best Fontevrault students – you've heard of Bruce – he is a scholar at Abelard's college. He exchanges scrolls with a special chapel outside Paris called a Paraclete. Abelard built it for his star student, Heloise. There she perfects her own order. Paraclete comes from the original Greek Bible. . ."

Ellen was losing the two girls. She brought back their interest. "What do you know of Peter and Heloise? Their letters?"

Amira gave a wry smile. "Oh yes, we know."

"They are in Latin," Ellen said neutrally.

"We are studying their longest sentences," Eleanor said wryly.

"Sure you are." The executive admired their tight grins. "These 'love-letters' were copied and carried from Paris by Bruce in recent years." Their vivid love fired many a young mind and greatly motivated learning the ancient language of Rome. "Shall we lift our eyes from the rain-gutter to the bell tower?" They giggled. "Let's return to the Abbey's re-search of faith." Ellen waited for the girls to look for her direction.

"The Fontevrault orders are – how do we put it, Eleanor – like a code that purifies itself. The order is sustained actively by followers, as the best minds of our generation see it. Rather than have a plethora of rules and laws, they make as few principles as possible. Basic principles can generate a larger number of laws."

Eleanor liked the idea. "Who writes the principles and defines the order?"

"Good question. Robert Arbrissel lived the original precepts. Some of his rules were based on prior monasteries, like the ancient hermit Saint Benedict. Some of Robert's codes came from his acts, written down by his followers. A code prescribes exact action. They compile to a program for a manner of living to face the future. The program for one's own ideal behavior is not as easy to write as you may think. There are Robert's codes and his followers' codes, such as Love All Creatures. You may have seen around here tamed deer eating from our hands. That's why our forests are peaceful. Animals may not be killed on our grounds. All from one code. We'll meet the young woman who practices it."

Eleanor bubbled with ideas. New orders were everywhere, with masons, chevaliers, winemakers, sects. Their codes were written by men and women. And principles? She had not considered that fewer laws could express more.

"Girls, I have never seen so much curiosity. You have time to explore, but sadly, I do not. My promise to your father is to teach three things: the Founder, the Order, and the Franchise. Will you help me stick to this?"

Both gave the sign: fingers on lips draw out and become a palm. *Promise.*

"The Founder?" Amira urged.

"The mysterious beginning of Fontevrault is with the life of Robert Arbrissel. He died a few years before you were born. As a young priest, he was full of ideas from the Paris college, Saint Geneviève. He enjoyed the comforts of the Latin church. One day, he gave it all up. He went to live in nature. Ragged and poor, he suffered with those who suffered. His followers habited forests, limestone caves, and ruins. Imagine living only from nature like a cave person."

The two girls had met runaway orphans who had survived this harsh way.

"To Robert came the children of woe – rejected women, escapees of family harm, suffering souls who sought his aid and lived with him. Thousands. I am going to say this more directly, so you understand his heart, but I don't mean to upset you. He received wives beat bloody by husbands, boys crippled by fathers, girls tricked into having sex with priests and cast out for being evil, women forced to have babies. Children born blind, the unhearing, the voiceless, the sick – he received every suffering soul, young and old, male and female."

Ellen paused to see if they were troubled by her words, but truth and compassion were in their blood. She continued as if speaking from her life. "Where does a poor young person run to? I was told, 'to the forest to seek Robert Arbrissel.' Broken people begged for shelter and safety. His charity was meager, but I found room."

"I?" ever-vigilant Amira noted.

"I was one of the orphans schooled here before William discovered me."

Eleanor thought, from noble places came noble people – *Ellen is noble.*

"One remarkable thing: Robert did not give salvation in Latin, and he rarely used the words of the Bible, unless writing to an authority or a noble. Suffering is too personal. He spoke directly with a generosity of spirit, his presence. No words in scripture matched his; they came from his heart. Was he a heretic for this?" Ellen could see they wanted to know more.

"Girls, there are two kinds of priest. You can tell almost immediately by their presence and action. Do not confuse those driven by The Good, with those who speak in the name of God. The first kind are like Robert, and you might meet Abbot Suger someday. The second kind are like Bernard of Clairvaux, whom you will surely meet." The girls squirmed in consideration. "Goodness is eternal in the heart," and Ellen made the sign: hands facing, thumbs at the heart, shaking joyfully. *Lief.*

"Life?" asked Eleanor. Ellen corrected, "Lief – deeper than life, deeper than belief, it is in yourself. These are the signs from lief, to love, to life."

"Lief!" Hands facing, thumbs pointing to breastbone, vibrating with energy.

"Love." Hands folded over one another, palms to heart.

"Life." Hands from naval, rise to the sky, shaking joyously.

"I have good news. Later today you can ask more of Robert's dearest follower and chosen successor, Grand Abbess Petronille de Chemillé."

Eleanor was glad; her mind held a trove of questions.

"The Order?" Amira minded.

"Why thank you, Amira!" Ellen said, then cleared her throat.

"Robert's poverty, his life in the wilderness, took him beyond holy words. Amid wild deer and wolves, he learned first hand of suffering. He got to know human nature from families, men, and woman of every age. He tested himself and others–"

"Tell of Arbrissel's test, no one will tell me," Eleanor interrupted.

"Please wait for Grand Abbess de Chemillé. I could tell you, but she lived it. The truth is best heard from the source, oc? I can tell you his conclusion was this: that men and women live in balance; that women govern as authority, men in service of women. Those living quarters there were not divided men from women. They all slept under the same roof. The principle idea, Eleanor, is love. He did not see this virtue in men. He saw this as natural in the caring hearts of mothers. Fontevrault's ideal governess is the mature woman who has had children, knows actual love, and kens the ways of the world." Eleanor puzzled, 'Why only a woman? Men are capable of love, certainly my father.'

Ellen paused, looking for Amira to prompt her. The girl giggled, lifted her eyebrows and then mouthed, 'Franchise.'

"Many saw the good in Robert's works. He lived as a new type of Saint. While tending the suffering, he proved men and women can live together in spiritual harmony. Many liked his original beliefs, but outsiders did not."

Ellen rested her hand on Eleanor's shoulder, "Your Grandfather William, who cut and cleared the first ash-silver trees here, negotiated Robert's spiritual mission with the King and the Church. Lest you think he did it entirely out of generosity, William expanded the northern borders of Aquitaine by building this Abbey. He secured it by franchise. A franchise is a charter of Frankish immunity, free of any tax issued by the King. His deal with Rome was to build the chapel without tapping into their treasury. He paid the church to use its masons and builders, as long as all donations directed to Fontevrault stayed within its walls."

"That's smart," Amira said.

"Today girls, there are six Fontevraults. You look surprised. Ours here is only the first. Petronille and I manage and plan their general operation."

"How do you start them?" Eleanor asked.

"Ah, but what is being started? The mission. Sainte Radegund's mission?"

Amira said, "To serve the poor, but mostly to do housework for men."

Ellen laughed, then grew earnest. "I tell you this. All is first born in a reality, more awonder than its retold myth. Die Heilige Radegund. The German Princess ran away from her castle to found a convent in Poitiers."

"Why escape?" Eleanor frowned. "Radegund could have created a monastery in Germany."

"Because great orders have a purpose. It was necessary that she flee her murderous husband and his bevy of 'wives.' She created a monastery for runaway femmes. The Church made it a sanctuary, as is Fontevrault. Her life was a heroic achievement in the 6th century. Back then, Aquitaine ruled from Toulouse to the edge of Paris. Her deeper mission lives on at Fontevrault. You will learn of it from Petronille. Back to your question of starting new Fontevraults. With Robert's franchise charter, we start small abbeys of balanced order. We train missionaries by his example. He was too controversial for the ancient customs of the church. To build the abbeys, donations come secretly. Today, Fontevrault is one of the fastest growing franchises in Europa. We have 20 franchise inquiries from wealthy lords and seneschals of major castles. Each will have one of Paul's pigeonniers."

"Amira, your father's birds!" Eleanor said. "Why secret donations?"

"Most donors are ladies who have chosen Fontevrault to spend the remainder of their days, like your Grandfather's difficult wives who rest in peace. Rather than give their wealth to an already rich, far away church, each donor picks a program dearest to their concern. They invest in where they will live with a community that also gives young women and men rare chances. This is why the franchise succeeds. Shall we meet someone?"

...

"Oh, a storm is threatening again." The large silhouette of a woman in colored robes unique to the order stood at the grand office window. Her eyes swept the sky over the cacophony of chapel construction to the sheltered courtyard below.

Grand Abbess Petronille de Chemillé was a key power of Fontevrault since its beginning. At fifty-five, the happy lines of her face told the world that this force of nature had known many forms of love. She was no Psalm singer. Laid out upon her desk was the scrollable and pageable world of the Abbey.

Ellen brought in her guests. "Grand Abbess de Chemillé, this is Eleanor and her confidante Amira. They are both upon their teens. Ladies, this is Grand Abbess Petronille, the rock of Fontevrault. Madam Abbess, we have been speaking frankly about Fontevrault's order, franchise, and quite directly about Robert."

"So you have earned the confidence of Ellen," the Grand Abbess said, relishing Eleanor, who peeled back a sleeve to reveal a flamboyant orange under-sleeve. Petronille pulled open a concealed fold. A crimson strip ran over her heart. The Grand Abbess gave a face of mock alarm.

"So you are the one concerned so much about love. With that outburst before the bishop at the trial, good heavens. Now, what's this, Amira, bars in your hair, one over each ear holding your hair back?"

Amira explained, "A farm tool of some kind. To hear better."

"We are honored with such pretty ears. Yours too, Eleanor."

As mannered girls, they gave thanks for the hospitalization of Edeva, spoke of progress at the Abbey-school, and inquired of their senior's well-being.

Ellen said, "I am going now."

"Not yet Ellen." Abbess de Chemillé took her to the door with raised eyebrows. Ellen said for all to hear, "They are honest damisels. Speak the naked truth. Your time is well spent telling it all. I promise to see you girls later." She left.

Damisels. They had never been called damisels. A damisel was a responsible girl, a damisel on the verge of being married, available to flirt with suitors. The two girls took the meaning as 'being older,' and grinned at one another.

"So, it took the daughter of William to save Berry and Guisana from the cold snows. You make me remember why we are here, and, why I need to leave my office." Petronille, carefully studied the damisel girls, assured that they were capable of deeper thought.

"Before we go. Pilgrims and Saints," Petronille said. "Eleanor, do you know it? Let's play." Eleanor shrugged at the crude game of bawdy acts.

"All right, Eleanor. I am a pilgrim, you are a saint. Make up one. Play your saint with a divine stature. We pilgrims will take turns to tempt you, and make you fall from grace. I can make you laugh the very first time. Saint . . . who are you? Tell us your shrine and dedication."

Eleanor stiffened a sanctified visage before the great abbess. She chose a safe character. "I am Saint Peter, Church of The Rock, and I forgive all your sins."

"Let us test the Holiness of the Saint." Abbess de Chemillé leaned forward. Amira frowned, pilgrims in this game relied on unmentionable gestures, tickling, and swearing. To play a game of sacrilege, what would the Abbess do?

The Abbess bunched her shoulders and acted a humble countenance. "I am but a meek pilgrim." She winked at Amira. "Saint Peter, repeat every word of my incantation and do as I, repeat after me." She came right up to Eleanor's face, and with each word Petronille tapped her nose. "This - is - a very - serious - business. This - is - a - very - serious - business." Eleanor tapped her nose in time with Petronille drumming hers. Yet, seeing The Grand Abbess mash her nose while intoning 'This - is - a - very - serious - business' made Eleanor laugh wildly. The abbess shared her damisel laughter and removed the neck collar from her robe. Pressing back the hood to her shoulders, she pulled out her long silky black hair and let it fall. A few silver strands ennobled her vigorous age.

"Let us go to the forest!"

In no time, the Abbey grew smaller as they strode under the great Alder, Ash, and Elm trees.

"This could be the biggest sky I've ever seen. What do you think Amira? Eleanor? Oh what a pleasant spring wind." The girls appreciated the woman who could express herself as a child in joy. They walked into a meadow glade.

"What a troubadour your grandfather was. He had a thing for love, too."

It struck Eleanor. Petronille knew him personally. She asked, "Back in the times of William, when there was no Fontevrault, how did Robert make you what you would become?" Young Eleanor liked questions of origins; it was how she understood a heart.

The elder touched the grasses and pinched soil between her fingers. The whispers of nature brought forward a remembered familiarity. "Please, sit. It was here." The sun glittered on a rippling stream.

"You deserve to know the truth of Robert and William. Our ancestors deserve that if ever their lives are to have meaning." The abbess was risking a lot now and had to be sure.

"Young damisels, before we talk – we are speaking honestly. Amira, I hear you have a great memory, but please write none of this. If letters circulated, we would be shut down. Robert is misunderstood by everyone; slander prevented his Sainthood. What he did, what we did, well, this was our way. I trust my words to you in secrecy because your grandfather, William, and Robert, my Saint, made this place. You are their future. You are to be great ladies someday. This I give so you will be greater." She put her hand on her heart. The damisels touched their own and tapped their lips, making the promise sign.

"Well, honest souls with manners, let me tell you in short. I kissed Robert. We were lovers, but not in any way you could imagine." The damisels were surprised to hear this from an abbess. Kissing love was shunned in the people's church; a double sin if you did it there, a triple sin for clergy. The lady's cheeks flushed with happiness. Moved by the Petronille's revelation, Eleanor brought her wrists to her chest, pulling on a self-hugging gesture of joyful excitement. 'A woman to be trusted.' "Ah, heartfelt trust," the abbess acknowledged. "This gesture is more inclusive." She circled a double-round hi, a circular gesture ending with twinkled fingers that made the girls look twice. "Ask the orphans about it."

Petronille fingered grass roots, and continued.

"What character these two men had! Dangerossa with us, well that's another story. I see her in you, Eleanor. Robert Arbrissel had deep spirit, a thin honest face. Being in his company he was fully present, always listening. When he acted his good will, you felt beautiful sounds, bells. Have you met such a soul?" The girls shook their heads no. The blowing grasses shished around them. "Not yet? The world has so few. He was fair to all. He looked directly at the you in yourself. He did not live as an authority though he was. He never struck anyone. You always felt safe with him. As he saw into your soul, he let you see into his. He lived by the two-way truth."

The two girls looked at each other, as they lived by this bond already.

"Like most hermits, Robert turned away from the towering church. He rejected celibacy, believing love in all forms was to be celebrated, providing rules-codes to govern its exuberance. He found in poverty, in life, what he could not in the church. Sainte Radegund did charitable deeds and lived cloistered in a poor cell. We had no cell, we lived open to the sky in the harshest weather, poor and free as Adam and Eve. In nature, we felt as children, loving all life, discovering the Earth as if for the first time, hip free and shoulder bare."

The abbess looked at the ledge rocks by the stream, hearing again, the lightness of birds, the wind's sway, animal sounds, the clicking of leaves.

"How many wretched begged, 'Give me shelter!' None were refused. They were grateful for safety and what little charity we could afford. We helped in every way. Our shelter might be a cave, an abandoned ruins, a forest lean-to. Often we slept in the fields. Our idea of child's play was to tinker with broken bottles in the rain." The two girls pressed hands. "You know what I mean, don't you? To follow Robert was to be like him, so we gave away everything. We lived just like our poor refugee runaways. We spoke the truth and gave comfort."

Petronille looked about, wanting to express something, but it was further on.

"Robert taught of goodness through action. His words were few but chosen and true. His slim smile, his deep eyes, every heart remembered. He spoke in the language of the sufferer, rarely in Latin. His sayings and spiritual discoveries did not work for the church. His purity was beyond the cross. He lived close to human nature where every act is a potential heresy. How to explain this? The

Abbey order you see today is not how we lived. Back then we possessed nothing and tested our nature. Today, we preach easy morals. Under every moral prohibition lives a deeper truth that few have the courage to face. The trials of our boundaries made us greater. Facing one's nature yields enduring character, much like when you freed Guisana and Berry to show their will to love."

"I was ten winters, and you patted my head, then. Was I right?"

"Yes. That was who we were. Sadly I fear, the order is being reformed to appease the higher church. Now we keep a man in men's chambers and a woman in women's. This is easier than the test of habitation that lies at the base of human being and family. Unless we test ourselves, we will never ken who we are. With Robert's guidance we found there is no wrong. There is only truth."

The stream bubbled through rocks. "Sometimes listening to nature is better than talking about it. Let's for a while." The three held hands in the fresh spring wind. Trees animated their greening limbs, swaying in the peaceful sky. Forest animals peered at them. Feeling the sun and air, Petronille mused: "The wind once blew so young, the brightest sky, the biggest ideas."

Eleanor empathized with the lady trying to bridge time. She squeezed the lady's hand saying, "What you have to say is important."

Petronille fluffed Eleanor's hair. "Oh, so you are my confessor." Clear-eyed, they laughed. "Perhaps the world could be better if adults were forced to confess to youth. How to say this so you will understand? You know the tale of sailing Odysseus roped to endure the alluring sirens?" The abbess unlaced and loosened her soles to bare her feet.

"Arbrissel's Test is like that. Eleanor, you are of marrying age, so I am going to tell you of a form of love. This test exists in no book, nor will it be written. Remember how lost Odysseus, knowing he would sail past the sirens, wished to hear their ravishing voices. Their allure was so strong that no sailor could resist crashing into the siren's shore. They tied him with ropes to the ship mast so he could hear, but he had put beeswax in their ears so they could not. When the beckoning calls neared, the ship sailed on. The rowers could neither be tempted by the sirens nor take his mad orders to steer the ship into the shore."

Petronille de Chemillé stepped into the brook. *Was it ever this cold?* She cupped a drink of water. Ankle deep, the water rippling her hem, she turned to them. "Robert's test came from our poverty. We lived in nature, exposed. Every starry night we slept together feeling desires. We were the sailors. We had no ropes. None of us did. We accepted the mark of naked poverty. Robert knew this is how we must live, to follow the naked Christ on the cross. At night, as young women, we slept with little on. Unrestrained, we slept mixed, bodies next to one another. Some slept with the smell of women, others the smell of men. At times, we reached out for another's nearness. Robert helped us pass the siren test. We tempered the urge to procreate." The standing abbess took a deep breath.

"When you possess nothing, if all you have are the cold needles of the pouring sky, the sun burning your skin; with every thirst and hunger upon you, never deny the power of naked beauty. When being allows being, that is when you become human and pure."

Footing rocks in the stream, she wobbled from one smooth surface to another.

"One day when the sun was highest, in a brook of faithful followers, Robert asked us to stand facing, ankles deep in cold water in our rags. I stood next to his trusted counselor Hersende, a real fighter for our lands and rights who ran things. She married twice and gave birth to Heloise, who shares her erudite letters with our Abbey. Robert trusted women like Hersende and me who had married and birthed children. In the stream, Robert looked at her but spoke to all; he held open his arms saying, 'Behold the sapient body the Creator has made, the one you are, the one before you. We are the poor and the naked. There is no shame in feeling desire. If you deny it entirely, you are dishonest; when you lose that feeling, your spirit is dead.' He walked down the stream and back again looking into our eyes to see we understood in our own manner. When he came to me, I was so young, and I am not sure what made me say it, I dropped my rags entirely. Maybe I wanted to be seen as I am, to endure all of women's nature. My test. So much I wanted him; in every sense I loved him. I stood as our lips kissed without bodies touching. I could see the sweat on his brow and heard his swallow. I felt my desire with his. Then his words came. 'Only she who lets herself be naked, wanting without being wanton, only she will be our rock. Petronille, love gives you strength to lead our order. It is I who must go on. Put on your clothes and find everyone robes. Hersende, when I leave, follow your leader'."

"And here I am in so many more clothes." Petronille walked to the grass, pulling her long hair back. "I tell you, it is easier to put beeswax in people's ears and deny their humanity than to have them face the desires they are born with. Only a consecrated spirit can walk into a feast and mitigate between gluttony and hunger. Take liquor and moderate riot with sobriety. Listen to fiery music and soothe one's spirit. Step into tempting love and experience divine pleasure. I tell you, the pretense of chastity is a farce. Robert's ritual order was that humanity test every form of love and for brief years, we lived it."

"It began. Why should it stop?" Eleanor said.

"We found the issues of love challenging, the church overpowering."

Eleanor became boldly present. "You cannot give up. Resume Robert's quest to explore the order of love. When I rule as Duchess, I will protect you."

"Oh, I marvel at your intent. It takes two people in agreement to love."

"You teach balance between man and woman already."

"Young one, love has so too many spirits in life: friendship, desire, sex, birth, family, compassion, charity. There are too many variations."

The unstoppable Eleanor went on. "Ellen says when there are too many laws, you write key principles. Principles of love, each person by their own code. Don't you see? Stay young Petronille, don't get old on us."

Abbess Petronille rounded her cheeks, chuckled, then gave her concerns. "Persistent one, you may be right. You must know, even in Robert's pursuit of the order, Bishop Rennes tried him as a priest for sleeping in the same space as women, the essence of his test. In Catholic faith this is deemed a sin, but not in our order. Regard. We habited together for years in poverty, no different from any peasant family. After all the charity he accomplished – to comfort the frail in residence, to tend the sick in the hospital, to raise children in the orphanage, to train our followers – the church denied Robert's sainthood. A problem with religion is it forbids spiritual growth that exceeds the vision of its prophet. Who has the strength for humankind's passions? Love is a risky business at all times; beeswax is cheaper than rope." The Abbey bell sounded.

On their way back in heavy thought, Amira had the sense to be light.

"How long before the church chapel is complete?"

"It is a temple we build for generations," Petronille said. "We depend on various donations of wealthy women who retire to help finish it. We work our charity, comfort the frail in residence, tend the sick in the hospital, raise children in an orphanage, and train followers. Damisels–" The abbess halted. Touching grasses, she surveyed the compound. "Consider this. An injured runaway girl – we give shelter, but you have to wonder, as Robert did, why was she forced to run away in the first place? That is beyond scripture. That is our real mission, our true cause."

Eleanor strode the grasses with conviction, *somehow love*, that was it.

In the refectory, clear light broke through a half-laid black slate roof, flooding long tables where a hundred robed men and women quietly ate a simple, meal. Eleanor and Amira found tasting each soupspoon of bean, each chew of bread, a magnifying sensation. Mechanically they ate, savoring thoughts in pure light. Eleanor swam with sensations as the spiritual world were unfolding. In this new orders, love had a principle nature, the mission has a cause. She thought of Robert's trial and his test. Eleanor received a pat and looked up. Men and women congratulated her.

"Thank you for speaking out at the Chauvigny trial."

"I just spoke my mind."

"And what a mind that is. You speak with focus. Petronille says you have novel ideas." Eleanor grinned. These followers had laid together at night and proven their character. Could she pass their test? The specialness of Fontevrault was apparent. Unlike convents and monasteries she had visited on progress, these holy men and women did not fear gender. Flirtatious camaraderie was their union. They accepted Berry and Guisana having a child. Amira, regaled her amusing childhood experiences, prompting others to share a few of their own.

"Eleanor, we are most impressed, you have chosen your friends wisely. We cannot get over Daena and Calbi. Daena is almost worshiped here. Did you know her beau sang touching serenades for Edeva Franklin, and everyone in the hospital ward? Oh, when he sang for his Daena, such delight. They slept together making the lovely sounds, a practice of veracity as Catharics. Still, he wants to take the test, without her it must be. They know we do not choose a life of denial. We live with enough desire to care and keep balance in the pleasures of life."

Eleanor said, "If ever there were a miracle, it was that trial. To see Danae in such mannered behavior that we learn here. Danae is a builder who comes from a line of Viking ship makers. They met building a wall."

Grand Abbess de Chemillé came into the clear light descending from the unfinished roof. "Daena will apprentice to the builders of Fontevrault, regardless of what the mason's say." Amira said, "I've watched them build the roof from the trees. Were she in charge it would be already finished – ready is the hrad." After a Psalm, sung in Occitan, as tables cleared, the damisels gave a long hug to Petronille.

Ellen waited out in the bright side yard, mashing a honeycomb in a jar with a spoon. She watched her damisels come out and look at the social activities around. Making their way over, they had added depth in their eyes.

"Too much to think about?" Ellen said as she worked the pot.

"What smells of honey?"

Ellen pulled out white beeswaxed twizzle sticks. As the girls played the sweetness in their mouths, Ellen brought them to a near finished circular tower. "One of Paul's pigeonniers." Amira swelled with pride. Ellen pointed nearby.

A young nun in a white new habit worked gracefully under the warm shade of a silver ash tree. Visitors in colorful clothes watched. She gently pet and fed a baby deer. Silently, the girls approached. She motioned, and they understood to approach the animal. Its tongue extended, licking their honey sticks out of their hands. "Where are you from?" The nun tilted her head, lay a hand across her smile and shook her head indicating she could not speak. Mutely, she led the ambling deer into a sun shaft and knelt in straw to mother the deer with milk.

Ellen said, "Poachers, hunters trespass our forests. This sister leads a new Fontevrist sect, cultivating a code to shelter animals. She instructs visitors from Italy. You would think she could speak to the animals." The young nun gestured. Ellen interpreted, "It is all in the hands. Love is the language of all creatures."

Ellen graced the sister's cheek exchanging a smile, then set forth the honey pot. The nun fanned it away then rubbed her stomach making a sour face. Ellen interpreted, "Not good for the deer." She and the girls nodded farewell and walked off to a distance as they chewed pieces of honey-wax.

"There is so much to think about, Ellen. When do we take Robert's test?"

"Eleanor, we will have time for that."

"I doubt you would pass," Amira said.

"Why not?" Eleanor pulled out the glob of white. "Beeswax." She thought of Odysseus, then licked her honey lips thinking of Mathieu.

Amira said, "Ellen, she talks of teasing suitors and twistles her lips with bur rose stems to make them red."

"Once in a while. Rose is more natural than oils; the color comes from me."

"Suitors we'll talk of later. Just know damisels, as you may feel drawn to men at times, many feel this impulse for you, often too strongly. Those who've not taken the test play upon desires. Save this to mind, all right?" They nodded.

"You are being trusted to keep this yourselves. If you need counsel about the order, what you've heard, ask me, your parents, grandmother Dangerossa, elders at Fontevrault. We have been through it all."

Amira spoke for both, as was her position. "We understand. We thank you."

Ellen offered a new honeycomb. "There is *official* and the *unofficial* side of this order. Officially, Fontevrault serves spiritual and commercial purposes. Men and women live together by a new code that explores balanced spirituality. We have our famous seasonal market to sell our famous colorful two-sided quilt, the Auqueton. Sewn here, these beautiful quilts warm our finest beds. And they are worn by chevaliers to pad their chain mail and to sleep in the field." In the distance nuns lay brilliant patterned auquetons to air on a line.

"Officially," Eleanor teased, bringing her orange-lined sleeve to her chin.

"Unofficially, in light of your talk with Petronille and knowing your natures, think of the abbey as a love hospital." The damisels giggled. "Regard. Fontevrault is the church's dark secret. We receive the outcasts and the runaways. Our care for poor Edeva is a hospital of ex-wives of bishops and lords, maimed prostitutes. The orphanage affords their forbidden infants, abused and abandoned, boys and girls. The infallible church could fix their own problems by sending the perverted priests to King's court, by asserting love rather than celibacy. We are the check, but the cause goes unchecked. The Church executes a program written a thousand years ago that runs for eternity, forbidden to reexamination, prevented from growth. Fontevrault houses the result from a lack of spiritual guidance, to teach properly of love. The Abbey is big business, my doves. Eleanor, one day you may be asked for program advice by the order. By your time, there may be sixty franchise chapters, and Amira, just as many pigeon towers your father is building.

Ellen gave final caution. "This vault over the spring is a safe place, a sanctuary. The chapel is always open to men and women to further Arbrissel's cause by dwelling on one's own story, one's own tests. Fontevrists are who we are, but never say that to the Catholic. They have little toleration for other temples of their faith. Speak of us simply as, 'The Abbey.'"

〰〰
〰

Summer Fields

The spring rains fled, making May the month of mayhem when every greening thing pushed itself haphazard to the sky. A field of wild honeysuckle blossoms peppered with bees thrummed outside the wagon-house near the knight's stable. The summer was full of life and Eleanor wanted it to last forever.

Dim in the looking glass, summer-happy Eleanor, in a simple knee-length kirtle, let herself turn and be, her typical wondering self. Honey twigs and Fontevrault's mission was three months ago, but it seemed a year had passed. Love letters and long hair; hunting belts, new dresses, and family history colored her young damisel world. In the glass she twiddled her lathe basket, practicing hot and cool looks to attract handsome maleness. Men looked at her differently these days, and not always in a fun way. In suitor court, her father said, 'good character alone makes a man worthy of your love.' Never did court seem so vapid and the courtyard of knights seem so full. The men she wanted were not the class of suitors father offered for arranged marriage. How hotly these men trotted out, how slyly they asked, 'Can you feel my heat?' She insisted she preferred coolness in men – her secret truth.

Men becoming Chevaliers – nothing appealed to Eleanor more. Not boys who knew nothing, nor privileged men breathing tooth rot who said they knew it all, but males becoming eighteen. They showed muscle, intelligence, wit, and daring. They wore brilliant auquetons – knee length, colorful two-sided body quilts The best were made at Fontevrault, and the best men had cool tempers.

'Hot' was the worst thing to call a chevalier. Tolerating intense heat, compounded by battle, armor, horse, in sun and summer, was the price of invincibility. Cultivating a chivalry of keeping cool, a 'frosty' had the quality of practiced movement in combat. Never letting the heat of battle get the better of him, an 'iceman' waited for the decisive moment. Chevaliers only played with heat; they did not absorb it.

The knights of the realm, training for chivalry in her father's court, were Eleanor's preferred companions. They took her on play dates, improved her riding skills with her mare Limona. At times, they almost came to blows with their overzealousness to keep her safe.

She twirled, feeling brash and hrad again, yet something troubled the little girl she had been. Aching to let go, when she turned to look into the glass, and no matter how much she turned, she could not find that older one she felt within.

By the round stables, Eleanor ambled out with her basket to a wildflower field and stopped at the hazel tree. The vast Aquitaine sky never seemed so blue. In the high midday heat, sheep lazily sauntered into the stalls to be sheared. Oxen took a shady break, their furlong day done. Stallions gathered after a hard ride to be groomed. Eleanor teetered on the fence, the pulse of her neck quickening. She placed the basket near the fence post. Men were splashing nearby.

There had been a skirmish with outlaws, and the Chevaliers had returned to the stables. Their bathhouse songs were bawdy – sagas of women they fancied and favored echoed as they washed. This circus of men, removing armor, unsaddling horses, sloshing buckets of water, wrapped in towels, ended by cavorting half-nude poses for their girl mascot. She pretended not to notice, but she was not ashamed to peek; horses and men were invigorating. Posers emerged from the bathhouse, praying with soap, taking humor in Catharic rituals. Their roman antics made her laugh, a silent score for them.

Eleanor lay her hand on her simple belt and sighed. It was not an iron-strong horsehair belt, the kind that knights wove from the hairs of their steeds for their favorite ladies. Hopeful at the wood post, she pulled honeysuckle vine growing around the hazel. Being infatuated with knights, she had her teases well-rehearsed. All knew her game, all except the new horsemen – the ones she might have a chance with before they learned her stoop-your-head title. The new were always the last back, cleaning up after engagements. She glanced up the trail.

A chingle of iron mail and hooves approached, clopping to the livery yard. Eleanor took up her basket and thought, *bright armor, strong horse,* a new one. The knight rode, slowly in thought. He stroked the neck of his horse. *Probably his only friend.*

"Don't pet your horse too much or she won't take you anywhere!"

The chevalier pulled rein to attend. She was coming to meet him, near a chest-high fence, a shy but beautiful young girl with an eager grin. A faint flush rounded his cheeks. He challenged for good measure:

"Now why would you say that?"

"You don't handle her well. Looking *hot* there, I would say." She looked from her wicker rim and leaning forward on the fence, probed in quick nervy patter, "You're not Aquitaine. Bavarian, umm Alsatian!"

"Yah," he said. Being called 'hot' by a quizzical female, well, she didn't know better. Or maybe she did judging from how the long red-haired damisel leaned on the fence, nipping nectar, seeming to ken something. Into the yard, fellow chevaliers crept to see how their new man would deal with Eleanor. She dawdled and looked one eye to the clouds. He squinted up to see what she was looking at. She pondered, "You like it here."

"Yah, well, ah . . ."

She leveled her eyes. "Fight? .. Joust? Slay a soul?"

"Ho there. You a priest?"

"No." Enjoying his handsomeness, she shot a cheerful look of understanding. Her smile pushed him over the edge. He had to confide.

"Oc, Ja. We wounded four men. They fell quick."

"I knew it!" Proud of her guess, she also felt his lone woe – men were hurt. He seemed even more handsome by opening his heart.

So that the listening knights could hear, she dipped her head with authority and said to him, "Your brothers there. Sad men. They are missing peace, that peace – you know – that having a lover gives you. That's a lonely livery you have there, you don't mind me saying."

The two exchanged nods, grimaces, then short smiles in wonder of who would speak next. The knight leaned forward on his saddle pommel.

"So, smart-talker, tell me your name!"

She rolled her eyes and turned her head away, giving a self-effacing "Eleanor." She burned a glare. *'Do you have any interest in me?'*

Struck by her willful look, the knight gazed into her young eyes that seemed to look right into his soul. *Was she playing?* For moments, she behaved like a woman, this girl. He cupped hand to ear and bent closer, gesturing he did not quite get her name. Her words followed fast.

"Actually, Alienor, by a mother I never really knew, but I'm Eleanor, just a girl named Eleanor." She played with her basket, saying neutrally, "You can call me Spark. They all do. It's easier for iron-heads."

He took the hit. The yard of men mouthed an 'ooo'. "How old are you?"

"They say I'm twelve, pains me to say, but I am older. I know I am. Do you know how old you are?"

"Ha, I should, I am eighteen."

"How would you know, were you counting when you were born?"

He chuckled, not sure how to take the quick of her. Eleanor had to set aside the bothersome age difference. She put her hands on her hips.

"I hope you know how to make a horsehair belt. I like chevaliers, not knights. Why are you so slow in the saddle?"

"Uh, well . . ." The young damisel leaned forward pressing the fence posts, wide-eyed, welcoming his confession. ". . . it was a bloody ordeal."

"Harsh!" she barked with a graven face.

"Outlaws cannot hurt travelers that way. I had to ensure they lived, that's all."

'Compassion,' she noted and empathized in a comforting tone, "You are here to keep the peace, not take souls." In a high manner, she raised her head and lowered it. *Sadly that was life.* He raised his head and lowered it as if in

agreement. She nodded, he nodded, together they nodded. Then as one, they laughed aloud at their noddingness.

"So what's your name?" she asked eagerly, playfully tilting her head.

"Ahm . . ." He turned to his brother knights, pursuing their contest. He gave a slight nod. "I am Armstrong of Alsace."

"Armstrong! I LOVE your visor!" she mocked with an exaggerated brow.

He felt proud. Asquint he wondered, *did she really*, was this girl serious? She giggled sharply. Played again. The knights roared and whistled at the damisel's scoring wins for putting Armstrong on. He threw a hardy laugh back. Yet even in this play, he could feel she meant something by the remark. He let his hand glide to his visor. "Uh, thanks." She smiled and coyly lifted her head.

"You are kind of hrad, you know?" she said in a throaty way.

'Is she putting me on again?' he studied her devilish smile, having no idea if hrad was a compliment or an insult. The men leaned forward. She threw her legs over the pickets very boy-like, set her basket down, and came to him. She reached up and felt the seam of his auqueton. She rolled her eyes up. "Are you hrad?" Back she went, picking up her basket leaning on a creaking fence, giving the basket a bounce on a knee. Her eyes glinted as she gave a nod.

Half-nodding, he pretended to know the word. "Um hrad, how do you mean?"

Eleanor pushed a shrug. "I don't know . . . hrad. It's just a Call."

A Call. The word struck Armstrong with the punch of a lance. Something was calling him; she was charming his heart. How amply and joyfully she flirted.

"Hrad . . ." he engaged, hoping it did not mean pride.

"You don't think you are?" She spied one-eyed, and gave a charming profile.

"Wooo . . ." the yard mused at his drawn-in confidence about to be tripped.

"Oc, No. Umm, yes, I think I am."

"Yes. No. You think? You are sure!"

Not knowing irked him. "Yes, I guess I am."

"Maybe you're not," Eleanor teased, glowering for a judgment from the men.

"You have been lanced!" The yard knights awarded her the score.

"Lanced," she giggled. With a sporting smile, she raised her basket and danced to his horse. It munched her yellow-throated honeysuckle and velvet green-leaves, then took them all at once. She went and leaned on the fence.

"Bye 'lance,' I am going now," She swung off the fence.

He watched her walk the field. "Wait, what's a hrad?"

She turned, "My nature, Chivalry" She mocked and waved, skipping away.

"Yah! I will see you around, uh . . . Spark!" He reflected as she left, *'Wait, Chivalry is not my name,'* then dismounted and sighed. The chevaliers clapped his back. He felt he'd passed some type of test. There was something about this little mascot and how she worked her charms. She seemed to know his mind. The stable knights told her she was the Princess. He marveled. She had not used her title or airs; she was simply being the girl she was. Like every knight who came before, charmed by her nature, he redoubled his vow that he do some deed to be called his name – Armstrong.'*What was chivalry to her?*'

To Eleanor, it was one more happy vacant day, gathering another knight's confidence. Lighthearted she could be, but she wanted more.

That night, she smiled into the hand mirror she kept by her bedside. Unlike any other, the pure glass gave perfect clarity that held her gaze. Mathieu, the adventurous boy-wizard had created it for her. He had really cared. They remained good friends, but he was a puppy in love; she was 'ready for men.' Yet, only in Mathieu's glass could she see deeper perceptions, the hints of her wished-for beauty. Her cheeks had lost their chub, her neck had curve and muscle, even her chin looked kissable. She wanted this thing in females that knights truly desire – was it merely curves? She fancied small pleasances, playful teases, and stronger yearns. Into the cool mirror, she looked. '*It must be summer heat.*'

Pretty women and their beaus would invite Eleanor on play dates with them, where she observed their affections, ones she hoped one day might be meant for her. Eleanor often brought a troubadour. "May, the month, the May of song, the May of women." Who could disagree with music's transforming power? They created feelings that all could feel. Those women of rose-twistled lips always brought a red bud, barely open. Their beaus always shaved. The women played the bud along their jaw to ensure their chevalier was rose petal soft. Inspired by their woman's flower, they wore it. What drew them to kiss, what appealed to these cool men famed for iciness, seemed to be an aspiration to redness, some desire for heat.

On a play date by a tree, alone with her recent handsome chevalier, away from his beautiful woman flirting with others, Eleanor asked, "Armstrong, kiss me as you do her."

"I cannot kiss you like a woman. But as a girl, I can. Stand still." She sulked, closed her eyes, put her arms to her side. She readied her lips imagining his masculine warmth. When their lips touched, and he tapped hers with his tongue, she giggled and broke off. "That tickles." He winked at her, and they laughed.

Growing like a May song within, Eleanor's sensitivity expanded. It let her know of other minds – dangerous men, gifts that were not gifts, as well as true friends and true gifts. Inside, a beautiful music swelled, clearly from what she felt was her ample heart. The humid day smelled of green. She wanted a new style, no longer hrad. It would be something glorious, something definitely red.

❋

In the summer morning at the river point where the Boivre meets the Clain, north of the boat docks, the sun was in its early rise. Princess Eleanor went to a chair on a broad blanket under the Poitiers elms. Amira was back from her time away. She adjusted furniture that servants had placed. The outdoor hair-wash station was set with tables for oils, brushes, bowls, and something new – a basket of personal letters of love. Eleanor floated her arms as if flying.

"Eleanor, do you have to be so damned beautiful all the time? Shives, sit still."

"You sound like your grandmother Lorraine."

Amira mimicked with vim. "Sit still child, behave!" Eleanor shook her head, pulling every gathered hair from Amira's hands.

"Eleanor, a green branch is about to become a switch!"

"I'd like to see that. For spooking Aigret, you sure got a good backsider."

"Thanks to you!" Amira was about to say something, but it was best to leave Eleanor with the last word. Amira again drew the tangly hair in short gathers from the hair's brill, then drew it to longer strands. Long hair was a slow, gentle business before the hundred strokes of a comb. Depending on Eleanor's mood, in chambers at least, from bathtub to dress was bell to bell. "Jesu, your hair feels like it has been two weeks in the wind!"

"You have been gone a week," Eleanor said. Then, changing the subject, "How are the birds with Paul?"

"Well. We have new stock from Spain, and more routes, including two with Paris. Mathieu says we'll have news of the world days before anyone knows. He has a new coding scheme for private messages. He is very clever. O, Mathieu sends you every best wish; he is in your court, Eleanor. He often wears your scarf. Just the thought of your lips on him when he passed out keeps him going. I like reminding him of it. That was a good kissing you planted."

"It was. Let me bring you up to date on the suitor follies. I met a 'manly man.'"

"Can there be a 'manly' suitor?" They watched a boat sail the Boivre.

"Not the toadish suitor but Francois, the man who accompanied him across the French channel. Francois and his brother monks worship, as he says, 'honestly, uncorrupted by the church.' The Northlands are in rebellion, and the troubles began last year when King Henri I died. He was the second generation of William the Conqueror. On his dying bed, Henri willed the throne to Mauthild. You'd think a king's will would stand."

"Famous Mauthild," Amira said, pouring honey-spiced wine into their silver-glazed cup. Amira sipped first – her duty as a taster practiced since the death of Aenor and little William. Eleanor drank from their cup and continued.

"Nobles swore allegiance to Mauthild. The archbishop too! When the King went to heaven, Stephen of Blois, just thirty leagues away, goes to London, nabs the Treasury and thrones himself. Poor Mauthild will have to fight to get it back."

"Yeah. Henri had twenty known bastards. It is good to be the King."

"For men, perhaps. What manner of family life is that? Amira, a King should have more honor than our best chevaliers, don't you think? The church is a mess to allow broken families. That's why Francois was so full of religious zeal. He says Mauthild wants religious change as well. He even prays with Mauthild. I asked him to pray her prayer with me. I liked how I felt with him."

Amira asked with a bit of edge, "How close did your feelings come?"

"It was not like that. You know how Abbess de Chemillé praises Good men and Catharics – like how we feel when Calbi prays? I felt valiant in my soul. You never hear genuine talk in confession – all that mysterious mope and shady guilt."

"Eleanor!" Amira minded. Eleanor looked up to the elms.

"It's the same old story! Francois said, 'Souls are not elevated, but remade in the image of the church.' And confession, he says they write down your sins to use against you later. My father says so, too. Mauthild marries the Holy Roman Emperor at eight. I am already twelve."

Amira said, "When the Emperor died, Mauthild came back childless."

Eleanor turned with peppered eyes. "Mauthild came back as an Empress! Imagine! Twenty-six summers and she remarries to a boy, eleven years younger. 'Come here little knave, put down your wooden toys and kiss me.'"

"Eleanor, get a marriage under your belt."

"I know, don't advise me. I told Francois, put the Empress on the throne; she'll fix things right, clean as stonework."

"I doubt that. Mauthild is pregnant again by Duke Geoffrey. They say he has striking looks, dresses in style, original and colorful. They say he even bathes."

"They say, they say – stallions, who cares! He's at war, settling the Normans while Mauthild must fight to retake the throne of the English-lands – and by her father's will. If she has any heart, she'll lead an army, even as a mother. I know I would. I tell you Amira, the limitations put on a woman for not being a man make me furious. As Duchess, I will change that."

"If you ever accept a suitor. I guess you don't care how the King's coin flips." Amira handed their silver-glazed cup to share a draft of wine.

"I do care how it flips!" Eleanor wiped her lips, thinking of knights – men with stamina like Armstrong, learning the code to do right. But suitors? The old pale faces came to her – so-called better stock, hot braggarts with sweaty looks, and those shiny birthday-boy faces with bad breath, all resting on their decrepit father's gains. It was dreary to consider a man without his own charge.

Father William's horse galloped loudly, stomping at their side. The Duke was elated. "Just received the bird's word. Eleanor, Uncle Raymond is crowned King of Antioch. Keep this news dear – he wed not the mother, but the daughter."

"Certs?"

William disliked her slang, rectifying, "Certainly. Ready for a marry age?"

Eleanor abhorred his puns, correcting, "Must we talk of my unmerry future?"

William shook his head and laughed. "I'm on the road to Mirebeau."

"Father, you have recovered from your deathly winter illness."

William glared, "We'll speak of that later." In a wind he cantered off, rippling their basket of letters.

Eleanor expressed concern, "Amira, I worry that father may have been poisoned by a suitor to get to me. It has happened."

"You should be his," Amira joked. "Well, news of your Uncle Raymond is surprising. He did not marry the Queen of Antioch, but her daughter of nine! How do you feel about that?"

"I wonder if she can love him. I think I could. My uncle was ever so much fun."

"Undercutting the Queen mother? Wedding her child? She must be furious."

"It wasn't his idea, the bishop insisted."

"I wonder how that works?"

"Let's ask a bishop, next mass."

"Since when does your family care what a bishop thinks?"

Eleanor grabbed the comb from the table and held it up to Amira's nose, waiting for her to snarl.

The comb always confounded Amira. Her mistress used it differently from its intent. Combs were supposed to remove lice from hair, as with any horse or pet. On some days, Eleanor audaciously wore the comb in her hair in broad daylight. It was a badge, expressing that Eleanor never had lice. She was a bather. Bathing was a suspicious act in the eyes of the people's church, and the act of enjoying the tub was near blasphemy. Body smells should be driven off like evil, by a purchase of imported and blessed church incense. Eleanor crushed in her hair a flowery fragrance like lavender that warded off every insect but the bees. She was accused of not smelling Holy. Although she used frankincense, she loved more the fresh flowers of troubadour song. After the sin of flower fragrances, Amira combed Eleanor's hair into further sins. She 'fashioned' it in shapes and added adornments: brushes, combs, and bars. Called a barrette when clasped, a pinion when open, the double bar allowed her to form shapes at the back of her head and cool her neck. To pinion her hair behind her ears, she availed her ear-gems, and she also heard better.

Amira seized the comb in front of her nose and rolled it into Eleanor's hair. "Oc, let your father see this comb in your hair. You know he detests it."Eleanor ignored Amira's subtle suggestion. "Amira, I am feeling a new style." Eleanor turned in her chair, her visage radiant. Amira looked at her sharply.Style was controversial, significant. Wrong decisions could make her look like a fool or even a heretic. Style was a power that challenged power; it sent waves of change to people who did not like change. The church fussed over it as a vanity. Grandfather famously opposed the church; to him, fashion was pride of lief, one's self. His words came: 'Being made to feel guilty for living is contemptible, why make a point of dullness? Never be broken from yourself.'

Setting her style was part of Eleanor's identity. Priests called her new looks a sin of indulgence. However, since Father paid out coins to indulge the King's church, she would be forgiven. It never felt right to Eleanor. Amira joked about making Eleanor 'damnably beautiful.' "Amira, see me as vibrant, active; clothes that work on horseback. Boots, not slippers, and no more veils. I open to Red, definitely Red. Think about it, will you?" Eleanor pulled the planted comb releasing her hair. "I'll not wear this today. Let the river run my hair."

"It will draw attention to bathing, and you do draw attention."

"My hair needs a good Clain wash. It has been too long without you."

Amira would leap into the river if she had to, so much she enjoyed making Eleanor beautiful. On this hot summer day, the Princess walked into the stream, lowered herself while holding onto a branch, letting her hair drift into the flow of the natural eddy. Amira walked in and followed its cool length with a broad wide-toothed comb.

Eleanor grew still as Amira pulled the comb through her hair. As the stream flowed cold, she felt the hot thoughts of summer. Damisels of her age were to marry, yet Calbi and Daena were united, not married. Their stories of love's exploration made her want to know about The Subject. Namely, everything about lovemaking, sexual encounter, and the possibilities for her own heart to run wild with another's body. Calbi's stories of Daena never ended. Last told, they played as animals uncaged devouring one another in pursuit of love. Would she ever experience such things? She pictured the basket of forbidden letters she was about to read.

The Princess drew herself out of the river. Standing steady, she spread her feet and put her hands on her waist. Bending over and flipping back, her torso let loose a wild spray of water from her hair. Her signature animal-like drying style always brought a smile to Amira and many onlookers. After a long, vigorous shaking, she stepped to the broad blanket and dizzily sat.

"Keeping the balance," jested Amira, holding out equal lengths of hair. She assessed if the weight was right for the next 'transformation.' "Needs time to dry. Pilgrims and Saints, or shall we read?"

"No, my hair must think."

Amira chuckled and thumbed through the basket of letters.

Love letters were everywhere, as never before in history; all at once, so it seemed. The writing of passions filled their world with feelings and let one understand how someone else felt. Eleanor liked to read heartfelt words. In the open vellums of personal emotions that hungered to be felt, lines sometimes held delicious meanings. Most love letters were hard to write, and many were as hard to read. There was one very famous exception, Latin letters of a man and a woman, clever philosophers, that encoded love in elaborate biblical allusions. The two wrote in the style of the pulpit, in remorseful, detailed sentences, of how they regretted enjoying the damnable pleasures of bodily love.

"Go ahead," Eleanor giggled. "Do Pat."

As was their ritual, Amira put on a learned demeanor, imitating the teacher's clear enunciation. "Class, I have never seen so much interest in Latin. It can mean only one thing. How many copied the poet Ovid? The strong hand of Abelard? The lettered student Heloise? Are we too tired to raise our arms today? Read aloud, let's hear some fiery Latin." Eleanor kicked the stream with laughter and retrieved Heloise's letter from the basket.

The Fontevrault courier had obtained the correspondence between Peter Abelard and Heloise. The Abbey was not of the strict Roman Catholic persuasion and had special arrangements with both writers; Fontevrists could speak freely on the writing. The Roman church frowned upon these letters, although they tolerated them, for the church wrongly believed they openly disparaged and chastised misguided love.

If their memorable epistles were too subtle, there was nothing subtle in the popular street songs inspired by their college love affair. A great variety of raucous song emerged about The Master and The Student of The Subject. Tavern drinkers learned as many nouns for male and female anatomy as scholars learned of vulgar verbs. To the lovelorn, Peter and Heloise were heroic outlaws who allowed a glimpse into forbidden knowledge. The eternal faith of one in the other was as strong as their vow to the crucifix. Between their lines, burned never-ending passion.

The princess read to herself quietly and broke out laughing, "Oh, his heavenly eyes upon her earthly body. What style. We must meet them someday. I want to feel these things when I am her age. Hear Heloise":

> ...for me, youth and passion and the experience of pleasures, which were so delightful, intensify the torments of the flesh and longings of desire. The assault is the more overwhelming when the nature they attack is weaker. Men call me chaste; they do not know what a hypocrite I am. They consider purity of the flesh a virtue, though virtue belongs not to the body but to the soul. I can win praise in the eyes of men but deserve none before God, who searches our hearts and loins and sees in our darkness. I am judged religious at a time when there is little in religion which is not hypocrisy, when whoever–

Both looked up, surprised to see Eleanor's sister Petronilla skipping towards them, giving a thin smile.

"Damisel Eleanor, consumed by her silly letters of modern love. A little Peter or a lot of Heloise?" Petronilla dropped a letter to the basket as Amira studied her for devious looks. Suitors did not call on Petronilla, only her sister. Resentful, she came to add fuel to her sister's fire, as surely the letter she hid in the basket would do.

"You know they were more than lovers," Eleanor said.

"I am sure sister." Petronilla as she sat down next to her.

"Peter is said to be able to debate a Pope! Heloise created her own order!"

"Is that so, big sister?"

With such unchallenged agreement, Eleanor eyed Petronilla suspiciously. Some masterpiece of mischief was brewing. Amira presented the newletter to her mistress. Petronilla seized it. "Big sister, ooh. From one of Abelard's disciples?"

The letter was addressed to Helienor, Eleanor's Latin name, and written on reused parchment with words piled new on old, parts were partially erased, as palimpsests are. Definitely written by a student. She broke the seal.

Divine Damisel of Deified Dominion

I think out upon you out there I think I am unable to attach a heavenly thought to your body that swells · like Holy bread in my hungry head I pray you like me are malnourished too tighten not your waist to avoid the pangs but peck this lettered feed my bird drop · Look for my pen is trying to find you move your writing hand quickly and fill my pounding heart as I fill you with truth · Quick my drunk let me drink your ink and thusly think, before I am caught by my Peter, not my Abelard but I know the beautifuller one · This letter flees to you

Signed by my very hand waiting to skin you

Onar the Legend.

The writing was a bit off, word choice questionable. Odd use of interpuncts, and sentences shorter than Abelard's. A love letter with a seal from Baris, Baras. Hard to tell. The writer of credit was Onar? – honor? owner? A legend, no less. It went to Amira's special cedar box for later reading.

Eight more letters of a vague Abelard nature arrived over the next half moon. Eleanor could have replied to "Halo-wheezer, my pleas-bud, mercify me in thine repline," but it was more fun not to. This encouraged a desperate creativity of unintended strivings. Alas, Onar's identity was too obvious to continue the pretense. She found the source afield, feeding his horse. From behind the fifteen-year-old boy, Eleanor buzzed: "Halo-weez" in one ear and "On-Ar, the Legend" in the other. "Have you ever read one word of Heloise or Abelard?"

Flush-faced Arno stared at the her. He conceded his evasion and acknowledged his hand. At least he protected Petronilla's involvement entirely. Although Poitevin Bruce, now a scholar in Paris helped write the first letter, Petronilla's many cheerful encouragements of Arno's writing skill made him finish. It started as a joke, but Arno masked a care he came to discover. With silly words, he first heard the divine throaty cackle of Eleanor, and in her lovely laugh, grew his attraction. As men sought her damisel hand, Arno wrote in guised affection for this impossibly younger, intelligent, beautiful energetic female. This unattainable woman of his heart brought a new pain to his face, a jealous hurt. He clenched his jaw as if chewing off his true feelings.

Other letters by more serious authors arrived for Eleanor. These were not as fun. They hounded her with desperate intent. Useful bottom paper.

❄

"What in creation?" Eleanor yelled her vast assessment from the wash room. Amira, two rooms away, ran to peer into her toilet pan. Curiously in the pee was red. "Piss and blood," she said and turned to Amira. "We are damisels now!" The bleeding months had begun. Their first moon blood came with alarm, but little surprise. Grandmother Dangerossa, the consummate woman, had explained that for three to seven days by the mark of the moon, the humors of their feminine nature would find a way out. As she was away, father advised of the discomforts. "I wished Aenor were here for this. Active girls girdle their loins with holding rags to take away menstrual blood." William comforted and made them feel thankful for their womanhood, as was the way of the better fathers of their heritage.

Other fathers in Europa locked bleeding damisels in towers. They could not face daughters at the danger age, the period before a match was made when an entourage of males surrounded young females. Long imprisoned damisels became anxious, wretched, maddened, some listless and dull, a condition called acedia.

William and Paul chose not to cloister their vigorous daughters, but instead to nurture them towards maturity, teaching them the traditions of Aquitaine. . Already proven as good horse riders, the damisels were taught to be willful in the careful use of dagger, confident in the sport of birds, and proficient in firing bows. The Chauvigny trial had been a cautionary lesson to women about the need to defend themselves.

The fathers encouraged the many arts of birds. Amira mastered messaging pigeons, and Eleanor flew falcons. After two weeks, Eleanor proudly brought Amira and the fathers to the falconer's field. The master falconer brought Eleanor's bird that flitted on his arm.

He proclaimed: "These fowl keep rats from moats and pigeons from fouling castle walls. When the bird is aloft warping her wing, she mixes the air with her sound. Quiet comes the gliding gyre, enlarged her eye to hawk the prey on the ground."

Eleanor explained, "A Falcon gives sighting signs in a flight of turns called gyres. He flies Skyla, who flies highest, then dives, striking fiercely. I prefer Karybdis. She gyres in long circles, taking time, tilting signs. After she tells us what she sees, she swoops. To get them to fly, they must be hallowed, making repeated, ever louder calls."

She nodded towards the pigeon tower. "Since falcons can eat Amira's pigeons, falconers must signal the tower before flight." The Falconer gave the signal, then set the bird on Eleanor's arm, its talons seizing her arm gauntlet.

She traded soft tones with the hooded bird on her arm. "Time to fly, Karybdis." Uncapping the head-blind, she looked steady into the large falcon eyes, then hallowed calls and urged her on. From her raised arm, the bird flew hard-winded off the gauntlet. The damisel chased from the ground, and hallowed up her hunter spirit, invoking ever louder, running under, waving, so the bird could see her master was serious.

"Go-shock!" Eleanor called Karybidis, "Kill-prey!" was the falconer's call to Skyla. Each bird had their own commands. Eleanor came back and pointed up. "Falcons seek rills of streams. They never fail to bring back moles, rats, or some half-chewed vile thing to my arm." The falconer said, "We trade that tasty bit and feed them only their prey – rabbit or bird, so that is what they hunt.

For days they practiced, making Skyla and Karybdis into good hunters who retrieved rabbit and quail. The falconer said, "Falcons must be trained to be heroes, not roosters who kill poop-birds. The greatest of these are warbirds, who go into battle taking down enemy hawks and messenger pigeons from the sky. But we are not at war, are we?" Eleanor was delighted to bring home her first rabbit, that fed her family.

. . .

On the first day of bow practice, the girls were excited. Steward Ellen joined with the daughters and fathers, feathers in their caps. The five walked the summer morning fields outside of Mirebeau. They rested under a spreading shade tree, leaning their bows against the trunk. Ellen said, "William, you had the worst winter fever. Mind if I ask, have you told Eleanor about it and our issues with the King's church?"

William looked far afield. "Damisels, it is time that you knew. When I returned from Parthenay, you heard rumors of miracles, devils, and every other thing. Ellen, disclose what happened at 'Bernard's trial.' I will tell you why."

"Your father, along with uncle Raymond of Antioch, cousin Roger of Sicily, and other Lords approved of Anacletus. He was the Pope elected five years ago at St. Peters when the last Pontiff died. Opposing the Pope was the one who now calls himself Pope Innocent, supported by Abbot Bernard of Clairvaux and King Louis Six. The Popes had a bloody contest for the throne. To unseat supporters of our elected Pope, Bernard came into our Aquitaine lands. In Parthenay, he uprooted your father's civil law and made his own judgments. It is no secret that Bernard wants to seize our mills and install his Templar knights to run them with his Cistercian monks. William rode to Parthenay to face Bernard. On the day of petition, in the audience held at the church, your father vomited a bitter foam and could not speak. Bernard raised his hand to heaven. 'A sign Duke William! The church will cease making land judgments when you halt making holy judgments!' We have some idea how he staged that."

William took over: "In other words, agree to Bernard's choice of pope. Our Pontiff is being deposed. Attempts are made on his life. I nearly died. It appears we must concede Bernard's choice. We arrested heralds who shamed me, but Roman pulpits are untouchable. Bernard declared his warning a miracle. You know how people love to hear of miracles."

"Miracle? You were poisoned." Amira said sharply.

William looked to Ellen; this was old ground. He brought Eleanor near.

"Does my damisel think this too?"

"Yes I do, Sir."

"Listen, it is not that simple. We cannot make the church look bad. Abbot Bernard has an overpowering spirit. When I drew my sword in anger, he projected the power of peace. In that, he was in the right. I was impure."

Paul said, "You are too noble. The abbot relies on underhanded helpers to create his miracles."

Ellen declared, "Bernard still wants you dead, William."

The girls squirmed. It was terrible to think that the church killed people.

"Daughters, the valiant lesson is to look to yourself. I did not see that without my voice I could not petition! Blame the hand of evil, but it is your own neglect for not noticing the devil's tricks. Be vigilant of what passes your lips. Learn this. Amira, I need your help, have the staff examine our food, our drink; know its source, its preparation. Observe purity; Aenor and Aigret teach us this." Crossing hearts, they gave a silent prayer. "To purity!" father resounded.

Paul looked to the sky. "We are losing the time when animals forage." They grabbed their bows. Ellen held up her hand. "Wait. Daughter and father must make their first hunt their own. Amira and Paul go this way, Eleanor and your sure-shot father, that." The fathers nodded thanks. With hands on hips, Ellen watched Eleanor carry her horizontal bow with William into the high grasses of Mirebeau. Ellen smiled at her own cleverness– the rest of the day was hers.

···

Duke William was a patient hunter. In the midmorning heat, Eleanor had her belly to the ground. Her father lay beside, having removed the Egret plume from his cap. They had covered themselves with leaves and moss, as much to hide as to smell like the earth, for animals have an acute sense of smell. In low talk, they passed an hour, then two, studying the woodland fauna in the field.

A splendid hart walked into the clearing, a red male deer of brawn of six years. The huntress steadied her crossbow, supported by a rock. Her father quietly listed:

"set your bow sight, higher, wind is up."

"aim, take distance, up a bit."

"aim, distance."

"aim."

"I see," she said.

"shhh huntress, only my voice. The hunter is always silent."

The deer foraged, darting among the bushes. Father looked at his daughter's hold and stance. She was ready. They saw with one clear view.

"Still your hold on rock, finger gentle to the trigger, my call to you is 'pull,' do nothing. This is my call on the target; you will hear your own call." The hart took time coming closer, raising its head, then stilled to sniff. Father's even whispers steadily soothed her ear.

"pull . . . pull . . . pull . . ." She felt wood, metal. The deer dipped ahead, hidden by a tree. His head peered around the tree, then he lurched into clear view. Its neck lowered to take in grasses, fully broadside in stance.

"pull . . . pull . . . pull . . . pull . . . p–" pressing the trigger, the crossbow launched hard. The arrow arched more than expected. Falling to the deer's front hoof, the tip struck and glanced off. Eleanor was furious and elated in the same instant; angry she had missed the body, happy the grand deer lived. It sprang for safety.

A long arrow hit deep its neck blood spraying, crippling it, bringing it down.

"Look! The Princess brought down a hart!" shouted a man's voice.

I did no such thing! My shot missed. I let the hart live! she thought.

A mustached muscular young man stepped forth from the trees, short compared to his long bow. This visitor from Lusignan, the castle south of Poitiers, had come for one purpose. One she knew all too well. He counted the yards, teeth showing. The Lusignan's boots strode in long paces through the high grass. "...sixteen, seventeen, eighteen..." The archer looked hungrily at Eleanor. His teeth did shine. His unwelcome glance was as upsetting as the attack on the deer. Was he a wolf or a fox? He had come to Poitiers as a suitor, and she was the prey.

A bugler rang out. From hedges and high grass, hunters ran to the fallen animal. "She struck from thirty yards at least," exclaimed the archer.

Father spoke loudly, "Eleanor, it looks like you downed that deer."

"Father, I glanced a hoof."

"Our people will believe you took the deer down, as this man testifies."

"I did not."

"Well, Eleanor, he says otherwise. What do you want to do about that?"

The question rested on her mind and stretched out before her as she walked. *What will be my code?* With every grassy step and rocky teeter she thought hard. She came upon the fallen deer lying on his side breathing rapidly, the large eyes steady, blood pumping out. In its helpless state, the head of the animal seemed to look at her and cry out, the spirit of its stricken soul entering her heart. Eleanor knelt, wishing she could give it more life. The bloodstained creature then stilled and its head fell. She put aside her girlish feelings. She knew the truth – there were too many deer in the forest. They came to eat the crops. The skill of good archery was necessary in these times. Providing such game kept families from starvation for weeks.

"Good shooting, Sir," Eleanor said, ennobled. "Thank you for acclaiming me, but I thrive on honesty." Swallowing the distaste of sorrow, she took a hard look at the hairy Lusignan. She had to appeal to all men, so she smiled.

"Sir, a true verse about hunting: I'll be your inspiration / shoot with your art / just don't aim your bow at me / and we'll feast on hart."

The hunting party cheered, sharing blood markings of the deer. Hastily, Eleanor swiped up her fallen arrow, cutting her right hand on its sharp tip. With the blood from her hand, she painted a smear from left cheek bone to hollow.

The archer beheld the archeress with her red stripe. He wiped his mouth on his sleeve. He would do anything to get under her gown. Anything on earth.

Eleanor studied the deer-slayer. She was firm. "Lusignan, better your manners. Show grace to be in our company. Your hair. My horse groomer has a lice comb. Shave off that gruesome beard, if you want me to see who you are. Attend me with song in your heart."

The words both challenged and pleased the bowman. A highborn female would be the best bagging a hunter could hope for. He knew he had to appear polite for her father. "Lady, your desires are mine, but let's improve your shooting. Lord William, may I improve her bow?"

William said richly, "Me? Ask her, it is hers. Best you take her damisel advice before spoiling her with your charms." Eleanor sucked in her cheeks to keep from laughing. Charms. Father bound her wounded hand. "I will kiss it every day until it heals."

The suitor found the best barber in Poitiers. By blade and stropping leather, he cursed the shaving. After the pain of losing the beard, he kept his mustache. The barber explained a tutor could teach him mannered ways, but paying a troubadour to sing her favorite songs was faster. The archer paid.

At the set appointment, the now handsome fellow attended Eleanor, giving a deep bow and a frill of his hand.

"You did not bring me flowers," she said, showing a demonstrable shock.

"Damisel Eleanor," the suitor lilted with forced affliction, "to take the life of such sweet things. It troubled me. I could not cut such stems. Let me take you to a glade of flowers to enjoy a picnic today."

That was good. I'll get the name of his tutor. Though outwardly charming and appealing, the mustached suitor still frightened her. The Lusignan had a stealth, a cruel strength of force over all creatures. She was getting to know this type of man well; the world was full of them. She existed simply for his gain.

A flowery midsummer field in a meadowy rill of the Clain spread about the party. A manservant took care of wine, fruit, and cheese for the couple. Cercamon prepared to sing. Many things came to Eleanor as she sat by the stream looking at the hunter. Heart was her standard, it never failed to measure truth. She could read his distaste for women. The slain hart and Arbrissel's mission to end suffering came to mind. What caused men to be deceitful, wrathful, and violent? Could she mend their motives and improve them? The answer would come in later life, but today the universe permitted her to see the question and made her laugh in a glade at a deer-slayer who avowed feeble compassion for flowers.

Troubadour Cercamon strummed his fine lute. A steel-eyed chaperone observed at a distance, a woman Eleanor would never employ otherwise.

The Lusignan's candy-like voice neared, "I feel a magic when I touch your gown." Eleanor dashed a thought – she would love to hear those words from the kind of man who truly meant it. She gave the deer-slayer a sidelong look and said loudly, "What a line! Do you want to strip my dress off and see me naked? Why do you look at my chaperone?" She sensed his fever. *I see your desire for me.* Like many hunters hot to bag a kill, they had little to offer beyond the hunt. The mustache smiled falsely, trying to ward off the hot feelings she named so aptly. To make the best of her situation Eleanor petitioned, "Your troubadour has further words. Please, grant me my desire." Cercamon's poetry of nature deliciously affected her, and 'sweet air turning bitter' had no effect on the suitor. When the music came to its last couplet, she brushed off her gown.

"Lusignan, I see how able you are. Please, call again in Fall. Shall we go?"

He wanted her more than anything, but he could tell by her set look, her mind was too strong for him. All his snares were sprung. Music, so fair to her, unsettled him. There were some things in this world he would never understand.

The Lusignan exclaimed, "To honor the hunt, Cherished Eleanor, I render a gift. I will rebuild your crossbow in two weeks time. I'll true the sighting, strengthen the pull, and recurve the bow for proper balance. I vow you will shoot straighter than before. May I?"

It would be easy to say no and never see the wolf again, but the universe made Eleanor of different stuff. To be champion to all striving men, she gave the flat of her hand that he kissed. She presented her weapon with a flourish.

True to his word, the hunter masterfully reworked the crossbow. It was so powerful, the instrument took a windlass to load. At close quarters, it could penetrate armor. Its true aim could strike down wild boar in one shot. Who could guess this very crossbow would one day change the course of a crusade battle? Eleanor learned how noble is man when set to achieve what he truly loves best. Cercamon played: 'Sun damisel keep gifts near your heart / to save a giver's soul takes art.' She accepted the gift, giving a graceful kiss. And so he bestowed, "A crossbow fit for a Queen." And so it was.

Day after day, Eleanor, the prize of Poitiers, was surrounded by troubadours and suitors who pitched tents by the castle. Duke William raised the stakes to make his daughter worth the trip to Poitiers, where music lived in its stones. Hunter-scouts spread word of a silver purse for a troubadour competition. On route to the capital, musicians sang for their suppers, danced for their dinners, and traveled with every hope to make the Palace their home.

By these chances, the realm filled with feisty jongleurs, jesting fools, singing troubadour bands, and tumbling dancers. Hearths of taverns and family cottages warmed with grace and jibe. Music overflowed the roads, wild streams, and flowered fields.

To win the composers purse, all were chastened: never use Eleanor's name, and avoid the word love. Therefore, the songs and stories were all about Eleanor and every aspect of love. Intended for her young ears, some verses were Platonic, some erotic. The best were both and sung aloud for laymen and called lais.

To clergy, as if music were not temptation enough, the lais did not warn of the evils of devil dance. Even reverential affection was not for the ordained. The new verse inflamed desire, with new rhythms, a new way to move one's feet. Vibrant, artful dance spawned a new class of graceful gymnastic dancer.

Over the roads to Poitiers that brought dance and song, there came another breed, the men of short purposes – clans of outlaws, makeshifts, ransomers, and robbers. For the silver purse, the glint of happy flute and sword did equally shine.

Marching ahead of her friends in country fields, Eleanor was easy to spot. Red as a flame was Eleanor's new scarlet cape. An azure-green underlining increased the intensity of the cloth of red smooth satin soft as her skin. Satin was a new fabric and scarlet a new color. Both were recently discovered in Crusade lands. Not even Dangerossa dared to wear such a full-bodied thing, head to knee. Eleanor, empowered by the bold and vivid, changed the fashion of her hair.

The attractive curls, were set with a new process of painting boiled flax seed on her hair at night and rolling it in a towel. Running along, the cascading twists of energetic waves filled inner collar and the flaring hood. The raised cape freed her gold-crimson hair from the neck. Cut for summer, the cape's arm seams were open. She lifted to see her light armpit hair, damp with perspiration. It made her animal, Dangerossa said of scents that drove men to hunt. Her new style underscored a radiant transformation as a falconer, crossbow archer, and witty mascot of knights. Gone as the snow were her tired scarves, simple gowns, and soft slippers. The new clothes were rugged on horse, sturdy in harsh weather, tailored to fit her active body.

Summer fields of flowers bathed her in every color. Red poppies reached up to brush her knees. Bees buzzed through honey-rich banks of yellow broom. Groves of cream Dogrose buds and white Hawthorne bushes tilted the breeze.

Humming, far ahead of the others, confident Eleanor bent to gather fragrant flowers to fill her lithe basket. Tender new ideas and feelings were brought on by soft smells and brilliant colors. Troubadour songs of perception made her evermore aware. Everything seemed the unpicked flower of discovery. She brushed a red poppy to her lips. Troubadours sang the new verse of PRINCE JAUFRE RUDEL. He lived in Blaye on the Garonne. The master composer made her imagine love in nature, love a thousand leagues apart, love across time. LOVE ACROSS TIME. Imagine? Rudel's longings for unfound love! He improved on ancient poems. Ovid the Roman wrote about one-sided seductions to trick Venus, giving suitors simple ideas, not worth a tune. Far more interesting were the new ideas of love: vacillating attraction, the far and near, the dance of flirtations, shared sensations in the fine lightness of being, the savor of the long Aquitaine kiss. Rudel found female facets worth singing of, upholding another's view of the world. Never had such music existed!

Far behind on this picnic day, her friends hammered the bushes in play of winter's wars, fevers cured, losing sight of scarlet Eleanor as she dropped from the view of her protectors. In her world, she gathered her red folds to travel down the banks. Yellow daffodils waved from across the stream. The muddy waters of spring had given way to the sparkling clear of summer. She raised her hem to enter the shin-deep river. Scores of watery rainbows streamed across the river bottom, a pleasant a bobble worth a dictone. Calbi described Daena making love in many ways. In pretense, Eleanor incanted their words out loud. "Rove with me, give me the shovel, summer work you know." Exhilarated by the power of her own voice, she came to a stop. The stream flowed cold against her knees. Suddenly, on the other bank in the bushes... Danger! Men! One rogue in plain view, eyeing her, ready to give the order to attack.

On a hill overlooking the fields to Poitiers, Trobaritz Mirielle Denni let the wind blow across her even-tempered face. Her round thick eyebrows and lashes caught a length of her long black hair. The dark-eyed woman of seventeen with large jaw and firm chin keyed her voice for a great wail. Her voice could flow a river of sorrow or make you feel the rill of joy. Four other troubadours took a knee to the grassy knoll. The musicians, ready to ascend in the world, cued by their inspired singer, tuned up the scales of flute, heavy-strung viola, resonant lute, and low sack pipe. From their vantage, out to where Poitiers should be, a rowdy band of youth advanced rapidly.

Below in the near stream, a red-hooded young woman halted mid-ford. A vagabond swordsman paced the bank spying to take her down. His troop in the woods made wide tracks to surround the prey, ready for his order. By the time the approaching clan sighted her, she would have been well taken. The damisel in danger did not flee. As all creatures know, only those who act the victim are attacked. The swordsman stilled at the water's edge gauging her. This woman could stare down a lion, but not a den of them. The siren was compelled.

Flipping a coin in the air by her custom, Mirielle readied, able to sing the same song in every way – anger or tenderness – one view or the opposite – the flipped coin revealed. Mirielle understood the testing fates. She rang out a tuning line to all creatures of field and stream a clarion voice: clear, tempered, and strong that fit the musician's war drums and luted chords.

♪

MMM'WELL Hiih'nn'low

As I rambled along rivers blue the leaves full green

I overheard a young woman converse to me it seemed.

Her hair was gold, her eyes were blue, her lips as red as wine

And when I gazed upon her, she saw smile sly old Reynardine.

She said: kind sir be civil my company please forsake

For in thine own true purpose say what purpose I may take

He said: no talk of Venus train, conceals this heart of mine

I may be a young wolf but not a fox so sly.

Fine Sir, you look a little hungry, your teeth do brightly shine

In forest I fear you would devour me like sly old Reynardine.

Your beauty so enticed me I could not pass it by

So with my sword I'll guard and valiant be thine.

♪

The troop on the river halted their headlong advance on the red-caped woman in peril. Mirielle's sure-voiced song settled the hottest blood. By then, the entourage had found their princess.

The two troops leered across the water. The rogue leader struck his blade to his boot, signaling his gang of highwaymen to shoe. They fled in scuffled protest. He planted his sword in the bank and tipped his brown fox hunting cap, giving a high nod to the musicians. Eleanor signaled her court to move to higher ground and retreated from the chop-haired men.

On the hill, the troubadour band received the woman in the brilliant red cape. Protected by her worried clan, Eleanor hovered, her eyes fiery bright. She exchanged silent hand signs to Amira: *I am fine, talk to the musicians. Be wary.*

Amira strode up guardedly. "Travelers, what song is this?"

"I am trobaritz Mirielle Denni. Reynard the Fox is our tune. We hail from beaches south of Aragon on our way to the troubadour contest in Poitiers. Yon?"

With possible ransomers around, Amira had to conceal identities, though she sensed their angelic intent. "You are nearly there, two leagues on."

Her silent mistress summoned Arno with hand signs, 'go to the stream and find out their game. Peace, keep it.' Arno showed his hard jealous look and bounded down the hill. The scarlet princess gave the scoundrel on the bank a tilt of her bonnet, having seen in his eyes how he checked his hot desire. She thought, 'O Arno, keep the peace.'

Eleanor whispered to Amira, "He is bold and handsome," letting her think she was talking about the vagabond; a counselor had to be kept vigilant. "If you see through the dirt," scoffed Amira. Eleanor nodded for her to question.

"What is your inspiration for Reynard?"

"Our song is a lay from my forest heartland. It tells of a damisel's enticing beauty and the trouble beauty brings. I dare say my verse will contain your scarlet womanhood with the tamer's power to keep wolves at bay." Looking to Eleanor, Mirielle said, "You have the alert eyes of a scout. Do you speak?"

Eleanor smiled, "I could speak, but I'd rather hear you sing."

Mirielle winked, "Sometimes, classic hunter tunes are best. I have new songs for Eleanor of Aquitaine. Damisel, who might you be?"

"I am Amira," interjected the head maid, "and you speak to Lady Spark."

Splashing sounds turned their heads. Arno waded the stream to reach the leader with the long sword who stood unmoved. Mirielle looked to Eleanor. "He regards you from afar. He is struck with you as I am."

Scarlet Eleanor turned to vibrant Mirielle and looked over her playful band. A colorfully cloaked girl had been standing quietly, with no instrument.

"Do you play anything?" Eleanor asked of the silent girl.

"Oh, she is special," Mirielle said. "Play Sirq's tune." The musicians struck a beat followed by fluted notes.

Stepping out in white patched hosiery, a thin twelve-summers girl with knotted-up long blonde hair, let her cape float and fall. Arching her eyebrows, bending low with the music, the young female sprang up, twisting into a flip. Gracefully, she somersaulted the hill in turns that measured the song. Her maneuver crossed their view of the stream and rolled back up in perfect circles. She did a playful dance with circular arms as if she had done the entire magical act a thousand perfect times. The feat was as utterly amazing as it was arresting to see a young woman dance in slender underwear. "Sensational," Eleanor said. Amira whispered, "You had your father stipend this singer and dancer when we were young girls. Remember re-enacting battles in the snow?"

Eleanor nodded. "We know who you are. All will do well in Poitiers."

Arno marched strongly up the hill to report, "More so-called Crusaders looking to do 'good deeds.' The lone wolf says you enchanted him by your presence. Mirielle, he says you sang so sweetly he wanted to die."

"We're all dying, aren't we?" the trobaritz said. "I sing to live."

"Eleanor, let me teach the foragers a lesson," Arno said.

Scarlet-gowned Eleanor said firmly, "There has been no offense. Be proud in keeping the peace. Aquitaine needs every man on its side, even salvageable villain." The words sliced across Arno's face. His jaw clenched ever harder, held back his jealousy. Eleanor patted his shoulder. "Cheer up, Arno."

That evening, Eleanor's court applauded her bravery. As friends, they gently reminded the stunning woman she had come close to being taken in the water by a horde of men. Eleanor confronted her own impetuousness. She had eyed down a wolf's glare, and once was enough. She willed to venture safely, thanking her friends for tending so closely. Reyna lent her new collie Rip to improve her vigilance, especially at night. Petronilla became enamored with the dog, so much that Eleanor called her sister Rip. But Arno's serious glare and avoidance troubled her. Why was he so moody?

In summer country fields, there was much to glean. Walking with Rip, red-caped Eleanor did not let her wariness of marauders halt adventure. She kept her keen ears and eyes open in the long days of heat. On a trip, she came upon particular acts of vivacious human nature worth reporting to her inner circle.

On a hot rendezvous day, a conclave of hrads came to meet in the cool spreading shade of the prime Oak at Reyna Chasseigne's watermill. Looking anxiously for Eleanor, Amira gave Maryam the latest news. "Mirielle and Sirq have joined the court after winning the troubadour contest. Danae, champion of the Chauvigny trial, has construction troubles at Fontevrault chapel."

"What troubles?" Eleanor queried, arriving in her flash of red.

Maryam sang simply: "Have you seen the well-digger boss / light-catching hair of angel floss / spritely in joy about her work / she brings spirit to every smirk." Maryam stopped. "As my lay goes, in spite of her earnest work, the Catholic Masons of Paris refuse to let her touch any tools. When Mathieu lent his, there was trouble. The Parisii are confounded by Danae, an able builder who wears a dress that can turn heads. They rudely call her 'well-digger.'"

Eleanor said, "I like your songful meter. Fours and fours – the charge of horses, the flight of deer. Daena should build the church of her faith."

"No man of the people's church would be permitted to work with her."

"She is a woman of hearth-legend. Good men will work for her."

Amira taunted, "Well, here comes most beautiful."

From the Chasseigne mill-house, Reyna swirled toward them. "Hi, Scarlet."

Eleanor said to only them, "Look what she's wearing! Piss and blood."

"Mind your tongue," Amira said, following the line of her friend's glare.

Eleanor had wanted one forever. Around this damisel's waist was not one, but four horsehair belts! The blonde-haired beauty spun into the branch-shade, one arm strumming her colorful belts, the other raised as if being twirled by a beau. The dancing damisel teased Eleanor:

"How divine you look in Crusade Scarlet. Feast upon what arrived. Four beautiful belts, each from a different beau. Aren't you happy for me?"

It was easy to believe that every man wanted the hand of the miller's daughter. She was famously beautiful, and her family business produced steady wealth. The Chasseigne mills ran every sort of water machine, day and night. Reyna watched her friend's envy rise. "Help me choose the best one."

Imaginative Maryam said, "A lady pursued by four suitors. You must encourage them to a tournament, a fight to the death. Oh, the unfortunate victor who wins your love. What is this? There's a tag on each belt."

Reyna lowered her head. Eleanor said, "You are putting us on."

"I am. Time for the living truth. Four is our quorum."

Amira conducted their private ritual and executed a double-round hi - a truth sign. Of the gestures learned during voice lessons from unspeaking orphans, Abbess de Chemillé captivated them with this one.

Reyna said, "You did that after we met. A farewell sign? What does it mean?"

"The first time you gave this secret sign is when you depart a 'person of interest,' someone you wish as a friend. Only a truly interested person meeting you again will ask what you mean. Which you did. It is not a farewell; it is an invitation." Eleanor added, "To enter the cloak of truth. The double-round hi begins with a heart-side hand arc across her face completing the circle at the mouth then circles again. The hand finishes in a twinkle of finger-falling stars to the side. It means: Let us joyously speak of what we truly think, but tell only of direct experiences. No hearsay or other knowledge is permitted. You try." The girls drew stiff circular double spirals in the air. Eleanor said, "Good. Now a lighter wrist, with the palm up." She demonstrated with a broad smile. "With elation, then twinkly. Playfully touch forth the song notes of truth."

Reyna confessed, "The living truth is: this morning, Armstrong's girlfriend arrived with these, made by four anonymous beaus. They are to be worn by the four most cherished damisels of Eleanor's court. Of course, I tried them all." Reyna unbuckled and handed each damisel her belt. "The tag is your name."

Eleanor realized. "Ah, the mystery is to discover who made them. Meet them. Put on your belt. Their eyes will give it away."

"Let's put another's belt on," Maryam added, "that will drive them crazy."

"They are already crazy," Eleanor assured. "Just stick to my test."

Amira admired her colorful braided horsehair belt. As Eleanor's maid, she was beginning to feel invisible. Gratefully she bristled the hairs. They were all stunned, turning over the newly burnished colorful horsehair belts with patterns and symbols on the leather ends.

Amira said, "We're not here to slosh in the trough. The sign was made. Who has the next 'truth'?"

"Boys and smells," Maryam said, pulling a flower from her sash.

"Boys are naive," Reyna injected, "they don't love, I'd rather talk about beaus."

"No wonder," Amira proclaimed, "Reyna has kissed all the knaves away."

Eleanor noted, "Kissed away, but what of love beyond the kiss? It's daft. Why do we have to appear defenseless, dumb, and doft of clothes to be the women we deftly are?" Maryam joined, "In all our combined travels, is there anywhere in the world that a woman can speak her mind in front of a toad?" After trading further derogatories about the idiocies of maturing boys, they agreed that the charade of playing dumb and helpless was bearable. They traded names of the few worthy males with whom they could speak their mind honestly: Calbi the Squire, Mathieu the Maker, Arno stern-face probably, chevalier Armstrong definitely. Then they realized, One: they had named the likely belt-makers; Two: they did not have to play dumb to receive this most sought-after gift; and Three: a ray of hope existed for mankind.

"Smells?" reminded Amira.

Maryam presented a sprig of Hawthorne blossom. "The odor of these white flowers is alarmingly strong. I asked Cercamon why troubadours began songs with Hawthorne buds and he said, and this is no joke, that it smelled like a woman's sex." The damisel's passed the harsh bud around uncertainly.

Amira said, "No woman I know smells like this."

"It is a bit foul. Maybe it's men smelling themselves," Maryam said.

Amira roundly waved, "What more do we ken about The Subject?" In conclave, this meant sexual encounter. Reyna exclaimed, "First, Eleanor, tell us about the suitor business. All we damisels have been 'suited upon,' but Eleanor most of all." They cringed as she spoke of the torture having to talk to careless old and mannerless men. Never had the nature of toads been so well-described.

Reyna said, "I told father a suitor has a crush on me. They came to blows."

"No wonder!" Maryam said. "You cannot say crush; the word is obscene."

"Ooo, crush," Eleanor said, to stir things up.

Amira coughed. "I hear-tell, hear-tell mind you, that to make a thumb-sucker, a man has to jump naked on a damisel, then crush her. I don't want anyone jumping on me. That does not sound like love. Um, does anyone have a direct experience?"

Eleanor cleared her throat, "Now, about The Subject . . ."

A ten thousand leaf wind wove shadows across the do-tell faces. "I saw the act with my own eyes." Her eyes arched a brow. "When I traveled in Bordeaux to visit a cousin's vineyard, I made a side trip to Blaye. There lives a troubadour prince named Rudel. While my escorts waited for him, I went walking with Rip, safety you understand. Deep through a vineyard, I took a wrong turn by a salt house. I never did meet the composer."

Amira said, "I see a truth coming."

"Never curse a missed meeting. Never scourge a wrong turn. Keep mistakes dear and your eyes open. Well, Rip went to the stream to drink. An old gander nibbling crumbs passed me by. The male goose led me to a dell of grasses matted down by a half-naked man talking with a half-naked woman."

Reyna asked, "Which part was naked?"

Eleanor whispered. "Their bottoms were off." The damisels covered their mouths. "He was no knave, and she was no girl. They sat propped up next to one another, legs folded high and close; their bodies touching, you know. O, he looked at her so tenderly and listened to her every soft word. She hung on his every response. Such serious sweetness between tender friends. Her face was flush saying something, almost crying, I guess some true secret. He touched her face softly, and she felt his clean jaw. He spotted her tears with his kerchief, a blue sky of clouds that he kissed. They looked into each other's eyes, speaking lowly; I could only hear the music of their words. Both scooted closer together. His fingers climbed her long hair to her ear. She petaled his cheeks and gathered his head to kiss. Oh, they were a couple, kissing slowly for a long time. They rocked back and forth in soft moans. It was beautiful lovemaking." Eleanor stopped and cherished the conclave's wide open eyes.

"Go on," Reyna summoned, scooping her hand.

"Well, I felt ashamed. This was their privy thing to do. What if they caught me, Eleanor of Poitiers in the blinds looking? Lucky was I to see that much. I quieted my way back with Rip. I will tell you this. There were exaltations of purification and beings of the firmament! Certs!"

Amira and Maryam asked at the same time: "Did he jump on her?" Reyna wondered, "Were her glances quick and fiery, or slow and cool?"

"There was no jumping, and her visage, she was in a sorrowful type of joy."

"Maybe the jumping came later," Amira said.

The damisels cooled in the sway of high shady limbs, waiting for Eleanor to say the next thing. She said thoughtfully. "Lovers must begin as friends. When fine artful love takes place, they become naked, unashamed of plain desire, for their hearts are radiant and true." While they pondered, Amira repeated her every word and tone. Maryam spoke with surprise, "Why Amira, only Petronilla can match her sister's voice. You remembered every word."

Amira confessed, "Eleanor, there is no one like you. I find what you feel, say, and do, is somehow important. What you say, must be said or written down."

"I am glad you think so. Written? Pewp! The voice is all!" Eleanor put out an arm. "Now, put your hands in as one. Damisels, who shall be true to love?"

They committed in gesture, fist on fist. "We damisels shall be true to love! Piss and blood, damisels! What do we oath double round and true?"

"Piss and blood!"

"The conclave is over."

Reyna said, "Take me to Bordeaux next time. I'll bring a nice picnic."

Maryam disclosed her churchly puzzlement, "Where's the sin in love?"

Amira crossed her arms. "No one is jumping on me!"

Walking to the Palace, Eleanor smiled at Amira. Every note of her life was safe in her counselor's memory. With an ear for Eleanor's audacity, Amira captured her intensely original views. The skillful recitation of her words had an unusual effect. Eleanor's first impression of a subject expanded in reflection, affording a deeper look to comprehend essentials, like the growing intuition that love in all its forms was the driving power of the universe. And for any worthy code to endure, a clearly reflected idea could purify itself.

Gusts rolled the grounds; soon there would be color in the leaves. The fields of summer had been a growing experience, and she had the belt to prove it. Starting as a honeysuckle damisel, she was fast becoming a desirable woman, with every healthy want. Her confidence would not be shaken. Eleanor had come to know suitors, knights, letter-writers, falconers, dancers and troubadours. With her conclave of friends, she surveyed men of better qualities, giving them more than an idle thought.

Riding Limona slowly, Eleanor pulled open her amazing scarlet cape, its red gleam in the sun attracting looks. She exchanged glances with her counselor on her horse, who leaned aside to listen attentively.

"Amira, I am feeling a new style, a season of red. Next season I will wear green."

"But that is a spring color; the next season is fall."

"Yes, a fine gown of verdant emerald green."

"Why, that is contrary, Eleanor!"

"Exactly. Contrary Eleanor!" She lifted her chin. "I'm a force of my own nature. Let's see how much trouble we can get into with green."

"We?" Amira rolled her eyes. "Well, it can't get any worse. I'll begin at once."

Eleanor pulled aside on a ridge. She rested a hand on the bristle edge of her horsehair belt. She thumbed the belt open and peered at the secret 'A,' the symbol struck by its maker. There were many possible A's, both men and women. Eleanor loved life's riddles.

Another mystery was Daena and Calbi. They had great hearts and knew much about the coupling Subject, yet for some reason that summer, no one asked Daena to tell of lovemaking. Perhaps everyone felt that if she did, the humor and charm in Calbi's songs would lose their power. Perhaps true love was personal. Still, everyone was curious to have a working understanding.

Calbi and Daena had joined in a union of their particular faith. It was not a marriage according to the dispensers of marriages. Their religion prohibited vows of any kind. The only outward commitment was to wear silver rings cracked from the same mold, the same way a sailor shares one earring with his mermaid.

As summer ended, Daena was asked by an anonymous foundation to break ground for the first Catharic church in Poitiers. When Daena replied her faith did not believe in churches and worshiped under the sky, Eleanor felt, at least, they should have a temple. Fontevrault chapel felt like a temple, for it had around dome. It was a place to think about what love and life may be. Pure water was a key element of Catharic ritual, and the Aquitaine was full of springs. Instead of a church, mason-apprentice Mathieu went to scout for a water-bearing site.

South of Poitiers Palace, across from the Roman Coliseum was an island of the Clain with an ancient church. Just south of it Mathieu found a spring-fed Roman ruins of a sunken garden. A fountain surrounded by eight columns once channeled rain water. To many minds, this could was not a church, for it had no roof. It was a pagan open-sky water temple acceptable to Cathars.

Daena led a willing crew. Many were proud to work alongside the well-digger, whose line of fathers had built legendary Norse ships. The fore-woman and her spiritual husband Calbi, an aspiring chevalier in training, worked hard, like any Good Catharics of the Albigensian sect.

The Scholar

'The love of learning is as dangerous as the learning of love,' began his letter. She could see his Paris hand in her mind, having spent last night translating his Latin manuscript. She felt the silvery ink of his letters in her hand. She brought the parchment up. The florid pen-work held an optimistic force that voiced words beyond his challenging college life. He would arrive at her class today, and she wondered what this bold letter-writer looked like, now. She'd ask the legendary student of past years what he meant between the lines.

Cream-colored courtyard gravel crunched evenly under her steps. The late morning heat of the heat rose through her dress. Their warmth would linger pleasantly into the night. Still bleary from translating his difficult Latin, she inspired. Autumn colors seemed cheerfully brighter; tree limbs waved with mirth, splendor filled the great blue sky.

It was the time of year before bonfires, when roses flower their second bloom, and birds sing their second tune. Amid the leaves of scarlet and gold of the Fontevrault compound, the only green thing fluttering was the robe of a willful woman of twelve, walking with letters. Young Eleanor in verdant green headed to school, a short morning walk from her Fontevrault apartment.

In 1136, France possessed what the lands of the Spanish, English, and German did not – a college. Italy had one. Paris had three. Combined, these church-colleges aimed to be something far more, a university. The foremost was Saint Geneviève whose teachers produced Robert Arbrissel, founder of Fontevrault. It attracted Peter Abelard, the vibrant philosopher, and other great minds. The colleges drew trusted students to deliver papers between schools. The courier to Fontevrault Abbey rode his horse to his former school.

Bruce Giles breathed in deeply and dismounted his horse. The man of eighteen flexed his broad shoulders straining his dark tunic lace binds. Shaking out, then fingering back his shoulder-length brown hair – the look of every virile Aquitaine man – he gave a handsome puckish grin. The little school at Fontevrault had been his beginning, a foothold for his curious mind. A monastery was normally the next step; each had a specialized practice. To acquire more general knowledge, a college in Paris would have sufficed a vigorous mind. Bruce desired to ascend to a new and higher form of education

– universal knowledge attained from all three colleges. Although he could not guess, his three Paris colleges would be unified by a green-sleeved damisel he was about to meet. She would reflect on this stimulating day in years to come when making way to sanction Europa's first university.

Bruce tied up his spirited horse. He was back on familiar grounds, a place of accomplishment without worry; all of his Paris struggles faded. Here, former teachers and students idolized him. With jovial acting skills, he could pretend to be like his masters, and profess his own direction. The dilemma of becoming his teacher or himself, any perceptive soul could see. He was in search of his life's calling. For all that Paris offered, the scholar missed one thing most – to commune again with the mannered, vivid women of the Aquitaine. After a refreshing night, he placed her rose on his saddle.

Bruce was a dedicated, full-blooded, living, breathing scholar.

Repressed, if not forbidden, was much of the knowledge that he and his kind uncovered. Their rediscoveries – of histories, sciences, art, machines, and for Bruce, classic Greek plays – were changing the world. This wanting to know of all humankind made such men dangerous in the eyes of the powerful church. His master, Peter Abelard, was not content to merely uncover Greek philosophy, he dared to read from the earlier sourced Greek Bible. What challenged authorities was not merely the unearthing of spiritual ideas, once source to Christian faith, but the rediscovery of anything before the time of the current religion. The papers Bruce carried were in many senses, the fires of the gods.

That she would soon be thirteen, pulled Eleanor forward. A broad-backed man came off his horse. It had to be Bruce. Revitalized, he disappeared into the schoolhouse. Girls said the returning star was irresistibly handsome. She understood that. She also understood because of such scholars, life improved. Aquitaine grew by their rare ability to rediscover how the past worked.

Her teachers had given his correspondence to any student who promised to interpret his every page. Proudly she picked up her steps. Now that she understood his letter, Eleanor shared many of his sentiments. Emerging was a glaring truth, and it meant everything to her aspirations: knowledge is power. Firsthand knowledge made her arguments irrefutable. Grasping facts comprehensively, reasoning, and judgment gave her an advantage. She could make the decisions of a man. She desired more: the volition of a woman, the skills of feminine nature, and everything about love and beauty. Eleanor's finds about her creaturehood were limited, and in some cases, like the quest of a scholar, buried, forbidden. She felt his loss for the unearthing of ancient books crumbled by the church as easily as the fertility stone-dolls that Amira collected.

Eleanor wished to comprehend it all, succinctly stated in his letter: a love of learning, and learning of love. Why did he call these acts dangerous? The letter observed, 'Women in Paris dress fully covered head to toe. Even among such women, their desire to learn is rare...' On Eleanor's travels, the desire to learn among women was indeed rare. To know their feminine nature was feared. Amira concealed stone dolls to 'hide the woman;' to protect her father she said. Eleanor countered, 'But if a woman hides, how can she discover the world, and how could she flirt?' Eleanor favored troubadours who made women witty, bright, attractive figures. She followed storyteller Alberic's advice, his code: 'don't live by other's stories, put others in your own.' Bruce's letter continued, '... except for the beloved Heloise. For when a woman seeking knowledge appears, she is the flower of scholars.' Here was Fontevrault, a school that let young women pursue knowledge. Eleanor could see the door.

Sure, knowledge is power, and sage academies were needed, but father made a deeper point for students to flourish. To be curious and ask questions freely meant evicting ridiculers, blind obedience, disciplinary education. Teaching was mindful. These points she grasped, even as she and her class received the benefits. So much she wanted to ken her world, her time, her mind, her body, her heart. They were all related in some wise way.

Eleanor touched the beveled wood frame of the school room door. She tucked his letter under her horsehair belt. She pressed aside her red-gold hair that fell to the back of her knees. Adjusting the green gown and azure scarves on her sleeves, wrists, and waist, the damisel arrived perfectly on time.

Light fell in the classroom from one large window into a square room with benches, desks, stools, and a large teacher's table. The room buzzed with an aspiring scholarship. Some had met the athletic, cheer-faced Bruce when younger. That he once attended this very class and returned meant: you could survive in the outside world. You could make it if you could be like him. Bruce swaggered his presence and charm, speaking respectfully with Pat and Genet, his former teachers. He bristled with pride at his achievements strewn across the table.

Eleanor studied the puckish scholar: dramatic, handsome, eighteen and famed enough for a – that wicked word – crush. Like Armstrong, Bruce would be fun to tease. She looked deep into his truth. Beneath his male cockiness, the scholar gave unsettled glances to his teachers. He enjoyed acting who he once was, but who was Bruce now, and who did he aim to become? She pulled her green scarf under her nose and blew a puff at him. He raised a brow. She was practicing.

Bruce flexed his shoulders dramatically, knowing how to use the light of the room – moves everyone learned from Genet. About to speak, he found perverse pleasure eyeing the students would have to copy his groan load of Greek and Latin scrolls. He gestured with emotion as if he were going to cry:

"I've seen things, people, you would not believe. Prometheus bringing the knowledge of Heaven, Icarus on fire falling from the sun, Vestal damisels making the Olympic gods hot in lust for love. People! A thousand ideas from so many times are regained! Here are my college scrolls from Saint Geneviève. My copies, my gift to you to copy. O, you fortunate, fortunate ones!"

Arno surveyed the table of pain, and brought his fist to his head; mouth agape, his pen hand twitched. College was a school for old people, not doers, not men who dealt blows of the sword.

"People," Bruce implored, "I know you are aching to edge your hands to parchment. Aren't you ravenous to know everything? Hungry brains and thinking hearts, go ahead. Harvest from me. Widen your universe." He became unnerved by a woman in green, winking. The class rollicked whispers, "Roses." The teachers prompted: "Bruce, say your dictone about roses."

"Ah yes, the dictone." He grit his teeth. A labor of his concern, his personal anthem, his signature poem – now with a new dedication from last night. He was here to make them think! He tapped his lips. The prospect of being charming, to become again that imagined flower within a woman's bosom, yes. He silhouetted his angular profile to the window, knowing how dramatic he appeared. Without revealing any emotion he lilted the air:

"a rose arose a bloom around, a rose of a rose aroused ah, Dangerossa."

The sighs, flush-faced Eleanor did not hear. What did he know of grand-mère! Amira wondered the same.

Arno, to fend off the torture of writing, but more to make Eleanor's face redder, as he was greenly jealous of her interests, asked for the glory of the class, "Please Sir, repeat your dictone."

"Yes please," the boys and girls resounded.

"I only repeat, when I have learned something new about my subject."

The class 'gee'd' with disappointment. Eleanor rolled her eyes. What a stick.

"You complain. I .. elect to grow. I .. restrain for your enlightenment."

What An Ash Stick!

"Now, now, people. I have decided you need to hear something new. The ancient Greek tongue. What is your choice? Pick from four of the ancient Greeks! The history of the decline and fall of Troy by Dares Phrygius! Poetry from Homer's sailor exploring the world! The nature of love by the philosopher Plato! A play by Euripides tells the plight of women at war! A count of hands?"

It was not even close. Philosophy was on everybody's mind.

"I am Plato. I write of my wise master, Socrates. Some say Socrates was a figment of Plato's imagination; he never wrote anything down. The story is of a dinner party that friends hold for Socrates: a symposium on love's nature. Hear how he learned of love. From The Symposium:" As he turned the scroll, his eyes fell on those most interested. The girl in green leaned forward. *Good!*

Young Eleanor's mind was always ready to learn anything about the greatest force in the universe. The *stick* could be forgiven. She put her green sleeved hand to her chin, elbowing back Amira's mockery of her fascination. Although it was Greek to her, she felt something, and not just Bruce's eyes that kept sweeping to her. He intoned the oft-repeated Greek 'Diotima,' – the woman wise in love, teacher of all lovers of wisdom. Eleanor thought, a *woman, master of man on the subject of love.* Speak, Bruce! Speak Plato, Speak Socrates, Speak Diotima! Initiate us to love's purpose.

"Love is that which prolongs life and leads to immortality." '—*YES.'*

The class showed moderate interest. Eleanor was positively alive.

Bruce gave a small debate with his teachers for the benefit of the class. He used the dialectic taught at college, a method of proposing convictions that allowed for two sides to conclude fairly. His teachers were considering performing harvest-time morality play. He persuaded them to consider a Greek play he was translating into Occitan, the local tongue. Master Genet was moved but was at a loss for casting a king who kills his father and marries his mother. Eleanor challenged Bruce to quit translating and write something original. She told the drama of her family. Her grandfather abducted his married lover. Forbidden to marry, they brought together children from prior marriages who fell in love, wed and gave birth. Ergo, Eleanor.

"Where does the story of love's child lead?" the scholar asked.

"Write the ending. Write it as a new play for Diotima."

"I like fresh." Freshly in his handbook, he wrote down as he spoke:

"A, New, Play, For, Diotima." He had Eleanor sign her name. Cooly, he folded the book to his breast pocket. They agreed to meet after class.

A warm slant of pale sun came to the autumn Abbey trees. The scholar and student greeted one another by a wall of fragrant roses in second bloom. Across the field, a verderer assembled laborers to shape a grove of ash.

Eleanor asked straight out: "Did you ever kiss Dangerossa?"

Bruce said squarely: "Damisel, that is for me to know and you to find out."

What a stick! She would not let his rudeness get to her. She decided to look him over cooly. "You could save me the time. I am curious."

"Of what, Abelard's forbidden teachings?"

She answered yes and no with her eyes. Unsure of what they confirmed, he smiled puckishly, "The Master and his Student know of you and Fontevrault. I carry their letters. Heloise wants to learn about the Abbey. I want to learn about you. Their latest street song that he composed, I added a line."

"For Heloise?" she said coyly.

"Perhaps I'll add another verse. You are far prettier than Heloise."

He seemed sure. Eleanor was sure, and said so: "Of course, I am!"

"Heloise has a blemish right there." The scholar reached to touch her cheek, looking for her eyes. *You are so obvious*, thought Eleanor. "Go ahead." She raised her cheek, slightly wanting. They endured a sapient moment.

A rake-saw slowly cut back and forth, zipping limbs that began creaking.

"You sweet angel." He tweaked her cheek with a pinch. She recoiled with alarm. He was seeing through her coyness. She was seeing through his charm.

The teeth of the blade in the limbs ripped both ways, slowing as each sideman called "Pull!" to the other's "Pull!" Distant branches cracked.

"Heloise knows four languages. She is the most sentient woman I have ever met. Like Diotima, she is wise about love, only she wanted to be in it."

"Do you have a girlfriend?" Eleanor asked innocently.

"Well, why do you ask?" Bruce toyed.

So he does. "Oh, I don't know," she said, bouncing her shoulders arabesque as Maryam. She had his eye and squared her shoulders racing relentless words:

"Am I right? You have ridden back to the house of fame, to play out before your teachers some personal decision? A scholar's dilemma, so to speak." A remote axe banged fresh on the tree. Bruce's mouth hung open. Eleanor gave him a sidelong look. He stepped to her.

"You think you are a highly observant girl, don't you?"

"I don't know about that." Hands on her hips, she said, "I won't be a girl for long." Eleanor let fly her curious torrent of words. "So that big decision, are you going to be like your teachers or become yourself?" Arborists shouted their distance pulls. He laughed nervously, *how could a young woman of such arresting beauty know his mind?* Only in Aquitaine could females challenge him so, and he relished being with her. Another river of innocent words:

"You taking that girlfriend with you. What's she like?"

He scratched his brow wondering what to say. Axe blows struck. He charmed over her irresistible smile, "I have many women friends. Sad it is, you cannot ride with me to visit Paris." The remark brought intrigue. He walked dramatically about her as if speaking to a sculpture. "The woman I seek has not been born."

"Or has she?"

The scholar laughed aloud at her victorious confidence.

Together they gamed a roman antic commentary on the tree work and the verderer's surgeon skill – blows, cut lows, laying on saws, pulling on ropes, watching the fall, twigs on their backs – all the while exchanging glances and throaty laughs. The green sleeved damisel stepped back to the wall of roses and playfully twirled her verdant scarfs wafting the scent around her. She toyed with the idea of a scholar who knew fine things. Could she forgive this for-me-to-know-you-to-find-out man, hiding his Dangerossa knowledge? He was rude, and she was proud. Her able heart could take strong feelings. Wanting this man of ideas, articulate words, and humor to play with her, she extended a fine scarf that he drew through the air. She tugged, pulling him.

"Teach me something!" Eleanor challenged.

In his questioning college way, Bruce persuaded her, against her will, with the absurd idea that men make everything the opposite of its intent. School keeps you from learning; it is a watch-and-spank service to relieve parents. Heaven is an invention to keep you from being happy on earth. History is the process of misunderstanding the past; it is how the dead entomb the living. Teaching music destroys all pleasure. Church keeps you from understanding the prophet's true life. Rewriting in Latin prevents anything from ever being known. She was offended, yet charmed with his many college-learned evidences. But, when Bruce said teachers were torturers and rulers were robbers, Eleanor protested.

"Look at Pat and Genet! Our teachers brought us to a higher level in every way. Duke William improves the lives of all. Sir, you missed the premise, the premise of love. For when that is present, anything is right and true." He could not disagree. As if she won a tourney, she demanded her prize. "Now give me a kiss." She darted her heavenward eyes, mind on fire with his rude appealing ideas. Bouncing her irresistible beckoning angel look, a deserving sweet kiss it was. He looked deep into her eyes and addressed her: "So, Lady Premises, learn the axioms." His words stimulated her; as much and as real as touching skin. She kept the thought to herself, *axioms of love*. Later she'd consider the profound idea. From his hair, she brushed an imaginary insect.

In the tradition of Aquitaine men and women, they pranced out flirtatious natures, played scarves about waists, traded troubadour verses. He gave his level green eyes. "It is time to talk about theories of friendship. The bond that Cicero defined between men could, Cassian testifies and he's always right, apply to men and women." She rolled her eyes and hand-crabbed: "Ya, ya, big talker. Just put peace and love first, friendship follows. Male, female, who cares. Oc, you want to be friends?"

The young woman's speedy intuitive mind positively excited him. From her quick lips came the essence of a three-week-long study of Greek orators.

"Eleanor, I have decided. You will study classical friendship and love – with me."

Eleanor teased with her brows at his veiled solicitation. "What if I said . . ." with a teasing flutter she waited for his assertive devilish charm.

"Yes . . . Yes . . . I can see. You are thinking..."

"Perhaps . . ." She felt the vanity of her footing slipping, her heart about to crash on the rocks. Bruce flourished his shoulder-length mane and pressed aside her red-gold hair past her ears, rolling his palms on her neck, fingering the roots. She closed her eyes: my weakness, my hair, *he could teach me the heavens*.

"They say you are a princess. You don't behave like one."

"How am I not?"

"You are not haughty. You don't gather friends to worship you. You don't expect the world to serve you. And calf boots. You ride a horse. You move me," the scholar said. "Ride to Paris with me in two days." He lifted her thigh-long hair, his fingers spreading her strands, feeling the heat that let cool her neck. "Be loved, damisel. I can bring you the universe."

"Promise?" she fingered the green folds of her gown. "I will let you know. I am going now." She walked off shy and cool.

Eleanor tried not to fly across the cream stones of the courtyard into her apartment, heart beating wildly. She revealed the details of her exchange to Amira, then hotly ordered her to pack so she could leave with Bruce.

Amira was as still as an autumn leaf on a windless pond.

"Say something!" Eleanor demanded. With disbelief, she watched her counselor leave the room. *With all the nerve.* Amira returned and pressed a thorny red budded stem to her hands. It hurt. Amira mimicked his scholarly male voice: "a rose a rose .. nay? a rose of a rose, uh Danger Rosa?"

Eleanor glared at her counselor and ran out into the last rays of the red sun. Blast, Amira was right. He'd had her grandmother in some intimate way. Had Eleanor been a mare, she would have stomped, whinnied, and neighed.

At the heart of Poitiers stood an impenetrable four turret keep. Elsewhere it would have been a watchtower or a donjon. Called the Maubergeonne Tower – for its entry was surfaced in marble and marble nude sculptures populated its garden. This was the sole residence of marble-white skinned Lady Bouchard of Châtellerault, Eleanor's vigilant protectress and grandmother. The notorious fortress of amorous legend was built by her deceased lover of a husband for her adoration and her protection Duke William the Ninth, Eleanor's grandfather. For many good reasons, the Maubergeonne Lady was called Dangerossa.

The tower, a stone's throw from the Palace, had survived the wrath of two ex-wives, one ex-husband, a cavalcade of priests, bishops, summoners, and an edict from the Pope of Rome himself. When trouble brewed, Dangerossa and staff would bar the door, climb to the upper level, pull the ladder behind, close the trap door, and seal the floor off. It had to be love, for what mother would live this way. Any other woman would have demanded marriage or beguiled the Duke to be declared Duchess of Aquitaine. In spite of the efforts of the world that thought it knew better, the two lived in a union by their own shared code centered in love for one another. Alone now, Dangerossa lived in the tower, tending her gardens, entertaining family, guiding women by her code, and even a few men. She saw whomever she pleased. She loved the Maubergeonne. The tower guaranteed something few woman of any time ever have, a place of her own.

Eleanor came urgently to ask about Bruce. Seeing Dangerossa busy with father preparing roses inside, Eleanor cut the morning beds near the open window.

Side by side, William and Dangerossa trimmed stems; she bare-handed, he with gloves. The early sun warmed the room of ready candles, colored hunting tapestries, stone fire hearth, marble-carved statues of nude gods and goddesses, and a high bed. Shields and vases were painted with Grecian nudes. On a table of many kinds of cut autumn roses, William placed flowers while throwing disapproving glances about the stylish tower boudoir. When Dangerossa turned to her stepson, he rested his eyes on the woman whose glamor could not be denied.

Past fifty, Dangerossa dressed like a youthful virgin and pulled it off well. Rich auburn hair fell to her revealed marble collarbone. The scrubbed vibrant skin was as vibrant as the sun glowing on her fine bed cover. A perfect arrow-bow of small lips puckered light red. A straight thin nose tipped up at the end. Faint lines danced about her lively eyes when she spoke; an extra line when she smiled. With the figure of a young woman and deliberate posture, her moves were as carefully chosen as her words. Scarlet ribands wrapped about her waist, matched by a satin bow tied loosely on her white gown. The captivating story of how William brought her the new fabric back from The Crusade was for later.

Dangerossa was among the first women ever to wear scarlet satin, the cloth of Catholic foes. That took nerve, the kind William the Ninth possessed and William the Tenth appreciated and shone well in Eleanor. The subject turned to Eleanor's future, and the lady of nerve had no problem dressing down Ten.

"You are a good father to speak of female matters to your daughter. Daily, you kept her hair to the hundred strokes, and her face to a hundred washes. What are you up to with my sweet granddaughter's hand?"

William ignored the playful delicate tones that other men so readily answered. What could he say about love and marriage that Dangerossa did not already know? He gave a half-hearted sigh and cleaned thorns from roses.

"Dear William, Eleanor could have been married at ten. You missed her big chance. The Duke of Anjou surely wanted to make the deal with his knaves."

He pulled a large thorn from his glove. "To fight his wars, and send more knights to die up north? Look what it has brought Anjou. Very little. Chinon has not seen a new building for a long time. We stay at peace and prosper."

"Why should marriage stop him, or you, in truth? It did not stop my father. He took you straight off your husband's land. You certainly are desirable. No woman I know has tended to a body with so much care. Losing your touch?"

"No man has that kind of passion anymore."

He snapped a thorn sharply, wanting to say that's not what I hear. Instead, he said, "Thank you for such a fine daughter. Aenor was a gentle soul."

"You loved her well," the stunning woman said. "William, you need a lovely female of stature in your life. Your two girls will leave soon. You are too much a gentleman. Be like your father. Go out and grab some beautiful rose."

"Now Dangerossa, can there ever be a belle like you?"

"William, regard. Eleanor is twelve and unmarried! You know where that leads. Name one girl married past thirteen. Soon, bang. Into a nunnery, if you prefer."

Outside, knees in soil, shearing blade glinting, Eleanor cut dead heads from the rose bushes. The dictone of Bruce was like a bee in her cowl. As her family debated, she sulked a truth: I am in the middle age of damisels.

"Dangerossa, Eleanor will rule Aquitaine. At fifteen, Grandfather William became Duke of Aquitaine. At fifteen, cousin Geoffrey became Duke of Anjou. Eleanor can wait until fifteen. I am in no hurry. Who knows? The rose may choose the hand that picks her."

"You are not thinking. A Duchess in her own right?" She kicked a heap of faded roses into a corner. William ripped through a stem. They turned to the doorway. Stepping into the flowery room, Eleanor glowered. William spoke self-consciously, "I'm sorry if you heard this." She threw the basket to the table showing her red horsehair belt. The elders inhaled her harvest.

Without a further word, the three went about preparing the flowers. The women carefully pressed off thorns bare-handed in a certain light danger called 'touching roses,' a practice of stemming that gave more time for conversation. Damisel Eleanor glanced sidelong to grandmother with a 'there is a thing to talk about look.' William read his daughter and put on his brim-cap and went to the doorway. The white Egret feather swayed. "I'll let you two finish."

"Think about a new honey, busy bee. Love keeps you young."

"Bzzzt!" he intoned with a finger snap of leather glove, shuffling outside.

"Not that he isn't trying. Limoges, you know about Limoges. The town hid that woman from him. If William had his father's heart, he would have taken her." Eleanor scratched an itch from her horsehair belt; fingers pink from touching roses.

Dangerossa continued, "So, who are we in love with this week?"

Eleanor wanted none of it. Taking a stem, she conducted a scornful tune:

"A rose arose a bloom around, a rose of a rose aroused, ha Dangerossa."

The shock of surprise in her elder's visage said it all.

"I knew it; I knew it!" Eleanor said inflamed.

The mannered woman was never shy about The Subject. Experienced and seasoned, every lesson of her life, for better or worse, enlightened her grand-daughter. Over the years, the expert gave Eleanor further proofs and ideas about every aspect of love. It was time to graduate from 'Love is harmony; desire is the key,' to the 'Crush and fall of lovemaking.' Eleanor's life would depend on such mastery. With head held high, the satin lady turned up a palm.

"The Rose . . ?"

Eleanor yielded the red thorny wand and sat on the edge of the bed.

"Well, my sexual damisel it is time for our 'Thorns and Roses' and art of love talk. First, I must tell you my side. Is that not fair?" Dangerossa lightly tapped out the highlights of the bedroom. "This marble-statued room was built for love. That bed is the height of the frame of a man's hips. The shield at the fireplace, a memento. The draw-rope from the ceiling, that is my escape ladder when things get touchy. Up there I have hidden from summoners, legates, magistrates, and . . . irate wives."

She drew the rose to her collarbone.

"In here they call me Beautiful, in here they call me Belle. I told your grandfather, 'Come, take your boots off, you may not have time for that later.'" She pushed the door closed. Pointing the flower from Eleanor to the bed, she teased. "Lie there my lover. Lie down on my bed for the big time. Ready, set?"

Eleanor laughed and leaped to the bed, enjoying grandmother's elegant directness. Dangerossa flourished as she spoke.

"Young Eleanor, you are so dear to us. Your body bleeds, saying it is ready to know, and I am privileged to tell you about love and lovemaking. Marriage is so near now. Few damisels learn until it is too late to live well. To rule your heart, to advise the ladies of your court I'll tell you how an Aquitaine woman uses her body. Ask me anything about sex, love, marriage, creating children. A caution, I tell you only of my experience, what works for me. Everyone has their own sense of what's enjoyable. What would you like to know of how a man and woman make love?" Dangerossa twirled the rose and put it down without a prick.

Eleanor asked, "Do men jump on you?" Her mentor laughed. "We ride. We rise and fall. Me, I enjoy a man's working backside. I live for a man's crush on me."

"Crush?" Eleanor recoiled. "That's a wicked word."

"Few women understand this lovemaking remark used so meanly. I learned its meaning from a farm woman. She never had a shortage of strong backs to teach in the hay of the barn. Pitchfork in hand, these were her unashamed words . . ." Delicate Dangerossa pulled her collar lower and romped the room mimicking a deep voice. "Ready, set your heart to go. Lady Bouchard, once the door is barred, just the sound of the key in the bolt, closing rusty shut by my turning hand, that man is hardened to make love. He has nowhere else to go. In the straw, my breasts burn his beard; my thighs rub him to enter paradise. He knows he is going to make love to me and, by God, I make him desire to take me to heaven too. I'll fork him if he doesn't. I hide in the hay to let him find me half-naked; I dare him to 'crush' me. I wrestle him until he falls." The impersonation ended.

Eleanor could not help but laugh.

"Sweet, you laugh at her crudeness, but she teaches a damisel important things. First, choose your own place and time to make love: never let the man force you; stay in control of the time; you unroll love's story. Second, few women know the pleasure of their own sexual release. It is not just for the man, who easily enjoy a sudden spurt. You must teach them how to bring you. How could they ken a woman's body that we know so well? The men who handle horses are best. Seek them out. They naturally groom and care for powerful alien creatures, which we are to men. A chevalier combines his power with his creature, much like vivacious love. Third, you talked of a man jumping on you. My farm friend would mount and ride men, then brag about shaking a man's boots off. In public! That is unseemly. A true lover never brags. When made public, love rarely survives, remember that." Eleanor took it in.

"Finally, the crush and fall. Sex is bold; it is tender; it dances in between. My art is to tempt the man to crush me. A good lover knows he must be forceful to crush you and yet gentle enough to avoid crushing you. You are the muse of in-between. After you have made long love, you strive to release him and feel the thrill of his strong arms in fall. For unless he falls hard, you have not totally aroused the entire animal force in him. You have not made him want to completely give you the all of his body. This way to pleasure some women mistakenly call surrender. It is not that at all. The art is teasing the man's crush, and galloping together to let him fall into your release."

"Grand-mère, you are so open with me. Some say sex is exhausting and boring."

"Invigorating and pleasurable! The wrinkled people say that, nay?" No man in his teens will say those words; I know first hand. With age, people forget their spirit; the church finishes off their soul in my view. Keep alive your chain of being, back to your earliest childhood, and then you will never lose sight of your birth-given lief. Lovemaking is a rare and joyous act."

"Spoken like Calbi." Eleanor turned sideways on the comfortable bed.

"Eleanor, let's not fox-fool ourselves, remember last fall at the trial of Chauvigny? Or this summer, what men tried with you in your red cape? Some men behave like a pack of dogs, as you've heard some women behave as polecats. Often men force a woman into having sex. The people's church confesses them and they go on sinning. Meanwhile, the pulpit condemns honest lovemaking as evil pleasure. From them, hide your true spirit away."

"Why hide, love's nature should illuminate. Shouldn't it?" Eleanor was cross with uncertainty. The image of good hunters, violent hunters, church words, all conflicted in her heart with images of love and intimacy. She was thinking for herself and someday for others, how should it be?

"Sweet, do not despair. That is why this spring, we had you and Amira meet Grand Abbess Petronille de Chemillé. Now you know Fontevrault's origin. The Test separates the fair in love from the violent. By next moon, you will be tested and may well have no idea you are taking the test."

"Really?"

"Yes. Now I will tell you some delicate things about women's nature. Consider, you may have a large court someday and you may need to counsel your ladies – out of earshot of nuns, except the elders of Fontevrault. Since you are a horse-riding girl, you will not have a problem when it comes to lovemaking, as your thighs are well stretched. Advise young women of your court to be avid equestrians. For indoor girls like me, I spread my legs and felt myself before my teen. There is wisdom in knowing pleasure and a sad ignorance in accepting pain."

Eleanor marveled; could she ever speak so unbound? Grandmother was liberal with her art. Eleanor returned to her point.

"So Bruce; tell me, what is he to you?"

Dangerossa poured a glass of wine for each. "You are persistent. We like that about you. He is a friend. He teaches me things as I teach him. Here, take this. From golden Aphrodite to you, bright-eyed Pallas Athena. From ancient love to youthful wisdom. To purity."

Eleanor knew the Greek goddesses. She scrunched her nose trying to appreciate the unhoneyed 'pure' wine that Dangerossa enjoyed.

"Love! Sweet, we've talked about lovemaking, but not love. You must command the favors and stages! Your grand-mère is no great example, but I am real. When I was young, I learned from Cathar women – you know, the bathers, their great ritual. Her sect believed that you are not born until you first make love; until then you are nothing. Southern damisels I knew ran away and took their first man, so their lives could start. Not that they disliked their family; they preferred to sleep with a lover. How noble to believe that life is best lived in love and that men can love. Males who seek your bed are easy to find, men who know love are not. Of everything, I have learned this — Friendship is the first stage to the next step."

"Then we will have a school. You can teach them all."

Dangerossa smiled at the innocent impossibility of such an idea.

Eleanor drove on. "A Southern woman, Guisana, told me: 'When I ran away, I tried men on like new clothes. I could never find my size.' She found her fit and is married in love with her husband. They have a child and live with their order at Fontevrault."

"Famous Guisana. A divine match that is rare, Eleanor."

"She told me her favorite prayer. God, I want you inside of me."

Dangerossa laughed. "I have heard that. Some say he is already. Oh, you look like you are falling asleep. The damisel does not want to know the art of making fine love?"

Eleanor laughed at the jest. She could not be more wide-eyed.

"To be bodily loved by a man, their sex stiffened easily onto me. Their hardness can hurt even the exercised woman, primarily because they do not care how you feel. Take control of him as you would of time. Pet and caresses equally to become warm and your kisses moist. You will both become equally pliant, hard, and wet all over. Without that, sex is exhausting, boring, a be-drudging thing. Take the time, your finest of time, to build an orgasm of consummation, where everything comes together in supreme lovemaking. God sure knew what he was doing when he made us for love."

On the bed, young Eleanor touched roses breaking off thorns by feel.

Dangerossa touched a petal across her wrist. "Smell. Make yourself fragrant. Every point of the body has its own way of Eros. With as many areas to explore as courses in an Aquitaine feast. You must enjoy longingly, finely, and savor," she put her wrist to Eleanor's nose, "it is a sin against Love not to."

"A sin against *Love?*"

"Yes, Love is its own force. It has an honorable code that must be obeyed. Love can deny nothing to Love. You can never be deprived of any act you desire without the very best of reasons. The acts of feeling, stroking, kissing must be cultivated; pleasures are the truest mysteries to favor. Keep the book of love open."

"Grand-dame, tell me of your love with grandfather."

Dangerossa showed concern. "Our life was this keep of many years. William, my troubadour, brought me first to this room filled with roses and candles. He knew how a woman wants to be made love to and sang to me bawdy and true. We were mad for the other, alive; never being boring. How dead were our heartless marriages? First marriages are by your father's choice, never your own; forced and rarely felt. My second had no veils. It was a plain union to see love's true spark. I was too much for my first husband and not enough for my second."

"Tell me more of your true love, will you?"

The stunning woman calmed. She put a large rose petal to her neck. "This figure has been drawn many times. Pure, no tattooed mark of the slave. He never liked roadsigns; loved the mysteries. A temple dear is washed often, kept to its own fragrance. I clean my mouth and chew bay to kiss purely. I took care of this body so it could be ours. Before his passing, he insisted I stay ravenous with desire, for as we believed, love keeps you young. You have the power to restore the other's chain of being. He liked to draw me naked and teased I be drawn unclothed with every lover after him. Do you want to see a real drawing of my lively animal womanhood? I fear my valise has gone missing. Surely a manservant took what is by now church-smoke."

Eleanor thought it best not to mention the missing drawings yet. Amira had them in safety. "Is that you over there, on that shield by the hearth?"

"Naked on his battle shield. No, it is not me; that is a myth, a Greek deity, William's inspiration, like the statues he brought back from the Crusade."

Eleanor eased off the bed to the striking, proud nude figure drawn in curve and line. As a child, she had once drawn the image on a bark shield. There was a fair likeness of her grandmother. *Strange, that a man in battle would proclaim so boldly for a woman.* Eleanor revolved the bronze shield on its axis.

"Bold is love!" Dangerossa trumpeted.

So those really were drawings of her. Naked as Amira's buried fertility statues Amira hid the woman. Was she right? Or was grandfather – driven to show the woman in her vigor through song and image. Eleanor leaped back on the bed. "Troubadour William took you from your tower to elope. I have often imagined that bold night. Do you think any man will seize me?"

"That's not what happened, sweet. Seize you? You allow yourself to be taken. It is an ancient Pictone custom. Never forget who is in charge. When William came for me, what really happened was different from what everyone repeats. You know, he who is not jealous cannot love. That is why it was easy to leave my marriage. Sweet, listen. There is never an excuse for not loving. Sex keeps our blood bold. Marriage is no excuse for not loving."

The last comment made Eleanor take a breath. Marriage was a bound church rite. Perplexing questions came to mind trying to connect sex to life to marriage to love. It made her head swim. She sat back on Dangerossa's bed.

"Grandmother, how could you tell grandfather was your love for life?"

"In true love, there comes a mutual paleness of shock, the endless thoughts of the other – both heavenly and wicked. You cannot eat or sleep, the heart skips. You are nervous seeing one another. You check yourself. It is right to find out, will he beat you, has he beaten others? Is he jealous, in a healthy away?"

Eleanor propped herself up on a pillow. "You have so many great codes; you should pen an Occitan tome of love."

"Danger writing that."

"Why? What more can there be?"

"It is a battle with the Church, sweet. The story of that will come later." Dangerossa pressed her lips in a line, trying to be polite and disengage. She overcame her reluctance. "Abbess de Chemillé told me all about your expressive ideas of love when you learned of Arbrissel's mission. The abbess and I go back to the beginning. Dare I say? I've had two men love me at once. Chemillé and Hersende loved Robert at the same time. Ultimately, I got William; Chemillé gave herself to Robert. A new love often puts to flight an old one."

"Tell me. Grand-mère, you ken love, I do not. Be fair."

"Eleanor, here is my problem. If I tell my story, I have to confess to God."

"Confess to God?"

"I vowed silence to the white priests. I formed a union outside of marriage."

"Love is not a sin. Did you feel it a confessional wrong?"

"No, they made me feel guilty. They said my soul will not go to heaven unless I renounce my union. William was cast out by the church; he was braver than me. If ever I tell my story, they want the names of any who listen, to confess them, and keep them from damnation. Believe me, I want you and your sister to ken the truth. By my vow, I cannot. Silence is my only way to heaven."

"I wished there were no heaven!"

"Eleanor."

"It is unfair! I want to hear the truth, but I must honor your vow!"

Dangerossa was vexed, wanting to tell her tale of thorns. The people's church forbade talking of their past. The one person that could help her now was Abbess Chemillé to share her story of abduction, loves, and motives. It would save Eleanor from the Church's version that damned her so.

"Eleanor, know my sadness. My wish is to teach you everything in life. Grant me time to weigh my vows."

Eleanor nodded unhappily. Dangerossa took her daughter's hands on the bed.

"I see you wear a red horsehair belt, strong as steel." Eleanor glowed at the prize. "Yes, be proud. This is a chevalier's rare gift. He loves you. Your maker had to get the agreement of every knight, which he and he alone would present this to the Princess of Aquitaine. Love demands you honor him for what this belt promises."

"I don't know who he is."

"Some mystery? In time. Bristles itch, don't they? May I suggest." Dangerossa went to her dresser and pulled a beautiful wide red satin scarf. "Stand." Eleanor stepped off the bed. Grandmother ran her fingers on the belt. "Yes." She wove and folded a smooth red satin across Eleanor's belly, forming a guard that revealed the belt. "Turn." Across the hips, she tucked the satin. Scarlet tails flowed behind.

"Thank you." Eleanor sat back on the bed, smoothing her guard. "It looks—"

"Alluring, feminine. That you are. Sweet, I know you bleed. Piss on blood."

"Wait, isn't it piss and blood?"

"If you are going to curse, give it properly. We are women; we piss on blood. Say it under your breath. Men hate to hear of feminine acts." Eleanor laughed; how often she misguided her conclave. Dangerossa gestured further.

"Be very clear in your mind at your tender age. With as much pleasure as you may afford, if you are to bring a man inside you, you are in the act of giving birth to another human being. Know full and well, this act makes you a mother. Few women, in the throws of hard-driven men, give a wit about it. They love, in desperation. Eleanor, mate with a passionate will for creation! That's how your mother made you. Regard. You are now a birthmaker to any man. You are the grantor. A man must achieve the sacred right to be a birthgiver to you. Choose well. If you let his stalk inside you, a child is likely to come, wish or not; their nine moon birthing requires fortitude. Motherhood and suckling expand your love for children and their longer lives. If you do not desire to be a parent, by all means, enjoy love. Tell your ladies, undressing entirely is not necessary to enjoy the great pleasures. Give your full sex only to a man you can see as a father to your children, a man who will last their ages, that you are proud to be seen with. Create a family lineage, improve on your parents' will that had you. Some care goes into this. Eleanor, you maintain your beauty, he will seek you out."

Eleanor said, "Sex for you, Dangerossa, you risk becoming a mother."

"Sweet, women in elder ages who have flashes of fever for many months bleed no more. When the womb is spent, we are no longer birthmakers. If your heart is big, you can let blood to stay youthful."

"Blood-letting?" Eleanor puzzled. "I am not ready for that."

"Of course not. At my age, we still draw men. Lovemaking at my age affords the pleasures of creation without concern for any birth or a child to raise. Damisel, we become the roses in fall that bloom again."

"And marriage for you?"

"Love, not marriage, is what William and I found. We had three children of our own to prove it. The Roman Church prevented our marriage and our divorces. They excommunicated us, meaning no priest or follower could communicate with us in any way. We could not attend church or partake in the rituals. The intolerable part is priests telling everyone that we are evil."

"That is madness. True love and family are good, always, Grand-mère."

"Our hearts prevailed. We joined freely in love. Here is the beauty of our union. Your grandfather and I brought our children together from our prior marriages. With our love, our children came together in a passionate mating, married, and bore you, my damisel! When he died, after two years of mourning, by our promise code, I was to stay happy, free to have lovers again."

Eleanor came off the bed and whispered in her grandmother's ear, "Before I go, thank you for mating and giving me a chain of being."

Dangerossa pressed back he granddaughter's hair. "Make fine love." She startled, "But dear, you did not ask of Bruce?"

Eleanor looked up. "Fine love? I hope you shake his boots off." In the light autumn laughter of the marble room, two women across time, a rose of a rose of the other, embraced to share the double pounds of their hearts.

As the year ended and came to be new, Eleanor at thirteen remained untouched in matters of love's consummation. After a round of troubadours, everyone gave desire more than a hum. She had teased knights playfully before their belles, lingering long to observe the sapient language of love. Their women received every form of aspiration in voice and gesture. Chevaliers softened their words, brimmed trembling resonant chests, they fingered their hair, stroked their angled jaws, rubbed their riding legs; unlike her suitors who begged, demanded, prayed, gave offerings, or made beastly advances. Cooly, chevaliers waited for a feminine response, refraining yet on the verge of acting on their desires.

Eleanor considered many dares often testing the edge of forbidden. Moon over moon, her teases tempted her yearns. Pouring into her new teen blood was a heat; men of all ages looked on her hungrily. Some tried to get under her vestments; they were foxes about that. She was smart and wary.

From the winter new year light Eleanor entered the kitchen side-closet of Poitiers Hall. Amira was on a small ladder.

"The next dish, the next dish, and the next, whew. Oh! Eleanor! I am examining heirloom pieces, setting aside platters with chips or breaking seams."

"Let me help." Eleanor seized the plates. "Amira, now that you have had a 'Thorns and Roses' talk with Dangerossa let's talk of intimate touches given and received -the accidental, the actual, and the desired." In the closet, they squeezed by one another examining the dishes.

"I have nothing to offer but counsel." Amira clattered plates.

"We damisels are not at the level of knights and their ladies." Squeezing by, Eleanor said in a high tone, "You were right to chasten me about Bruce, Dangerossa's lover. The scholar's rude ideas appealed, but he was so arrogant."

"Here set this plate over there."

"In my off chances with men, I have slapped away many a hand. I only have to tell them once now." Eleanor sorted plates. Amira came down the ladder.

"What did you say?"

"A woman's body is her temple, only a clean and proper hand is allowed." Amira laughed. "Clever, no male ever washes. Saved by your code."

Eleanor teased, "But the few, fresh hands . . . Amira."

"So how did you end it with Bruce?"

"I told the scholar, 'Inky nails, leave.'"

"It's for your own good. Crowncrabs! So much is at stake for a Princess."

"Crowncrabs? I haven't heard that since I was six. You saw me?"

"I heard. Your father said that you'd get crowncrabs if you wore his coronet too much. You pushed it over your nose and wore it like a collar. Hmm, now, tell your counselor of these freshest hands."

"An innocent one I let caress me .. on my own terms. Only those who voice the poetry of their nature may come to my ear." Eleanor let Amira pass. The counselor said, "I can't tell. Is that a troubadour gibberish, or are you speaking your mind?" They moved the plates from the closet along.

"I shan't say. Oh, what sex must be like, and how old people waste it."

"Tell me how a kiss should be," Amira said, trying to simmer the conversation.

"A kiss. I seek its flavor. I wish kisses. Let them be long and full of time. One measured Aquitaine kiss, potent with love. Regard, should one take charge, or, wait to be kissed? How many soft strokes must a lover give at the fireside."

"I can't see what I'm doing," Amira said. "It's hot in here. You thirsty? We'll do better in the dining partition." Amira gave Eleanor a stack of plates, then grabbed a clay-fired bottle of wine and their silver-glazed drinking vessel they shared in travel. In the hall partition, at make-shift eating table, Eleanor set plated, poured wine while Amira continued to bring dishes out.

Eleanor jibed: "Dangerossa says love should be pure. Listen to her beau. 'Love ever-fixed in a soul travels tempests unshaken. It is the star to every wandering back. True love is a timeless two.' Then he crushed her."

"Don't curse. Dangerossa will get you in trouble. Was she quoting him?"

"An aspiring troubadour. Amira, a woman should find her own lover and seek her own man to marry."

Amira's exasperation was as expected.

"Are you cracked? Love is one thing; being a man's property is another. It's your father's choice!" You have wealth and concerns." She pulled a worn plate.

Eleanor took a plate deftly. "I will never be a man's property, and you either. I may allow my land to be joined. Amira, I can only accept the glances of a few. You are free; you can exchange glances with any man."

"You don't know my father. I've seen your glances. That's for the good pile."

Eleanor set the plate for her maid. "Amira, it is not our father's choice, but our wild hearts freely felt. That is how male and female should pursue love, not with matchmakers. Horses and birds, their parents do not choose for them. For us, with so many to choose from, how does one settle on a mate and call it true? Why must a man always be older? I consider it daily. Did you ever stop and think that your true love may live far away – you don't even know the person's name? If you don't go on a quest, you will never find out. Maybe the best lover is the one you just passed by, and you didn't bother to engage. Maybe your lover has not yet been born. You might miss any of these."

Amira considered. "You listen to music too often. Your parents pick the bone-brain, and you marry the tooth-picking fool as you are told."

"Like your mother thinks summoners can arrest your father whenever, for no good reason. That's not the world we will make."

Amira took her point deeper. "You say a young person has a voice in love, which no elder decides for you? The idea is alien. I've never seen it done."

"You forget Calbi and Danae. Their love was not arranged. Our generation will write our own book. We will make the law."

"Hmm, you can, I suppose. You are a highborn princess."

"Well yes, I could." Eleanor leaned on the table. "If I had the power . . ."

Amira's eyes glimmered. "Given lordly power, how would your rules go?"

"Let's see. The blessed Arbrissel learned of nature. He started the order of Fontevrault." Eleanor said casually, "He had a test . . ."

"You mean, The Test." Amira drew her out. "Eleanor did you . . ."

Eleanor whispered her near. "Yes, I did take it, in a way – or maybe I gave it. I can't tell. At a nightstay on the Abbey floor, after a bark boat trip and hike with elders, boys and girls lay out to sleep. That night I let a boy touch me, right here." She touched her collarbone. The finger traveled three inches lower. "He spent a long time playing with my ear. It was delicious. My ear! He gently twirled and tugged my hair and traveled my neck. His fingers smelled of flowers. A clean hand permitted to my chest and no more! It satisfied me immensely to be touched so softly. All night, my mind went to his words. 'If everyone lived by an order of love, we'd live in an untroubled world forever.' Rules of love! Fair principles for all, and judged in a court!"

Amira could not resist a lively howl.

"Don't laugh!"

"You are saying, some hard-nosed judge would try cases of love, in a court?"

"In front of everyone. Why not?" Eleanor was adamant. "A court embodies the will of its ruler. A ruler can do anything. All my father ever hears are tribunals of hateful crimes and deceitful claims. Why judge hatred when you can judge love? The verdict has better consequence and the proceedings more interesting."

Amira had lit the fire and had Eleanor on a run. She pushed the flame along.

"Then why settle for one royal court?"

"Yes, that's right. We will need franchises of judges."

Turning away, the maid set dishes on high mantel places. "Books of love?"

"Yes Amira, many fine books."

"Schools of love?"

".. and taught in every abbey-school."

Amira laid the dishes out. "Castles of love, donjons of love, love farms, canons on love, a love mass in a cathedral of love." Amira studied the back of a silver-rimmed platter. When she turned, her mistress stared at her with crossed her arms:

"This is serious! I'm not speaking to you anymore!"

"Eleanor, to the Holy Church physical love is a sin. It is a forbidden subject."

"That should not be. Not at Fontevrault. The Christ teaches of love. If his life was not interrupted, he would have explained it all. I was thinking."

"That can't be good," Amira said. Eleanor glowered. Taking their favorite silver-glazed cup, Amira poured honeyed wine and proudly drank. "Taster's first."

Eleanor took a sip. Her words ran like a river. "Mathieu speaks of knowledge as growing. He is of the physic like Arbrissel is of the spirit. They both go to nature and figure out things for themselves. However, when Mathieu reads Archimedes, he is encouraged to go further by those who saw he could. The problem is when Arbrissel or Calbi read a Bible; they are stopped from going further by those who fear they could. I encouraged Mathieu to stand on shoulders of giants. A boost, if you will."

"From a brush of your bust," Amira said, recalling her tease of Mathieu.

"That was our first day in class. It was an accident."

Amira touched the rim of their cup, pucking her doubting lips.

"It was for his imagination," Eleanor hastened and took a deep swallow from their cup. "Less honey from now on, please. I am learning to taste the honey in wine. And the boy who touched me was not Mathieu. Amira, the point is this. It is dangerous for me to encourage spiritual natures. Remember when we were small, Calbi's scolding at church? Unless religion changes, no man will ever stand on the shoulders of Jesus, who stood on the shoulders of Moses, who certainly stood on other shoulders. The new heart-faiths are the future; love is the Next Testament. The prophets only started. See, the spiritual world can advance! That's what the Catharics are doing. What do you say?"

Amira rolled her eyes. She picked up their cup and goaded Eleanor. "Only in Aquitaine. What you are saying is pure blasphemy."

"I know I look heretical. This is between you and me."

"Good. So when will you have this figured out?"

"Figure out what part?"

"Love," said Amira.

"Just Love? Soon enough. We will benefit as women, eh old friend?"

"If they don't lock us in the donjon."

"You have summoner's block. Donjon, hardly." Eleanor finished the last swallow. With both hands around the vessel, her eyes looking joyously over the brim, she resonated ghostly: *"Ammiraa, Ammiraa,* I own the keys."

During harvest feast in the Poitiers dining hall, Eleanor toasted the new guards. In response to her father's request to protect her against overzealous men wanting to claim her, she increased their numbers. She included female guards. Someone had to lead them; someone trusted from her generation. Reliable Arno could, but all Eleanor ever saw from him were hard looks. As they ate, the muscular squire of fifteen avoided her eyes. She knew how to straighten her friend out.

Sturdy Arno went to the library, after dinner. He threw himself on a large settle and read aloud to himself by the hearth-fire. Eleanor walked in and shut the door. He registered hurtful disdain. She stood before him. They were very alone.

She looked down into his averting eyes. "Your hair is uncombed. That is not like you. Arno, look at me." He lay his book to the side, looking up warily. A familiar jealous passion washed over him. He clenched his jaw.

"You have become so moody. Why do you look so hurtful around me? You made my horsehair belt, didn't you? Arno tell me, what is it?"

He nodded slowly. But what did she want him to say, what could Arno say — that he could not have her, that he had wished ever since last year, every breathing day, to take her damisel arms, kiss her sweetly, and know her beauty? Eleanor patiently waited for his words. Arno beheld her warm face. He studied the brushed crimson, gold hair. Her body could be measured in lengths of it, as he often did: neck to knee, shoulder to fingertip, head to naval. Sitting at the settle-couch edge, she stood close. The miserable knave dug his nails into his palms. Her presence flickered before him; he wanted to run from the room.

She fanned out her tender fingers. "Arno, do you remember my dictone?" How could he not? Her dictone was in his mind that school day when the words first left her lips. There were ten words. He breathed life into every glistening nail.

'Silver Signs Through Rolling Palms Touch Forth The Silent Senses'

At the sixth word, *touch*, he tapped a finger. "I am proudly remembered. A secret, Arno." She bent her mouth and cupped his ear, "Whisper anthems close to a lover's ear, with sibilance, like this: *'silver signs through rolling palms touch forth the silent senses'.*" She waited, then pulled back to see. His eyes were closed in bliss. Arno felt her eyes probing him; relishing the animal heat of her eyelashes, the undeniable scent of gardens, bay, and honey-sage. He wanted so much to come to his feet and thrust her to the couch.

"Do it to me Arno. I want to hear."

As the damisel pulled on him to rise, he slowed to join her budding curves. He pressed back her clean combed red-gold hair. Inspiring her sagely scent, he sang back her ten whispered words that sweetly tickled her ears.

Gently, Eleanor pressed him away. "Do you know what a service kiss is."

The muscular Arno swallowed. "No."

She unbuckled her horsehair belt and let it fall. "Find out. I want yours."

Eye to eye the two searched, saying nothing for a while. He'd soothed many a night away taking her in his arms, imagining everything, but never her initiation. Eleanor was no longer twelve and the budding chevalier no longer fifteen; what age they were only eternity knew. She faintly swayed a stance before him. Her eyes sparkled a tempered joy. He wondered what was within his reach. His hand, she turned away. They peered into the other's sparking eagerness.

"Ooh!" Eleanor uttered, being lifted strongly and swept off her feet. To the settle, he laid her gently. Would her heart melt from beating so fast? His weight rested beside her. They let time be.

In joy, Arno looked down into her intense blue eyes. She looked up into his hovering smile. He savored to kiss her, burning to know her skin. Yet as much as he wanted this woman, he wanted her fairly. He could tell; she was not completely there, wanting, and unable to give herself entirely. Still, her beating heart, her roving eyes, her scent, and available lips maddened him. And if she spoke again, her voice would drive him out of his mind. Unexpectedly, Eleanor pulled him straight on top of her. She said softly, "Can you protect me?" letting him wrestle with the impossible question. He looked for the serious stars in her eyes, a moment forever. She voiced, "Be my bodyguard." He felt his desire swell upon the frame of her hips. "Arno, be my champion and prove yourself squire to knight." She rocked him playfully, "You would be Limona's horse groom first." She pressed her thighs on his and gave her siren whisper: "I give you permission to ride once. Sir, your service kiss," and offered her neck. He set his cheek to her peach-skin fur, inhaling her sage. He nosed her neck and nibbled her ear. He stroked her hair to its roots and gently parted her lips with his. Little sounds came from the back of her throat. They darted their tongues in play. She corrected his hands, there would be no further undressing, yet she wanted her curves to be caressed entirely as much as he wanted his firm muscles to be felt. She allowed her collar to be taken down below her shoulder, then lower. Arno vowed long ago one kiss would satisfy his life. Now she lay beneath, responding to his hands. He removed his tunic, and they explored one another, their mouths ever-widening. He kneaded her with kisses. She broadened her hips, rising up, and hummed her breathiness in his ear, "Crusshh. Crussshh. Crusshh me...," encouraging him, kissing him down onto her until he was engorged with impossible wishes. He pressed on top of his gorgeous beauty, trying not to crush her, yet wanting to. Their bodies entwined in tempo. She closed her eyes and let him take her lips, throat, budding breasts. His palms felt like silver. Arno rubbed the full length of his body on hers, and they thrust their naked hearts together. He felt her darkness. He felt her light. The charge of horses filled his veins. In heavy breathing, gallop with her gallop, he urged her on into his gasping finality. Thrilled by the rush and might of his crushing fall, she owned her empathic moan of release. When he settled, his ear pressed on the wet skin of her beating chest. Both felt they had run up a mountain and at the top were angels. Wrapping crimson-gold long hair in a glow around him, she tended him with kisses. Arno felt pulled into sleepy angelic heaven feeling her lips upon his crown. He knew what was being asked, what he had to do. Kissing her breast sweetly, he untangled her hair from his. Arno stood, then helped Eleanor up. They peered at the marvelous flame lit in the other. She said firmly, "Friends forever if there is no further affair between us. Your deeds will be for our court. I will speak to my father and make it so. Before I go now, friend, what is your wish?" Arno, at fifteen, knew the call of higher destiny. He kissed her lightly, and they embraced. A voice, sure as fate passed through him. He would protect this woman for her life; for his life; for the rest of their lives. He would never have her, except for this once, her gift. Arno felt just in his heart, his voice filled with emotional words. "What I wish is what I will do – your long life. Friend." "Friend," she replied, eyes bright. With tears, they pulled apart and laughed at the wet stains each had made of their clothing. He clasped her hands, pulled her near, and kissed her chin, lips, and crown. With moist eyes, she accepted his wish. Thinking of his crazy love letters, being called 'halo-wheezer,' 'pleas-bud,' bright-eyed Eleanor gave a throaty cackle, "Arno, make me laugh again and bring your joy to our court. That is the you we all truly miss. True Friend." When her palm touched his heart, and her fingers opened wide, he felt the angels of cheer return to his breast as if saying: *You, I restore your chain of being.* He kissed her palms as a priest blesses a sacrament, then let her silvery self go.

They never spoke of this episode again.

Duke William gladly welcomed Arno to Eleanor's growing court as the head guard in training. Arno groomed and trained Limona as a trekking horse. He acquired a page, for there was travel ahead in Eleanor's close guard. Sir Armstrong drilled Arno, Calbi, and the guards to become expert men-at-arms. As fierce as Arno became, he never forgot his purpose nor the evening he got to know the body that he vowed forever to protect. His pranks got better too.

This intimacy Eleanor would bestow on a small set of admirers. She mused on this deep force that pulled with trembling pleasures. In the attraction and the thrill, she felt a person's epic character in formation as if she were birthing a star. This force she deemed majestic love, and she was determined to be its master. Her form of personal affection may have seemed calculated, and in some ways, it was. She chose trusted friends who cherished her and made use of her inspiration. She judged that men improving their character would make a difference to the larger world. A bond of personal pleasure sanctified deeds. To her, as for the Cathars she knew, love was a religion and she the novice learning the sacraments.

The aspiring princess knew her actions were dangerous. Not so much with whom, for she judged character well. Danger and betrayal would come from outside, from those who did not understand her alien idea of love, particularly the predominant pulpits of the world that proclaimed human love sinful. She got to know her ritual well. It was never gratification, it was transformation, and bolstered by Calbi's peculiar Cathar rite of catharsis, she knew the difference. She told no one where, or with whom or the age when she first experienced this rite upon her person, but the ten whispered words to her ear were hers forever.

At their scholarly conclave, the damisels shared little beyond the names of their belt makers. Deepest knowledge is best kept between those who share lips. Maryam kissed a boy she first met in Perigueux, tall Mathieu, the builder. Amira's embrace came from the spiritual aspiring swordsman Calbi, whose Daena gave kind permission. The beautiful Reyna kissed brave Armstrong. Eleanor peaked happily at her horse belt marked with an 'A.' When asked, she would always say it meant Alienor. Years later, Aphrodite, and later still, Athena.

Arno watched Eleanor riding Limona, proud when she rested her hands on his horsehair belt surrounded in red satin. The aspiring warrior had no desire for school, yet he remembered her ten-word dictone perfectly. He had kissed the song of each word on her fingers. And when she whispered, oh when she whispered, he felt his mind grow with wisdom – just like a scholar in commune with the universe, pleased as it reveals its deepest, most ancient secrets.

◆

Lief and Liege

Falling loosely across her face, Eleanor's strawberry flaxen hair tangled past her knees. Twisting strands by her nose, the odors of clover, leather, and horse were sharp from the spring morning ride. It tickled her how men tried to guess its color; words beyond yellow and red, only troubadours and her mirror-maker knew. The young life, full of the world's sensations, floated in her new gown.

Eleanor of Aquitaine was beautiful, but it required others to assure it. None were more caught up in it as Amira Neas. As her dresser, she drew Eleanor's long red-gold hair back; it did not shimmer enough. She adjusted the silvered hand glass in its lemon-wood frame, and the two exchanged a cheerful smile. Preparing for her hundred strokes, Eleanor raised to resettle her gown and sat, flattening her palms along the length of her thighs smoothing the new lemon-colored dress. Remarkably clear: on the verge of her curves, she had slapped bony childhood well behind. And now, a serious day.

Into the mirror, the woman of thirteen springs searched. Pressing her cheekbones, she centered her face. She set a steeple to rest her chin for the bell and comb hours. The bright window flooded her sculpture of Frankish genealogy.

The brill of Eleanor's eyes opened with youthful awareness. Fine red hair roots framed a broad forehead of Bretagne ancestors. Two boyish eyebrows with a bit of pluck had thinned to proper female Celtic crescents. A hint of a scar above the right eyelid ratified her childhood riskiness. She scanned from the piercing black pupils across her blue star iris to her violet rims; the wide white circles signaled her observant nature. From a thin Nordic bridge, an almost aquiline nose tipped up, lightening her measured smile. Above the slight dimple point of the chin, lips drew full pink bows. Her elvish ears were naked to the world and accentuated an almost square masculine jaw. Two vocal muscles traveled to the tender v of her collarbone. Her fresh-scrubbed skin, the prize of young Aquitaine females, glowed like a fresh-cut white Anjou peach.

The collar and gown were infused with lemony frankincense; her own fragrance insinuated earthy sage and wild honey. All eighteen dress gowns in her wardrobe matched her physique perfectly. Freshly threaded, they were renewed in spring and fall. She fit well into number nineteen, a cream-lemon silk embroidered Damask gown, sent from Antioch by her Uncle Raymond.

A bell pealed as she pulled up a perfect posture, shoulders set back, pronouncing distinct femininity.

In 1137, the conventional model for a girl in the teen of her age was to be docile, blindingly obedient, reverentially still as a coffin. The little, gowned adult, no better than its parent, was grateful to be that way.

Then there was this teen-of-age Princess of Aquitaine. Snappy in style, sharp and sure of voice, assertive in mind, she had a readiness to play any game, many of her making. The Princess was forming her own code of manners, as glad to learn a lesson as to give one. Her sexuality was unapologizing, challenging, and proud. Because she was honest, her teases could be infinite. At times, her vibrancy and daring gave to a forceful temper, easily angered by a world that could not keep up with her.

The comb began at the crown of the head. The wide teeth traveled to her shoulder, then finely to the ends. "mmm, love that." By her code, pleasure received must be acknowledged; it brought better stroking. What most damisels wore as flat, Eleanor often styled in ringlets, serpentine tresses, or up in a reveal of her neck. Today, she would proffer a fullness of long waves, set last night in flaxen towels. Disciplined unturning sleep was the noble price of beauty. The Princess listened to the crackle of comb, well aware of her nature and what was said of her.

She knew how to look, and she knew how she felt. Her mindfulness – noted by knights, visiting scholars, and suitors – was made greater by her uncanny ability to read hearts. With quirky bravado, often preceded by a joke or a tease, after a few guesses, she knew both your doldrums and desires. Such intuitive skill gave Eleanor an aura of calm clairvoyance. That is when she was not being vainly desirable or sulking, cross at the world.

A bell pealed in the distance announcing: come witness.

Her growing entourage, the long train of young women, for which Eleanor would become famous, was based on ritual friendship, accepted in stages. The number of circles testified to her winning manner.

To claim that her amplified youth attracted a burgeoning court would entirely miss the greater cause of her popularity – the wretched state of humanity, a society in fault of its ills. A surprising number of women escaped a world of abuse. Without a childhood, such girls suffered horrible bouts with their clans. As if teenage awkwardness were not enough, fathers made fun of their pubescence. Mothers kept quiet or were beaten to keep the 'harmony of the house.' Made to feel disgust and horror of their monthly purges, the girls were assaulted, accused of lustful attraction. The official church was no friend. Clergy were alarmed by the sign of the unclean devil's illness absolved females monthly from Eve's curse, the original sin. Doomed to a life of permanent guilt and suffering, the weak sex was said to be lesser than men – females were made to feel like grave dirt.

Eleanor and her court confronted cruel beliefs and led by counterexample. She showed bravery and humor in sharing the same transformation happening to her body as her other pubescent women. To keep the simple peace, Eleanor supported the steadfast mission of Fontevrault Abbey, providing sanctuary for runaways. Such youth first received fair love and felt safe – away from prying church confessionals, away from unwanted advances of relatives. Her staunch inner circle interpreted scripture differently and provided alternate spiritual guidance. Calbi and Daena gave great hope in their burgeoning faith where men and women were two shells of equal spirit. In the people's church, whereas heartless men drew blood in combat to kill, women endured monthly blood to give life and needed absolution, However to advanced minds like Abelard superfluous humours made females superior.

"Love that," she said as Amira stroked down.

As Eleanor's generation turned teen, their generation separated from the prior ones that theologically abused females, where graven men assumed misogyny was a way of life. They had no place for women. Of violence upon females, her father Duke William administered stern warnings to fathers to leave beaten wives, daughters, and nieces be. Violent incest was a serious problem, and in this, he worked with known faiths. At times, church elders mishandled young women coming of age. Sadly, Catholic clergy could not be corrected for they answered to no court.

Eleanor's young culture was pure. Court troubadours voiced love's appeal and celebrated men and women who showed the possibility for love. Trobaritz Mirielle sang of a woman's heart in glissandos in the forests of Fontevrault – an Eden orchestra, a secret garden chorus. Eleanor's women evolved as she from the smallest care to cultural identity. She taught women her daily routine – bathe thoroughly, wash your face in a hundred small circles, rag out your mouth, brush your hair a hundred times. She groomed them for sentience and sapience, ability, and supported a firm sexual identity. With wealth behind her fresh ideas, the Aquitaine showed every promise of becoming a stimulating court. In time, such confident females would become the most prized women in the world.

"Eleanor!" cried from outside. Today was the momentous day to celebrate her promise. Her resilient hair glistened with every lengthening brush. "I adore your care, Amira, never let me forget this day." Music floated with murmurs of followers in the courtyard. The birdsong trees rustled to and fro with vigor. Birds called sharply, making love in March flight, bringing laughter to the busy salon.

In the somber distance bells rang.

The brush-through now called for a dab of preen oil. Amira applied the bird's feather-strengthening gift lightly. She let William stroke his daughter's long hair. He stroked from head to floor. The fine comb ran clean and clear.

"You treat me like I am a horse on parade." Eleanor turned her neck playfully.
"Don't you know that? You are the prettiest mare ever."

Eleanor looked sidelong over her shoulder. "Crowncrabs."

William laughed, "Crowncrabs?" He set the comb down. "That's been a while." He moved the stool around to the front. "You wore my crown in play."

"I wore it around my neck." Eleanor gestured, making him laugh.

"Eleanor, you know I made up that affliction. Admonish privilege! Now, I owe some restitution after such a hair-tangling horse ride." Amira offered a bristled brush. William applied a counter tease to full the hair, and then long rolling strokes. The red-gold flowed with the endless charge of life.

"Love that too," Eleanor said as her father stroked down.

The last time Eleanor was this happy was with the same smell of leather, horse, and clover when he read to her as they first progressed the Aquitaine. He brought ancient history to her stylish life through his controversial views that were solidly hers now. When she reported that Catholic teachers said Rome fell because of silly gods and foolish rituals, her father made a wry remark about history repeating. To him, Rome was built on the ruthless succession of murderers. Why continue to repeat the bad habits of past times? William knew an unwritten history of Aquitaine Franks. His ancestors, like the Greeks – his favorite civilization of the past – were a conquered people made slaves by the Romans. True Franks wore their hair long to oppose Romans Catholics who cut their hair short, nearly bald in tonsures; women clipped theirs to the mid of neck. Father concluded: 'Style is important to history.'

William finished brushing. "You make your ancestors proud with your hair to your ankles." He held the bristle-brush before her face and smiled sardonically. "Let's fashion this tool into your hair, right here for the bishop to see." Sporting a game of snatch-the-brush, he put it down and gave a deep, serious look. "Sweetheart." Her heart melted hearing her favorite name. They both understood the importance of the day and the hundreds coming to see her. He crossed his arms, proud of her potential. Amira resumed combing.

"Eleanor, you have the makings of a first-rate court. Grandfather William became ruler of Aquitaine at fifteen. For thirteen and beautiful, you look ready."

"I feel ready."

"Do you now? You sound confident."

"I am!" She said offhandedly. "I was talking with Dangerossa."

"Yes, how is the grand amoureuse?"

"Don't you think she is beautiful? When I become her age, I hope to be as pretty. Why do women and men let themselves go?"

"Spark, you get to choose the elder you want to become."

"Hm. Grand-mère was giving advice on that thing that keeps you young, you know." William listened open-minded to whatever risqué thing would come.

With the hundredth stroke complete, Amira set the comb down and tended errant hairs. Loudly, bells pealed.

William admired Amira; his daughter was in good hands. "Spark, I look forward to my pilgrimage to Spain. I will leave this evening; the moonstar sky will be clear. Abbot Bernard says that praying in Compostella will make up for our contentions, now that his Pope is in place. Louis our King requires such penance before even thinking of sending his son to meet you."

Eleanor knew she should be smiling, but for the thought of suitors. With a sable brush and powder, Amira smoothed the skin, eradicating minor blemishes.

He said richly, "Most damisels are bargained off by their fathers to some rich geezering hag-maker. I have seen that higher ranks of suitors bid for your hand. It will be your marriage, not mine; I want you to know that. Your heart will have some say about the man we find. Yes, we. It may take a few years, but you will receive a promise crown today as Duchess. That should shorten things. The King's son wears one." Amira twistled a fine-burred rose stem to redden the lips. "The Crown Prince of the Franks might well pay a visit to a Crown Duchess of Aquitaine. Of course, you'd have to pray more, wear only long gray gowns, and obey, obey, obey." He smiled, knowing her response.

"Father, you jest. I hate that in suitors." Amira lined the eyebrows.

"The King feels somewhat the same way. He admits your troubadours might do his over-prayerful son some good. Favor the Prince with a promising song or uhb, one of your letters of affection. You know, Aquitaine will grow by you now. You will create the next William."

"Crowncrabs!" Eleanor rebuffed. She contemplated her lineage and dread her soon-to-come role in motherhood. Damisels her age already had infants by wandering men. To be fox-fooled and let your clothes be tricked off, had they no will to create? "Father, when you are in Spain, find a bride. Make that William yourself." Dutifully Amira cleaned the ears with scented swabs.

"You know Aenor was my only. I'll be back in a moment."

Eleanor shared his smile. It was mostly true. After mother died, father once called on a noble woman of Limoges-sur-Vienne who was said to have born his child. The Citadel refused his visit. Father did not believe in taking her the way grandfather would have. Was that being strong or weak? William never had affairs when Aenor lived because he vividly recalled his mother Phillipa's tears. Father despised his grandfather's unfaithfulness capturing Dangerossa and installing her in a palace tower in the sight of his mother. William hated him and willed never to be unfaithful. How could parents be untrue and not consider how their children felt? Bending the family tree was a scar written deep in Eleanor's heart; she would never make that mistake. She had let Arno's crush be short. Why couldn't adults make love with clothes on, as she? Child-making and lovemaking were clearly different. Eleanor calmed to fair-mindedness. Was her mother exciting? Eleanor never thought so; not like Dangerossa. Both women loved. Deep in Eleanor's hold was love – big enough for her half-brother Will if he was actually spawned by father and this woman from Limoges, a boy she had yet to meet. Why didn't father remarry, and was he Will's father? It was not the time to ask.

Amira said, "Your ears are almost perfect, I will return with the jewelry."

Eleanor stood up to stretch. It struck her that her parents had no ambition to search for love beyond cousins and neighbors. Like Cercamon, she wanted to search the world. *I will simply be better than my parentage.*

William returned, hands behind his back. She said sharply. "Father, I promise three things! I'll not marry a cousin, all my births will be church-cross true, and my first will be called William." Surely he understood her declarations.

"Aquitaine river-blood surely runs in those veins. William would be a strange name for a girl." They shared a laugh. She batted down her temper.

Tu-tah, a first trumpet blared. It was almost her time. Amira entered.

Duke William produced his daughter's golden crown. "Eleanor, you'll see, when this gold is set on your head, you will feel different, and you should. I rarely wear mine in public. A crown is ostentatious. People should discern you by their lief and liege to the majesty of your character, not by a bar of gold on your head. Pitiful is the young crown on a high horse instilling fear, demanding favors. You've seen this, haven't you? Loyalty earned eye to eye brings forth virtuous deeds. With crown and vestment, you will be far more. Let me lay out our social obligations. When a person bows, never think your rank better. Did you deserve that bow? When you are called majesty, highness, grace, or noblesse, did your action truly earn that title, or is it usual flattery? Privilege, when properly used, accesses further plateaus of noble character. These are rare views of crown nobility, and as you are a forward-looking woman, I hope you will look back on what I have said."

Amira said, "I'll not let her forget." *Tu-tah, tu-tah,* trumpets blared.

He held the glittering circle high. "It is time to fit the crown." Amira fastened earrings, gems she found of pure Merovingian crystal caged in gold she afforded, and crafted by Mathieu. Eleanor leveled her head to balance the clear crystals. The lashes of her eyes opened wide. Coming into view in her perfect mirror was the Aquitaine coronet. The thin circle that rested on her mother slowly landed on the sheen of her blonde-carmine. The sighs in the room, she felt inside. "How powerful is the visage of beauty and promise beheld in one's self.

"The coronet brings out your golden edges," Amira said. After a minute, she lifted it and set it aside, then shaped the hair slightly. "It fits."

❖

The Basilica of Montierneuf was built by Duke William's lineage. Outdoor on the platform steps toward the Palace, he regarded the high box of the church where his daughter would appear with the ancestral title of Crown Duchess to promise eventual rule. The Duke reserved the full title of Duchess for a venerable wife; he was thirty-eight and able to remarry. Mixed bells clanged city-wide. *Tu-tu-tu-tu, Taa-taa-taa-taa*, a cavalry horn trumpeted.

William stood on the platform, clean-shaven, long hair well-combed. He looked grand in his cream-white and rich blue leather tunic, embroidered in silver wheat and circular water patterns. The Duke rested his fine gloved hand on his hilt, his face registering many emotions. He surveyed his people as they filled the outer yard on the half-cloudy day.

A deacon on stage mustered the hushing crowd. "Hear and heed! Aquitaine, Lord William the Tenth speaks for all to hear and vassals to answer in fealty."

William boomed, gesturing dramatically with deliberate diction:

"A Holy Pilgrimage to Spain, I vow to take! Who rules should I not return?"

"No Lord! Speak of life!"

Scattered heartfelt responses were gratifying, but he had to appeal to all.

"While I am away in Spain .. to travel on a Holy Pilgrimage .. or to find a new bride." The courtyard laughed at his lightness of this important day.

"My son, my wife are lost by the pox. Hear my will. The heart of this court, you ken. With me, she has progressed through your villages and ruled." He gestured to the green and white flower high balcony.

"Our Crown Duchess! Eleanor of Poitou! Eleanor of Aquitaine!"

Her young arm broke from the balcony trellis greenery. Out of respect, rows of people bowed as the little hand waved.

His glowing daughter came forward in sun-bathed virgin-white and lustrous gold. A choke came to William. During cheers, he took water to clear his throat.

"Be Good to Her! Or Eleanor may preside in court with her l-ov-e."

Cheers filled the yard at his levity. Everyone knew how she expressed herself in hearings in her unpredictable, heartfelt way that achieved rightful justice. William emphatically motioned with his arms, opening his hands in a calming please-listen gesture. The courtyard stilled in hushes.

"Vassals. I ask your Lief again for this Liege of our lands .. which shall be ours and our children's. Honor to them, as your ancestors honored you. Vassals. Kneel to your Crown Duchess, Eleanor of Aquitaine." Vassals in their colorful auquetons gave the powerful kneel in homage. "Protect her .. for she will protect our realm. Holy Bishop, we beseech your highest blessing." Everyone showed some form of respect – hats off, a nod, a curtsy.

Young, vital Eleanor shimmered lemon-white in her Damask gown. Her heart was in her throat, feeling the power of such allegiance. The gloved hands of the Bishop of Poitiers gently raised the Coronet to his lips. When the diadem aureola contacted her ruby-gold head, the crowd stirred. The Bishop raised a hand-held cross and gave a Latin blessing. Coming forward in the high garden box, the Princess poured her light into the courtyard. A priest raised a large crucifix. The thousands signed the shape over their hearts.

Duke William drew his sword over the courtyard and boomed:

"I must hear from my vassals. Your Lord asks you to swear truly! Not like the shabby English to Henri." A hail of humor passed. Allegiant cries filled the sky.

"Those Lords oathed to obey! A will! To a rightful heir! To break an oath before the Lord, is that right? Here in Aquitaine, an English slave spoke out to honor a family's will in Chauvigny, still on your lips I'll wager! Tell me, does Aquitaine not have a voice?"

"—AOI" filled the air, even women nursing children at the fountain hailed.

William raised his sword straight to the sky. "Vassals of This Aquitaine from Bordeaux to Poitiers! Will your lief and liege! To the Crown Duchess of Aquitaine .. Princess Eleanor .. to Aquitaine law! Witness, what we do by cross above and sword below." He downcast his sword; a cross raised high. In ritual, each vassal clan showed individual gestures of allegiance, homage, and strength, no two alike. Hand grasps, fists to shoulders, chest strikes, arm hails – unique signs of each clan, formed to allegiance. Kneeling knights like Arno, Calbi, Armstrong made blood vows, a sliced hand to chest. Eleanor put her hand to her hard beating heart, overwhelmed to receive such charge of trust.

William led; his vassals echoed. "I affirm by God .. I pledge my lief and liege .. to Princess Eleanor! Upholder of Aquitaine law!"

"So the Almighty will hear! Roar you lions!"

The vassal tribes affirmed their almighty lief and liege to Princess Eleanor.

The Duke bellowed: "That is a vow!" He reached wide addressing the serfs. "Heed your liege lords, respect their liege, honor Princess Eleanor." William signaled the Bishop of Poitiers. The miter tipped forward declaring "Witness our will, Lord God." He kissed the cross, as did the Eleanor.

William commanded, "Arise and act as you have willed! Honor the ways of Aquitaine!" He held his hands high, the crowd returned gestures of solidarity, hails, and praises to the Duke and the Crown Duchess.

Petronilla hugged her Liege sister in her box and led Eleanor to a token court in the great hall for fealty congratulations. Eleanor summoned a platform realizing she was young and short. For the next hour, and unique to her early court, she exchanged a bise without a bow.

. . .

Life's patterns returned to normal as carpenters sporadically pounded and moved lumber to change the fealty court into a platform for the evening celebration. Troubadours rehearsed for Eleanor's promise dance. Music colored the feast-smelling air. The sun fell into the golden clouds of the western sky.

Enlivened Eleanor bounced about the ancestral dining hall. It spoke of many past times with family and friends. On a stone wall, shields were set, and a rack of lances stood with streamers of every clan. Across other walls hung vibrant tapestries of the hunt, mills and river lore. Placed on mantels were silver goblets, a rock crystal vase, and family relics. Gifts for Eleanor fanned out – elaborate flower displays, specially bound books, rich clothing. She touched a new colorful dress from Bayeux, illustrating Aquitaine castles. On this day of days, the Crown Duchess felt history within her, especially as she stood before the long family tapestry map of the world, hung when father married. Many had stood before its places, to tell the origins of castle-cities, the history of the Williams, the great adventures of The Conquest, The Crusade. Mathieu had said the geometries were wrong, and Eleanor chuckled. She pulled a blossomed dogwood branch from a large vase. Playfully she painted the grand tapestry, batting a few outlying frays.

William entered the room in thought. "How was the ceremony?"

Eleanor grinned, turning her dogwood branch. "I could barely keep my stomach from turning to water. A crown sure keeps your head straight."

"As it should." William drifted to the armaments rack. "I was thinking of the family. Take this Norman shield, rounded at the top, pointed at the bottom. Two cross bands of strength, its only design. Those clan streamers you can hardly tell them apart. What heralds the Aquitaine?"

Eleanor pranced with the flowered branch and took the shield from him and mocked: "Love! Imagine grandfather in combat. Painted on his shield is his naked lover. He says, 'In bed, or in battle, I bare your arms.'" Eleanor lunged and jabbed with the branch. In her stiff lemon coronation gown, she teased, "Come at me! Aye! Try to take Dangerossa from me. To arms! To arms!"

Her father dodged. "I have two arms!" He darted to seize her shield and tickled her pink. "You dare play with family memories, tauntress." Out of breath, she surrendered. She picked up her flower stick and settled. She simmered to listen, tapping his shield. Her eyes sparkled.

"You know, he loved her deeply. He drew Dangerossa on his heretical shield like a Greek myth. Yet her naked ideal lived on through his victories and defeats." William spun the shield and stood it back in the armaments mount. "Wouldn't that be some heraldry? Fierce warriors charge with images of nude lovers on their shields. 'Brother, that woman is naked, look away! Ugh, I am slain.' Might work. Knights in love, I can just see that." William laughed to himself, but Eleanor saw nothing but merit in the notion; it was the entire idea of the Viking circle defense.

"He left my mother, devout Phillipa, may she rest in peace. The Holy Church excommunicated his soul. I pray for him now. How I hated his infidelity to her. At first, I did not understand vitality. The church despised his passionate love for Dangerossa, even though he took the cross. His Crusade army was cut down by Turks in Outremer, yet he returned to find his greatest love."

"What does the stupid church know of love," Eleanor said triumphantly.

William stepped forward and grasped his daughter's shoulders firmly.

"Dear, think before your voice rules! Never doubt a man's faith. Of love, beware its true power. Respect the Church, Eleanor. My brother Raymond rules Antioch by their grace," he admonished taking Eleanor's hand to the Crusade end of the tapestry, tapping it on the Citadel, "by their grace." William calmed.

"Eleanor, do not blurt out what is on your mind. A girl does that. A woman thinks. Thinking is not what is on your mind just now – a voice bubbling to speak. Thinking takes those few moments longer. Think, my dear. Summon your mind, then speak fortified by thought." He held out his understanding arms. In the rumpled hug of his tunic, Eleanor peered at the woven Antioch depicted with grapes, river barges, pillared Roman temples, statues, lutes, and crosses. *Grandfather arrived here after barely surviving a mountain battle.* Heedful, she walked over and picked up her grandfather's songbook. Like a talisman, the book had a power within that made her want to sing. She lay the book on the table, her finger held on a line, her other hand brushing back her temple hairs. She came to a conception and looked up to her father.

"Grandfather returned from war, singing love songs. How can that be?"

"War is black-hearted murder. Better emotions keep the mind purposeful. Heartfelt experiences change you . . ." William was about to amend his thought when Eleanor ran a river of words:

"Killing and blood are things faith can forgive, but a man goes mad without love. This is in his song! A code centered in love within chivalry can restore vitality." She traced the fine white carvings on the book cover with her fingers.

William wanted to laugh, but when he thought to correct her, there was such charm in his daughter's ideas in blossom. It was not the right moment. "When I return from Compostella, I will tell you the seasoned truth. Today is your day. Just be." Glowing as he pet her head, Eleanor hugged the cover.

The songbook opened to the middle stitched pages, as freshly bound volumes do, filled with red and black inked notes of songs; lyrics penned under the bars. Eleanor stretched out on a pillowed bench, feeling the horn cover as she read. Holding it in one hand, the other stretched long over her head; she appeared like a colorful statue. Amused by the saucy words the girl turned a page and rolled her palm across the clean sheets. As her silver bracelets jingled, she sensed a discovery. She said, "His notes of love. This is the new code. It is all in my hands."

William thought of the imperfect man that Eleanor idolized. "Understand, The Crusade ended Holy fighting for all time. It was already over when your foolhardy grandfather came late with a small army. Without the protection of his liege, he lost everything, almost his life."

"Hmm. A King's Crusade army could march like Alexander the Great with 100,000 men. We would be invincible!"

"Not even Kings marched in the Holy War, much less a woman."

"Just liege lords?" Eleanor closed the songbook and hugged the cover, shaking her head. "How ignoble of the king."

William sat on the table edge, hands running his thighs. "From bad chances, good things came. When King and Church saw the price William paid, they granted a franchise to build Fontevrault." He gestured to her book. "Your contests of troubadour songs honor him. Psalm-singers will never understand warrior passions. To most, his naked songs are vulgar, silly, and heretical. Yet, these outlawed songs were his salvation. His heart was his life. He was driven." William pulled the gold crucifix on his chest. "He was happy when you were born."

"Father, I don't care where I was born. Where was I created?"

"Need the Duke!" came a call from outside.

"I have to go – final preparations. Arno and Calbi are traveling with me to Belin. Halfway from Bordeaux to the beach is where your mother and I created you. We couldn't wait for the shore. Aenor was lusty making you. That should make you happy. So what are we going to do with all of these suitors?"

"You brought them, even though you know I idolize young chevaliers. Since I am not to offend anyone to enlarge the court, to every man I will show my love."

He was fairly sure she was joking, but the way she intoned, 'love,' pulled on his heart. This love he cherished for her would go to another man. He held his daughter, knowing it was time to go. She looked up to him.

"Say it please."

He knew the word. Her eyes glistened. "Sweetheart." She smiled. "Eleanor here is an irony. I travel to Spain, the furthest point in the world from the Holy Lands, to worship the bones of a Saint who never lived there, not unless you know a horse with wings bound for Galilee? Enjoy your promise dance. Tell me all about it when I return." He wagged a mock finger of threat. "One day, a real coronation."

"Farewell" "—Farewell." A kiss, a long hug, a be safe, and he was gone.

Eleanor connected her champion thoughts. Grandfather's songs of unbridled passion for women cured his war heart. She felt like her roaming soul was given a key. Desire drove life, still yet, another form of love. She pictured the new breed of men who sang personal songs. William the Troubadour led Prince Jaufre Rudel. Their voices trumpeted orders to kill and gave words of vivacious personal love. William would live on, not by deed of sword, but through love of song that would become a new form of love song – reborn in the heart of new hearts. Holy fighting was over for all time. It would be her generation of peace to make songs dance with musical passion. How hot was luck – to live at the birth of music, – a time of no war. Her privilege was to sponsor a personal music: bawdy yet spiritual, youthful yet wise. She would inspire Rudel, Cercamon, and more. Outside, strings in the hall sounded the tuning moment of beginnings. Sirq clapped out a new dance for the court. Voices of a gathering crowd loudened. Eleanor jumped downstairs for Amira to make her up.

Petronilla sat squarely before Amira. She frowned as Eleanor descended in her yellow inauguration gown. Big sister wanted to be out there. A sisterly stall: "Amira, avail me to more preening oil."

Eleanor abided. "Improving your charm? Oh, the world I will make. When father returns for Poitiers fall court, the Aquitaine invasion will be in full force. Ellen can franchise stages, and we will launch troubadour tours all over Europa. Love song will conquer all." Amira smirked and shook a mocking head.

Petronilla scolded, "Sister has too much pride."

Amira finished tending. "Petronilla, by Eleanor's will, things usually came into being. A lesson there." Leaving the chair, Petronilla flaunted her neck, showing her sister's favorite clear earrings. Eleanor seemed not to notice, pulling off the regal gown. In her linen chemise, she through herself to the chair.

After combing Eleanor's hair Amira and Petronilla plaited an elaborate braid to form a crown, sharing glances in the mirror. While twistling lips with the rose burr, Eleanor thought of her style. Music swelled outside. The counselor set her ears in moon-pearls saying, "Father William is barely on travel and the castle resounds with party tempos with all the mmm of men. Sirq dances with roving courtiers, your party will become wild."

"Count on that!" Eleanor danced in her chair, looking squarely at Amira.

"You are tapping your foot."

"Can't help the beat. More to sing of now. More singers too. I'll bring back the interesting ones."

"Eleanor, this is your promise dance. Ellen will chaperone."

"Well, maybe. She trusts you, Amira."

"Crowncrabs Eleanor, I don't trust me. Not with what's going on out there."

"Amira, I have this idea."

"I smell wood burning–"

"No witchcraft jokes. Let's have that new Bayeux red stitch dress with the picture of every Aquitaine castle. I may not be able to love them all, but I will dance with every Prince." Eleanor raised her arms overhead.

Amira flowed on the colorful new dress.

"Petronilla darling, you are wearing my coronation earrings. Let's try them on." Begrudgingly, her sister obliged. Amira set them. The dazzling visage in the mirror was complete, her lips apart barely showed teeth. Her lower lip thrust and cleft as if in the act of saying, 'Live.'

Amira and Petronilla shared the beautiful moment.

"Oc sister, I've changed my mind. You may wear them. My ears want to be naked. I want easy whispers." Eleanor and Amira bedecked Petronilla's ears, and with a quick bise, Eleanor raced off.

It was becoming night, and it was very hot.

〰

Lady in the Lake

Eleanor was panting. Over sunlit branches hung her fine embroidered dress. Rich red Bayeux stitch-squares defined Aquitaine castles, towers, steeples, walls, flora and fauna depicting every colorful region. Within the redlined castles were sewn threaded figures, though no couples were kissing. From a distance, the shaking dress looked pink. Since promise night three weeks ago, by order of steward Ellen, the dress's owner had to be in the sight of guards at all times.

In the privacy of white dog-rose buds, Amira, her face equally flush and out of breath, hands on knees said: "It was fun to catch the guards dozing and tear out." Out of breath, Eleanor teased her maid, "I have worn that dress enough. Now I want to be naked." She raised her arms overhead. "Take my chemise off." With finality Amira said, "The shift stays on!" then left to tend their snorting horses, waving up the hard following guards. Courtiers were not permitted here.

It was an April midday in 1137. The familiar spring-fed lake southeast of Fontevrault gave a reflecting view of the Abbey, begging to be remembered.

The breathless princess of thirteen summers hurried through the bushes in her shift. Since father left on pilgrimage nearly a month ago, she came to swim a daily routine. Eleanor had done everything with her court she pleased, within the bounds of Ellen. The steward would arrive by next bell with corrections, certainly for dashing away from the guard. *No harm done.*

The dusty damisel took it all in. This day could last a hundred years in her mind. Clouds played out the light of the sun. Shafts rolled through branches across the lake on the rippling surface of distant bathers. Perhaps she and her court would travel to lands where every day was like today or better. Who knew the world? Real places were often more surprising than her imagination. *I will conquer the world in my time and lead with my Alexander.* Everything felt potent and possible.

She stepped to the ledge rocks overlooking the scene. Fontevrists Berry and Guisana performed water purification rites, as they called them. She had not talked with the couple for years. The lake-water looked clear and cool. The air was heady and hot, and Aquitaine adventures lay ahead. She was in a fever to jump in and wake the water.

<Splash!>

Diving deep into the cooling spring, she felt her loose gown rippling, the dust from the road washed away. Still feeling the pounding drive of her horse, the strong swimmer pulled herself ahead. Her physique pulled the drag of the heavy shift. She wished it the skintight body hosiery of dancing Sirq, or nothing at all. Muscling through the clear water, she swam upward. She broke into the air, blustering a spray, blinking open the thick forest trees circling the lake.

Chestnut Limona stirred with arriving horses. The guards had caught up and posted themselves along the bank. They removed their hot helmets, perturbed at having to give chase. With their task to route potential onlookers, the guards were the criminals of the hour. Watching the lady in the lake, one of the new female guards said to Amira, "A hard charge you gave us just now." Amira said what was on all their minds, "Look at her swim, probably lost in one of her dreams that we all wished we were in."

Arno. A handsome squire of sixteen. The bodyguard volunteered to lead the hard-to-find female guards. One wondered who would be in charge if any order were given. He wore his handsome tunic full as if it were his chest; a very different boy from the one who bragged of the one girl he kissed. He only spoke of Reyna, and only if asked. Only he and Eleanor knew of one more.

Armstrong. Eighteen when they met, the magic year of men for a damisel. At the knights' stable in Poitiers, she teased the Alsatian to learn her code of chivalry. Somewhat serving of her hopes to be near him, honor and conscience did make the better man. He needed no orders; he knew what to do. The valiant captain in armor had made Reyna's horsehair belt, a forward-thinking chevalier.

Mathieu. Smart, brilliant eyes, adventurous. Her tall friend made a beautiful mirror and set her clear earrings. Maryam wore his belt. They'd met once before in Perigaux. Mathieu hoped to leave for Paris to apprentice building the new cathedral at Saint-Denis. He invented a winepress to make red wine richer and brought a La Rochelle wine to the promise dance.

Chevaliers. Eleanor loved them all. She had some knack to shape them for the better. She'd never forget Armstrong and Arno who gave her a surprise picnic. Armstrong brought a spicy wine grown from Primitivo vines found on the pilgrim trail high in the Croat plains. 'What a woman does not ask for, strikes the best memory.' Armstrong's voluptuous woman had devilish jokes about men as playthings. Love was so easily in her reach, yet she seemed not to understand Rudel's ethereal poem-songs, not like Eleanor.

Troubadours. Cercamon long ago, nuzzling her ear in a game, "silver signs..." His invocation to 'search the world,' became part of her chain of being. Chevaliers serenaded their pleasant longing, with catching songs learned in Blaye from Jaufre Rudel, a master poet of the most sensitive imagination; what hooked her? Was it male fingers, their lute, the singer's voice, the song itself, or the composer's idea? Like meeting famous Cercamon, she would surely meet Rudel someday.

Calbi and Danae. In his years of pranks and larks, Eleanor once danced nearly naked in the rain-chiming wind with him. He could not wait to make love, wanting to kiss Reyna, actually kissing Amira, but finding total love in Daena, now round with Calbi's first child. The two handsome blondes were meant for one another. If there were more women like Daena in the realm, hard-working, hard-loving. Amira cared for 'kissing Calbi.' They would have made a good couple. Keeping her maid busy, Eleanor saddened at her friend's missed chances to sample men. How good of Calbi to make Amira her horsehair belt, and how good of Daena to permit an intimate gift. In Calbi burned something deep, a sense for love, and always the right approach to it. Eleanor still thought of Arbrissel's test that they took together that night at the camp. Calbi was pure in heart like Francois, the manly monk visiting from the English-lands. She could pray with such men and not because she had to. The water felt cold as she swam casually. Eleanor felt the consummation of thought – every assay of life coming together rightfully, as Dangerossa said of supreme lovemaking. A splash of consideration to her unclever suitors with long titles from far citadels of the Continent. These castle sitters had no sense of accomplishment, no real ambition, no true spark. *So much arrogance fills a lake of toads.* She maintained her friendship with the feeble smilers, feebler hearts, by her father's wish. They were rude but not interestingly rude, like scholar Bruce. By now, Calbi and Arno would have passed the borders of Spain. What flame-flickering stories would her father share; what valorous deeds would cause these squires to be dubbed chevaliers by her father.

Father. This pilgrimage was to atone to Bernard. Eleanor knew father did this mainly for her. Father had given Eleanor's mind greater weights to lift. Everything was some right to property, and judging rightful assignment was not naturally evident – there were contradictions between the once earned and the continually claimed. The dilemmas of taxation and production, obligation, and free choice were maddening. In governing, she had to deduce elusive justice from principles. Father made her think about the cause of productivity. What was the first principle, happiness or love? She'd studied Amira's family. The rule of love prevailed. Then father's regal idea of creating a realm *to allow* radiant potentiality. Failing to see Berry and Guisana, Eleanor nearly crashed into them. Unable to wit their words, she smiled, pretending to know what was being talked about.

"Spring, oh day. So they say," Eleanor spouted lyrically, innocently paddling chest-deep, askew of the robed Fontevrault clergy.

Tonsured Berry, with an odd tuft of hair jutting from his left ear, looked at the writhing water creature. "Welcome to the speculations."

That was no help. Eleanor turned to attractive dark-haired Guisana and played further. "Speculations, yes?" The three bathers tread water equally.

Guisana said, "Grand Abbess de Chemillé bravely upholds the order for our men and women, but the days to oppose these mandates are numbered." Berry touched her and added: "Only at Fontevrault is measured love allowed. Elsewhere, orders are commanded by Rome for clergy not to marry, to deny life and never have children, to divide male from female. Yet, Bishops and Popes secretly have them. Hypocrites against God omnipotent."

Eleanor considered and responded, "There should never be hypocrisy. Not if love as a principle is a pillar of faith. Why ignore the greatest power in creation?"

"Exactly as I meant," the monk said. "Can one counsel a family without having family experience?" Guisana added: "One cannot be spiritual without knowing love. I am certainly the wiser for this, eh Elle?" Only Guisana called her Elle, a trusted name from their talks of making true love, long ago.

Eleanor tread water and looked to them. "I can see how Roman Nazarenes can improve themselves spiritually, yet I must be careful in my position. They could learn from you. What more speculations?"

Monk Berry was stern. "The Latins are a danger to the Nazarene faith. They are intolerant and rage against any holy word that is not their own. They want control over all worship, what we eat, how we love, when we wake as if people's souls were for the purpose of the church rather than the emancipation of spirit in knowing God."

"That's enough Berry," Guisana said firmly, seeing the upset in her friend.

"Yes, enough for now, please," Eleanor said. She could not afford to confirm in public she felt that way; that would be risky. The views with her father and Calbi were best kept confidential. Even for rightful speaking in support of Pope Anacletus, her father was publicly poisoned at Parthenay by an agent of Pope Innocent. Eleanor gave a light smile to be playful. She cupped and poured the lake water on her neck. Competing with Guisana the teaser, she fluttered her lashes with a slight pout of lips, all the while paddling underwater hard until Berry felt her waves, "Ahh, refreshing, do you love how water feels?"

Guisana swam to Eleanor's side and slinked her shoulders back. "Ahh yes, water is refreshingly pure, Elle. Enough to feel reborn as we are, in marital bliss." Eleanor slipped her head under the surface; their twitter dropped away. Such love was theirs, not hers. She shed her smirk for teasing teased Berry. Cleansing herself deeply, she surfaced with innocent sensuality. Genuine sexuality was respected by the Order of Fontevrault. If you showed no lewd intent, you abided trust. Fontevrists were schooled in the skill of balance and toleration. Eleanor avoided Guisana's looks and smiled innocently.

Berry put his back into swimming. The two women followed. Arriving in sunlit shallows, navel-height in water, confident in their wet appearances, Eleanor shifted in the sand to get a better footing, thinking nothing of her nippled chest.

"At Fontevrault, how do you find a woman's rule, Berry?"

"Females govern with measured authority. 'All men of the order are in the Abbesses service,' by Arbrissel's rule, set the year The Crusade captured Jerusalem."

"Fortune's year," Eleanor noted, wading into a full beam of sun. The codes of Fontevrault crisscrossed her mind in a flash. Service to love's authority could be a code of chivalry. Men could be made honorable, just as wayward Guisana was made honorable by love in join with her secret womanly charms. The excess of woman's lust for men was why Guisana became a nun; her mastery of it was why she had a husband and a family.

The three stood at arm's length from one another. Guisana said, "Elle, did you know Arbrissel slept in the midst of women to endure their nature?" Eleanor, knowing far more about this than anyone could imagine, cooly turned her gaze. She let Berry respond. He tread water with her and replied:

"One woman is enough for me to endure, thank you. Robert found a just balance, as you must in your courts. Tell us about your order of the world."

"Well, I am just at my teen and my world is definitely unbalanced. Worlds collide in our courts. Of a recent trial," she pushed a wave, casting rainbow colors on the river bottom, "the Crusade, long ago, took our men. Their women run the lands, often more wisely." Eleanor pushed a cross-wave watching how the colored waves interacted. "Crusaders return in waves, claiming with divine excuse the bounty of lands they never knew. Sins forgiven, war-pride and church-law conflict with Aquitaine family rights." The hypnotic color pattern of water rippled and swelled into blues that fell into chromatic whites. "I sense the color of every heart. I seek where radiant hearts overlap. I look for a resonance that best suits the land."

"A colorful court. Of love, fair Elle?" Guisana teased, knowing of her hobby.

"I come young; my father says, as an outsider to the courts with a fresh view of life. My confession is that I rule for the heart alone, not by canon or royal law. Love is our true bearing. That I seek first in measuring a person."

She was proposing an interesting state of affairs to be governed by. In the growing era of persecutions, Berry raised a brow to Guisana at the revelation. He removed a wet leaf that floated on her robe and put his hands with hers, in a house of four hands, the double-prayer of Fontevrault.

Being their ritual, Eleanor dove toward multiple glints of a silverish rock. Amira would like it. The underwater world moved in six roving ghostly sun shafts. She reached for the stone. Amira, it was a false alarm. Nothing to take. Per Bleddri's Welsh superstition, she closed her eyes to listen for the Lady of the Lake. 'Bury a sought for treasure, count four things or make a greater wish.' Her hair floated in a watery cloud over her arms; she expressed her wish in bubbles.

The couple prayed with their eyes open, looking down on her beautiful arms. Intertwining fingers, Berry intoned, "To be ruled by astute love." Guisana said, "To the Saint-souls of Arbrissel, Pierre De Bruys, the Henricans, the Catharics: may their rejuvenating ways prevail. Let all Christians in Christ, and Christendom be manifest." He answered, "To every of the faiths."

Eleanor surfaced, happy with her lief, uncertain of what lay ahead. Father would know. Nearby, two bobbing friends cupped water with their hands. Distant Amira folded her hands in thought. Male and female guards teased one another. Two cats in a tree pawed branches with careful curiosity. Butterflies lit on spring blossoms. Eleanor skin dipping, trapped lovely water in a lake.

Fontevrault's bell tower waited to ring; she knew the hours. The cusp of Eleanor's Aquitaine life was emerging. Floating along, she dipped her shoulders back. In sparkles of the amber sun, the chapel reflected. The Abbey improved all life. As a reward for her charity to Fontevrault, the orphans taught her their hand language, the silent signs, the double-round hi, the four-handed prayer. At its workshop, Mathieu made new machines. Its hospital cured beaten Edeva. Its school gave youth voice. Boisterous Berry and Guisana, side by side, took turns teetering one another. This was why Fontevrault was special. Family fit the progress of the Abbey, and even orphans were given a childhood like Eleanor and Amira. As long as the couple worked toward Fontevrault's spiritual mission, their child was blessed. Others like Abelard, Heloise, and their child had to fight and were denied a family. What was becoming of the Catholic? A faith of wrathful men. They tormented lovers and troubled convents of women as Loudun did just thirteen miles away. Arbrissel needed to be made a Saint – the Saint of gender's balance and possibility. Eleanor felt born to bring into her era new faith, ideas, inventions, music, and fashion. She knew not how; she simply would. Dangerossa and her father gave her a confident will.

Her red-gold mane floated around her, glistening. She lay in a halo of waves.

Distant Limona neighed, then stamped. Joining horses told Eleanor it was time to return. She was due to confer with Ellen and be chided about forsaking her guard and other rants. As much as Eleanor wanted to swim into her future sea of Aquitaine tranquility, she stroked backward to go 'learn.' Live and learn. Shives, when would she start living?

"Eleanor!" a troop of voices shouted from the banks.

"Eleanor!" "Eleanor!"

Piss on blood, what is it this time? Am I on the wrong side of the water? She could no longer pretend to be a mermaid. Backstroking toward them she thought, *those were stony calls.* She glanced back over her shoulder and turned quickly to a chest-paddle to take in the super-real scene.

Columns of dust loom from arriving horsemen. A ruckus of guards points to her. Amira disappears into teams of horses. Hard-blowing riders clopped forth that she has never seen. Frantic guards at the shoreline, dive in, toward her. Up on the bank, banners. The Fleur-de-lys flutter of the King of the Franks, the Waves of Aquitaine flow, and underlying, a black streamer.

A black streamer?

"Fish out that lady of the lake!" It is Father, but not father. A hard breathing warhorse emerges from a chaos of horses. It is Jofree de Rancon, Lord of Taillebourg, next to the armed Lord of Sanxay. Why? His castle is four days ride away. The towering chevalier clad in helm set for battle commands Arno, who releases the female guards who jump in to reach Eleanor. Their pilgrimage to Spain can not be over. Calbi is armed astride an anxious horse, speaks harshly with mounted Ellen. It must be war.

Female guards splash closest. Eleanor, swimming her strongest, ignores them and wades the waters to the bank. It is a madscape. Horses will not be calmed. Ellen talks frantically with Amira. Warriors face outward, closing ranks, ready in arms. They expect battle. Rising from the lake, Eleanor takes a few steps. Attendants run a fence of linen around her. Arno just outside. Amira, biting her lips, face white, lifts the wet slurry of a shift over her head, dries her not speaking, places her in a full chemise. She presses out her hair. Eleanor furiously wipes the last spring water from her ears, glancing at those trembling about. In silence, Amira urgently flows the red stitch dress on Eleanor, then a heavy traveling mantle. All men are protective of her, drawing steel to ready. Heart jumping, it comes to Eleanor, an army marches upon us; death is near. *Father must be in the rearguard fray. Something is wrong; for all look away, none wish to lock my eyes.*

Hurried up to the privy hedge are messengers, priests. Eleanor stands among the clang and chingle; sword hands are hot.

"Are we at war?" Hard faces. Sir Rancon the only tongue: "Eleanor! Danger and alert! Your father lives no more."

What is he saying so urgently?

The words. The black streamer. The force. No air. And then an awful stillness.

Amira gives a towel to wrench and rend. *First her mother, then her brother, now her father.* What curse is upon her providence?

"Oh, Eleanor!" Amira tried to sooth her fitful friend, but Eleanor would not be soothed. The thirteen-year-old exploded, shrieking like a convulsing child newborn to hell, flailing its flames. Wretchedly wailing, doubled over, Eleanor grasped for her handmaid. They fell like sisters in mighty cries and heaves. Ellen pinched tears away and stood by her ward. Sir Rancon rested his hand on Arno to shore up his protege's manly speech. "You were there." Arno swallowed to say:

"Can you bear up good lady? Will you hear me?"

She nodded through her towel.

"Rise and hear, Eleanor," Ellen shouldered her up to strengthen her.

Arno endured her gasps. He'd felt as much, days before, seeing the corpse.

"Three days have I driven horses from the ocean end of Spain. Never have I stopped since the devil-cursed pox laid Duke William low under a Castilian sky. Priests did it–" Arno halted himself, caught by Eleanor's look, her chin wrinkling with a press of lips. She exploded into a storm of tears, and her legs collapsed.

Prince Taillebourg could stand off no longer and spoke her tribal birth name. "Alienor, take heed." She glanced up, blinking. "By lief and liege to the Duke of Aquitaine, William gave final words to be known to you now. Aquitaine is yours alone. You are the Aquitaine now." He waited to see if she understood.

Eleanor's throat stopped. In terror, she could not breathe. Amira gave water and spoke for her friend, "Rancon, Aquitaine passes to Eleanor, and?" The tearstained princess took her counselor's hand to her heart.

Foreign priests lurched forward. "The King of the Franks is entreated to be your protectorate. You are to marry his son, Prince Louis, quickly."

Marry? Nothing is making sense. Shocked Eleanor stung deep, recoiled realizing that a thousand potentials all within her reach were suddenly gone.

"Woe no. No! NO!"

Rancon steadied his cousin with both arms. "Alienor, your father would warn, peril is high! Relatives will rise to contest a girl's rule. Warrior lords will march to claim Aquitaine. These men are no suitors. They will take you. Hateful men, the kind your father and I trouble with. Brutal armies will invade and claim your property. Take our escort now."

Somehow she was placed on Armstrong's large horse. A hand patted her knee. With no time lost, with no words in memory, her hair was knotted to ride, and she was holding onto a chevalier, galloping hot, the long road south.

The sky passed through twilight and fell to black. Amid heels, hooves, and spurrings she closed her wet eyes. She felt raw to her being. The wind cried Queen-sized tears from her face. *Marry.* Blurry-eyed to the capital she hugged the heat of armor. The Keep of Mirebeau went by darkly.

Summer night leaves blackened the unseen sky. Terrible trumpets blared the Maubergeonne. The tower loomed. In torchlight detail: the marble bastions, the footings, the rusty keys, the door creaking open, the hard rock steps, the arriving soldiers. "Make way!" Ablither, taken off the horse, the sobbing princess was escorted within. The bolts of the castle wall thundered shut. Dangerossa's high bed offered its out-of-place loveliness. In Poitiers with no family present, Eleanor was alone. Faceless guards and servants pled her to rest. Round turned the throw of the Maubergeonne key. She felt no security; she was shut off, small, facing night's candles. Pillow feathers cushioned her fall. Wet in a lake of tears, sleep tugged her eyelids. With hair unknotted, blankets drew over her; questions whirled in continuance: *What has become of the world, and what will father do when he returns from his journey?* And then the room flew away.

〰〰

The Wait in the Two Towers

Alarms filled the dark tower as the castle readied for assault. Archers climbed, and watchmen lit torches along the crenel walls. Nearby trees fell to chopping axes making sight-lines for arrow-fall. Boots numbered in regimented marching about the citadel. In the dead of night, barking guard dogs, laboring horses, and the endless grind of shovels joined a relentless hammering and ripsawing. Inside the sorrowful Maubergeonne fortification, in the middle of it all, grieved parentless young Eleanor engulfed in shades of black. Duke William's sudden departure from his pilgrim journey, his vigorous body buried afar, made his death seem unbelievable. The ghost of his being habited her mind. Whips cracked, cart wheels rumbled, workers murmured — shadowy fears formed of dangerously tainted food. Alone in the dark marble tower, Eleanor sobbed in bed. The long pillow she shaped to sleep with was her only friend.

At day, swirls of summer Ravens plucked serpentine worms from puddles. At night, the menace of thunder cracked as black rain fell. Suspicions in darkness surrounded the lonesome keep on long watch.

On her better days, it seemed father was not gone; he was asleep like she was asleep. On her worst nights, she slept fitfully in a whirlwind of dark fear. Her family had been blotted out. Candle shadows conjured ominous black slippery eels rumored to have poisoned him. Yet, father had survived what his wife and son had died from. He escaped the malice of poison pox in Parthenay. Careful of what he ingested, his death seemed out of place. Whom had he wronged? Was his death chance? Was it to get him out of the way? In the hell brought to earth, Eleanor had lost the will to know. In years not far ahead, a monk with detection skill would resolve such questions; she would mark his name well.

The specter of Duke William's death loomed large. By fealty oath, men-at-arms filled the ranks to protect the Princess. Lord Rancon of Taillebourg took command of the defense of Poitiers. By his order, men built spiked barricades, laid half-wall stones, and dug ramparts. Knights galloped to the forest edge repeatedly until they knew the number of paces to ward off raids. Able bodies practiced sword and shield. The military prepared.

Meanwhile, the practicalities. Ellen scrupulously taught Amira to taste Eleanor's food and drink, to secure trusted sources of supply – a steadfast task for the rest of her life. The will of William came under scrutiny. The words of priests were said to be his last; nothing was written. The apparent offering of Eleanor of Aquitaine into a distant marriage left the thirteen-year-old white-faced.

Atop the roof of the tower, she lay on her back to watch rain clouds roll forth. Under a big Spanish sky he died, unable to cry as she could. All her efforts to build a circle of followers, her friendships, the young men she had an eye on – the sum of her ambitions were now lifeless as a dream. She was another ghost for Aquitaines to forget. She was to go on a journey like her father and leave the land she loved, perhaps never to return. Dark clouds boomed followed by the rain of days and the mud of weeks.

It was drizzling again. By the rising blow of the wind, Amira knew harder rains would fall. The great Poitiers hall was a chaos of chairs, screens, rugs rolled up. Mud tracks covered the stone floor.

Ellen moved the pail forward. Together with Amira, they scrubbed and washed to take their minds off the worry of waiting.

Amira was at her wit's end. "What will bring Eleanor back, Ellen?"

"Do you know what ray of light, what an able loving father, has been taken from Eleanor and Petronilla? Black time will pass to blue, the sun will also rise, and Eleanor, child of the sun, will awake. Rest on this: she's not like other wealthy girls, pampered and told what to do. She is independent, self-possessed, and makes decisions herself. That is who will come back."

As rains fell, Poitevins speculated: would the King of France invade and carry forth this rumored marriage? Despite royal silence, the Mother Church of Paris had every interest in procuring Eleanor for their ends. So much so, they came up against their own bishops in a plot with relatives to rule prosperous Aquitaine.

Fickle-minded Ermengarde saw her chance. The first wife of grandfather William was a fervent Roman Catholic. She was known to run off in a foul temper, shut out the world, then return as if her absence never occurred. She felt God-sent to be declared the Duchess of Aquitaine as she once was. Confessing her claim through her bishops and allied lords, they presented canon writs. The Church of Paris had other plans. They admonished her clergy, then wrathfully sent Ermengarde on a pilgrimage to the Holy Lands. Being unquestioningly devout, she abided and was sent on her long way.

Unopposed, the purification of Eleanor was the top priority of the Parisii clergy. The God-fearing Angels of Paris descended on the innocent of thirteen – a born sinner of Mary's sorrowful gender. To reshape her wishes, to take control of her decisions, a guiding hand was needed to prod the pliable lamb. Father and mother swept aside, where was the challenge?

The problem with purification is purity. Aquitaine had a deep-rooted sense of it. A pure mind had a conscious will to act of one's moral volition. Cathar knights were devoted to such purity – the ones Eleanor was infatuated with. A key point of Poitevin purification was: truth mattered.

Purification in the Parisii Church was quite different. Truth, that is, the actual facts of reality, were as dispensable as incense smoke. What mattered was belief, blind obedience to the word, to the authority. To conform the soul of the lamb, stories were told to induce her doubt, her wretchedness, her guilt. In method purification, Eleanor proved a most difficult soul.

The thirteen-year-old was isolated from her court. Not even Amira could see her. She underwent a week of praying cycles: nuns to wake her in prayer, put her to sleep in prayer, sudden prayers at midnight; silence otherwise. After fifty masses, her father's absence loomed larger than when he lived. Except for one difference. There was little honor in his being; only a remorseful life recast in sins.

"Believe, child! Fear God child! On your knees! Believe in your shame of being a woman! Believe you and your sinful family were born evil! Believe your grandfather is in hell for living in sin with the damned Dangerossa! Believe your father is a blasphemer for his support of an Antipope! Believe God's miracle in Parthenay condemned him! Believe he never reached Compostella and his soul wanders unable to find purgatory!" All these sins can be absolved by regular Aquitaine treasury payments.

Eleanor withdrew to herself and knelt in subjugation, never confessing to her overseers that her father inhabited her dreams. Hands together, she let him illumine her mind. He gave advice and soothed her memory of Aquitaine ways, restoring her chain of being. The obstinate, young life would not be broken.

To get the reluctant soul to believe false things were true, they gave daily confession to confirm sins, making her repeat phrases until they were believed and her former life erased. Contempt for her lief and her sinful parents was replaced by a new father and mother with all the right answers. A white-robed superior nun said softly, "Call me Mother. Next confession Eleanor, tell The Father you believe." The thirteen-year summers girl resented, "I will not believe." After a course of slappings, and knowing she would be struck again, she said: "I will never call you mother, and he is not my father." After her 'purification,' Eleanor was confined to her room. Shouting everyone out of the Maubergeonne, Eleanor cried until she fell asleep.

Or so, she led them to believe.

Amira was replaced by obedient Parisian nuns. The former maid could only visit the tower bedroom to clean when Eleanor was taken away. Her unmade bed was a sight of misery. Twisted and knotted sheets formed the picture of tortured creatures left from a cruel night's sleep. Amira ran her palms to smooth out the wrinkles pressing the invisible force of her hands to help gentle Eleanor's coming night.

In the Palace dining hall, Ellen listened to Amira's fears.

"Eleanor could not bathe until she had been purified."

A Parisii Father marched into the hall, followed by a Mother Superior.

"Magistrate Ellen, our lamb Eleanor has vanished from her room. She has already missed second mass."

"From the Maubergeonne Keep? In your care? What will the King say?" Ellen said with great alarm to upset them, but knowing what happened. She took them to Eleanor's tower. Arno and Calbi searched the room for signs of her departure. Her hand mirror and crossbow were gone. Ellen noticed the significant detail but let Amira discover herself. The missing draw-rope.

Amira pointed. "She's up there."

Ellen explained to the Catholic clergy, "Apparently, Eleanor climbed to the upper level, pulled the ladder behind, and sealed the floor off." After pleas and holy incantations to the floor above, no reply came.

The Superior Mother lost control: "Counsel that obstinate crying brat!"

Ellen studied them, cooly. "She is in your keeping. What can I do?"

"Get her down from up there," the Father ordered.

"Down from up there?" Ellen echoed to let them express their intent. Amira admired her tempered skill as she stroked her chin.

The priest demanded, "What are we going to do about this!"

Ellen and Amira looked at one another. Giving no specific order, the authority was yielding control of the situation.

"Only Eleanor can let herself down," Ellen said. "The builder made the tower that way. Perhaps you can pray her down?"

"Don't blaspheme the power of prayer. Now do something."

Ellen let it cool. "Here is what We will do. We will talk to Princess Eleanor. I am sure you realize, she will not answer with you here. She can spy on us from up there."

"We've had enough of this know-it-all Princess," the Mother jeered. Amira held back a smirk. The priest vented, "We'll go. You get her down! By tonight!"

Ellen realized the churchmen had a timetable. "I have good news. I know just what to say, and you will have Eleanor, willingly. She will never do this again. Wait at Saint Marie's." As the clergy steamed away, Arno and Calbi held a vigil at the tower door. No one had seen Eleanor for a week. The ladder came down readily.

Ellen lay a steady arm on Amira. "It is good you are here. Now we can counsel properly. Steady the ladder." Ellen climbed up and off. As Amira climbed to follow, the steward's voice was shaky. "Amira, hold on a minute." Through silence came sobbing. Ellen sobbing. Amira bounded up the rungs.

The dim room had a small grated window on each wall. A dusty table fit with two chairs. Ellen and Eleanor embraced on a small bed. Ellen let go for Amira to see. Her beautiful friend had dark circles under her eyes, blister marks on the back of her hands. Ellen lifted the gown. The legs were striped red from caning. Amira bit her lip and ran to hold her friend. "Are you all right?"

Eleanor was weary. "Do no weep. I am fine. I broke their rod over my knee."

Tinged with the girl's courage, Ellen began diplomatically, "You have sealed yourself in Dangerossa's tower. Yet, you have lowered the trap ladder to allow us up. May we leave it down? Arno and Calbi are guarding. I have made it so no priest will come."

"No one will get me to leave my tower!"

"And no one will. This tower is for a woman's protection. You control that."

Amira fret. Her young heroic friend, fatigued and beaten was showing her best hrad self, but she was the Crown Duchess, and this was her realm. She smelled bad, her clothes were filthy, her voice ached, the severe marks on her beauty made Amira erupt:

"It's not right! It's just not right!"

Ellen was firm. "Amira, tranquility. Are you Eleanor's counselor or not?" Amira muffled out an "it's just not right," and simmered. Ellen looked to Eleanor. "To see you marred. You have done nothing wrong."

"That's what I keep telling them!"

Encouraged by the twinge of Eleanor's pluck, Ellen proceeded as always, from the other person's view. "Tell us of your 'purification.'"

Eleanor recounted her torturous sleep deprivation; Ellen corrected, "— Pious devotion." Her social isolation; Ellen amended, "—Cloistered prayer." The prying and lie-telling that took place; "—Holy confessional." The forced days of starvation; "—Fervent fasting," Ellen minded. Then Eleanor spoke fast as a river, "I refuse to fear God. They said it was evil not to fear. They ordered me to obey and repent; they hated me!" Ellen minded, "They showed wrath, not hatred." – "What's the difference?" "—Nothing. Use proper words."

After venting, Eleanor admitted her secret comfort. "Father visited my dreams every night, reminding me, 'Aquitaine will not stay wealthy if you let anyone know where Aquitaine's wealth is kept. Only you and your progeny will know.' They tried to beat that out of me. I broke their Goddamned rod."

"Eleanor! Never say that again!"

"I will if they try and beat me again!"

"You are a difficult soul," Ellen summed. Amira was proud of her friend but worried about what to do. She studied the experienced steward.

"Prayer and beatings are my world now," Eleanor sighed. "I will never yield."

Ellen wagged her finger at Eleanor, but her voice was soothing:

"How are we going to get you out of this situation?"

Eleanor shrugged with listlessness.

"Duchess to be, what is your greatest concern?"

"The Roman church wants to take all of ur Aquitaine wealth."

"Surely not all. Specifically, how did the priests request it?"

"They want a sum of money for father's absolution. He never did wrong."

"Tell them the fee is too low."

"What?"

"The church does not show him enough honor."

"This is your council?"

"Unbroken Eleanor, heed me as you would your father. Ken the ways of the world. He told you about the high place the church has over its followers. Aquitaine has nine churches, and the one encamped here is the faith of your future husband. This, you cannot change."

"They say I have to believe horrid things about my family."

"I say this. Do not dwell. Gyre, free as the Falcon. She sees the field on high for what it is. When prey is spotted, she strikes the rat, but not until she hovers and learns the terrain first. Never forget the truth of your family, but accept that the faith of Paris requires Roman censure. They require every soul to be measured in sins. Your father and I never believed that, but most of your people live by this. Do not deny their faith. Few find their own way; they must believe in others."

Amira assisted, "Eleanor, you suffer I know, but heed Ellen, she is right."

"Here's how we play this," Ellen said. "You say their fee is unworthy of the intent. The Aquitaine has in mind a larger sum. Leave. They will talk to their superiors and see that more is at stake then your always-complaining soul. Let them seek you out. In the rounds, discuss the price, ask them many things, like the good that the church will do with the sum, ask them to be specific – the benefactor must always get commitments from the recipient. You are responsible for the wealth derived from your people. Ensure it is spent properly. Give devout consideration then name your final sum. Leave them for deep prayer.

"You mean you want me to buy them off."

"More than that, you must tell them you have learned a great lesson from them. You have, I hope. Eleanor, show a fervent Catholic devotion. Amira, remind her of her schooling in presence and voice. You must act in piety, Eleanor."

Amira advised, "It is the way of Queens."

Ellen resumed, "I am working on a compromise with the Parisii Church. They are fed up with your obstinacy, frankly. Name a great fee that you will donate to them." Wealth filling the pockets of foreign robes caused Eleanor to frown.

Ellen raised a brow. "Oh, I forgot to tell you, most will go to Fontevrault."

The three descended the ladder. Eleanor bathed righteously in a hot tub.

In the compromise, Eleanor's court was reinstated. The Grand Abbess of Fontevrault agreed to supply Eleanor an acceptably firm Catholic view of the world. A chapel cloister was built to sooth family bereavements for William.

Contritely attending every ritual mass, the young Princess gave obedient appearances as she did with her father. As if he were present, and as he would do, she called priests 'father,' in mercifully light tones. She realized it was they who needed to hear that word, to believe in themselves. Fellow worshippers rejoiced in her public devotions to mass. To see their bereaved young princess mourn, her father publicly brought them great relief.

Eleanor's grief was inconsolable. Troubadour song could not transform the blue heart of the tower prisoner. Such music was, as yet, unwritten.

To the rosy beds of the courtyard, Mirielle brought flute and tambour, Maryam her Gudok, a long-stringed viola. Mirielle painted shed tears on her face as did Maryam. They were tears of protest for the plight of Aquitaine as much as to grieve Eleanor's sorrowful loss.

Like sisters, they took turns painting each other's face. Maryam drew giant blue star-streams of tears. Along Mirielle's strong jaw she painted sierra patterns to a sturdy dimpled chin. On the Castilian coco-light skin of Maryam, her friend brushed tears bianco sopra bianco –white on white– completing a visage of small falling stars. They sang gently.

Maryam touched broken chords upon her gudok. Setting a lament, she looked up to Mirielle to confirm the way of their song. Mirielle took over her friend's Gudok and scratched the soundboard in a slower tempo. She replayed the broken chord bending down the notes and turned it back to Maryam.

Trobaritz Mirielle breathed upon her flute the cold loneliness of her lost childhood. She pulled long notes, Sirq came to the scene, seized the tambour, and folded to a sit. She unloosed and hid in her hair, and banged the three-beat rhythm. The strings cried naturally. Mirielle intoned deep hums of suffering. Sirq added a high girl voice, an ode to youth's desolation. Like childhood sisters, their music flowed many ways. Without beginning or end, they sang wild in sad play to the infinite sky. Sirq and Mirielle toned in parallels a siren call.

In the lament without a name, Maryam picked verse-less phrases out of the air and sounded them. Mirielle stretched them further, fingering sad chords, turning phrases as to wear out the meaning until only feeling remained. As the others chorus, Mirielle incanted purely — 'hair song' 'heir sorrow' 'her infinite' 'why hear sorrow' 'i'm first' 'oh sire' 'sirens swallow,' 'song dark' 'oh swallowing kisses' 'her heart falling garden.' They warbled voices singing one voice over the other, registers of mature feminine and young girl voices in discord. In drum beats, long sawed strings, a fluted breath, the three overlapping hearts swallowed sorrows for the princess in the tower.

Eleanor felt the smoky blue tabla tunes, in a recall of the sad songs of the ice ponds of childhood. Moved, she had her face tear-painted by her sister who brought a cithara-lyre. Petronilla placed the instrument in her lap. Eleanor extended her fingers and began to play. "Piss on blood," Eleanor said under her breath. "I can't get it right," and turned the instrument away. Petronilla soothed, "There is no right way, sister. Remember how we sang once, walking in the snow." She guided the fallen hands back to the strings. From the Maubergeonne tower, Eleanor's strums joined tear-painted Mirielle and Maryam. Three chords interpenetrated one another. She played the instrument on her lap for hours until she played her sadness out.

Calbi and the good men of his faith visited, reminding her young belief in the two-sided nature of things, and how her harmonious accord brought comfort to others. By restoring Eleanor's chain of being, her common senses began to return.

Eleanor became touchy about the problems of estate. William's closest of kin was his brother Raymond, too far away, and King in Antioch. Next was Raoul de Faye, Aenor's brother. Her uncle had local powers to act, and matters were getting out of hand. Father once subdued distant rebellions and settled claims. Now these unresolved decisions erupted into combat. North, on the Angevin border, Normans came south to incite squabbles. Nearby tribes of rude Lusignan and arrogant Parthenay stirred up easy passions. Suitor encampments in pursuit of her hand petitioned meetings.

In early May, night mobs and brigand clans beat their shields outside the gates. They made claims requiring Eleanor's judgment and demanded she take one of them as a husband. No one was killed, but blood did flow and squire Arno at sixteen received his knighthood dubbing from Princess Eleanor as the play battles of childhood were no longer.

Amira stole Eleanor into the attic office of the Palace to William's favorite den. Eleanor thumbed her father's papers. Here they had planned trials, she learned of the realm, and he gave council of life. Amira started politely, "Since his great life was taken, we all hoped for so much more." Tears came.

"Explain."

"A part of me is dying. This is not Aquitaine."

"What is it then, Amira?

Amira's worried words came in a flood. "A Catholic priest said your father dying was a miracle, and asked me to repeat that. I would not. His death was no miracle. He struck me on the back." Eleanor's empathy returned, and she offered the comfort of her shoulder. Amira continued, "These Fathers, why do they beat us, our real ones never did? Calbi says, 'False Father's fear God, true father's know love.' Once we could go anywhere and do anything. Remember when the sky was blue? The sky was big. We had the greatest ideas!" She drew back and looked at Eleanor directly. "Paris clergy sit in every class insisting only scripture be taught. They strike children in front of our teachers and demand obedience. We cannot discuss the slightest idea of our own." Eleanor expressed a face of compassion. Amira wept saying, "Last night I dreamed a yellow sky with orange clouds as if there were a forest fire. The wind blew fiercely. Your Falcons fell from the air; all my pigeons lay dead."

Eleanor could tell her friend held something deeper. "Compose yourself, Amira; you blubber worse than me. Now, what is it?"

"Terrible news. The Templars have begun to seize Aquitaine mills, just like they did in Toulouse. Reyna Chasseigne's mill was first."

"No! This is her family property."

Amira sniffled. "Reyna's father was arrested by summoners. They say she must marry a Templar, a hideous oaf who slobbers when he sees her."

Eleanor formed the picture: Bernard was playing on the lust in Parisian knights to seize her friend's famed beauty. After pardoning that lust, the Cistercian order would operate the watermill and obtain its wealth.

"Also," sniffled Amira, "building was halted on the Catharic water temple."

"Why have you waited to tell me all of these things?"

"Oh Eleanor, we've spared you from events so you could properly mourn your father. He loved Aquitaine, and it is dying. I have said my piece. Share my prayer." The two touched the steeples of their hands in a four-handed prayer. Amira incanted, "Wisdom and love hear us: help us feel, help us know. Is it right to become Queen of France?" After pressing interlocking fingers, they bowed heads together. Amira seated Eleanor in her father's chair.

Eleanor pictured father upholding Aquitaine law, but now it was she and the few she trusted. Though lieged, Eleanor felt no authority as the best of her generation was being laid to waste. As her father taught, she gyred long from afar to look at every side of the situation. With valiance she circled the big sky view of her life. As she swept over Fontevrault's schoolhouse, the best teachers Pat and Genet forced a whip rather than teach. Over Reyna's family mill, the famous beauty was ravaged into yielding her property – all for Bernard, poisoner of her father. Upon Daena and Calbi's work, their temple was stopped by scornful words from a wrath-filled faith. When she imagined these all at once, the strength of Eleanor's father gathered in her turbulent Aquitaine blood. She was ready to strike, yet she knew her emotional judgment had to be checked, something her father advised before great acts. She needed the trusted council of many.

"Amira, I have gyred over abbey, mill, and temple. I see what I must do. No other shall become the Queen of France, but I. This is how Aquitaine survives. This I must do. When you are yourself, call a hunting party for early tomorrow. Summon my elder council. Amira, secure the coronets, please."

"Yes, Majesty."

"Amira, what did you call me?"

"You heard. I felt its presence."

❖

Hunting kept instincts sharp for any assault to come. The Poitiers elders looked to the dark tower. Knowing she was lamenting her father, deceased not even a moon, the elders concluded dejected Eleanor could use the sunshine, exercise, and the challenge of a good hunt. Surprisingly, the request for a vibrant hunting party came from her. Putting on her satin-guarded horsehair belt, the heir of Aquitaine ordered chestnut Limona prepared. She asked her new council to head with her to Mirebeau and retrieve her falcons. It was the grounds where she once flew her birds and hunted deer with her father.

At first cockcrow, a heavy guard assembled in grand procession: a clatter of knights, lords, hunting hounds and high lances, drums and bugles, boots and belts. Horses rode with plenty of nerve, the guards ready to take wild boar. Short of the great keep at Mirebeau, Eleanor, Ellen, de Faye, Rancon set an overwatch in the fields.

"Eleanor, what are your war orders?" asked Ellen, "Tell Rancon."

"What do you mean?"

De Faye said, "You rule Aquitaine. Imagine we face hostile tribes. Your orders?"

She thumbed her belt. "I shall form a war council. Prince Taillebourg, Lady Ellen, Sir de Faye, please give me the names of your bests and their qualities."

"Fair," Rancon said. "Let's say thirty men charged out of those bushes, and—"

"I would not allow myself to be surprised. Where are your sentries? Out poaching, Prince Taillebourg?"

De Faye stared at his young cousin. "You have some boots!" Rancon chuckled and leaned to Ellen, "Her insolent tone is music to my ears." She replied, "It is as Amira says, Eleanor is back." Rancon studied Eleanor as if for the first time. Something in hunt and battle appealed to this rare woman as much as to him.

When they reached Mirebeau, Eleanor launched her birds. Their precise flight of purpose spoke to her. The excitement in the hunting party amused her. She took counsel about her Aquitaine concerns. Concluding she had to be vested with authority, they all returned to Poitiers.

Next day in a short ceremony, the Bishop of Poitiers validated the crowning of Eleanor Duchess of Aquitaine. The act was justified by her devotion to the church, the recent liege given by her lords, and that the title would simplify the upcoming marriage. As she was not yet fifteen, by law, uncle de Faye would act as a proxy for her rulings.

Acting Duchess Eleanor installed de Faye as Mayor of Poitiers, titled Rancon Lord of Taillebourg as Commander, and continued trusted family friends in their positions. Eleanor gave three orders to Chancellor Magistrate Ellen: "To cover Abbey, Mill, and Temple, invite Abbess de Chemillé to Poitiers. Summon my court for a hearing tomorrow. Include Reyna, the

Templar claiming her land, and Sir Armstrong. Let the Cathar temple builders know Mayor de Faye decrees they complete their works and will post a guard."

Ellen spoke, "Duchess Eleanor, as your Chancellor, may I suggest you meet Petronille half-way in the privacy of Mirebeau. Under your hunter's guard, you can fly your falcons, my Duchess."

"Good council Ellen, but please everyone, no titles for me unless necessary."

Amira's pigeons were dispatched to every Aquitaine tower. 'At sunrise, ring your bells for one hour for our new Eleanor Duchess of Aquitaine.'

The next day, the bells rang throughout Aquitaine announcing Eleanor's rule. A dozen friends of her Poitiers court assembled to hear the Templar appeal for Reyna. Chancellor Ellen announced, "The Duchess of Aquitaine presides," and stood behind a simple tapestry-covered chair. Eleanor judged by her fair heart first, the working laws second. It took but a few questions to find that the Templar exhibited a complete lack of affection for Reyna. As Eleanor figured how to resolve this loveless Templar case, a man stepped out that she had never seen.

An aspiring vintner testified his love for Reyna and challenged the Templar to a swordsman's duel. Though handsome, the young beau was clearly no match.

Eleanor proposed, "Templar, will you tourney for the hand of Reyna?"

The Templar laughed. "That's all it takes?"

"Please no!" Reyna softly cried. Amira shook a head no to the throne. The meaning was clear. This would be sure death to Reyna's beau.

Eleanor said, "A mortal tournament for the hand of Reyna, it will be!"

Shocked at the cruel sentence, Reyna broke into wails and fell into the arms of her beau. It was as Eleanor hoped. She read the clenched hands of Chevalier Armstrong – the maker of Reyna's horsehair-belt.

Armstrong stepped out. Looking put upon, toying with his mail, in singsong, he bluffed, "Reyna. Defend her again? Oc, I will represent her beau." He railed, "Templar, if you can survive my first blow by lance, which is unlikely, then I shall raise my sword and certainly finish you. Let's see; you will be the fourth soul. What say you for the honor of Lady Reyna, Templar?" The court held back comment; hard-faced Armstrong was making this up as he went.

The Parisian Templar eyed the situation. He did not know battle lance on horseback. Out stepped another Chevalier. "Give me the honor; I will lance your Templar heart if you have one. I am Sir Arno Allant, bodyguard of the Duchess."

Eleanor read the Templar's scan upon her and saw his contempt. The chevalier's had given him pause, but his vile eyes glared at her. The issue was herself – the little woman. An Archbishop had not ordained her as Duchess. To win the mill, an encamped religious authority would challenge her title and this decree. *Authority*? Eleanor needed to act her role.

"While you weigh your chances, Templar, I ask my court to kneel for my judgment!" A formidable mass fell to their knees, unnerving the Templar.

Eleanor saw into his heart, *do you still see a weak femme?* The jingling silver bracelet of her raised arm fell, pointing to his head. "Templar, you look upon the soon to be Queen of France, will the Chancellor record your name?"

He took a step back. Eleanor summoned a voice, noble as her father:

"I, Eleanor of Aquitaine decree: Sir Armstrong and this Templar shall meet in a tourney of ordeal for Lady Reyna. Have your horses ready within the hour at Trinity field. May God show mercy."

"Hail Eleanor," the crowd voiced. She summoned them to rise. "Chancellor, summon a doctor, Templar, summon one of your priests. I know Sir Armstrong. He feels remorse when taking souls."

It was a show of force. Unwilling to contest the forthcoming Queen and seeing no purpose in a combat of honor for a woman, the Templar fled Poitiers. De Faye worked with Eleanor to compose an urgent petition to the King of France:

> Attend directly to matters of Aquitaine providence. We must preserve the power of the state or lose all income and military authority to lands being annexed. Humbly, until such urgent matters are settled, please consider delay in asking for the hand of your faithful Latin signatory,
>
> Helienor, Ducissa Aquitanorum

The Chancellor wisely made a copy of Eleanor's letter for Abbot Suger – the King's ear in spiritual matters. A believer in the beautiful earth, Abbot Suger was known to oppose Abbot Bernard's austere Cistercian views. It was a shrewd political move. When the petition flew to Paris, Amira's messenger birds taught Eleanor a quick lesson. Rather than five days of couriers riding, in seven hours, the message hit. The advances of the Cistercian Templars came to a stop.

Paris received air messages from both Poitiers and Loudun. Loudun was an outpost of the Paris church that spoke for the King's clergy that warned of a gathering assault to abduct Eleanor. Messages from Poitiers conveyed Aquitaine concerns of independence. Paris sent an urgent message to Loudun. Take charge, negotiate a marriage. It never arrived.

The Loudon tower lost its carrier ability and quite by accident.

As planned, the hunting party returned to Mirebeau for Eleanor to fly her hawks. They had been kept there not to consume the Poitiers pigeons. On a late midday, cages in hand, the hunting party headed north in the direction from which invaders would most likely come. They stopped short of Loudun.

Eleanor laced up her arm gauntlet, "Shall we have a look?"

The Duchess introduced Taillebourg to her beloved birds, Karybdis on her arm and Skyla on her falconer's. A dozen more by hunters learning to fly. Eleanor peered into her falcon's eyes, charging the warbird with her hallowing phrase: "Go-Shock." She presented her warbird to the sky, running, hollowing everlouder "Go-Shock!" As guided, the hard pounding hawk went northerly. Her falconer launched Skyla to follow. "Prey-Kill!" was his call. Within fifteen minutes the falcons returned, fat-bellied with Loudun pigeons. This they did every day.

Loudun's air traffic halted, and without Loudun, Paris was in the dark, reading only messages of Poitiers demands.

In Mirebeau's hall, huntress Eleanor finally met with Petronille de Chemillé of Fontevrault, refusing to take the great chair. "I cannot look down upon a Grand Abbess. Just last year we were playing Pilgrims and Saints."

"Eleanor, you must assume the throne."

"Only if need be! Let us talk." They went to a quiet partition with a hearth.

"Duchess, hear my pleas. Paris priests have taken over our school. They strike orphans and force programmed obedience. Only biblical ideas may be taught."

Eleanor was unsure about being an authority before an elder, yet she ordered as her father would. "Continue. Pleas to petition."

"For killing our tamed deer on Fontevrault grounds. I petition eviction."

Eleanor thought deeply. She ordered Ellen to Mirebeau hall. In council, they determined that a law of property was broken. The possible claim that Catholics were a higher church order had no relevance. The royal franchise charter established the sanctuary of Fontevrault. Eleanor took the castle chair of her father. "I decree, all Fontevrault forests are a Duchy preserve. None but the Sovereign of Aquitaine is permitted to hunt those grounds."

When the Abbess bowed, Eleanor said, "You don't need to bow to me."

"It is to the office which earns this humble bend."

"My father would have liked that. Grand Abbess, I dream of him every night."

"Redouble prayer. Your harsh dreams will cease when his soul is at peace."

The next day, a troop of verderers and knights arrested every Parisii priest and nun on Fontevrault grounds for poaching and abetting poachers in violation of franchise and royal law. Banishment was immediate. The foreign clergy were carted in chains and dropped off, halfway to Paris.

Eleanor returned to Poitiers. A Parisii agent awaited. He made gestures of good faith and asked many questions, especially about her birds. The emissary handed over a bag of gems of betrothal intent to Eleanor. The solicitation was not heartfelt, and the courier left as quick as he came. Crestfallen, she had no chance to ask what her groom was like. She thumbed through the plain sack of pretty stones, then ran after the agent.

"Wait, sir! You tell Louis this. It is rude not to give me words! Worse, there is nothing wearable in this sad sack of river rocks for me to fashion as a pledge." The agent recoiled at her emotion, fearful she might throw the sack at him and nodded coolly, "I will tell him," and left.

How tawdry to engage the beginning of, could there even be love? Ellen reminded that as a great landowner, a Princess had to keep perspective of this relationship. As she listened, Eleanor was surprised to find a nice square-cut blue sapphire. Feeling a tinge of ingratitude that she told the agent off, well, too bad.

"Her Falcons are stolen!" The news sent Eleanor into a fury she could not temper. The falconer said a Parisii agent had a warrant to take the birds 'in violation of agreements.' The birds were removed to the family forest preserve in Talmont on the ocean. Its greedy verderer, William de Lezay, received the prized birds. He had the gall to send a ransom note. She barely had time to read it because galloping from Loudun. A courier presented a military order signed by the French King: Secure the Princess and prepare to receive Prince Louis for a marriage in the port of Bordeaux. She was to be marched to the high tower, which adjoined her family Palace – the Ombrière. Eleanor reflected, the Holy Prince Louis could never call upon Eleanor in Poitiers, not at the marble tower of Dangerossa that received a Pope's excommunication. It also meant he would cross and take the Aquitaine.

Under heavy guard, the last week of May 1137, Duchess Eleanor stepped up into her carry-wagon with her sister and counselor, her trek-horse Limona in tow. Heading southwest to Bordeaux, passing out the Poitiers gates, it was morning. From her wagon, Eleanor turned to the deaf orphans of Fontevrault, who came to see her off. They made their sign: the symmetry of one thumb and finger interlocks with the other thumb and finger, and folds to the chest. *Marriage.* The thought startled her. She touched her heart to her well-wishers.

Amira observed. "That's not a smile, is it?"

Eleanor pulled a glum face and leaned back.

"You look better dour," Petronilla taunted. The Princess bared her teeth in a quick snarl. The horses clopped the stones. The Duchess pushed back her hood and pulled open her collar. Petronilla echoed her move. Eleanor would have to look after her sister now. Jaunting along in a wary spirit, they headed 150 miles into the past comforts of Eleanor's seashell youth; a place once shared with her father on progress, now gone. Sunset beaches near Bordeaux, Belin where she was created, once past, would come again. It was almost June and Poitiers had surrendered to a devilish heat.

Near the Ombrière Palace, so named for the tall Elm shade of cover, and the breed of salmon colored trout, men cooly fished from the banks of the mighty Garonne. The shady Elms moderated the distant ocean breezes and sheltered the gentle river winds. The same cooling airs tempered the vineyards and rounded the natures of Bordeaux's inhabitants.

The hunting lodge had two turrets half complete, a vast improvement on the former ancient Roman officer barracks. In thirty years, the Ombrière would become a Palace. Grandfather William had added tiled fountains and a hanging gardens civil features he treasured from the great cities of The Crusade. One spent little time in the fancy hunting lodge, for living outside was its purpose. There was hunt in the forested preserves. Roman ruins prompted stories of its lost civilization. The gardens of Bordeaux, a picnic the vineyards, becoming beached in ocean sands – these were the lodge's adventures.

The Ombrière lodge-works joined to the ancient city wall that bent with the flow of the River Garonne. The wide river and stone protected the town center and its cathedral. Everything was a scenic walk from the lodge. Adjacent to the Ombrière was a massive Roman square tower that soared over the groves. The stonework was thicker than the six-foot thick castle walls of Poitiers, making the watchtower the safest keep in all Aquitaine. Built by Eleanor's forebears under the whip of Rome's centurions; after a thousand years, the slave's labors would protect their valued distant progeny. The chill of the trees awaited the weariness of the summer travelers.

After four days in the shifting trolley, Duchess Eleanor peeked up to see the high tower. The lodge gates swayed into view. Grandfather had made Aquitaine's first troubadour poems here, certainly over many glasses of wine. After the clatter halt of horses, coming off her wagon-carriage, the duchess looked at the lodge and said one word.

"Wine."

Amira minded, "Please."

Request given, they passed through the large quarters to the nine rungs of the draw up ladder. Up through the hole in the floor, Eleanor peered at the repulsive four walls of her cell. Dank and cold, there was little space more than the small straw bed and table. Her air and light would be measured through two grated windows – a waist-height portal that viewed the courtyard below and a small high square on the opposite wall, looking to the green Elm tops.

Eleanor occupied the space. She took one step and pressed her head to the bars and sighed. Birds flit about the empty garden courtyard in the middling light. Amira ascended, every time bringing something up the ladder to improve the room. A stool for the desk, a clothes chest she ordered placed, candles and stands, white day lilies, and the cithara Eleanor liked to play. Amira pulled out the straw bedding. Together they lay feathers and fleece in a mattress. After a cover of linen and light wool, they shared a deep glass of wine, but not until Amira tasted each glass first.

"Life of a Princess," Amira teased.

"You don't have to taste each one."

"Both glasses of wine are good." Amira toasted, "To the life of a taster who gets to drink more." Amira politely did not drink more than the duchess.

Eleanor contemned, "One tower, then the next. Seems to be my station."

"My Duchess, you are the most unmerry prisoner of love." After a glass of wine, they trued as friends, then laughed like girls glad humor had returned.

"It's cold for summer," grumped Eleanor, feeling her doldrums return.

"You'll miss this when you dwell in Paris. Summer's hot there. Treasure the chill. I have to stock the kitchen. Don't go anywhere now."

"H'ya, right." Eleanor looked out the bars – the sky overcast, the air damp, the cell cold and still. Feeling alone, she recalled the breezy, sunny beaches of Bordeaux from youth, when she was another girl. What had she laughed about then? She rested her head on the iron bars, letting her long amber-rust hair fall to the courtyard. She waved the strands at the birds. Her grandfather composed out there. She was here for a dull, short sunless summer walk to the church of Bordeaux. A high view of green leaves rustled in the overcast sky. She imagined the life-giving river outside. In sadness, she thought of her past, her present, and her future. To her unstarted life, she hummed out a tune.

♪

Summer leaves Ombrière · rivers brown sky is gray

Child of my sun born soul who always wants to play

I skip youthful summer · darkness along the way

The stone cold tower keeps · going nowhere today

Summer winter dreaming on a summer's day.

I'll step through a church · on the fish river way

I tread on love · intent to pray

The bishop's given gold · he knows I'll go away

Soon I'll be in Paris · on a day like today

Summer winter dreaming of summer yesterday

♪

Up the stairs, stepped the shapely woman of Eleanor's family tree. No stranger to towers, she brought her Maubergeonne homemaking skills to make the Ombrière Tower bearable. She appeared at the ladder top.

"Dangerossa!"

"Eleanor, my dear! No word from Paris yet? Then we will have our own good time. I have rose-scented rushes for the floor, rose-oil for the iron bars to stem reddish stains. Every aunt and abbess will pile into your Bordeaux donjon sharing their marriage-bent wisdoms. Soon sweet, you shall be very wise. I must hurry to market now. Cheer up, you will stay in the lodge. This place is only for a while."

The Ombrière became wedding central with the direction of Amira, Ellen and the advice of Dangerossa. When enough guards arrived, the Princess took an escorted walk to the river. That night, she locked herself in the cramped cell. Sleep brought dreams of her father as always. Morning brought sorrow.

To prevent the sadness of her mistress from turning to acedia, Amira sent for local troubadours. Many lived across the river around the castle of Blaye, the final resting place for many an ancient warrior. Bordeaux was the perfect city for songsters to compose profitable lyrics of battle valor. The vanities of wealthy families wanted their ancestors remembered. Among the local singers were the Plaganet Brothers. Busy at the beach taverns carousing, they sang of mythical dark lords before the time of Charlemagne. Of newer style was a composer of personal songs sung in present tense. Straight he came, on the last day of May.

. . .

It was past midday when Jaufre Rudel skiffed a craft over the water. Lute over his back, the twenty-four-year-old troubadour Prince of Blaye was handsomely decorated in a blue and gold gown belted with scarves. His huge blue felted beret entirely capped his long brown hair. The broad approach that the River Garonne afforded of the shimmering Ombrière lodge was most satisfying. He had left the far bank where a bird sang in the longest of songs. The magnificent reflection of tall trees, towers, and palace stirred memories. As a boy, he had met Eleanor's grandfather, the great Count, who inspired him to sing. His craft approached where they met at the Ombrière garden. Close came the trellis pattern of the silvery gate, lace-curtained windows, potted flowers on their beveled ledges. He kept in mind: he was a guest, a pilgrim to her bedroom tower. He hoped his humility would void the tinge of nervousness he would feel singing before the newly crowned Duchess, the prospective Queen of France. She was said to have favored one of his early songs, a personal poem. To honor her, he would mimic the lively style of her grandfather William. Rudel had gone out on Pilgrim's Night at the drinking taverns to learn all he could of his distant Crusade. He'd met some real characters. Through their slurs of speech, he made some sense of those returning from pilgrimages. Everything went into his triumphant song. The birds of May welcomed his boat to shore.

Rudel passed the guards, encouraged to see Arno who had sung his verse before. Arno affirmed everyone was away at the market except Eleanor and a few friends. Rudel gave a fold of white flowers to be placed. In the high elms he noticed – for the second time today, a bird was lost in the longest of songs. He whispered to Arno to only call him Jaufre Rudel, not Prince.

In the large room made whiter with just placed wild Dogrose and Hawthorne branches, Eleanor sat on her couch, glad to be free of the tower.

She wore a long sleeve blue and gold brocade gown. Two married friends from Fontevrault cradled a sleeping baby and presented a wedding vase. Outside, the tone of her bodyguard entertained the day's musician. A bird in never-ending song changed its tune. Eleanor fixed her eyes upon the doorway and let her cheeks rise.

Before he entered, Rudel had willed to count her every glance as an exercise. In the doorway, she was already looking at him.

In her first look, he searched to find her salient features. He was surprised by a clear-eyed young woman overcome by a wide impish grin seeming to say, 'Let's play,' just weeks from her marriage. Her age was as uncertain as the number of vigorous colors that made her hair.

Seeing no visible response, Eleanor turned back to her friends.

Rudel felt many things at once. He closed his eyes and beauty was all he saw. A voice sure as an angel said, '*you are in the presence of a special being, do not ignore her for your life.*' He opened to see an empty vase in her hands. Her smile had vanished. Holding the gift, she gave breathy thanks to friends far happier than she. In all of her snappy fidgets, one-eyed figuring, reseating herself in her vestments, he saddened, sensing no well of happiness in her countenance.

Her second flitting look at him peered right into his sad want. A place deep within, he sensed she also dwelled. Such hints of sorrow made beauty richer. She swayed her head in a sea of concerns: first hand on knee, then cheek to hand, listening to her friends. From a bundle of turns, she ran a gamut of looks: too-bored-to-wonder, too-sad-to-care, too-serious-to-play. All the signs of trailing grief: her father had passed. Feeling the sad dance of her spirits, Rudel had the remedy. He could not wait to bring her marching back to life. Eleanor raised her hand, a signal to her head maid, Rudel's employer.

This third glance seemed meant for the composer, for without introduction, her visage was full of respect and courtesy. She glanced down at her lap. Amira announced: "Jaufre Rudel of Blaye."

The fourth came with her upward gaze of wonder. It was all he needed.

"Princess. I will now sing, '*Why We Fight.*'"

Eleanor winced. She should have stopped him right there with that title. The colorful singer looked earnest in his large blue-felted, puff-rounded cap. His clean-shaven face reminded her – was he the young man she had accidentally glimpsed half-naked coupling sweetly in Blaye? She whispered her notion to Amira. They both pulled faces of sultry wonder and accepting his song.

Rudel did not know what to make of their looks. No matter, he drummed up a martial rhythm. The women were not feeling it. His mellifluous tones and expressive face came in a way they had never seen, and they gave his song to bold chance. Rudel sang forth a sad rousing saga of gut-wrenching sacrifice in desert lands and a distant ocean rolling shore, a place from which few returned. He banged of bloody crosses for bloody causes. When he got to the drunken Simeon monks spinning in circles, their blind faith revealed in slurs while intoxicated and naked, drumming ever louder on top of Roman pillars, and then moaning of impossible rivers of gore – even Amira was ready to pull the stopper from that tub. Especially when the infant broke into crying. The parents rushed the baby to the river.

"Amira, could you find me a bloodier troubadour? Gore, please more gore."

"I can pike a pig bladder with a pole," Amira recalled of road larking days.

Rudel wanted to say, *I have not yet sung of the glory fight*, but his patron was unsettled, losing all desire that he sensed initially. She unconsciously gave a sign: the chin rests on two thumbs that lurch out. *Denial?* Not me, Rudel?

Eleanor stewed in a puzzle of frowns. She had heard Rudel's love poems sung by knights, but this Rudel of today was a misery, or was that his intent?

Jaufre looked as empty as a wheat wagon in winter; his rousing words saw no sprout. Standing on ice, he apologized with hurt: "I have listened to every homecoming pilgrim. These are their lais. Lady Eleanor, I sing to remind you of your grandfather William and his troubadour songs of The Crusade."

Eleanor gave him a forward look and made room for him. "Come sit." She knew he would like that. He sat gently by her side. She liked his honest face; the sentient eyes coupled with the gentlemanly choice to feel. Few men had such a run of appeal in them. She felt being scanned, just like she scanned hearts. When Rudel pressed his kerchief, light blue with clouds to his perspiring forehead, Eleanor cackled nervously and turned her eyes to Amira. He was the soft lover she had seen on her walk in Blaye with his pants off. On the wrong path now, he needed her husbandry, a good goading; time to truth the beast.

"Do you want to know a secret?" Eleanor flashed it with her eyes as well.

Rudel readied to be taken wherever this honest visage of damisel led.

"A fighting man, a real Chevalier like William? 'In the far off desert,' you sang." She quested, "Do you know Why We Fight!"

Rudel was falling hard to her chiding passion.

Eleanor sensed his speechless want. "I will tell you! Grandfather William sang verses of love in war from his own true heart. He mocked combat with course songs of distant lovers, bedding two women at a time. Imagine that, sir."

Rudel attended the hard shocks of truth, emotions stirring within. It seemed impossible that so much passion about love, his dearest subject, could be boldly rooted in this bright-eyed, unjaded, young woman before him.

Eleanor, unsure if wonder-all-over-his-face understood anything, sallied on. "Only true warriors sing great love songs. Death tests life, lust in love tempers violence. Men sing with a mad heart to keep from going mad." In his eyes, she saw how deeply he drank her lesson, or maybe her. For his sorry soul, Eleanor let him feel her tang:

"What is not a secret is, that was the worst song I have ever heard! It is laughable. If ever you hope to sing for me, it must not be from drunken pilgrim hearsay, but of the evident. What we live and feel, presently; you must be in it! Sing not what you think I want to hear. Sing of yourself. For my court, let it be of love. Forget the titles, just begin. Bold with a true heart take my ear, Sir!"

Never had anyone spoken to him this way. Who was this soul in a young woman's body? He felt like dying. *Great bladed arrow strike deep my blood.* How often he chanted 'I must be in it,' and then raced to his inspiration. Like a muse, she had said the very words. Everything she spoke of were his values, his true poetry that he left behind – *You call to my very core* – would he have a second chance to sing what he truly wrote? Rudel managed to keep composed in her audience. He pled and bent for her hand. She granted not just the flat of it, but the whole round, as a friend does. Time stopped for Rudel. This was chance itself. With this innocent hand hovering before him to kiss, Rudel wondered how she might feel. This was his rebirth to sing another day. To her tender underside warmth, he tipped his finger to her pulse; her palm rolled forward. To the faint smell of rose, earthy sage, ephemeral violet, he inspired. To this wrist of silver bracelet, laced-in sleeve, he marveled at its youth. To the delicate vibrance of her light fingers that accidentally tapped his palm, he brought her slightly forward. *Your every impression will live in me forever, until the day I really die.* To her scented lief, he pressed his lips.

At that very second, onto the back of her hand fell a tear that matched the swell in his throat. Rudel stepped back speechless, mustering himself through a blathering fog of gratitude and forgive-me bows. His senses took everything in. Eleanor tendered the received hand to her lips; with a thin smile, she ingested his emotion. Reseating herself in her dress, she put him out of her mind. She stroked her crimson gold hair returning to her friends with their angelic infant. He put every impression to memory and gave himself to eternal aspiration – the birdsong, her parting folds. 'Berry' and 'Guisana' glad patrons, their familiarity to call her 'Elle.' How she frowned and laughed at their trials of sexual abstinence. The party exchanged words and hand signs as confessors to one another. Rudel was awash in jealousy of a friendship he desperately wanted with her. He noted coincidentally; her friends were named after provinces at the bounds of the Aquitaine Duchy. The poetry of the moment registered, as words came to compose later. He needed her last glance.

Eleanor flitted an awareness of the pesky troubadour still gaping at her. It was her call: she reversed feeling annoyed and gave him her heart. She flashed her underlook of desire that she had mastered from Guisana. She did not expect the glow of his eyes. Her little gasp Rudel did not hear, for he had already turned away banishing himself, repulsed that anyone could make him feel this way. Imagining she'd said the word 'Friend,' tripping on flagstones, he bumbled his way back to the river boat.

For both, it was the last calling glance that played that night in their summer sleep. The art of each came to the other's mind. With vivid certainty, he would sing for her again, and it would be with verse no soul had summoned before.

Eleanor awoke at first cockcrow, where was she? Night had brought dreams of an arid desert, of violent knights in white mountains, bloody cruelties, strange words she could not understand. A meandering river barge led to market stalls of exotic crimsons and strange birds; melodious towers of winds, mad monks singing, and now quite strongly, the settle of an ocean's shore. She bolted up. The courtyard fountain splashed outside her cell. '*Rudel's ill song!*' Her head rested back on her pillow, and she found herself strangely happy. She realized this was the first night her father did not appear in her dreams. Surely this meant, Father was at peace.

In her waking recollection, she felt having made a great decision. She concentrated, and the harder she thought –what was it– the more elusive became that resolution. In the strands of her warm dream, she swished her hair to bars, watching it fall. She rested her head, peering down at the cold court fountain. Surely that decision and its purpose would reveal itself one night, one day.

Amira brought up warm milk and looked into her friend's clear eyes saying, "Fresh pulled. I see the Spark is back." Eleanor blew bubbles in the milk holding back a smirk. "Spark ... that's good. Thank you, Amira."

"How did your sleep go?"

"Father did not come to me in my dreams last night. His soul has moved on."

"That's good."

"Odd socks, Rudel's dreadful song got me somehow. A singer of note, oc?"

"Eleanor, Rudel asked me not to tell, he wanted you to know him as a troubadour. He is the Prince of Blaye, commander of a chevalier's regiment."

Eleanor drank. The sweet milk warmed her breast. The air smelled fresh and sweet, sweeter than ever before.

The still beautiful mouth of Dangerossa smiled.

"Eleanor and Louis . . ." teased the woman of fifty, clad as a fairy-fabled queen in a light pink open-throated gown. A red satin jeweled choker encircled her porcelain neck. ". . . how principle a love would that be?" She pretended not to know where Eleanor hid in the room of the Ombrière Palace. On this warm mid-June day, abbesses and relatives fanned themselves, intent on giving wedding advice. Dangerossa spoke gently:

"The Prince is most Holy, and Eleanor is . . . words escape me."

Petronilla came forward, greeting her sparkling grandmother with a bise. In the perplexing way of sisters, Petronilla delighted at the impending marriage in one moment, reviled her sister favored over herself in the next. With fierce joy, she announced: "His highness, King Louis 'the Fat' must be carried by four men. Oh sister, how much does his son weigh?"

From a noble couch facing the fireplace with its back to them, up came a long arm making a thumb-knuckle fist. A dismissive voice made a "ppp-pp-ppt!"

Abbess Isabella d'Anjou discounted the childish drama. In her mid-twenties, she was nearly Queen of English-lands. Now she presided at Fontevrault as one of Eleanor's champions. She countered, "Louis-Seven was raised in a monastery. He is quite thin though his wit needs wetting."

Petronilla lilted dear words, "Grand-mère, how wonderful is marriage? You had a passionate love with grandfather."

Dangerossa said lightly, "He took me quite by surprise. We had both been very unhappily married. Arranged marriage is not at all interesting though I am sure Eleanor will find some adventure in it. The seductive powers – well, love is something else you know."

"Eleanor is getting married, mare-heed, mare heed!" Petronilla sang derisively.

The Princess popped up from behind the couch. Gripping the back, she lay her sad visage upon her arms, "I have more than land to give."

Isabella said, "The key to love is children; their special love is beyond the man."

Eleanor nearly puked at the thought, "Children? I want passion! I want love in marriage, the good in the good. I want to feel something if I am to have a man create life in me. It is at the heart of every troubadour song. In this, I truly believe."

Dangerossa said, "If you didn't look so pitifully crestfallen, we would laugh."

Abbess Isabella said in pointed tones, "Dear, how must the Prince feel?"

Petronilla was more obvious, "You are just a title. When he becomes King, Eleanor will be pumping out the princes, chanting with the monks; pumping out the princes, chanting with the monks, Oh-one, Oh-two—"

"Is that all you can imagine," Eleanor snapped, "you .. nun-bunny?"

"I'll not be a nun! I will marry, and a better man than you!"

"Girls!" Dangerossa sympathized. "In every one of our ten-thousand living days, we should love and be loved." Eleanor seemed the only one listening. The room fell out of sight as she flopped to settle on the couch, folded her arms. *What do they know?* Only the flame-licked coals understood.

A trumpet sounded. Boots stepped the courtyard stones. Women at the window said, "It is the three-lily banner, the King's fleur-de-lys." Arno entered formally making way for 'The Envoy,' an animated mid-aged magistrate in a dark cape, holy collar, and large jeweled cross. The envoy's sign language echoed his words, in case his harsh Parisii French was misunderstood. He had not yet learned to speak lilting nasal Occitan. Understanding was his business.

Arno heralded, "Louis Six, King of the Franks speaks through The Envoy from Paris concerning his son, the Crown Prince, Louis Seven, to all present and for his bride Eleanor to hear." The envoy swept in helpers and gift boxes. He flourished his thanks to a room of bows and curtsies. Spotting whom he thought was Eleanor, he gave Petronilla a double dose of flourishes.

The emissary began, seeming to invent a hand gesture for every word.

"The King of the Franks greets you this midmorning with warmth, cheer, and compassion. I will speak for him to Alienor the Occitan." He rushed to the pleasing face of Petronilla eager in her response.

"Your tongue is Parisii. You mean to say, Eleanor of Aquitaine."

"My apologies for my poor tongue."

"I can guide your hands to show you how to say it. How fares our King?"

"The King is in good spirits, but poor health," the envoy gesticulated. "Lovely Occitan voice, you are the famous Eleanor?"

Petronilla delighted with the assumption. "Aquitaine welcomes Paris. Let my hands teach yours. Here is how we gesture, Aqui-taine."

The couch spoke: "Let my sister be!"

The envoy showed confusion as the room lit with laughter. Eleanor stood on the cushions. Her sister fetched water and returned, "I am Petronilla. Here, for the heat of your journey." He drank, showing an overjoy of refreshment, returned the vessel, and stood perfectly still.

When Eleanor rested before him, he began, "Dearest Duchess Apparent—"

Amira interjected, "The Bishop of Poitiers has blessed her crown."

"Even better, my apologies." He swept into a richer tone. "Duchess of Aquitaine, The King compassionately grieves for your loss and the loss of all Franks. The church prays for your father's soul." The envoy was first to cross his heart. After a sea of crossings, he continued. "Like all matrimony, we join the wills of two fathers, two great houses, sustained in marriage. As for the main points of your union to the Capets—"

"Will you hear first," Dangerossa politely intervened, "Aquitaine nuptial terms?" The man appeared hit by a board to the face. "Not allowed." He did not cross his arms; he was not taking a position. Another woman stepped forward.

"I am Ellen, magistrate of Poitou. As you are an envoy, convey this to the king. That only Eleanor will govern the Aquitaine realm—" The man halted her, both his arms went to work, giving a reply.

"This is not possible. Women, to rule, and own estate over man?"

"It is, and they do," Ellen retorted. "Many Crusade fiefs are managed by maternal survivors. Princess Eleanor is expert in maintaining family continuity."

"Worry not, the King taught Prince Louis to run duchies at age thirteen."

"Eleanor learned when she was six. She is expert in laws and ways. Look at your tax roles. For the Crown, Aquitaine generates the greatest wealth of any Duchy. Only through Eleanor will the riches of France flow."

The envoy conceded, "I understand the starting points. What shall I record?"

Ellen dictated: "In brief, Eleanor of Aquitaine will, for France, retain the full title as Duchess to the county. Her office will settle final tallies. As dominant regent, she will set rents and grant properties of land, sea, and air."

"The powers of air belong to the church," the envoy said confidently.

Eleanor took a step forward. "As Duchess and Queen for Aquitaine, I will deem all bird routes, fishery areas, animal rights of forest for both fur and hunt. I will license all watermills."

Ellen continued the thread. "Good sir, wealth is a matter of state. By her vast knowledge of her people, she will obtain the steady revenue due the Crown."

The envoy said neutrally, "The issue of tithe to Holy Church?" Tithe he stressed with his hands. The financial stipulations of the church were crucial.

Eleanor returned gestures with equal skill saying, "Graceful envoy, we do give our tenth with all honor due Rome. Inside my realm, the Aquitaine Duchess will approve the direction of larger commissions, and plans for great structures."

"Prince Louis will become your Duke. I don't see—"

"I have been given the liege of my people. As ruler, the Lord Duchess prevails."

"Ah, a woman lieged, huh. Since you are lieged, that is different. What else?"

Ellen gestured vividly: "Eleanor of Aquitaine will deem all grants of franchise for Fontevrault. Goods made with her own Aquitaine seal will be spared the King's levy. Eleanor will bond any trade agreements made. As Queen of her duchy, she wishes to appoint all Aquitaine bishops." The last was said to concede.

Surrounded by the woman's flying hands, the envoy flailed the air:

"No. No. No. No. Bishops are King's work!"

The women bowed in tacit receipt of his position. The envoy concluded, "We will entertain every consideration. Prince Louis leaves his sick father. The King wishes the marriage here at Cathedral Saint-André."

Abbess Isabella nudged Eleanor a low whisper, "Bless."

"A blessing on the King's health," Eleanor crossed her heart. The envoy noted she did not bless the marriage. Amira signed the interlocking finger thumb sign representing her ring. Eleanor ignored it.

Isabella asked, "Of the wedding ceremony in Bordeaux, how many will arrive from Paris and by when?"

"Five hundred soldiers—" the envoy gestured.

The room went cold with shock. This was an invasion.

The envoy extended, "To escort Louis .. and to protect your land."

Arno raised an eyebrow. Everyone saw the mincemeat in the words. Abbess Isabella broke in with proper protocol, "Then accept our invitation for them to be our *guests*. They must all bear flowers. Do you have a date?"

"The King's army will–"

"Guests?" prompted Mathilda.

"The guests should arrive in two weeks." The envoy smoothly motioned to the metal-studded chest on the window table. The lid opened smoothly. A red velvet-padded wagon held twenty-four impressive fine blue cups and plates made from the clays of the Vienne. There were Silver spoons from Castile.

The emissary broadly swept his arms to the sky, then pirouetted his wrist to shape her slender waist. "Beautiful Eleanor, the King of the Franks gems you." He poured forth the hard contents on the table. Out clattered silver crosses and two blue stones. Eleanor stepped once to take his hovering hand to convey. "Generous Louis, receive my token kiss," and planted her young lips on his hewn hand. She concluded in songful voice:

"If in our token terms we agree, then a royal wedding there shall be."

The envoy gave an over-dramatic bow. "I am off to Saint-André. Abbess Isabella, will you join to set our date?" He left in a spin with the abbess trailing. At the door he turned, almost bumping her back saying, "Oh yes, how could I forget. You will receive Lady Jolietemps and her dressmakers today." The women smiled him off.

Eleanor drew rapid council. Ellen agreed to dispatch an immediate order: not to provoke the five hundred. Doing so would certainly bring five thousand. Eleanor felt the thrill of her gamble of politics and power. She watched her short-lived roll fade as a growing circle of women soon brought her down to her linens as others brought our ward-robes and powders.

The Ombrière main room glowed with brightly white hanging wedding vestments. Rustling aunts, damisels, and advisors bouted through hem-heights and haw-strings in a world of shifts, undergowns, midgowns, overgowns, surcoats, and lacings. As was tradition, each woman sat tenderly with their lovely doll and brush. They rubbed creams and feathered powders on her skin, applying both makeup and wisdom. Compounding blushers and concealers, beauty secret on top of beauty secret, Eleanor soon felt the weight of her face.

Petronilla delighted. Amid the bustle and abutting, in the center of the busy room, dressed no further than her underwear pant-gown, sat Eleanor in red-lip oil and rouge, rocking one leg over the other. They exchanged squints of sisterly fire.

Eleanor pondered, *doesn't anyone understand me?* Certainly not my sister, making sure every beauty consultant had a crack at my face. Petronilla grinned with a punitive smile.

Satisfied with their work, the ladies served themselves orange-peel tea. They gathered at a clear hand mirror comparing shades of blue gowns with tints of tea cups, making hushed remarks. Eleanor endured the cackle of women attempting to see themselves. She dreaded to see her image.

With fanfare, a tall empty frame from Paris wheeled near the window. In its mid-height groves, a large mirror was set. Even after five minutes of polish, the surface removed more light from the room than it reflected. Over the frame of finely molded Oak, heralds placed floral garlands. The mirror stood waiting to receive the images of the bride to be. The first to appear before the reflector was the mirror's commander.

"The Madame Queen Adelaide's Dresser, Lady Jolietemps of Medoc." The proper high-nostrilled woman of mid-thirty satisfied herself with her barely discernible image in the mirror. Behind, followed four finely clad garment tailors and a handful of mid-aged women of the Paris court, all taking short steps. The austere women wore the same murky Holy gown.

Lady Jolietemps flashed vexed glances about the dress-filled room – not a Holy gown in sight. She curtsied to Eleanor, for some reason painted as a clown in her underwear.

Jolietemps pronounced, "I am personally sent by Queen Adelaide, the mother of Prince Louis-Sept. These are my aides. We are here to help, here to help." God's Mountain, there was a great deal of help required. Passing her gaze – the room seemed filled by women obsessed with the constitutions of biblical harlots. She perspired, looking squarely at an elderly scarlet-collared woman.

Dangerossa slid forward in her red-riband pink dress, cleavage hinting. Touching her satin choker and touching her two granddaughters the stunning woman said, "We are family." Lady Jolietemps pulled a fan.

Highborn Parisii gowns of murk passed before each of Eleanor's ladies to take the center of the room. That they were married, or hopelessly unable to be married, was obvious with the chemise taken to the chin. That Aquitaine women were damisels of their own terms, was expressed in the lace chemise cut low, their chests allowed to breathe. Below the waist? A real battle. The irked Parisii women paced lockstep in long-hemmed single piece gowns. The femmes of Aquitaine gaited freely, each her own flower, no two vestments alike. The final insult that lowered the eyes of Paris were the colorfully corded sandals, rich colored socks, tight boots, and naked bejeweled ankles.

The room swam happily with Aquitaine delight and drooped with Paris long-sleeves. The straight gowns expressed righteous contempt at the belt-wearers. The suggestion of a woman's hips, back curve or any rise of her form was scandalous. Lord! Infidel clothes, the ethnic clothes from Spain with hints of Arabia and a separate shirt-bodice? A heresy. The Parisii women were fit to break out in hives. The fashion-starved tailors appealed with a gleam in their eye, "Lady Jolietemps, what do you think?"

"We are shocked! Shocked. I say, the hems of one court must be the same. This wedding court must dress by the standard of Queen Adelaide." The tailors bowed, opened their trunks and presented gown fabrics. The reaction was immediate. "Duchess Eleanor refuses to be fit in river-mud-ugly robes." This impudence to Paris did not phase Jolietemps. Here to outfit the entire court, she fanned herself into contemplation.

Amira could see this moment portended the bear claws of Paris fashion, into which Poitiers was headed. She weighed the forces in play. The tailors showed great interest in the Aquitaine look; Jolietemps was rethinking her attack; and Eleanor was beside herself.

Amira smiled at the dressmakers and took charge: "Tell them."

Dangerossa turned her charm to the austere tailors. "Fashionable men, for some weeks now, the dear friends of the inner court have been contriving a special Aquitaine wedding dress." Sad-painted Eleanor and her pestering sister wondered what was afoot. The curious raiment makers asked, "Tell us more." The stunning woman replied dryly, "You will get the details when she is ready," indicating the dollishly painted Eleanor.

"But I am ready!" The Princess scanned for mercy. *Dangerossa? Ellen? Amira? Maryam? Reyna? Anyone?* They mimicked Eleanor's permanent pout shaking their heads no.

Petronilla proudly presented Mathieu's mirror to her sister. Eleanor startled.

Amira addressed the well-dressed gown makers, "To understand Aquitaine, let us have a vestment review," and swept her hand. Lady Jolietemps puffed out, "We will sit for your drips and drabs of color." As if to please their master, the gown master said, "We have reservations and certain prohibitions against fashions in a pious court, but .. proceed."

Maryam displayed a Spanish surcoat layered in Moorish colors. Reyna exhibited lace-in sleeves that matched an ornate underskirt appearing through an overskirt. Her golden frills matched the gild of her boots.

Jolietemps kept smoothing out her gown as if mud had been thrown on it.

The youngest gown designer sat nervously. He wanted to get up and show the Aquitaine women what more they could make of their look. From bold color dress-gowns that hinted underskirt, he imagined elaborate reveals. Undershirts laced tightly could be relaced more attractively. Fabric restricted to accents could be bodily worn. But the dismal prospect of having to make the same old holy gowns for years to come, made him stand. "I am delighted! I suggest for the wedding that even Parisii gowns be pleated in falling rings."

Everyone turned to the freckled faced twenty-year-old.

"Vesteed Tisserand!" was all Jolietemps could say.

The lean man could not stop himself. "I see nothing but possibilities. I've traveled the world and the sea, seen fashions of Spain, Italy, Greece, and Arabia. I've measured the clothing of wealthy, poor, and every walk of life with equal interest, but what you have here amazes. What we want to do is–"

"What - we - want - to - do!" Jolietemps stomped a foot. "Vesteed? Sit. What we want to do, what we are going to do, is this. One long dark gown, one piece, no color, long sleeves with pedant embroidery, and soft black cloth slippers, like mine." She extended her leg. It was not a pretty foot.

"Nay," Amira said.

"Nay?"

"Wear shrouds? Plainly, nay. 'Celebration of the living is worth more than a mass for the dead'," Amira said, quoting her first lesson from Spark. "Jolietemps, this is a joyful marriage, not a funeral. We are in Aquitaine, let's live."

Jolietemps ignored the jabs. "Seriously dear, we must bring royal favor in the eyes of the King's church. The Queen prefers enduring family values to fashion."

The red hairs on Amira's neck raised. *I will give you enduring family values.*

Ellen intervened. "Lady Jolietemps, I remind. You are a guest of the Duchy."

"And none of you will visit Paris if you do not please me." Jolietemps sneered.

The unsettled tailors had much work to do, and the impasse between the Holy style of Paris and the vibrant illuminations of Aquitaine left little time. Ellen found a compromise agreement that evening. The Envoy helped persuade Lady Jolietemps of the deal as such. For the royal marriage in the duchy, Eleanor of Aquitaine would wear her personal vestments. Whenever the day came for a Queen's coronation for Paris, Lady Jolietemps would have unbridled reign. Jolietemps finally assented. Before mercifully departing for her mother in Medoc she left her obligatory threat, "Make her family values tasteful or you will never sew another stitch in Paris." The tailors happily showed her the door.

The next day, Eleanor and Petronilla went to chapel services. The tailors gathered around the dressing table, curious about the Aquitaine wedding dress. Amira spoke: "Family values must endure. We agree. We honor Aquitaine ancestry and her father's ancient-inspired themes. Can you help?" The guild master spoke. "We know of Greek and Roman aprons, diaphanous folds, laurel crowns."

Amira placed two stone female figurines on the table, the first of Celtic stone, the other of Greek ceramic from Crete. Both hand statues were bare-breasted women with long colorful skirts, doing what looked like cheers. "This first feminine idol is from her Norse ancestry. The second comes by her grandfather by way of Byzantium. Deep-rooted family traditions, gentlemen."

"Well, weave me a cross," the head tailor exclaimed.

Ellen drew two fingers through her brow, "Amira has drawings that are more to the point." From the next room, Amira brought a leather valise marked with a 'G.' Dangerossa leaned to the table wide-eyed.

Amira cast a serious countenance. "This is a royal wedding. Family values must be observed. Men and women balanced in style." Setting the valise on the table, she solemnly fanned out the drawings. "The Bible is taken seriously in these lands. We revere Adam and Eve." Dangerossa took a step back. She had assumed the drawings were missing. A sheen of mortification rippled through the expert dressmakers. They picked through the full-length drawings. A naked woman stood with an equally naked man, their birthing parts fully revealed. The horrified tailors squinted at straight-faced Amira, dead-serious Ellen, and the rising smile of Dangerossa.

After a golden silence, freckled Vesteed broke out laughing, as did the women. The tailors followed, nearly ripping their seams, feeling the worst pain in their ribs since they were boys. The head tailor gasped, "It would save on the stitching." Amira put the drawings away and kicked the case to Dangerossa who scooted it under her gown. After a good venting, and congratulations for the prank, Amira implored, "Sirs, can you carry forth her vestment along a Greek model in a tasteful manner? It must be beautiful."

Tisserand stood, "Master if I may. I have been to Crete. We understand the spirit you are after. Lady Eleanor told me herself if she had to wear the old gown of Adelaide that she might as well powder her hair white. I assured her that Paris did not fashion dressing like dead people, not just yet." The tailors bent in stitches suggesting the barb of truth.

Over the next days, inspired Vesteed led the effort, working with Eleanor's court. The thin man took Dangerossa's council to add something familiar and improved her scarlet entry cloak. He placed Amira's Grecian doll on the mantel. Directing the dressmakers to cut his mysterious designs, they used the finest silk and cotton from the Holy Lands. When Vesteed dangled parts of the pearly fabric in front of Eleanor for fittings, she got the idea. It would be her: brazen and fine; ancient and new; raw, feminine, and gorgeous.

That week, Eleanor's court grew by one. Amira and Ellen interviewed Vesteed Tisserand away from his masters. He conveyed his abiding belief. "Aquitaine vestments are liberating. After Paris, Eleanor's vision makes one come alive. Slippers? Women's boots are heroic. Short hair? Long hair holds great sway. Style is history. Fashion is power. I want to be part of the future realm, and I can help." He discussed the limitations and necessity for gowns in Paris and gave a new plan for variations in sleeve and hem handling, hair pockets, arm and shoulder lacings. He was perfect. Amira took him to the high tower. Appalled at Eleanor's tight quarters, he stood on the stairwell ladder. Eleanor flat her palm to his shoulder, "Vesteed Tisserand I invest you as the head dresser of the court. Will your employer release you?" Everyone laughed as he kissed her hand.

June turned into a heated July as the wedding dress revealed its inspiration. Eleanor turned her attention in consideration of her Prince. At the breakfast table, she and her damisels ate the fresh fruit of summer. Over peach and cherries, Eleanor announced she would pen a letter for Louis Seven from the tower in the evening.

Finishing strawberries and honey melon, Amira said, "I have good news everyone, tonight we shall have music. From castle Blaye, the Plaganet brothers will sing fantastic songs of dark years and forgotten battles."

"I believe I will listen from the tower," Eleanor said, thinking of Rudel's 'Why We Fight' performance. "Please, no battle songs from Castle Blaye."

"Like a song, a castle can have two meanings," Amira counseled.

That evening, Eleanor climbed the stairway. Father once encouraged she write to the Prince. She touched her crossbow and graced her mirror for good luck. By candlelight she composed a letter of poetic concern, wanting Louis to know her hopeful feelings. Amira combed her heavenly hair.

In the torch-lit courtyard, the two Plaganet brothers sang of the ancient battles of the Celts and Pictones. The verse told of a queen and her men afield in an epic battle. Eleanor felt drawn to the song of war in a way she did not expect. A young woman's voice sang, whispering battle skills to alert each man in the battle line. From the iron bars, Eleanor stood to watch Trobaritz Mirielle Denni chant her martial orders in her sweet clarion voice. The troubadours and the trobaritz, in an ancient call, joined their masculine and feminine voices in night song. Eleanor picked up her harp to finger the strings and feel the play. After they shouted "AOI!" and passed the spirited jug, Eleanor asked them to play again. The brothers started. Through the bars, she hummed with Mirielle's return, of the dread song of generations past and forevermore.

♪

The queen of light went forthright, to dance the dark of souls,
Alone she rides in force tonight, he reds the stir of coals.
Woe-o- the winds sigh, war-o- comes the cry,
Come into mystic dreams dark-light, breathe in her deep moonlight.
Her mare she thunders into camp, hallowed in horses' whoa,
Ardor readied tent to tent, arise in the Eastern glow.
Pallas Athena calls upon the Angels of Amasons,
Sing as you raise your arched bow, shoot straighter than before,
Hail as you pull back your trust'd spear, hurl harder than last soar.

Skies fill with good and bad that every war-falcon knows,
Side by side we join in might, take heed the flurry black of crows.
Hard charge the striker rides, plant deep your bannered lance,
Pull back your blood hammer bold, throw down a heavy crack.
Bring back on winged victory, bring your heart home to me,
Ares see the blood foe we give thee and name this realm to be.
     AOI

♪

The party had long gone, but the music remained. The martial nature of the young prisoner in the tower stirred. Standing in the moonlight, she regarded the spent candle husk and the red coals of the courtyard below. Through the grating, the damp chill of midnight air breathed on her face. Turning about, she let loose her ankle-long hair to fall through the cold iron bars. The red strands caught moonbeams that glittered like gold on the Ombrière gate. Wolves howled high in the hills. She had been writing a letter for a face she had never seen. The music inspired a new direction. Unfinished, she needed whiskey. Before closing her tired eyes, she asked Amira to have by midmorning, four jugs for the Plaganets. She knew her musicians well.

Late in the morning light, two musicians sat harshly in the courtyard like unknowing knight's apprentices. The page, Jem-James, looked a scrappy yard bird. The squire, his elder brother Robert, wore the feathers. Eleanor let down her long flowing strands of red-gold mane from the high tower. They leaped up, asking permission to climb her hair. Through the bars, she chuckled. "You just try." And they did. "Thank you both for last night's serenade. I appreciated the balance Mirielle brought."

Robert spoke, "We've never sung with a woman before. Mirielle's desire was to sing for her queen-to-be, in her dark hour, for the battles surely ahead."

Amira brought forth the jugs of hard drink for their delight.

"From on high, hear my commission," Eleanor announced from her tower window. "I want a song to match my letter. Play it personally for Prince Louis to help him on his long ride from Paris. I have a melody." She played, knowing they would improve it.

"No, no, like this!" Robert took the lead.

She floated down her draft verse. Gandering over it, tapping into the hard spirits, the two musicians rewrote their battle music to match her love-verse. After three shots. "Our song is good now. Timing is key. Go now!" "—How many more times?" "—A new cup tastes better than minutes of whiskey ago. Go!" They downed and sang.

Eleanor held out a cup from the bars, whispering to Amira, "We have to drink like the fellows, let them see that you can take it." Amira ran up the stairs with drink and to help finish the letter. The four shared the firewater as Amira lit up a wax warmer for sealing the letter. Eleanor imbibed, "AHH" and forced a satisfied face. "This is not a love song!"

"—AOI!" They spirited, "It is for love we drink." She wrote the final words, cut a trim of her temple hair, and attached it to the page with her wax stamp.

Amira scanned the note and said, "How bold to tell of oneself to an unknown person; especially in your way." Eleanor smirked, "Show The Woman; that is my code." Amira folded the letter, closed it with wax, saying, "I used to say hide the woman." The two broke out in complementary laughs.

As the musicians wove about, readying their horses to leave, an Aquitaine-born message arrived from the Bordeaux pigeon tower. Matthieu announced Prince Louis the Seventh, called Louis Sept, was on the march, calculating he was a week away. The troubadours would be able to reach the prince in four days, then return directly to the tower with the prince's response. The musicians rode up, weaving in their saddles. Amira ran down with the letter.

"We paid and primed Plaganets, armed with sealed charters, and jugs plenty full, gallop off into the Eastern sunrise to plant the seeds for your success, to find a prince without a princess."

They saluted and charged off. Amira walked a few steps then stopped to watch them fade. She turned to her friend and counseled nothing.

Eleanor simply had to wait.

◆ ◆

The Short Wedding and the Long Feast

The midsummer roads leading to peaceful Bordeaux trafficked in steady accounts. Bearing down on the wealthy port city, a mile long war train marched battle commanders, Counts, Abbots, and five hundred knights on five hundred horses. At the end of the convoy in a halo of luggage wagons and a devoted entourage, rode the young Crown Prince of France.

Two abbots of two colors minded the Holy Prince. At the head of the train in robes of gray, rode a jovial God-loving Abbot from Saint-Denis. The other who stayed behind in Clairvaux was a God-fearing Abbot whose white-robed priests represented his absence. No two spiritual leaders could be furthest apart.

The knights of Paris had a strange combat mission this month. They were to wear full armor, yet show no sword, flag battle lances, don colorful ribbons, put flowers on shield and visor, and decorate their horses.

Commander Thibault, the supreme commander, grit his teeth. The seasoned warrior in his salt and pepper beard was famous for melee and plunder. Beloved by his men, the testy forty-seven-year-old Count of Champagne shared their suffering. He did his best to march at peace. Thibault always rode with white priests, not gray ones. His armies were obedient to Cross first, King second. These hardhearted men – lieged to fight for the crown of Paris, doing their worst in feuds, raising castles, raining death, and putting to sword many in bloody kills – obeyed the killing cross. It took hard-cursing white priest confessors to discipline such brutes, for a code of honor was unknown to such warriors.

For Raoul, Count of Vermandois, King came first, Cross second. The handsome, heavily bearded Chancellor of France was fifty-two. He dressed like the King of France because he spoke for the King. Thibault permitted Raoul to admonish his men-at-arms, for this reason, and that the Chancellor was married to his sister. Gesturing a royal gold-sleeved tunic with an air of authority, Chancellor Raoul proclaimed:

"You shall not rob, harry, or spoil these people. That would be a great folly; for in a matter of days, they will become the King's subjects. Take nothing, lodge and live from your tent, endure any insult, do not provoke."

This stony order given to hard Parisii knights was as repugnant as bedpan contents, a warmth they would face as shit-mixers, should they disobey. The stirring staffs would be issued as fast as a circuitor poles by the Abbot in gray, Adam Suger.

Administering the counts and commanders, Abbot Suger made sure nothing slipped. With graying beard groomed as well as his tonsured bowl cut, the well-rounded abbot of fifty-six was a consummate organizer with a fix for any problem. In gray woolen robes with blue and gold tippet sashes, he blessed any and all as need be. This event was so important that Suger rested the construction in Saint-Denis of France's newest cathedral.

Suger mapped their march south, around Eleanor's homeland to avoid any chance of hostility in Aquitaine. A good call. Few wished the removal of their fair Princess, and many rightly feared the imposition of Parisii law. Aquitaine bowed to Duchess Eleanor, not to a foreign king.

The most amazing result of Suger's march of peace, was not that Raoul's order was obeyed, which took on its own form of bravery. This would be the greatest military victory of these warrior's lifetimes. Children in school learning of great wars, would not be taught that this conquest would acquire more land mass than any three generations of carnage-makers combined. As Suger might well say, 'The screaming, bleeding, killing – the woe of war. Children! Just kissed away!'

. . .

Eleanor's curiosity for the King's son lay in the hands of two troubadours on horseback. After four days, they arrived on a hilltop to behold the long march of the war train. Sighting an ashen-gray horse on which bobbed the young Prince, they pulled out their instruments. From a ground tone, they droned and scaled their notes. Having tuned their strings, they drove through the austere lines.

Louis, auburn-haired and lightly groomed beard, wore a simple gray habit and cowl over a white gold-embroidered tunic. The seventeen-year-old Prince sat heavy in the horse-hooves of a sorrowful prospect. His treasured life of the monastery was gone. His mentor, Abbot Sugar, rushed him to become next in line to be king, replacing his elder brother, killed as he was thrown from a horse, a horse very much like the one Louis rode now. This clomping man-killer was taking Louis further away from Paris, further than his soul had ever been, far from the familiar, away from his sick corpulent father. Elderly priests suggested how to run the kingdom to come. His earthly father crazily ordered him – in spite of the many obedient Parisian women he prayed with – to suddenly march off and marry a wild woman he had never seen. Louis looked high to the trees. "God-oh-God." He would bear the cross.

Two colorful riders appeared giving respectful introductions. Prince Louis dismissed everyone to take their private riding audience.

"Royal Louis Sept, your bride-to-be, even though she has lost her parents, prays for your ill father and presents her comforting words. Hear her song, to set your mind to a new beginning. Here, from the hand of Eleanor, to open shortly."

Louis received the small scroll, reminding himself, 'open shortly.'

Feather-plumed Robert played lute-mandolin, his brother strummed a lute-guitar. As did any of Eleanor's commission, the troubadours shared the state of the audience first. The Plaganets gathered the Prince's nature and matched his downbeat mood in ever heavier descending notes; their music seemed to slow the horses. When the road leveled, the troubadours broke to a bridge, picking out notes, tempo, and measure. Robert began with a musical sigh.

♪

Down the summer road, a woman waits fair
    with love in'er eyes, flowers in'er hair.

Never let them say each path is the same
    that women of the world are just one game.

The way west is best to take a long war train
    through crossroads straight as the ocean's vane.

Pass mud-brown rivers, pass clouds ever gray
    to find how tomorrow becomes today.

♪

Louis looked aghast. "This is not Holy verse, does she know who I am?"

"Not yet, but she believes you to be a man." Louis had to think, and then he laughed like Abbot Suger. The troubadours played couplets in a variant chord, signaling the Prince to break the seal and read the tight scroll written in Latin. The hand flowed:

☙

Come to the Gold Coast of France by your heart
My mind I have made to make our new start.
I am a poor prisoner in a tower keep
My hair is let down for you to climb and seek
A lock of it for you, this seal a kiss from me.

The Prince frowned, then mused as the sender intended. He lifted the red double bow of her lip-print to his face. Scents of summer lavender, sage, and honey broom rolled off the turned paper. Was it the music that moved him? Under his thumb, he felt the thinnest beeswax and a rough, colorful curl.

The note continued; he opened further.

Climb no tower of falling hair, unless it matches this key.
The children of the sun have begun to awake ☙

How could he be smiling and feel this way for someone he had never met? Louis rolled the lively strands of lemon and raspberry between his fingers, listening to the spirited music.

"Oho, this is a snippet of her hair. But why for me?"

Robert was used to patrons and having to explain everything. "Sire, she is actually locked in a tower. She jests about the *lock* of her hair as the *key*. My brother and I have seen her ankle-long hair and joked with her about climbing it. Her hair falls for you, and only you, to climb and take her away." To the musician's surprise, Louis laughed long and hard.

"She has some wit. She is informed that my grandfather King Philip stole his new wife from a tower. He was excommunicated for arranging his own marriage. The Duchess is a rascal to write of eloping."

"Not rascal. Hrad, sire. She is hrad."

"A youth in spirit, yes. Now wait. She wrote these letters. She is thirteen?"

"Yes, sire. Eleanor is wise. Her mind is beyond her years."

Louis looked her letter over again. "Play more."

♪

To find a queen without a king

She plays cithtara and cries and sings

  Al ah al ah

Ride an ash mare through the steps you are sworn

To quest for a woman who's never been born

  Al ah al ah

Stand on a hill in your mountain of dreams

The road West won't take as long as it seems

  Aaa al aaa, aaa al aaa, al aa al la.

♪

With his horse bearing downhill, Louis found himself looking up. He whisped her hair to tickle his thin beard and cast a grin. "One more time, please. Sing more of this woman who cries and sings." As the hooves crumbled ahead, the troubadours improvised. Mountains appeared, ravines dropped, the woman laughed, then brightly sighed. Forests grew wide; the sky changed colors, but in the end, Louis flew over the hills in the mountain of his dreams. He got used to their verse and sang the coda, *"Al Aa, Al La."*

"God in Heaven!" the white bishops shouted, catching wind of the tune. "There are hints of the unholy. It sounds like Allah in the air. Are the songsters taking Louis in through the out door of hell?" The clergy turned back. Light shafts fell through the trees. Louis cavorted between patches of light and shadow, saddled between the troubadours, one on each side, singing in tenso style. Back and forth in a musical dual, they sang in polyphonic canticle one over the other of love and war.

The sacred in white stormed up in a holy huff. Guiding the soul of Louis was their way to paradise. "Air-fillers, out with your leaden asses!" The shoe of shame was held over Louis for taking false delight in musical enjoyment. Suger in gray would allow this, but not the whites.

Robert held out his hand to Louis. A priest offered a coin of bribe. He refused. "If you please, Prince Louis, give us something for Eleanor to show of yourself."

Louis searched for a gift, something the white mitered frowners might assent to. His agent said she liked words. Some light travel reading; this he could share. His handler fetched from his wagon Bolland's Latin '*Alphabetical History of the Saints: Volume 2 of 47.*' The priests were shocked to see the hagiography leave his care. Louis knew he was being a little forward, it being volume two. He allayed his holy counselors. "To find my betrothed in the rapture of its comforting thoughts would lead us to a divine conversation."

Ten days at Ombrière.

That was the time allotted for Princess Eleanor and Prince Louis to conduct interviews with one another. The engagement period was primarily for their courts and planners to discuss their union in every detail. The wedding ceremony was quickly agreed to. The real issues ranged from the statutes of law, assurances of title, taxation, worship, and governance. Given the necessities of the royal kingdom and the affordances of wealthy Aquitaine, some matters seemed unreconcilable. Her advocates declared Eleanor keep her personal rule of Aquitaine with its lively customs. Ministers on Louis's side demanded Roman Christian sacraments in every church and that no other faiths practice. In the no man's land of property expansion, common law, and trusts, compromise agreements were partly reached. One accord: the church may expand holdings if frank-lien trusts were recognized along maternal lines. One concession: former canon cases like the one in Chauvigny required royal review. Unvoiced grievances would certainly erupt into feudal violence. A fortnight of days in talks would be time well spent. They had ten.

Eleanor spent all morning with her attendants of the bath in expectation of meeting Prince Louis. Scrubbed, soaped, rinsed, dressed in flower oils, she fit finely in a garden-inspired gown. After a precious hour spent with Amira's finish, servants perfected her visage and drew out Eleanor's ankle-length hair. The dresser talk was: Parisian Jolietemps was so upset at the wedding vestments, she dismissed Vesteed. The dress was placed under Aquitaine guard.

The prospect of the day's visit with former monk Louis weighed with apprehension. In Poitiers, the Prince's clergy had been harsh, brutal, and in some matters, unforgivable. Aunts counseled that God-fearing men were the worst; they conducted wrath into all life. Holy husbands gave the worst beatings, and Louis was rumored to be the most Holy. Amira encouraged: a God-loving woman will prevail. Eleanor was resolute to endure the days, no matter how mean-spirited her groom may be. They put talk behind. A garland of fresh flowers was set in her hair, and to be safe, frankincense on a scarf. The Princess walked into the small courtyard. Obtaining the approval of her chaperoning relatives, she withdrew into the Elm shade with her damisels. If Amira watching the riverboats approach with as much apprehension as Eleanor, she wasn't showing it. Her visage was placid as the Garonne.

The first time Eleanor saw Louis, she was unsure. The figure of a lean seventeen-year-old climbing carefully off the barge clutching a long rod staff made him seem feeble. *If I could just see his face*, she thought anxiously.

Her noble party assembled before the Ombrière lodge, Eleanor in reserve. Far off, he did look the Prince, walking tall in a clean long gray mantle over a gold-embroidered vestment. Although she had been beaten with a rod by his Catholic clergy, she put his heavy staff out of her mind. She was thirteen and determined. Abbesses and ladies received his party in style and grace.

Eleanor stood back, radiant under the Ombrière arch gate, shimmering in a light green and blue damask gown stamped in silver. She was adorned with silver bracelets set with small emeralds, a light silver necklace and cross, a ruby embedded on her center belt. Ears naked without earrings, a stunning blue sapphire strung in thin silver at her forehead.

The Prince approached studying her long red-gold hair, intertwined with light violet and yellow rose buds. He was in Aquitaine, the land of dances and long mouth kisses. Nervous Eleanor's heart soon skipped beats – his face was radiant and gentle! Not mean at all! She flushed a shame and held back a giggle to ever think such a gentle spirit malevolent. She swam in her first impression of his dreamy blue round eyes, wavy auburn hair, large long nose, and trimmed fine beard. He looked pale but youthful, saintly against his cloister of holy chaperones. Her chest breathed rapidly. Abbot Suger, smitten with her beautiful charms, gathered all the priests back to let Louis proceed.

As manner dictates, normally the man performs the first courtesy to a woman, but a person of a lower station must respect the higher.

"Prince Louis, lovely to meet your highness," curtsied sparkling-eyed Eleanor. They wondered through unsure smiles and questing eyes. She lowered her head saying, "Praise be to God to have watched over your long travel," staying her bow.

Louis received her direct presentation, her composure, and her joyful nature with a glisten in his eyes. Such a spirited uninhibited women could never flourish in Paris. "Eleanor of Aquitaine the beautiful, rise." He looked to the magnificent clouds. "God's face," and pressed his young beard lightly. "Thank you for sending your music upon the weary road." Louis beheld the letter writer's lovely blue eyes. He doubted he could sigh any deeper. He gripped his staff. "My-damisel, your words made me feel something."

"Your grace." She humored, "Are you going to beat me with that cudgel?"

"This is my holy staff."

"You don't need to tell me. It makes you look infirm! You are healthy as me."

Eleanor watched his wide, gentle eyes look over her focal points. They were looking at all the right places.

Nervously Louis said, "God-Oh-God. I am in trouble now."

Eleanor gave an unsure smirk; was he .. praying or joking? She made a hand sign: two first fingers in-join rising side by side.

"Both," he interpreted unsurely: "Oh, I said God twice?"

"I meant both of us are in trouble. Don't deny it." They laughed roundly. He was definitely shy. She probed his sense of humor.

"So, you are the Saint-studier."

"In their lives are the clues of our obedience to Him," he said gravely.

"I did get your message in Bolland's second hagiography."

"It was a little risqué," he said, afraid to reveal a bit of the lust in his blood.

"What shall we do about that?"

Louis offered at the edge of his young nerve, "Read every line together?"

"How about we read between the lines?"

Louis knew the passage. Perspiring, avoiding her tempting eyes, he asked politely, "My damisel, do you need to retire to your tower?"

"How considerate. Let's have fresh air." Eleanor scored the change of subjects as a light victory. On second examination, she felt he seemed unsettled, remote and detached; a guilt fixed in his mind. She noted his left eye was larger, and a telling mark of men: ornamental slippers, not boots. They would not be going anywhere soon; she would fix that. He seemed – she could not escape it – a bit simple and timid. His soft thin groomed beard was irresistible.

"Gracious Prince Louis, I see you find our high summer heat unsettling. I know the river walk well. Share with me the tall cool Elms of the Ombrière, and my family's lodge." Louis said nothing; his head was in the elms. They walked. Attendants and guards tittered near. Amira shoed away bystanders to a respectful distance for their private conversation.

Patient, open-minded Eleanor had many favors requiring his attention.

"Have you ever been to Aquitaine?"

"No, never."

"I hear we have ten days at Ombrière. I will show you its pleasances. If you can free me from this tower, we can enjoy the pleasures of the land together."

"Bordeaux has peaceful air. I like your air fabulously. It is not humid. Paris is humid." They watched the boats drift on the Garonne's perfect mirror.

Eleanor noted his increasing nervousness, his more simplistic responses. He would no longer look into her eyes. His heart hid something.

"You must have hunting lodges near Paris like the Ombrière."

"There is one. Outside the city walls. It is an old fort."

"My father hunted west of here toward the Ocean."

"Bless his soul. I have prayed for his soul. His soul is in heaven now."

"Thank you, Prince Louis. I am sure. He was dear to my heart; I trust as loving as your father. I hear your father is in repose."

"He is sick. He is not well. He is fat and not well," Louis stammered, straining to see the clouds through the trees.

"I am terribly sorry to hear that. We pray for the King's health in mass."

Eleanor studied him. Louis had retreated to a basic childish nature, unable to connect speech to thought. Words turned into prattle perhaps because he did not want to see his words connect in her eyes. Eleanor had experienced this before in suitor. Such avoidance came from priests that feared God and hated women. Louis was minding an instruction, yet trying to be kind. Eleanor said warmly, "Prince Louis, Duke William served your father the Lord King well. William made Aquitaine greater. May the Aquitaine count on you for continued assistance?" Louis did not answer. Avoiding her, his eyes were lost in the high Elm leaves. He would probably break out in another bumble of broken sentences. Eleanor knew what to do. He had to pay attention.

"Look at me. See how I smile to hear your answer."

"My damisel." The Prince flustered at being told of such a simple thing to do.

"You do like to look at me?"

"Yes, I do."

"Then do so. There are many lords who have looked on me rudely. You have the gentle gaze of a good man, Louis. I was speaking of land cases that need your father's attention. Only the King can adjust these matters." The Prince looked intently at her, and she gave her radiant grace.

At ease, Louis talked of his courts, and they shared past times of their youths. She gestured over the Garonne, "From where you ferried, just north are great vineyards. In Blaye, troubadours sing valiant songs of battle. We can visit the relics." The Prince lit up. "Louis, you know Charlemagne's man, Rollant, and the Roncevaux fallen. All their battle relics are kept at the Church of Saint Romain; their tombs run all the way to Belin." He showed passing interest. Clearly, not a military man, but relics and praying for souls drew his attention. Ready to paint the picture of a day trip in the direction of the beach shores, she smiled to please his mind. First, she had to urge him to a troubling request.

"Further beyond Blaye is our hunting preserve at Talmont, but I fear it."

"Mmm, fear what."

"My mother and brother died there. Dark rumors say they were befouled."

"I am sorry to hear that. What can the Prince do?"

"My hunting falcons were taken by my vassal at Talmont." She picked up his fingers admiring his cleanliness. "I would so love them in my possession again."

"Consider your wish my first quest," Louis said.

"O my falcons are so dear. Louis, you have such chivalry. Find out if the castellan hides anything about my mother and brother's death." She crossed her heart as did Louis. Eleanor halted their walk. Much later she would ask of the concerns about her father's death. The thirteen-year-old pulled the seventeen-year-old to her body and whispered tipping to his ear, "It would mean so much to me." She lightly grazed his beard and let him go.

Never had Louis neared such a sweet thing, held such a warm, tender hand, or ever imagined that a warm whisper in his ear would be a thing to look forward to. He could not resist putting his arms around her. He felt a temptation to kiss her, but this was not his constitution, nor hers to initiate. Instead, their eyes glistened at the river, and the two felt the tension of closeness between a man and woman in the nervous doubts of arranged betrothal.

"Let us go to the beaches of Bordeaux, a day's ride there, a day back. I shall love to have a seashell necklace." He appreciated her moderate request and smiled deeply. Little did she know what great gift he traveled with. In silence, they beheld the Garonne flowing past the busy port of Bordeaux. She told how the river flowed around the bend out to the seat of the Ocean. This led to a discussion of exports, imports, trade volume, and taxable income. All along the walk, each feared the other could hear their heart's beat.

Initially, they disliked how the other spoke. Louis wanted her to talk slower and use more Latin. Eleanor explained resenting the language. She was a Gaul; they were the Romans. Memories of her ancestor's conquerors ran deep. Forced to speak Rome's Latin was as repulsive as being stamped with the tattooed mark of the slave. He assured her those days were over. The Church of Rome caused her family difficulties, and Latin-speakers undermined tribal law. Eleanor preferred French, always Occitan French, her tongue. Latin! French! Latin! French! There is nothing written in it! Then change that, you will be King! In respite, they held hands making a language of their own. Of caresses, holding, and feeling, Louis was her student, looking forward to every graduation.

The trait in her the Prince cared for least was what he learned to love most – her thoroughly feminine country Gaul. Her self-possessed witty vibrancy came from a mix of Celtic and Southern blood. Her desire for native tongue made her more French than any Parisian. Unlike devout women who professed charity, Eleanor had genuine concerns for causes. Affronted by her ability to read hearts; her hands-on winning way with people; her openness to be vulnerable and engage empathic feeling; her constant honesty – Louis found such virtues alien; and he was falling in love with them, with her. His advisors noted her uncanny skills were a statecraft that would help him someday. That is, if Louis could get a handle on his bubbling bride.

"I believe I have found the woman who has never been born," Louis said earnestly. He was not the type to think of anything original, nor introspective to recall the phrase's origin. Eleanor smiled, hearing her words flourish, that the Plaganets had inspired her to write. She valued how sincere he boyishly said the line that she planted in his heart. Practiced and clear in her arts, she created memories to play with, scenes to enjoy being in. She said softly, "A time will come when I will say, 'Remember how you kissed me on the sunset seashores of Bordeaux?' "

That night as Louis settled to sleep; he went over her words, realizing he had not kissed her yet. He dreamt of sunset breezes, sea shells, and rolling ocean waves.

On a sunny morning in July, the last days of their interview arrived. Although it took some effort to travel beyond the city walls, Abbot Suger blessed a heavily guarded ten league trip of Louis and Eleanor to the ocean and back. Suger and his Chancellor were full in political negotiations with the Aquitaines.

In the middle of the convoy of guards, priests, and servants, the Prince and Princess rode, sharing stories of family and state. Riding past a Roman amphitheater with a spanning aqueduct, they revealed they were the second choice to rule their realms, taking over for fallen brothers. Louis drew rein and led a prayer for their souls. Ridding on, Eleanor observed both grandfathers abducted their favorite mistresses and suffered excommunication to marry them. Eleanor cantered ahead and then trotted back, circling the Prince. "Louis, will you be like your grandfather Philip, as my grandfather William? Will you take me, come heaven or hell? Prove it!" Eleanor dug her heels into Limona. Though excommunication was a serious matter to Louis, he could not resist her passionate game. The Prince galloped her horse-riding dare. In stops and starts, they and their guards raced until they found the cool ocean breezes west of Bordeaux.

Off her horse on the sunset beach, hot and breathless, her naked feet apart in the sand, with one well-timed chaste long Aquitaine kiss, Eleanor enrolled Louis in her magnificent pleasance.

As tents were set near the beach for a nightstay, Louis took honest Amira aside. "Look at her swimming so strongly in the ocean. Cold water does not bother her. What is all this Jacque-foolery about troubadours? She told me as we rode the beach length, 'once I put my legs around a horse, I am in love.' What is that, a chevalier saying, a troubadour verse, or one of her beliefs?" Amira replied, "You can never tell. Prince Louis, she is a force of nature."

Inside their tent, after a good toweling, and fireside prayers, Eleanor and Amira blew out the candles and listened to the ocean roar. They talked of Petronilla in a mope, a captive of chaperones in Bordeaux; of Louis's gentle eyes and soft beard. Amira noted his odd habit of looking over people's heads, nervously to rafters, as if to avoid eyes, and how he desired to look at Eleanor. They spoke of the sensational wedding dress that promised a grand ceremony. Unable to sleep, they pulled on wool blankets to join the guards outside.

The tents rippled with the evening breeze. Arno and Mathieu brought wine and bread to the campfire that the four shared. Facing west with the vane into a long sea wind, Mathieu set bread to be toasted. They tossed wine on it with Arno's words about bold young life in friends, then ate the toast, a tribal act of symbolically partaking of words to become part of your life.

Eleanor observed, "The moonlit ocean was golden at sunset." Mathieu countered, "Not a sunset, but an earth-roll. The ancients say the world spins; the sun is still." Eleanor smiled gracefully. He was full of old and strange ideas.

Arno asked, "Amira, give your impressions of Louis and Eleanor."

"They are an interesting young couple. They are drawn to each other's airiness. He probes the holy clouds; she toys with a hundred ideas of love. He is incapable of lying because it says so in the Bible. She is incapable of lying because truth is her code." Mathieu added, "Then too, Louis seems remote, austere, and plain. Eleanor is direct, present, and voluptuous." Amira finished, "Voluptuousness has no pious value to him. Eleanor has a spirit where piety is not as important as honor." The rolling ocean shore broke.

"A toast to what is over the horizon," Eleanor said. They partook. She pivoted her soles about in the sand. "I do not care for the end of the world. I like the idea of it always turning." Louis could be seen quietly praying with chanting monks before relics of blood-martyred saints. Eleanor stretched her arms long. Jaufre Rudel's music came to mind. Arno sang lines which strangely felt comforting. Talked out and bottle empty, the women let Arno and the guards secure their sleep.

In the ten days of closeness, Louis held back on his Godly views. Unlike the religious-minded women Louis had been permitted to see, Eleanor was beautiful, treated him like a wanted friend, and he fell into deep admiration for her views.

Louis had his surprises. Not the seashell necklaces he placed around her neck, but how he assaulted Eleanor's perfect Aquitaine Frenchness. His words! What a blow! Next morning after tenting near one another, they cantered back from the kissing beach of Bordeaux. They stopped at the Roman aqueduct near Bordeaux to let their horses draw water. Comparing Parisii and Aquitaine ways, Louis looked up to the mid-arch of the aqueduct.

"Do you have plumbing in your castle as we have in the royal palace?"

"Plumbing?" She knew what it was.

"My damisel, water pipes, hot baths."

"You have that?"

Eleanor felt the vain arrest of her sensibility. Louis gently placed her hand on the sun-warmed arch stones at the base of an aqueduct span.

"Feel history, my Aquitaine Princess. A thousand years before us, the Romans transported water long distances over these arches. Fountains and gathering butts poured into heating cauldrons. They had pipes in their villas. Your Aquitaine servants boil water and lug pails up steps to your tub. In the royal palace, we pipe hot water to rooms so that you can have a hot wash anytime."

Delighted by the idea, Eleanor also felt the depth of her royal ignorance. As they walked the grasses, she could not help but notice, at last, Louis spoke long and coherently.

"My damisel, you say you dislike my Latin speaking and mention of Romans. Do you not see that millennia ago they had all of this figured out? Yet you hear this as something new. Your tribes, you are blind to think of Romans as your enemy. There has been a great forgetting, a thousand years lost. In Paris, great scholars are recovering knowledge of the ancients who in some ways, lived a better life than ours. Eleanor, you must come to Paris. Live with me. Give Paris a chance. Come see how great faith mixes with knowledge."

His shocking truth hit hard, challenging all she had been taught. Romans were barbaric and to be despised. She stretched her mind in consideration. She recalled handsome Bruce, the scholar in Paris who inspired her with how the past worked. By her code, harsh truths made truer friends.

"You said knowledge; you mean the cathedral schools like Saint Geneviève?"

"Yes."

"Can I, can we attend?" she asked with a zeal that surprised Louis.

"Certainly, if you wish." He leaned to her. "We do rule, you know."

"I will chance Paris with you if you take a chance to kiss me. Kiss me deep." Eleanor stomped on his boot, which put Louis on the wrong foot. She ran off like a rabbit in the field making him chase her around the spans until he took her down in the tall grasses. Guards watched their mirth.

That night, the Princess thought of her wrestling, her back on the grasses his tunic on her gown, and the kisses that followed. She turned a happy thought to Petronilla. While she and Louis were at the beach, the centerpiece of the Ombriere was her sister hosting Chancellor Raoul. Petronilla was enamored in bringing the Parisii administrators along. Tomorrow would come practice of the wedding ceremony. Eleanor imagined her marriage; spurring Limona through the gates of Paris and falling into their royal bed. Today she gave chase, let Louis win, but most exciting – how he made her reach so far.

❦

On a warm Sunday, July 25, 1137, the peaceful city of Bordeaux awoke to the well-posted foreign army of Paris. No military bravado or skill of combat was required to occupy the wine-famous city. The army achieved every major objective of war. The no-drum victory was decisive. Love had done the business of battle. All would be settled today by placing a ring on the understanding hand of Eleanor.

The tall trees lent ever-needed shade to the wedding arrivals in the high hour of the great sun. Horses, wagons, and helmeted men stood guard outside the boxy Cathedral Saint-André near the river. Like all cathedrals, the length called a nave, received the sunset; the arms, called transepts, lay north and south. Sunlight streamed white from a high clerestory onto the vibrant pillars of burgundy, aqua, gold, orange, violet, and light blue. Flowers tied in bows lent fragrance to the humid air. Festive vested lords and ladies of Aquitaine milled about. A singing chorus masked the general tension.

Abbot Suger, seeker of harmony, directed everyone. The Archbishop of Bordeaux, who would perform the ceremony, waited for his nod. Suger had separated the forces at the altar point. In the south transept milled the colorful diversely dressed, clean shaven Aquitaine men of with long shoulder-length hair. Sir Rancon of Taillebourg and Chevalier Arno calmed their courteous soldiers.

In the north transept, the bearded short-haired Parisii knights, Count Thibaud, Prince Louis, his counselors, priests, and ranking relatives discussed the merits of acquiring the outlying realm.

Across the altar transepts, the Latins faced Occitans, each side believing their tongue superior. The armies made some game of putting one other on. There is nothing like a good misunderstanding. Suger went to Eleanor's bodyguard, doing his best to speak in nasal tones with his Occitan rolling lilt. The two nodded.

"Eleanor's defender, nervous you are?"

The harsh, almost Germanic quality, verbs at the end, made understanding difficult for Arno. He recovered from the Parisii assault on the Aquitaine ear.

Arno replied: "Ah, Paris, you are speaking our Romanz? Me. Never .. oh Nervous? Never nervous. Now nerves, I have." The Abbot frowned. To help him understand, Arno clarified meanings by gesturing, using fewer words: "People - want Eleanor - to stay. Want stay, yes, you understand? Your swords - out - fear. Some vassals - not impressed."

Suger heard otherwise. "This is bad - vassals not in prison - stay - who? You mean, not yet, ah - should we fear them - or their cursed swords?"

Arno troubled the dialect. "Cursed words be damned." He gestured a grip of his hilt. "Sword. This–sword. Cursing cuts the Lord's ears deep. Not cut the ears off. Oc, forget I said that. Paris! You arm yourself with sword – avoid fief-lands. Regard." He stomped like a horse. "bad - lot. they, you. sword. bloody. kills. Uhh." He drew a line across his neck with his thumb.

The two retreated, tightlipped. With beard-stroking movements, they retreated in apparent comprehension. Suger, embracing the chain of misunderstandings, instructed: "My son, you - the Parisii tongue don't know. Sir Pierre Argent, him find - talk, every knight's name and location for Paris he should note, you go?"

Arno nodded with vigor. "I now go." Turning the odd request over, he would find this Pierre fellow and ask him where every one of the Parisii knights lived, after the royal wedding. Out the main cathedral doors he went.

. . .

TA-TA-TA, ta-ta-ta, taaa. Trumpets blared and muffled.

Common weddings were held in a house not a church; an agreement of fathers affirmed by a priest in a few words and there was a small feast. Noble weddings were often held on the steps of a church. However, the becoming of Prince Louis and Princess Eleanor as the new blood of France required public evidence. This staging and procession brought every emotion – flush elation, perspired excitement, tearful sadness, happy delirium, pride in becoming, and anxious hope for the of the thirteen summers girl.

For this altar-bound event, Eleanor's personal guard appeared first. Two sets of male and female guards in polished armor held lances high for a white canopy of silk covering the bride. Harping arpeggios announced the opening light of the cathedral door presenting the silhouette of a mantled Princess in her chosen wedding dress. She would not be given away. This was her ascension. Eleanor was the Aquitaine preparing to become France.

Stiff gowns turned. Her serene steps unbroken by alarmists.

"Red?" "—Crusade Scarlet." "—No bride would " "—Yes."

The wedding Princess walked with steely nerve, knowing her leaving was her becoming. In her amazing red cape, she took thirteen steps in the narthex entry and halted. Arno removed the mantle to show sewn-in her new Aquitaine heralding of blue waves and white silver caps, the same as those hanging from the canopy lances. The heraldry announced her presence forevermore. Folding the red cape, a sign of her damisel youth passing, he bowed. The thirteen-year-old took a swivel turn and stepped under the guarded canopy that moved forward with her, presenting her gorgeous radiance.

"Can't see." "—Out of my way!" "—Manners." "—Only Eleanor of Aquitaine could ..." The gown was wildly full of her and coursed with her nature. Inspired, of classic Greek origin, her vestment carried her father's beliefs mixed in feminine allure.

She walked the wedding aisle in waves of "Oh!"

Splendid silk brocade from Damascus alternated with fine imported cotton from Egypt, sent by her uncle's prosperous colony. A white silk bodice-form ran up from her naval opening to frame her white veiled chest. The frame's piping traveled her shoulders, ending in a fine necklacing. The skirts. A series of seven thin hooped bells fell upon the other, suggesting fuller hips. Each silk hoop tiered in warm, faintly dyed multi-colors. A white apron curved to the front, overset by an embroidered belt that fell to a 'vee' entwined in sea gems. A larger waist belt circled her in silver and dark gold, inset with river-blue gems. Each white-sleeved arm had six ties; almond-shapes revealed glimpses of shoulder, arm, and wrist.

"Separated sleeves?" "—To see her arm-flesh." "—What?" "—Press aside!"

With her canopy in motion, she stepped toward Sir Rancon's confident smile.

Around her neck was a thin necklace of a hundred silver-wrapped pearls. Her blonde-red hair was fulled and woven with strands of fine silver chains, and tiny garlands of white, red, and violet rose buds. A white veil fell to the middle of her eyes. Beaming young Louis received her. "What style!"

As she was meant to rule, she walked in thin white calfskin boots given by her countrymen who ruled Aquitaine by horse. They fit as if they were her feet, ingrained in chevalier's style with gilded rims. Hard soles for stirrups; she was going places. There would be no fault in her steps.

Her canopy stilled to a hush. Stepping out from under, she took the hand of her wide-eyed groom. Music of flute, harp and choir swelled, then feathered away. The two took their places before the altar. The silence was magnificent.

The Prince and Princess steadied their stance on the large carpeted stage. They beheld the beauty in one another – Louis in robes of white, gold, and blue, young Eleanor in her sensational light-colored silks. Through half-veil, she looked to the Archbishop of Bordeaux in his gold miter and white robe.

Tipping up to see, the edgy Aquitaine and Parisii knights were transformed by the moment of marriage. The Archbishop turned to the altar and put Eleanor's coronet to his lips. He declared in Latin: "According to God's law. Witness Eleanor, Duchess of Aquitaine, Duchess of Gascony." In white gloves he pulled back her veil, enchanted by her gaze.

Eleanor touched her father's coronet on the altar table. The Archbishop. declared in Latin, "Almighty God cedes the domains of Eleanor, enjoined to Louis, Prince of the Franks as Duke of Aquitaine." In white gloves he lay the Aquitaine coronet on the Prince. Louis spoke his words exactly: "The royal kingdom of the Franks takes Eleanor faithfully in trust to rule her Aquitaine realm." Eleanor said: "To Lord Louis, I give my lief and allegiance eternally. Over my Aquitaine realm, I grant your trust by my father's crown." Behind their heads, priests floated two large gold disks symbolic of their titles to be. At the altar, the Archbishop tapped holy water to their rings and blessed them with a mute kiss. He put a bejeweled ring on Eleanor, then a gold ring on Louis.

The Archbishop pronounced in a voice that knew walls well. "Magnify God, Louis and Eleanor. In the life of our Frank realm, may He grant your

Grace to come. Blessed are these rings. The church grants he who receives it and she who receives it, the bond of faith to abide in peace and glory. Grant these lives be lived together in His faith and His love and all that His glory brings until their lives end. Let us all exalt our faith and exalt His name. In unison: The Lord God, Jesus Nazarene, and the Holy Spirit. Amen."

Eleanor blinked warm, wet tears at her glittering hand.

"Peace be on this union of land, liege, and lief. The Holy Church weds Eleanor of Aquitaine to Louis Sept of France. Eleanor, praise to your Lord."

Eleanor had thought to fall like great Alexander on a gorgeous rug the way he honored marriage to the tribes of the East. The Archbishop said Greek prostration was out of place in the Latin church. Eleanor commended her own ritual – extending her arms to either side and bringing them together in a bowing kneel to her heart. Louis came to a knee by her side. Amid myriad Latin phrasings, they rose to embrace in the kiss of union and peace. A choir welled the mass to the couple's majestic promise. They stepped off the platform to the protection of the Parisii transept. Bells rang. Then came the unexpected.

Arno rushed to Eleanor's safety as men and women ran forward, some throwing themselves, sliding before Eleanor's legs, clinging to her skirt. Eleanor motioned Arno to stand back. She alertly bore the adoration of her subjects in close contact. Her rich beauty and daring dress radiated with life. "The virgin's blessing!" It was manifest in Eleanor's presence – her wedding smile, flowered head, expressive gestures of grace – conveyed hope and felicity to all. Some were overcome and fainted as the Archbishop conducted the blessings. Louis shared the veneration of his wife. He looked to the rafters mixing saintly thoughts with less saintly ones. As the deluge rose beyond any hope of control, Abbot Suger forced the necessary exit.

Trumpets mixed with bells from every Bordeaux high place. Louis guided Eleanor down the Cathedral steps into sunshine then safely up into the wagon. Masterminding the marriage, Abbot Suger felt he was in heaven. He had accomplished his King's order without incident. The painted interior of their wedding cathedral affirmed his colorful direction of Saint-Denis. Perhaps his brand of Catholic faith that loved the joys of the Earth would prevail. How grand, if loving hands and rings of conviction could settle all sword-feuding wars. Paris could grow this way forever until it ruled the world. He wrote vividly of the marriage in his chronicle. Later sacrists would excise his details and speculations.

By sunset, Sunday, July 25 in 1137, the vast Aquitaine – its busy Atlantic ports, vine-clad hills, fish-laden rivers, deeply wooded forests, fur-bearing preserves, high mountain silver mines, many-river powered mills – became a French domain. To the Parisii, the victory of the Holy Union was a miracle. To the Duchess of Aquitaines, Duchess of Gascones, the ceremonial splendor and riches exceeded her imagination. Of the ring, Amira reminded Eleanor, it was not the one around her finger but the circle around her head that would count. France already had a living King and Queen. A Paris confirmation and coronation would be required. As for now, Louis was the Crown Prince of the Franks and the Duke of Aquitaines. Eleanor was merely a double Duchess.

Thus ended the short conquest by Paris,
so began the long occupation of Aquitaine.

Conquest differs from occupation. Invaders, whether by war or peace, inevitably take on the ways of the greater mass of inhabitants.

Thibault's warriors had never traveled so far and been thrown so deep into enemy territory. Hard-fisted, the Parisii ensured a peaceful Aquitaine marriage.

Aquitaine was a land of dances and long mouth kisses. Bountiful Aquitaine enjoyed, what in dark Paris would be forbidden. It confused many with its exotic entertainments, opulent styles, sensual aromas, spicy foods, passionate music, and unusual faiths. Here, a smile was not a form of weakness; judgments were not severe. Here was wine, not beer. Aquitaine women teased with unusual hilarity. People loved to dance; they could not get enough of it.

Conversation at wine tables passed into many a night. Rude warriors were sent off; the kinder were invited to stay longer. In telling of the Prince's marriage, they learned of the enjoined land of exuberant experiences, plentiful with resources. Talk came of further postings for knights to administer the realm. Some spoke of starting new lives as furriers, lumberers, fishers, miners, millers – avenues not available to them around Paris. The real table talk, well appreciated by good wine, was of the number of fair women who held trusts of assets. Laughingly, as some knights found out, these women had to be approached in special ways, and Eleanor's court held the key. The soldier's Saintly Prince was moved by the preciousness of Eleanor. His deep regard for his damisel came to fect their minds. The pleasure of Aquitaine being seemed that of an alien civilization. Compare: In Aquitaine, an honored code led to prosperity, pleasure, and family. The cross led to denial, endurance of pain, eternal poverty, and abstinent loneliness. These two ways of living challenged the core beliefs of the obedients. Talk of Eleanor's so-called codes of family, honor, and love lead to opportunity – and they spread like a contagion.

The wedding party at the Ombrière gardens received visits from the great houses of Bordeaux into the evening. From the vine-clad terraces of the wide Garonne came forth their famous drink. The purple fruit was transformed into a special wine, and there was plenty for an army in celebration.

"Blood of Christ!" Parisii men-at-arms drank a body-full. Instead of wild intoxication, they became mellow, talkative, and found pleasure in ordinary things. "More dregless wine!" Civil red ribbons were poured in celebration from vineyards in La Roche, Benon, Blaye, and Bordeaux. Dregless? Why call it what it's not, rather than the pressing, clarifying and aging process that it is.

"May I have more of that claret?"

As Amira reminded every table, Aquitaine wine was safer than water. The vast production of fine claret improved Aquitaine's wealth, and the small tax improved Eleanor's disposition. You could say this was done for Eleanor's dislike of ale and barrel froth or her desire for purity or the beauty found in clear rubies, but she had lost her family to impure pox. Making safe wine was such an obsession that her offices wrote vinicultural laws, the first codes for wine. They were improved by men like Mathieu Nouville, whose pursuit of taste over drunkenness was a firsthand lesson.

"My pleas, to raise a glass to Eleanor." In the red glass of celebration revel, he had seen more: a way to extract and increase the distinct flavor of grape skins, using a gear-leveraged winepress, powered by the watermill. No more foot-stomping, this was an exact science. Late-harvested grapes in cellared casks revealed a civilizing secret – wine improves with age. Mathieu compared wine's taste to imaginary ruby lips; ones said to have kissed him while he was asleep under the moonlight upon Amira's bed. So when Mathieu gave the toast, he brought the toothy glass rim to his mouth, recalling his Endymion moment. He did not drink wine; he kissed it. Closing his eyes, he knew. The more his casks slept, the more mature her lovely mouth would be.

Abbot Suger announced the departure of the newlywed wedding train. In two days the couple celebrated their first night together in Taillebourg, Commander Rancon's castle-city. Impregnable, built high on a steep rock hill, the fortress surveyed the encampments below. In the castle, Rancon showed weapons and battle relics. Louis chastised him for not having holy relics.

Eleanor said, "Rancon protected me when father died–"

Louis was curt. "God is your protector now."

Candles at the grand supper cast their golden glow on the royal couple. Rancon raised a glass, "I confess Abbot Suger, Eleanor has a smile that could drop a man's heart." The table of lords gazed her way and gave affirmation. The bride smiled gracefully. Louis glared at Rancon, for the first time feeling the stabs of jealousy. Eleanor kissed away his sour feeling.

Sister Petronilla sat quietly. Chancellor Raoul made her laugh. Eleanor asserted, to the surprise of her sister: "Chancellor, on the way home, my sister and I are going on a hunt to my father's preserve in Talmont on the ocean." Before anyone could speak, she recanted. "What was I thinking? You men go, take a royal hunt. Though I am a great huntress."

Raoul asked: "How do you hunt?" His eyes betrayed his male attraction, one to which Eleanor was accustomed. Mercilessly, she lilted her words with tilts of her head. Petronilla watched her sister's masterful flirtation.

"I hunt by bow, but my hunting falcons are ruthless, far better than your hunting hounds. My birds gyre in the air and give battle signs. They strike prey faster than the arrow. I launch them by my gauntlet. Amira?" A glove appeared. Petronilla seized it, handing it to Raoul with her touch. The Chancellor fondled the gilded leather. Prince Taillebourg said, "Eleanor, can you show us how you use this?"

"Alas good sirs, my prize Falcons were stolen. William de Lezay holds them for ransom at Talmont." Raoul handed back her gauntlet gently. Eleanor feathered it, looking about the room. Taillebourg volunteered, "It would be my pleasure to bring home your hawks. I shall fetch them for you while you and the Prince continue to Poitiers."

"Oh, would you do that for me?" Eleanor said, holding high her glove.

Louis snapped the gauntlet from her hands. "This is the deed you were talking about in Ombrière. On the morrow, I'll take a small party to Talmont."

Rancon protested, "Prince Louis, stay with your bride!"

Louis glared at being told what to do. "Eleanor, you ride on. Let me deal justice. Lords, let's have a royal hunt." His knights resounded to join.

"My champion." Eleanor smiled. "If I may, a bit of advice. Present Duchess Eleanor's falcon gauntlet. Drop it and look into his eyes; see if he picks it up. Try his ransom by his face, not by his words. Be wary of water, my mother and brother died from Talmont's pox."

Louis said, "Worry not, dear. God rides with me. To hunting, we will go."

Eleanor fanned her arms out. "Louis my champion, great lords all, promise to return by Sunday to Poitiers for a great feast."

"It is Tuesday," Louis said. "We will have plenty of time to hunt. Dear, shall we go for a walk on the bastions?"

Eleanor winked to Amira to get Louis's handlers to allow the couple to sleep in the same room. Consummation of marriage was required by the church, a point she made for her determined mistress; a point that Suger conceded.

The couple walked the high ramparts of Taillebourg's wall, overlooking the knight's campfires to the twilight stars. He could not say, as he said to girlfriends in Paris, 'You are dearer than treasure,' for she already had a wealth of her own. As he searched for words, Eleanor appealed, "You may join me in my room." Louis frowned, but after her soft kiss, and his outline of consultations, blessings, prayers, to begin a long progress for their conjugal felicity, he found his hand taken to her bedroom door.

Eleanor's room was lit with a dozen candles. At first, the two played, uninterested in their newly acquired license to practice the arts. She was not sure if Louis was kidding or teasing about his holy vexations – no lewd kisses, try not to enjoy pleasure. In close stance, soft kissing comforts begat alert embraces. Eleanor wanted to know, and Louis was unable to resist her want to know.

"Why are you trembling so, Louis my love?"

He looked to the rafters. "It is a sin. I have never seen a woman undressed."

"You don't have to see."

She blew out the candles. Sheets flew overhead. In her throaty playful urges as the linen settled, they felt the shapes of their dark nearness. She whispered in his ear their newly shared memories. "Remember how you kissed me on the seashores of Bordeaux, how you chased me down in the Aqueduct grasses. Louis, you made me reach so far. I was naked then; I just had clothes on." She gave him a long Aquitaine kiss, and the man was done for. She tickled him into a tumble-turn of kisses; her seashell wishes granted. They tussled and urged on wet ecstasies until Eleanor felt her arms reach all the way to Paris. As silent as starlight, they were consumed.

All her hope-gathering years, Eleanor had imagined a capital love and a ceremonial marriage. Now she could realize her felicity in a real Aquitaine wedding celebration. Bordeaux had been sanctimonious, Taillebourg memorable, but Poitiers would be cultured, ribald, and exciting. Her place among her people and her high regard for Louis earned the trust of Suger. The Abbot had wisely put Eleanor at the head of the five hundred knights. She led them through victorious village receptions in otherwise contestable lands. Along the way, Louis and a party departed to hunt in Talmont and engage in Eleanor's task to return her falcons, promising to return for the wedding feast.

The first day of August, exactly one week from the wedding, the train was in Poitiers and Suger could not be happier. He'd met gifted Mathieu Nouville, who accepted a station to help build Saint-Denis. Prince Louis returned in time for the feast day, the captured falcons en-route. He embraced Eleanor, secretly looking forward to the bed-end of night, the time of naked-play when he took to boyish climbing and spurting about, then running off to confess the sin of pleasure.

Pierre Argent-Lutèce marched into Poitiers with his 500 rough knights. Gruff, with dark eyes, bush-bristling beard, hair short, he wore a chain mail hauberk to his shoulders with a dark tunic, belt dagger, and low cavalry boots. He was only eighteen, but hard drink and ass-kicking ages one prematurely. He was not a Parisian, but part of the Parisii tribe that lived north on the River Marne by Vitry.

The knight counted himself among General Thibault's whore chasers, drunken gamblers, angry cusses, and brawlers. After nights of bawdy celebration, Pierre was a marvel of confession. Nowhere in his litany of prayers was written the salvation he was about to face. It was a matter of time before such hard-fisted Paris warriors would succumb to something alien and utterly an Aquitaine quality of its women, genuine heart-beating love. Surprisingly, a force in time that would make this aspiring warrior invincible.

Rays fell lower on the castle walls. The fountain waters in Poitiers market square splashed with soldiers, refreshing and stretching from the long march from Bordeaux's wedding and hunt. Thibault's Parisii army had traversed fortifications, the gate works, six-foot thick walls, and stood in its courtyard – dispensing with a six-month siege and the loss of a thousand souls. The intact palace a hundred paces ahead begged an assault plan. Every door of the castle was open, nothing guarded. Curtains flowed that you could easily ladder and vault through. It was too easy; it was unnerving.

Into the courtyard poured savory smells, rousing the burly knights.

The Paris knights blustered their martial wares before the colorful Aquitaine chevaliers. Hand on sword, helmeted, Pierre looked like his cadre, ready to get roman and brawl with these impossible to understand Aquitaine. The knight of eighteen ground a heel on the fountain step. Another boot stepped on the stone.

Bodyguard Arno Allant seemed more than sixteen, freshly shaven with lengthy combed hair, wore his gold-colored full-length tunic proudly. Leaning forward, wrist-banded, hand on knee, he asked what he took to be Suger's request of Pierre. The knight scowled at this hard-to-make-out questioner. Pierre would give no answers about his knight's home locations, if, in fact, that was what this no-beard was asking. Arno, finding himself unable to explain to the rough-bearded oaf about the fiefs likely to oppose the Parisii, politely left.

Arno entered the side door of the feasting hall. In the amber hour, he enjoyed the sensations – cooking fire wafts of Oak, bustling sounds of silverware, heavy chairs scuffling to their places. Within the high vaulted dining hall, the sun fell on the royal spanning table set on a platform with high chairs. Two trunking runs of trestle tables with benches joined to the main table for the lucky two hundred. A guest table was added under the royal console for entertainers.

Outside in the square, the Paris knights gave ravenous looks. Woodsmoke and roast smelled of a feast. Stomachs churned like horse hooves in mud. Hungry enough to storm the main dining hall, they envied a side door. An Aquitaine Chevalier held out a feeble drink.

Arno tilted a clear glass to Parisii Pierre. When the knight moved, the rest of the men meandered cautiously toward the side arch of the hall. Hearing music, they entered. Captains and barons of both sides busily exchanged words. Festively decorated Aquitaine women curtsied lightly, and to the horror of the Parisii, men bowed in return. The folk had names like Maryam, Mathieu, Daena, Calbi, Reyna, and Armstrong. Clustering in talk of the wedding progress, Prince Louis, his Counts Thibault and Raoul, and Abbot

Suger shared drink. White clergy stood distantly. Few paid attention to the excellent performances of minstrels, troubadours, and acrobats scattered about the anteroom.

Pierre scoffed at the clean-shaven Aquitaine, a potential enemy to subdue if need be. Arno held out a glass. A clear goblet of red wine.

"For me?" the Parisii said, not wanting to break the thing. Clear glass was rare. The Aquitaine lifted his glass to the candlelit chandelier and spoke:

"Note sir, the smooth ruby red. This is Eleanor's art from her lands, claret."

"Clear, eh?" Pierre gave a quick eye and gulped it down.

"You slake the gem of the vine. Did you taste anything on the way down?"

"Didn't gag," Pierre reassured, backhanding his lips from the quaff.

Arno summoned the wine pourer. Mathieu happily smiled, pouring a swift red ribbon of his distillation. "My press, the very best."

"You give good wine to me?" Pierre said warily, looking for signs of trickery.

"In chivalry, we are generous," Arno said. "To the maker." The knights raised a glass to Mathieu. "Pierre, the great heart gives. I live by the code of a chevalier." Pierre had heard of this chivalry thing. It was tavern talk, stories of rollicking cavalrymen singing of honor and rowdy love for ladies. A crock of woman's ways. Pierre was a hard helmet.

Mathieu put humor into his words: "Parisii knight, the way you dress, are we going to have a war?" To Pierre, nothing funny was said; on the other hand, there was no tone of insult. After a hoist of wine to his sword-brothers, he looked about. Arno and Mathieu had disappeared into an ever-growing crowded room.

Music stopped. Small metal bells rang, and finger symbols clapped to meter.

Youthful Eleanor of Aquitaine knew how to walk through a doorway and take a room. She moved into the golden sunlight. By training, she was always aware of the ordinary stage that life presented. Empathetic to all, radiant in fashion, glowing in smiles, freshly in love, Eleanor was a picture of joy in her gown of yellow with rose braid weavings, a vestment of aqua-blue waves scalloped in white caps. Her long, ruby-gold hair was plaited in a crown. She wore her Aquitaine jewelry famously. She let everyone feel her musical thirteen-springs gait.

Arno raised a glass. "Flowers do walk! A drink to Eleanor's beauty and to beauty's long life." He felt his old jealousy for Eleanor turn to gracious envy. If she could join the rough Kingdom of France, so could he.

Eleanor smiled demurely, encouraging all to enjoy, taking a higher ledge to extend courtesy to her guests:

"From Aquitaine to Paris! I raise a glass to Prince Louis and to Louis, our King. To France!" After a cheerful downing, the troubadours drummed up a rhythm as gifted entertainers gave forth their best acts among the milling crowd.

. . .

HER ACT could be called Dancing Ribbons. From the end of thin wands, the acrobat tossed up immensely long silks of narrow colored ribbons high to the stone vaults of the entry hall. There, she shaped standing flames, rippling rills, flying wings, keeping them floating in the air by a deft vibrating hand. Her fine white formfitting body hosiery gave to restrictive minds the illusion of a dancer in her underclothing; to other minds a perfect Olympic body of marble. Most ignored her. The Parisii men-at-arms passed racy glances while showing off their swords and scabbards to Aquitaine lads, trying to impress, if not recruit them.

The adroit acrobat gracefully reached to a high table of wands. She conjured a silver ribbon-sword rising from a rippling blue river. In the roped-off area that circled her pedestal station, the graceful gymnast silently cycled her perfect arms, giving a light ballet of rising and falling colors, all in a rhythm of some internal music she governed.

Eleanor discovered her. Both thirteen now, she and Sirq had met in times before. The dancer assisted friend Mirielle to win the troubadour competitions. Eleanor endowed the graceful dancer, a specially made wardrobe of white silken hosiery. It fit tight about her body from ankle to wrist, so her movements could be free. After ten thousand hours of dance, balance, and practice, the young acrobat mastered every range of performance. Eleanor always worried about her treasured friend, attractive with long eyelashes, sweeping blonde hair worn up, enchanting when let down. The dancer cared not for anything other than the joy of performing. Alongside her, fellow jugglers performed and stilt-men walked. She danced with the troubadours. Sirq's formfitting moves accentuated their meter; their tempo enhanced her springs. Her graceful tribal leaps added to the world's pure joy.

Pierre had passed jugglers in fairs. About the hard-hearted knight now were the ones of the high stage, the ones who made you watch. Never had he been arm's length from such artists, as the royal wedding feast afforded. He was so close he could smell their powders and creams if he were drawn to that sort of thing. Quenching his thirst, he downed wine gruffly, weaving past comrades. Typical chain-mail swordsmen, they gave Aquitaine woman the vulgar eye, as he had a time or two himself. He filled his glass, red again.

On the far side of the entry hall, over helmets and helms, shot long fires of brilliant ribbons, riveting they floated, then fell through the air in magical ripples. Pierre adjusted his helmet and muscled in to see the act of this woman rumored to dance in her underwear.

It was not what he expected.

An athletic woman in white hose from ankle to wrist moved a contour of her white form. A fierce grace all her own, she beat her wrists and long arms rapidly like a hummingbird, her back arched in deliberate form. She was a woman unique, no sweet cheek, no wench of round desire, but one able to enchant the air with a volley of colors. Something in her skillful way, a thing he could not name, something of her magnificence reached out to him. He inched closer to how she shaped the air. Her every minor tilt of head, shift of arm, tense of knee, caused Pierre to gasp and feel lost in Sirq's range of commanding movements.

She flowed white with purpose, giving a total program of human muscle and nerve. He felt bothered that no one was paying any attention, yet she danced with prowess and precision in move after artful move. Pierre wanted to shout to the sky, 'Angels in heaven, behold what she can do!' Then, confusing feelings came to the knight. She was a young female, not a lass to be whipped – as would his drunken father, nor to attack with violence as his male friends made game of. This was a fragile beauty, a woman with a beating heart that should never be touched. Yet, he wanted to touch her. He felt a deep urge to shelter and protect, like a knave who saves a sparrow from the forest floor. No! Just witness – leave her be. But see her legs strong as a steed, her arms falcon's wings, a face determined. Pierre's eyes shut down, ashamed to witness such fine grace. He wanted her, but in a way, he never felt before. He worried: is she seeing me? She sees no on. And then he glanced up, bright as the sun he saw her stance. It was not her sensational gyrating dance with color ribbons that called him. That was not it at all. It was her silent presence.

Pierre's throat had gone dry. He raised his glass as if to drink in her spirit. Was Arno's chivalry right about honor to such feminine creatures? O, such a beautiful being. Seeing his brother knights give forth their lecherous looks, Pierre was of a mind to strike them. O, but am I one of them? She surely must think that. He wore the same mail. How to show he was different? He put his goblet to his back, lest she make him out to be a lip-licking sot. He had to prove himself, to show this magnificent woman. . . his what? It was confusing. His heart pounded, what must I do? She deserved more than a glance! I could watch you for hours. He fancied the silent, determined acrobat was dancing for him in her white momentum. He attended her every move and beamed in awe.

The dancer glanced at a bearded intensely admiring knight hiding a wine glass behind his back. She let her knee dip naturally, and back, lest she lose her balance.

What did she see at that moment, a drunken hulk? A bearded fool? Pierre was so close he could touch her ropes. My God what am I? A rough-hewn man who only knows how to destroy things. He nearly made an angel fall. Pierre stepped back in anguish, thinking worse of himself. Being hot, he stripped off his helmet. Flailing his hair loose, he looked over the room of gabblers and time passers. Did they not realize the greatest dancer in Europa was presenting herself? OH BUT WHAT IF. What if his men saw him looking at this bird. He was a fierce knight of Paris, after all. Safely he scanned to see if someone had seen. Eyes locked his; he'd looked a second too long at hers. Pierre cast his head aside as if he wasn't doing anything special. He glanced. She knew. Eleanor knew and read him like a book. Pierre reeled, feeling like a downed stag. Eyes to the floor, he left in full retreat. *If I knew her name, where she hailed from. Will I ever see the sun again?* He dare not ask, for he was nothing. He turned his helmet in circles.

Eleanor had a sense for love. She saw it begin just now. Firmly believing all love good and keeping an eye on aspiring women, the young bride raised her glass goblet for all to share.

"Sirq de Béziers! Your grace inspires all who walk to fly. I dare say knights would put down their swords and never fight again just to live for your dances."

"Cheer to mirth and splendor be!" the revelers roiled.

In the room filled with ayes and claps, a sigh came from one knight, a sigh of exaltation – 'Sirq of the Sun' – Pierre's breast filled with joy.

When the room took a noble bow to honor Eleanor's toast, Sirq saw the one man standing. Transfixed on her was a lost knight of Paris, his helmet by his heart. In the time it takes a bird's wing to flap, she allowed his chaste attention, not that she needed any. Moved by Eleanor's words, the dancer presented to the Princess and out to the wedding guests her invisible bouquet of thanks from her chest, her graceful, joyful arms extended.

Her fingertips would burn in Pierre's dreams for months to come. He would feel her reach to him every night. Eventually, Sirq would realize this was the only man who ever made her knees lose balance.

. . .

Amira was nervous; the wedding feast had not yet begun. She was busy as a summer bee and proud of her promotion to First Maid. Her hair was cut to her shoulder by Eleanor herself! She would never again doubt the mind of Eleanor in love, the surest sign of ability. Everything could be done; even in the chaos of details right down to the exact flower in every vase. Amira ordered carpenters to add new tables in anteroom and courtyard to catch the overflow of former suitors and guests. She got to know Suger the Fixer well.

The feast plan flew quickly with decisions. Poor Dangerossa was convinced by the white priests to avoid the wedding celebration and pray for her soul. Amira had told her worry to Suger. He gave immediate absolution.

Dangerossa, Vesteed, his fellow tailors, and fussy Jolietemps sat in the entertainment hall. At side tables, Maryam and Mathieu, Reyna and Armstrong. Calbi and Daena – always ready to dance, Amira's parents, sat with teachers Genet and Pat. Amira helped Tova with the recipe of the last dish. Plenty of butter was needed. Four long-handle pumping damisels in their evocative chore drew ten knights to help. With love in mind, everything could be done.

The evening plan was for each dish to match a performing musician. The plan for the final dish – Tova's orange butter-sauce crepe – depended on the timing of the arrival of the greatest and most unpredictable troubadour Woofan. He failed to show for the reception. Amira set a damisel of Lusignan to find him. The fan, all too eager to help was instructed, "Confine the musicians to the gardens, and keep other guests away. It is a surprise."

Amira's next item was to make a close check on Eleanor. Good, properly dressed by the staff. Amira wanted to give Eleanor the night of her life, and whatever she couldn't set right, Abbot Suger could fix. Nothing could go wrong. Confident Amira signaled to fire up the first course and for the seating to begin. She raised the hem of her gown and hurried on.

The standard bearer ran the rung of chimes. The starving Paris knights rambled through the arch into the dining hall, led by Sirq in a ribbon dance. Gnawing on meaty food sticks, they tossed the splints over their shoulders. Sitting down roughly, they bounced flower vases, heavy candles, pewter spoons, and, amazingly, eating knives – knights had their own belt cutlasses!

Aquitaine chevaliers escorted ladies who received assists to be seated in heavy hewn chairs. Arno was most courteous. At the main table were Suger, Raoul, Eleanor, in wait of Louis, and Petronilla. Aquitaine lords and ladies sat about the hall. Sirq took a place at the entertainer's table in front of Eleanor.

Curious Pierre noted Sirq from his bench. He studied her carefully and WHAM! Arno sat squarely. He flapped Pierre's beard to test the bounds.

"Why you .. umm, skin-face baby," Pierre said with clenched fist, but the jest in Arno's eyes changed his mood mid-sentence.

Arno stroked his naked chin, mocking a beard and said, "Do not scoff at youth. Some advice, friend. I see your eye wonders at yon Sirq. I know not elsewhere, but Aquitaine woman love best the skin of gentle babies. That's a weedy bristle of thorns around your neck; you don't mind me saying." Both took in each other's playful sense. "Ah, be friends, Parisii. I am Arno Allant" he said with arm outstretched.

Grasping back, "I am Pierre Argent Lutèce, friend of Aquitaine." He leaned forward for only Arno to hear. "A warrior flits about to seat a woman?"

"Courtesy is the way to manners."

"Man her then, why bother?" Pierre said.

"When you can take her?" Arno probed, unsure if he was that type of man.

"No," affirmed Pierre. "Why fuss for what she can already do herself?"

"Ah, those are called .. man-nerz."

"Ah manners, I get you." Pierre heard of them. He scratched his rough neck.

"Dear Pierre, the benefits of manners, you cannot imagine. You will never ken the pleasure of carefully seating a woman's bottom."

Pierre knuckled the frown of his brow. "That makes no sense."

"Let me explain," Arno pressed on. "These women work the land. Their men never returned from The Holy War. We all reap their great bounty." To Arno, it was not clear the Parisii understood any of this. Giving a good dose of Aquitaine manners, Arno relished the administration. "Pierre, lifting heavy chairs is a light charity for us. From a woman's point of view, a ninety pound solid Oak chair is a task. I noticed Sirq struggling with hers. You could–"

"Do you know Sirq? Tell me about her!"

"Pierre, you are putting me on. A brutal knight like you in chain mail? You? Manners? Now that one over there has strong manners. First rule, love always brings a gift." Pierre followed Arno's glance down the table to Eleanor.

Giving an elaborate curtsey to Louis arriving, Eleanor whimsically took the servant's place and seated him herself. After the laughter, she clapped open two velvet pillows revealing a faceted crystal globe vase, crown-footed in gold. He turned the opulent dotted crystal over to see its colored gems and pearls.

"A treasure from my grandfather, a victory gift from Spain."

Arno walked up. "Prince Louis, if I may suggest, fresh flowers if you please?" He looked to Eleanor's thin smile of assent. What it really was, well ... a flower vase would serve. Arno took the crystal glove past Sirq and gave it seated Pierre. "Fill it with every beautiful flower you can find."

If a pile of dung were slapped into the hands of Pierre, he would look no different. He boasted for his fellows, "A warrior does not harvest flowers." Arno goaded, "You sir, are in a different land! For King and Court, Pierre, and pretty, please." Pierre strode out; the only virtue of the thing was being little.

At the supper bell, as was the style, servants proudly danced-in, they paraded cooked platters about the room. The large oval plates were filled with undulating, Sirq-like, flat ribbons of crepe noodles and thin flats of red, yellow, and purple vegetables cut long. The hungry Parisii knights stabbed for them. The servants successfully defended: "Wait for the summer-nut and basil sauce, their final saucing."

Pierre heard the dinner bell. He came back running to the banquet hall and planted the vase of flowers before Prince Louis. Starving, he benched himself by Arno, salivating, eyeing tables. No food served, no one eating, good.

"Pierre, you did notice Sirq when you placed the vase?"

"Didn't notice."

"It's why I gave you the job."

"Flowers. So?"

Arno chuckled and pointed at the scene at the wedding table unfolding.

Overjoyed Eleanor and Petronilla plucked flowers from every vase except Pierre's. They handed stems to Prince Louis and Chancellor Raoul. They named the mood the fragrance inspired. Eleanor held the flower to her nose and gave the pleasure of her face to Louis; Petronilla to the Chancellor at the other end of the table. As the women inhaled, they conveyed meaning in facial expressions and airy gestures – gladness, remembrance, sadness, light love, sweet love, mad love.

Pierre slapped his head. Arno's words sunk in. His friend had given him a choice chance to be near Sirq. He did not even notice her. Hungrily he looked at the head table to see Sirq, happily sharing the facial emotions. He let his stomach growl as a penance.

"Flowers mean all that, huh?"

"Feelings Pierre, feelings are part of chivalry."

Prince Louis mimicked his wife's wide eyes and praying hands. "Hope."

After presenting tender emotions, Eleanor finally picked out Pierre's weed. She opened her eyes wide, frowned, shriveled her face, then held her nose. Sirq laughed loudest and turned to Pierre and give him her greatest grin.

Arno said, "She likes your humor. You *did* know that was stinkweed?"

Pierre wished he did. One thing true. Sirq smiled a smile meant for him. Pierre was someone. He thumped his chest and rapped Arno's back with hardy satisfaction. With a twirl, servants set forth plates of noodles exotically sauced. Before a blessing, the knights dug in. With both hands, Pierre gobbled down the bands of bright colored whatever. Talking as he ate, "Arno, the tables" – Pierre belched– "are barren. Was there poor hunting?"

Arno rhymed his answer: "What is the hurry, we feast through the night / a bit is worthy, more than a bite / when you dine with a lady, keep your appetite." Arno leaned closer. "Savor the evening, Pierre. Savor."

Pierre smiled pointing with his knife, guessing he meant to save her.

Arno continued his ministrations. "Sir, do you not see that this ribbon dish you ate honors Sirq? Yet, you devoured her horribly." Pierre formed a frown as he picked peppercorns from his teeth with a dagger. Nothing seemed to get through.

"My Parisii friend, Sirq has not even begun her plate. She enjoys the conversation of her neighbors. Could you ever sit at her table?"

Pierre slammed the dagger into the wood. Seizing Arno's wristband, the Paris knight steadied. His face ran the gamut from murderous intent to grateful trust.

The room filled with the loud badness of Parisii knights who ate loudly. The din was unbearable. As if the Parisii cavalry leaped a charge upon the tables, the thunder of hooves hammered, divots of noodles banged up, while fists struck down. Plates broke, metal dishes rolled on the stone floor. Digging with both hands, they spat chunks about, elbowed neighbors and cussed aloud in hoarding shouts. The Poitiers court was appalled at the absolute lack of manners.

Eleanor stood in disbelief, angry at the charging brigade of slurping bowl lickers. "Grace! Abbot Suger. Before further feast, I think we need some Grace! Grace if you please." There was no doubt the kind of grace she meant.

The great Abbot got up from his chair. "In the name of God, Ahmen." He bent to sit. Eleanor flared at him, only to be caught by his humor. Erectly, he made his presence known; his lifted napkin signified prayer. The room hushed.

"We are thankful as we celebrate the divinity of Your heavenly world visited upon ours. Please guide our hungry hands with artful grace to partake of Thy abundant gracefulness. We remember Thy Cleanliness when we behold our napkin's grace." He wiped his lips carefully to be sure. "In grace, Amen." His tone set the room at ease with far less din and a lot more delight.

Arno teased his puzzled friend who noticed the cloth. "Pierre. Napkins. Good. Fingers. Bad." Pierre grizzled a laugh. Arno asked, "Well, what are your plans?" Pierre wiped his hands and beard. Arno acted the mirror tapping to a missed spot. "On the morrow, a tithe to some fountain abbey. Louis will present Eleanor's falcons. That was quite a capture. Come join if you can."

From outside the room, a rolling instrumental of oval fiddle and soft drum sounded as a woman announced, "L'on dit q'amors est dolce chose." Four troubadours entered playing. *They Say that Love is a Sweet Thing,* long black haired trobaritz Mirielle Denni translated, wagging her finger at the crude Parisii knights like a teacher. The men abided her lesson, scolding one another in mock play. None had ever been sung to by a single woman.

Mirielle wore a colorful tunic and a billowy white unlaced man's top shirt. The Parisii were bothered by a woman wearing a man's clothing. She soothed about the room, "This is part of the song." She lowered her gudok, turning the oval fiddle into a lap harp and played sorrowful chords. Her rangeful voice could express the sweet tenderness of a lover, the passions of hurt, the comfort of a mother. The trobaritz strummed, "Lady in love and gentle Prince, hear a song of tenderness. From The Crusade, I sing of happy lover's hurt, embodied in this lover's shirt." Mirielle stroked her blouse and waited for her feeling to rejoin the measure.

♪

> So sad my love to take the cross
> Our fond farewell we well miss
> His Shirt he sends from far away
> That he wears, that is he, that is this·
> At night when lonely love is thin
> I bring to bed near naked skin
> Your sandy hold to tend me near
> To sadly soothe my torment dear
> Desert Shirt, fill my dreaming core
> I pray your sleeves be full once more
> I believe your arms will hold me once more

♪

The image of a woman in lament embracing her lover's shirt enchanted Suger and the high table. Turning her warm eyes to Louis, Eleanor held his hand. Louis turned back – the white priest sneered; Holy War should be sung about sacredly. Commander Thibault, sitting with his Paris knights, was also of that school.

"I see," Louis said blandly of the performance.

"Don't you feel it?" Eleanor invited.

There were other interpreters of the song.

"The Shirt stinks! Wash the rag out, woman!" uttered one of Thibault's knights. His fellows roared at the benches. Thibault fought back a rise of cheeks studying the royal table.

Seeing the hurt in Eleanor's eyes, the Chancellor of France came to his feet, "Prince Louis, allow me." Raoul stood behind the bride and groom's chairs. Gripping the back posts, Raoul addressed the jesting knight:

"Sir! Your humor is not noble! It is not mine nor any at this table. Perhaps we expect too much to invite a horseman. Will you share the Prince's wedding celebration, or do you prefer the livery?"

"I take your meaning," the knight said. "Manners in the manor. My apologies to the court and to a song well sung." Waiting for the Prince's nod, he was approved to sit.

Petronilla's heart beat loudly; that a man could be so strong with words in defense of her sister's heart. She reached for Raoul's wrist in appreciation for his gallantry. His surcoat was far finer than Prince Louis. She caressed his silver and gold spun sleeve and slipped her hand into his. She looked up, doe-eyed to Raoul's well-groomed heavy beard.

Commander Thibault eyed his cousin Raoul, not sure he liked that dressing down of his man. Now the obvious, that Raoul married to his sister was showing more than appreciation in a tender handclasp of damisel Petronilla.

Eleanor took note as well. Scooting her chair back, she broke their hold. "Trobaress Mirielle! Come, share a place next to Sirq! Enjoy the next course that befits your song!"

Petronilla was on a cloud. Raoul's regal hand had been warm to her; he had touched her pulse, a sign of love. The pinch she felt was her sister. Petronilla gave Chancellor Raoul an even sweeter smile. Eleanor opened the crab of her hand. Petronilla curled a pouty lip. Raoul showed his teeth and smiled.

The herald announced, "Shirt of Beef with Spices from Outremer."

The crowd awed, and rightfully so. Outremer meant from across the sea, the exotic tastes of Jerusalem and Arabia – the recently conquered lands of the Franks. The food servers poured flaming filets of beef skirts onto plates with a saucy swirl. Eleanor smelled the earthy mushroom in cardamom spice, and syrupy wine. Louis tasted and was as pleased as the next man. Pierre had plenty to get his hands on. Arno nudged his burly friend only once to halt his cutlass from stabbing the server's plate.

Abbot Suger remarked, "Eleanor, spices from the Holy Land. This is um–"

"Exotic," completed Eleanor, explaining to the table, "The spices come from my uncle Raymond, the new King of Antioch."

To Suger, hearing the blessed word 'Antioch,' the largest Crusade principality after Edessa, meant the empire of France was strongly allied to Jerusalem. The Abbot felt the heights of exilient joy. "Holy bounty from The Crusade! What a rich piece of beef, and served with such style. The Aquitaine will be a great addition to the French Realm."

Eleanor bristled at the Abbot's phrasing. It was drowned by Parisii cheers: "Long live Aquitaine!" To the Occitan ear, no resolution ever sounded complete without some affection. Chevalier's boltered: "Long live Paris! Long be lief, long be liege, long be love!"

After many fine entertainments and plates, and promises and good will, the final dish was on the ready. Eleanor was pained. Every eye of her court was cast upon the entry arch. "What wild costume will he wear?" "What proper song could he sing for a wedding night?" Whispers of Woofan filled the air. It was rumored that Woofan Rhyser's playful gaze went straight to a woman's heart, and his voice reached deeper. Eleanor looked about frantically for the most talented musician of the era.

"Amira, where is that godforsaken troubadour? This is his dish. It might as well be pressed cat and sour dog."

Amira asided to Eleanor: "I've just been told – I am part to blame – you know the Lusignan brother's young wife-to-be? I sent her to seclude the troubadours. With all our merriment, Woofan and his band serenaded her in the moonlight. You know how he is. She gladly sat to inspire them, well, you know." Amira motioned 'top off.' Eleanor wanted to smile – muse-singing was a tradition as old as the Greeks. "The white priests caught the serenade in the garden and scolded the sinners. Not even Suger can fix this one. No one knows." Eleanor huffed, nothing could be done now.

Friends came by Eleanor's chair. "We saved our appetite for the last event."

Amira said, "There's been a turn. He is not coming."

They replied, "You were bold to invite Woofan; but, there will be dance!"

"Of course," Eleanor said half-heartedly and received comforting hugs.

"Louis, there is no living music in the world like Woofan's. He is the restorer of ancient youthful traditions, the creator of new forms, bringer of mirth. He would have been the talk of the feast." Eleanor sat heavy in her chair.

Louis tipped up her chin. Touching her Eleanor hair, Louis said, "I have something to cheer you. Your falcons are secure. I was there to see to that. I will present them tomorrow. To show you I have not forgotten the good of our courtship in Ombrière." He motioned to an administrator who presented a sealed document. He was surprised to see the light shine in his wife. Eleanor loved charters, sight unseen; such documents were the lifeblood of the state.

Eleanor broke the red seal and regarded the cloth tail: The King of France. She opened the sides. Her fingers traced the words, then brushed up her throat into a kiss of fingers. She waved Amira over to see. Side by side, the thirteen and fifteen-year-old read the heavy parchment with delight.

"A Writ Grant of Land, Title To Edeva Franklin, a Lady of Chauvigny."

The black ink penned over the silverpoint outline setting forth property bounds, order to heirs, male or female, in perpetuity, stipulated tax agreements, and prior invalidated claims. It was signed by the Royal penman himself.

"Aquitaine has a precedent case," the Prince said. The implication was that all Franklin properties could be granted to their rightful owners.

This was power her father never had. It was seductive. She could go places with Louis. She would not have to hide forever in fear of church power. This was royal law. This was history and marked the beginning of their story.

Louis, overjoyed to see Eleanor's delight, wanted her to really smile. He produced a sparkling gem. "This diamond set in gold replaces that sad sack of river stones, I first sent." The overjoyed crying bride pressed it to her chest and gave a wealth of grateful kisses. She took her gift, the faceted crystal globe that served as the flower vase. Amira cleaned it and summoned Suger.

Tearful Eleanor said urgently, "Louis, this crystal globe, I must tell you, is no vase. This is a lamp that once illuminated the Holy Sepulcher." Louis brought it to his forehead, then kissed reverently. Tears fell from Louis and Suger. The white priest standing behind Louis nodded begrudging approval.

Crepes were brought, troubadour be damned, sauced brilliantly with exotic blood oranges of Moor-held Spain and the lemon blossom-honey of Poitiers. The crepes were lit afire. Grandmother Dangerossa bravely spooned a blue-flamed crepe down her throat, to the cheer of Parisian knights.

Trobaress Mirielle shouted a Spanish "EAARGH!" With a friendly nod, Sirq performed fiery ribbon leaps. Knights cleared back the trestle tables. Flutes played notes, strings strummed vibrant chords, and Mirielle shouted, "Aya-Baya!" Tambours beat the bawdy drums. Sirq gyred in a whirl about the floor first dancing with Eleanor, then leading the wedding couple. Dance, how Eleanor danced. The rowdy room filled with zesty claps, budding infatuations, dives, and passes. By night's dancing end, every arm of Paris experienced the wild flavors of Aquitaine, and Louis learned how best to embrace and savor.

Fatherless Children

The stride of Woofan Rhyser was as long as his swinging arms. The troubadour's gait reached far and fast, late in service of his patron. His band kept up with as much huffing vigor as the gaggle of girls hot on their heels.

Outside the Palace wall, Eleanor looked wistfully toward the morning haze, hearing horses and men in the mist at the bend of the River Clain. Last night's August wedding feast was a lively memory for the year 1137. She would be Paris-bound soon. Only a few could come with her; most had to stay and manage new roles. As the wed Princess, she could call on them officially for the purposes of France; as Duchess, for purposes of Aquitaine and Gascony. She thought of the heartache of goodbyes to come. Today, the women of her court came to celebrate their last time together.

The air was pregnant with a light fog, the kind that lingered as if never to leave the ground. Down the slope at the river, past the half-removed barricade works and fresh-stumped trees, Parisii knights cleaned swords and shields. They had returned from the hunt and skirmish at Talmont to rejoin Prince Louis who had galloped ahead for the feast. Nuns had struck a cauldron fire and pulled white steamed towels to wash out the light wounds. On the bank, lay deer, boar, braces of pheasants. Prince Louis commended their retrieval of two caged falcons.

Princess Eleanor awaited in her calf-length yellow kirtle-gown with deep fur-lined sleeves. She awaited the returning warriors, and could hear them assemble on the river bank. She cooled her back on a low stone wall. About her, friends laid out a grand picnic. Sister Petronilla, Maryam, Reyna, and counselor Amira poured wine for one another with more to come later. The women of her court set out creamy cheeses, late summer fruits, cured meats, and fresh breads on colored blankets scattered with dogwood blossoms. Eleanor looked for wedding friends and, if by chance, troubadours. She leaned forward and growled.

Out from a trail of road dust came an impossibly long-stepping music-maker. Through his black bobbing hair, Woofan gave hungry eyes and serious lips. He turned to send his giggling fans to the river with a woof and urged his band on.

Woofan Rhyser. Who knew where this troubadour came from – not that anyone would want to know, except most every young damisel. Passionately bad, sweetly mad, he exuded a danger you wanted to know. The troubadour dressed in every color of the known rainbow; colored silk scarves, great plumes, a dark ornamented tunic, multiple belts, and metal studded boots. The artist mastered every art of lute and lure, possessing an amazing sense of music. Few noticed the enchanting power of his player's instruments. His lutes had extra, sympathetic strings. His boxy round guitar was as wide as a young woman's hips. Called a barbat-oud, the instrument gave the basest sound. Playing the music of young hearts, he pulled on feelings forbidden to words. Woofan's voice was a gift to the music lover's ear; not just his singing voice, but perhaps more-so, his dangerous speaking voice. It reached into your chest, sounding stone cathedral-like until he was spine-deep. He could resound your soul. You were at the mercy of whatever he felt next: a booming vibrato, a tender whisper. He held your eyes guessing.

Woofan was part of the circuit of troubadours that reached from the castles of Spain to the enlightened castles in Aquitaine and forbidden in Paris. Lords cursed the mop-head, despising music, not of the King's church. His mores that led to youthful music were scandalous to the men charged with God. Therefore, his words would never be copied in monasteries. If ever he laid his music down, it, like any mention of him, would be erased. His life would never be part of history. Rhyser's beat would live as long as he, as long as humans were sapient beings. His brilliance would die with his fan's last breath.

Aside from grudging him for not performing last night, Amira thought the troubadour special at first. Any man coming before Eleanor with hair afright would be dismissed. Woofan wore his hair wild, playful, and clean, something to run one's fingers through – Eleanor's true standard. To be fair, he would have played at the wedding feast had the white priests not banned him. Still, for missing the wedding song, everyone composed composed choice words.

Eleanor glowered to her friends. "Here comes one colorful gipsy! The nerve! Such a willful walk, like he has urgent business with me. Huntress Amira, those feathers in his cap, do you recognize any of those birds?"

"I do not. They are all fantastic."

The colorful troubadour swung his arms sharp and shear, arriving with his bangled band who tried not to look ashamed. Woofan stood attendant before his resilient young benefactor. He brushed his hair back with long troubadour fingers looking over the ladies.

The steam from Eleanor had not yet begun. She addressed him stridently:

"We are exilient today," then turned to Amira, "Will he play me by pleading with his eyes or deny last night's performance with his lips?" Woofan was unfazed.

"Jourbon, married lady. Bonjour damisels, I see you're sitting pretty."

Contempt from Eleanor's young court made the musician lengthen his smile. He liked raw emotions. He swam into them, denied them, he mastered them.

"Today is not last night," Eleanor said sharply.

"The muses." He gave a shrug of helplessness.

"That's all you'll say?" She studied him from knee scarf to head plume. His charm was hard to fight. "I see such ordinary colors. Quills, ready for verse? From which bird did you pluck that one? Looks like a pheasant but the barb is all red."

"Oh yes, the color is fresh," he resonated. "I plucked that bird carefully by moonlight. My rosy friend plunged it in red berry ink for some savage reason."

"A dangerous friend? Clearly a peacock here, but the tail-feather is white."

"Painted it. Too much color for my taste. She was a pretty bird."

"Now, this is not a purple shaft?"

"Oh, it quite well is. Purple as can be."

"And how purple was the bird all over?"

"She was right well ruddy."

"In this feather, I see nothing but vane, Woofan. What, no down?"

"Vain is all I have, alas."

All eyes were set on the two. Eleanor stretched her arms to the sky as if tired.

"Trouble-doer, will you saw your lyre for us?"

Careless came his almost nod.

"Woofan, I could find you an egret, a right fine plume, but you look best in black fish scales. So many dogwood blossoms on our blanket." She took a fresh cut branch, and dangled it under his nose. The ladies frowned at the singer.

"What a beaut, my femme. Let's put that right .. here." Instead of the shoulder, she stabbed the quill low under his heart. "You finish-it." Woofan followed her syllable joins and adjusted the flower, "That's wicked. No smell."

Maryam humphed, "Why bring your foul instruments today?"

Woofan the star began only as Woofan could, with a long pause ... a swirling spoon of whatever would come next. With throaty resonance, he captivated the air: "Ohhh ladies, pleeesz. The priest said I was naughty last night. Have you ever been naughty? Last night you would have heard nothing with crosses around. Nothing can compare to what I sing now. No crowd. Just you, just us. Hear up close the Rhyser, and he will sing. Woofan Rhyser and his band of troubadours are ready for you."

The damisels had ready in their eyes. Eleanor glared unforgivingly. Between the bawdy and the sublime, Woofan could not resist pouring it on.

"Oh, damisels. I am so inspired. I hear last night you ate well. I starved for you. I had but a sip of the jealous wine of love." He looked at their hopeful faces. "Which song of mine is your favorite? I can give you any; I can sing them all. Shall we play? Or do you want to feel love!"

No one breathed, for his was the only breath that mattered. Eleanor said coolly, "Lover, last night your song might have played for my marriage dish. Whatever fish-rotting song did you come prepared to hurl? We are in need of something not expired. I am just now married. So, compose as you feel. Let's hear your rhyme. Louis is my husband yon; newer is our love. Can you find us in it?"

The hit-smitten damisels would have settled for anything, but Eleanor was giving the master challenge – to compose music in the present. She waved up Louis for the concert.

Famous Woofan strummed his lute, watching white-robed Louis climb the grass past the giggling girls. He would someday become the King of France and she the Queen. This meant little to Woofan. More real was how the Prince sheepishly held two cages of sputtering falcons before a short white priest, and his jag-walk to avoid fresh cut tree stumps.

Louis thought about how to present the caged birds. It was the least he could do, he assured himself, with all the nonsense to forget. While hunting at Talmont, Sir Jaufre Rudel came to call. The troubadour was not like the bandy on the hill. Gentlemen Rudel presented a poem for Louis to sing to Eleanor. Before the prince could read one line, the short white Templar priest Thierry wrathfully scolded Rudel away in his high-pitched voice. Thierry told Louis the letter was nonsensical, not even in Latin. Something about long days in May, long birdsongs to remember, flowers to forget and such. Thierry spared Louis the heresy. 'You are never to see the dangerous words 'd'amor – of love.' There is only Christ's love. Strive as a Saint. Kings sing holy songs.' The Templar tossed the page into the nun's station fire.

"Templar, join me on the hill?" Louis asked. The Cistercian sidled a decline, reminding the prince in his shrill voice, "There is only Christ's love. Kings sing holy songs." Louis ascended the grassy hill, a cage in each hand. The poem-burning could be blamed on the Roman church. Better yet, forget the events ever happened. Just present the hawks. 'Kings sing holy songs,' he repeated.

The court rose out of respect. Louis set the cages down fussing jealousy with contempt. The wheat-bending attraction the women showed the musical harvester was below him. Eleanor's eyes probed Louis; he looked away.

"I am your colorful troubadour, Woofan Rhyser, at your service." He strummed. Prince Louis said, "I would not want to halt everyone's mirth. Please sit." Everyone sat a little too quickly. The Prince stood on unfamiliar grounds. He threw the bird-launching gauntlet on the blanket as if to claim his wife. "There! That's the last gauntlet De Lezay will ever pick up! He looked up to the clouds feeling cold in a white mantle; he had always worn warm gray wool. Eleanor knelt up to her husband. Rhyser gathered and presented the gauntlet to the Princess. She folded the glove and spoke to her statuesque Prince in a way for the troubadour to understand. "Sire, this trobar will compose a memorable song. We must speak bravely for the record. 'Louis my brave Prince, rides back from the battle of Talmont' yes?" Eleanor turned. The composer was lofting lip-lobbing air kisses to the women. "Woofan! Now, a troubadour's song of courage. Lionize Louis. Tell, sing, how he fought for his lady to save her falcons."

Rhyser was clear about his troubadour style. Most musicians would break at having to compose on the spot. Without knowing the melody, he probed what he experienced. As he composed, he looked into the eyes of his subjects seeing how they reacted to verse, then summed it. To Louis, he tuned up with chords.

"Brave young Louis. Heart set on his lady." (some feeling, how about...) "Set on his lady dear." (no reaction, a dramatic line:) "Princely he rides to first battle." (they loved that, a gamble) "fearing–" (Oh Louis, fear struck a chord.)

Eleanor knew the method and stood up. "You can stop that." She embraced Louis, saying in overly sweet tones, "Oh, my Prince. You fight for your lady's honor." Woofan groaned at her overacting.

Louis spoke: "A lady's honor had nothing to do with it. We were lost. De Lezay trapped us in a field of cows. I saw high dust in the trees, prayed like a Saint, and somehow we smote everyone as in a miracle. There." Louis jabbed at the battered bird cages. Yanking off a chain hauberk, he pulled his mail over his head. Eleanor fluffed back his hair, encouraging he continue. "I spared De Lezay for attacking a prince. Foul-mouthed he was of your mother. For stealing your birds – a thief's justice. Stumps for hands, by my order."

"Rhyme that," Eleanor said with a doubtful look to Woofan. She played her fingers across Louis, taunting as if saying, 'try any verse now.' Rhyser strummed.

♪

Prince Louis first time he battled · rattled forth in armor and shield,

Drew his hands from the saddle · cattle to make foul in field.

High birds hear prey his word · heard high in tree … he–he

♪

"How do I get to stumps and bandages?" The couplets of descending inter-rhymed meter were drool. Woofan was toying with her, and she knew it.

Eleanor said, "Just recite The Chanson de Rollant."

Woofan stroked his long plumes. "Do you think?" The war saga was a six-hour ordeal. Eleanor had teased him. He was in her debt. He would deliver.

"I am going to the river," the troubadour said. Summoning his band, Woofan left for the water nymphs. As the musicians frolicked to the stream, embattled knights in newly oiled armor strode up. Smelling of lamb fat, the soldiers were tolerable picnic ravens. They charmed their potential girlfriends in the Parisii way, talking with mouthfuls of pheasant. Eleanor rubbed her Prince's back, sing-songing gently, "My hunting birds. So much chivalry. Louis in verse. Everyone will think of you as King Charlemagne." She did not say Charles Martel – no hammer for Louis. Nuns moved the towel station close. Green stems were passed to the eaters, and the grounds began to smell of mint.

By the half day, the light fog settled about the wedding party. In the fresh country air of Poitiers, Louis dozed like a dove in Eleanor's lap. She soothed the Prince with her hands. She groomed him and into a light sleep. Woofan and his troubadours sauntered up from the river refreshed. Sensitively, he played simple Spanish string figures for the napping newlyweds. Fawning ladies and bandaging nuns tended the resting knights in the soft light of day.

In the distance. Galloping. Eleanor came awake. Through the haze, Abbot Suger led, his gray robes flapping. A herald flew the fleur-de-lys; under that, a black streamer, black as the pennant on the lake that announced the fate of Eleanor's father. Her heart jumped. She rallied Louis. Beyond the white fog came unmistakable thunder, the trample of armed knights on a hundred hooves.

Recognizing the King's messenger, Louis came to his feet. Eleanor brushed away the twigs and flowers from his white robe. From out of the haze an entire field of knights appeared. The Abbot spurred his horse. The couple walked off the blankets to receive the news. Half-listening Woofan pulled a flat slate coated in hairs from his pocket. Rasping the asbestos over his strings, it screeched.

The Abbot trotted to a halt before Louis, the cavalry cantered to a line. Every rider came off his horse. Hasty to their knees the field of iron men clattered. The entire troop put their hands together in prayer. Louis had never seen this before.

Abbot Suger stepped to the young Prince and looked squarely, summoning his holiest intonation: "I bear the saddest news of your father's illness. Louis-Sept, yesterday, he could take his life no further. The King of the Franks, Louis Six, is dead." A field of armor clanked with the crossing of hearts.

Louis looked to the miserable clouds, then broke into staggered cries. Feeling her touch, Louis turned to Eleanor's open arms and buried sobs on her bosom; a warmth rare in his memory. Into turbulent waters, they fell into the well of grief, her strokes familiar with the depths of her own father's dying. With hot tears, she bravely tried to stay above it all.

Suger's rosary beads passed through his fingers. He was no longer the organizer, the builder of cathedrals. Moved by the souls of two fatherless children, his eyes moistened. He readied to give a prayer.

White-robed Thierry Galeran asserted his presence, crossing himself harshly. Short and middle-aged, the Cistercian Templar priest scowled, *What is this woman doing to these men?* This entire wedding had been a journey into hell. Thierry knew with God's certainty what this woman was doing! By heaven above, her temptation was clear: dressed to finesse, open-collared, tempting with soft words, comforting hands, womanly tears. Suger in a weeping throw! Sweet mortification! Thierry fumed. The Prince's gate to heaven was rusting shut; Thierry had to kick it open and save the Prince's soul. Thierry cared nothing for newlywed feelings for mere flesh-fathers. He caught a whiff of their lowly emotion; their bonding was obscene. The temptress of the garden of Eden made his skin crawl. *Father Louis, your death was a sign to heaven. Thierry! you are called!* With God's wrath, the Templar reached out and yanked the young Prince away from her.

Abbot Suger was amazed at the insensitivity, but he understood why. Sly and wrathful Thierry was to keep an eye on things for his master Abbot Bernard. One day, the white cowls would have Suger's job. The stakes were high in vying for the Prince's soul.

Thierry held his hand high to heaven. He'd beat the Abbot to prayer. The small white priest cleared his throat before the heaving wailers of self-pity. When Thierry spoke people often laughed; he gave the pitch of a little boy. They did not laugh for long. Few appreciated the theory of self-castration. As a devoted eunuch, he would not be tempted. He was God's man. Averting his eyes to avoid unsightly passions, he beadled his little voice in a high squeal:

"Be stout. Strive as a Saint!"

Louis trembled. He cared little for Thierry, but Strive as a Saint was a confessional phrase that never failed to bring him back to stern master Bernard. Strive as a Saint was the key. Through obedience, he would prove better than his indolent father, and be canonized a living Saint. Louis warm with Eleanor wailed in the depths of empty loss, unsure of what to do.

Eleanor felt his sorrow deeply. She held him, and they suffered quiet sorrows.

"Louis!" Thierry nailed. "When you were dancing, last night – your father lay dead. God's lesson speaks my son. Saints do not embrace women. Strive."

"God-oh-God," Louis moaned. He pressed Eleanor away and broke into sobs. Feeling her husband in such pain, she could not resist giving the comfort needed.

"Take your hands off our new Lord King," whined the little voice.

Willfully, Eleanor embraced Louis. She gave the little man a sharp look and laughed in his face. "You sound like a baby." The priest gripped his cowl, ablaze at this woman with the arms of serpents. He burned with a hatred that fed a new wrath. She would be sorry. He raised his hand to curse her.

Suger asserted his spiritual authority and brought down Thierry's hand. "You have made your point." His looming voice left Bernard's cleric in silence. "New husband, new wife, take heart. Both your fathers are where they must be. Grieve we must; grieve we shall. You will see they have left you a way to follow to heaven. Louis-Sept, we have higher duties of the crown. Regard now."

Lost in a confusion of emotions, Louis pushed his bride away. Feeling sour, he stood alone. The most inappropriate emotion of the hour was summoned for reasons priests only know. Suger put his hands together as if to applaud and the white priest beamed, "That's a good Saint." They owned his soul again.

At this point, Eleanor and her court no longer existed. She felt as if in a game as priests as she watched Louis being marched away. She walked to the blanket. With Woofan's strumming of the sad moment, words drifted to her ear: "The King father lay on the ashen crucifix. His last rites . . ." more respectful strumming, ". . . aware of his passing to heaven . . ."

Eleanor stood on the blanket's edge, stunned as much by the death as watching the rudeness of ministers take her husband away. Rhyser's dark strings tugged. Poor Louis gave sobs she could not comfort. A doleful music. Her agitated friends. He in the thick of priests. The net of notes pulling on her nerves. The blackest of news. Raw maddening emotions she could not share. The situation being unbearable – she wiped her cheeks. She was losing her sense of mind. In all the chaos, the music had to become something else. She stepped back onto the blanket. She covered her ears. The music stopped.

". . . coronation may be, if the Queen Mother approves . . ."

A carry-wagon arrived with room for four. Eleanor could see herself riding with Louis and Suger but never the dreadful Thierry. She could order Amira to pack, Arno to fetch Limona, then she realized, there was far more to consider to move a royal household. She felt something deeper: *When I heard my own father died I needed to be alone.*

Eleanor ran to her husband and stared, chasing away the priest's gazes. "It is rightful Louis that you return to Paris." The couple hugged a cherished farewell. He stepped high into the wagon and bitterly faced forward. Suger gave her a compassionate embrace, pulled his weight in, and sat next to Louis. Thierry lifted his leg and took his position in the center bench facing rearwards. He stretched out his arms as if to say there is no more room. Suger turned, "You will follow soon, dear child." The Parisian guard assembled in the distance.

Eleanor in her fine clothes trudged and melted down to the blanket, her back to the half-wall. Petronilla sat on her heart side in a hand-me-down white wool sweater, consoling in banal tones: "It is common for men to disregard women," then collapsed forward in tears. Eleanor brought her up. "Don't cry sister, not for me. Cry for fatherless Louis." Everyone seemed lost in a roaming void.

On Eleanor's right, Amira arrived presenting a large, mint-infused steamed towels from the nun's station. Amira, proud of her personal hair cut Eleanor had given as ritual for becoming First Maid, pulled steamed towels with Petronilla around Eleanor's legs. Amira tucked the white cloth. "A wrap for the Queen of France." Eleanor frowned at Amira's strange words – *Queen of France?* In waiting perhaps, but still. Poor Louis, now King Louis Sept of France! Her leg muscles warmed. The three women felt the sudden bright sun. Touching palms they watched the royal wagon clop away over the main Clain river bridge. The army of guards joined to head to Paris as the ground fogs lifted.

Woofan Rhyser gestured the curve of Eleanor's hair. He could emote every range of her emotion, but what music fits an insulted wife – brave enough to become a Queen – lost in the cave of her heart? This was his moment! To pull her from a roaming void, he would try something new. The troubadour sat atop the half-wall, holding out a white slate-rock. Amira smirked. She recalled having sold it to him long ago at a merchant table. His fingers fell to a rapid play on his lute. Petronilla, Eleanor, and Amira joined hands. As if one, they let their eyelids fall into the soft red world of the sun listening for his tune.

The convoy distanced from Poitiers. Louis gave a final wave to his wife flanked by two damisels sitting perfect posture along the wall. Lit by the sun, eyes closed, chins up, they held hands reminding him of angels over a church facade. Louis closed his eyes to keep the picture in mind, to comfort him in dark days ahead. Branch shadows passed overhead. Thierry smiled. "I relish the obedience training of Eleanor to come. She best enjoy her last strum, for the Church permits no troubadours in Royal Paris." Louis drew on the image fresh in his mind: *The pretty one in the portal entry, mine, all mine.* He opened his eyes. "God-oh-God, they are praying for me." Abbot Suger weighed the words. Thierry's words were closer to the truth as they carted away.

The leaving army stirred the forest to sounds. The damisels swayed to the musical rhythm Woofan was making of their world. By touch, by holding palms, they trued their balance and basked blissfully in the warming sun.

With the heavy news of the tumultuous departure, Arno came running with Ellen. Through the half-barricades, Mirielle and Sirq led Mathieu, Vesteed, Calbi and Daena to join the court. The listened to the rarest of troubadours.

Woofan Rhyser ran the river rock down a string. He passed an imperceptible heartbeat to the bass player, a rhythm to drum. He touched out three notes – three notes – a short rest, – a beat, interchanging a meter of seven. Sure-handed and lightly played, it planted a melody into one's mind. His rock rasped across the bridge of seven notes. A slow saw, a faster release. A player picked up the bass undertone of melody. Chords colored next. Woofan's words: A woman in a void sings a sad dream; she runs in her dream through a forest prime, a forest of swamps and snakes to test herself. Seven notes; a saw of the long bridge, back and forth, torturing the strings like the caw of seagulls, then letting go – a near erotic release of the neck. His music filled the air with all-feeling pulses. Lost in Rhyser's spell, the listeners rolled to meter. He picked color notes: releasing sorrows, pauses for breath. Eleanor's sympathetic thoughts ran with increasing tempo. 'Blindly we two joined as one / he thought I would be holy / didn't know I was lovely / shoved me away like a knave. / This void in my damisel heart / he will become that place now / I can call when I'm lonely.' Stirred with Rhyser's words, awareness came on. The purifying septemeter transformed Eleanor's spirit. The tambours drummed in sevens: 1 2, 1 2, 1 2 - 1, music of the fatherless: *We live by our forebears, now. Aquitaine parents are we. Damisel I'm married, now. Husband I'm Francia, now. Foreign lands to travel, ahead. To my fore-born hear me, now.* The end came with a freeing release. The troubadour had done his deed. Her state as a woman had come present, ready to go. She opened her eyes wide and alive. All of nature was born, and Eleanor's place in it had meaning.

Rhyser greeted the passionate court with eyefuls of joy. He was looking at the future, and she was smiling. He nodded to Amira, pocketing her rock, feeling it roll to his hip. To youthful applause, Woofan and his musicians bowed and left. The music in Amira made her recall when it all began. Ian Chaenus chanting 'Elixirs, Restorer of Youth.' Warm by her heart was her friend, so full of spark. "I am going to my new home," Eleanor expressed, looking toward the eastern sky in wonder of Paris.

On the blanket, Eleanor eagerly took off her ring for Petronilla to pass around the circular court. She examined her freshly bare hand. The brilliant jeweled ring captivated. Each person held the royal band in different angles of light until the glamor of the circle fell at last to Amira. The counselor held it, silvery in her palm, rolled it, and weighed it. The signs of promise shone in the sun. Two gold flecks in the Aquitaine quartz sparked and sparkled. Amira felt in her breast a new call: *'Show the woman, and you will change the world!'* She put the marvel back on Eleanor's delicate hand, touching forth her friend's rose-pink fingers.

Through troubadour song, through her ring, the circle felt her feelings; they beheld glimmers of their destiny. And if you lived in the age of Eleanor, although you may not know her exceptional thought, her budding capacity for majestic outcomes, you knew her compulsion.

"Yah'AOI! Woofan Rhyser!" Eleanor raised her arms to her gathered friends. "The girls will be as jealous as greenwood when they hear that Woofan serenaded us. Nothing so original has ever been sung. We all feel it, don't we?"

Eleanor wished she were a chap squire on a wood wagon to Paris, just to see Louis, to stroke his soft beard, to comfort his grieving heart. She wanted him to hear her music; to share her revelations of ecstasy, hope, and fine feelings about their possibilities. The army had gone, and forest life ranged rich with sounds. Natural thoughts came. She looked upon the bedazzling ring fresh on: *'Oh our fathers, my hand, my friends, love, oh, the idea of it. I summon you forth, ring round and true.'*

She was just thirteen.

1137 & Beyond

Acknowledgements

The 1100s was a long time ago. Little is known of Eleanor of Aquitaine with any certainty, much less her young life. This story brings her obscure childhood forward, based on enormous conjecture. Be comforted; she certainly had one. Carefully tracking Eleanor's well-traveled historic achievements and her passionate lineage provides clues to the code of a human being strongly motivated to blossom in the productive Aquitaine. Girls of independent nature are easily observed. As Eleanor achieved so much in her life in a female-resistant culture, it follows her self-determined upbringing must have been strong.

Civilization's advance depends upon the well-being afforded by its children. Childhood is not interesting until society prospers enough to afford the luxuries of culture and education; otherwise, only shear survival matters. Throughout medieval Europa, children were set to labor when they could walk. In The Young Life, 12th century Poitiers developed a fair form of self-government, allowing families to prosper and acquire wealth beyond necessities. The innovation of childhood as a passage to adolescence, overseen by parents in Eleanor's Aquitaine, was rare and fleeting.

Our setting is always under construction as this Light Renaissance permeates the dynamic Aquitaine spirit. Improvement and innovation permeate the times. Personal music and children's stories were coming into being, truth, and sources mattered. Historian James Burke noted that the Aquitaine duchy and its hydropower economy uniquely afforded time for troubadours, fanciful storytellers, stylish dress, the education of youth, and dance. He notes: "Dance. The Aquitaine could not get enough of it."

The story of young Eleanor fits the medieval mind when life was short. It is natural that little Eleanor and her friends question as children do. Through their probing experiences, readers understand key medieval social ideas and concepts.

This is all to say, the substrata for interesting childhood adventures to take place, and for the natural complexity in children to exhibit their unique abounding, curious probing character.

Young girls need a father's approval and attention. Their self-image and decisions they make correspond to the relationship values and how their fathers treat them. It is hard to imagine how Eleanor would become so powerfully assertive without William's affection and care. She lost her mother and brother at age six, and it is likely her father kept her from retreating to her shell. William Ten, a man of law and battle, has a relation more like Atticus Finch with Scout in *To Kill a Mockingbird*. When he dies, a close, supportive court evolves, a hallmark of her sovereignty. In short, a positive foundation is laid for Eleanor's girlhood, for she will face unmentionable times to come.

Dedicated readers of Eleanor's life always remind me she was not a one-note woman, which is why a pampered, cosseted, spoiled slippered Princess Eleanor is a poor myth. Pampered girls often turn out overly dependent and live a life uncurious, untravelled, and unexplored.

The novel is faithful to the actual people, places, and actions in the sequence of occurrence. No facts were ignored; rather the story was made to fit what is known. I can't tell you how much grief went into rewriting what I thought was the story of a fifteen-year-old girl becoming a queen, only to find in recent research of improved authority that she was thirteen, likely born in 1124.

Readers are entitled to know the facts apart from conjecture and pure fiction. The staff around Eleanor is mostly fictional. Historian Ralph Turner gave insights into her household. Records show by the time Eleanor reached the English-lands, a head maid was employed by the name of Amaria, though I use Amira for literary purposes. All family relations are historical. Although Eleanor had a steward when her father died, Ellen is fictional. The abduction and escapades of grandparents Dangerossa (Dangereuse de L' Isle Bouchard) and Troubadour William Nine are historical. Their controversial union and their story are detailed in the next novel. Mathieu Nouville is fictional, although the new industry of the light Renaissance based on water mill machining would have required such inventors who were undoubtedly young. Calbi Lebeau's faith, Catharism, is factual though the term was affixed later. In the 12th century, they called themselves Good Men. Many Aquitaine chevaliers and lords were Good Men. Maryam Assiri from Castile is fictional. However, a woman close to Eleanor's court called Marie de France wrote the famous youthful Lais of love and gallantry. Reyna Chasseigne is invented, although an ancient water mill stands north of Poitiers bearing the surname. Edeva Franklin's trial is a work of fiction. Such cases of dispute between royal and canon law occurred. No record remains since these are aural ordeals. That Eleanor spoke up in the trial is pure drama. However, she did sustain maternal property lines of women Franklins, mostly Crusade widows. To own land was a law unique to the Aquitaine.

The Fontevrault order for men and women and its controversial founding is historical. Robert Arbrissel and his followers Hersende and Petronille Chemillé are factual. Their interactions are conjecture. That Fontevrault Abbey provided Eleanor's schooling is unknown; however, she did place her children there.

Peter Abelard and Heloise were Eleanor's senior contemporaries. The letters are factual. Eleanor is said to have met Abelard. She just as likely met Heloise. We meet them both in the next book. That Eleanor read their letters is likely. Hersende was the first leader at Fontevrault, and Heloise was reputedly her daughter. Recent historical evidence supports correspondence taking place between Eleanor's Fontevrault and Heloise's Paraclete. Scholar Bruce Giles is a fictional composite of a likely courier of this liaison.

Thierry Galeran, the eunuch Templar Cistercian priest, may have come through history as a composite. Abbot Suger (suJAY), Chancellor Vermandois, Commander Thibault of Champagne traveled with Prince Louis and the army to wed damisel Eleanor and Louis in Bordeaux. Adam Suger's historical account is the basis for much of that chapter. Bernard of Clairvaux and the battles to the death between competing Popes are historical.

Troubadours like Cercamon – first introduced in the chapter Magicians of the Abbey – did sing in the Poitiers Palace when Eleanor was a girl. Troubadour Jaufre Rudel and Rancon, the Lord of Taillebourg, both had a historical relationship with Eleanor of obscure intimacy. They travel together into the journey of the Second Crusade, explored in the next novels. Wholly fictional are Mirielle Denni, the Plaganet Brothers, Woofan Rhyser, Sirq of Béziers. The mostly infantile poems of '*The Young Life*' are a literary device to ready the reader's ear for the beauty of actual troubadour song-poems Eleanor will hear in Paris and in the rest of the books.

Words

The Occitan O-XSE-tah) language was spoken more widely than formal French in Eleanor's time. Occitan is now in its extinction. Daniel Everett lectured on endangered languages and lost knowledge at the Long Now Foundation on March 02009. "Once these languages are lost, we lose ways of life, and records of ways of life, we lose solutions to problems, we lose classifications of plants and animals and folk knowledge of the world. We lose myths, folktales, lullabies, songs, poetry, and literature."

'Hrad' is a proper medieval word for tomboy. It cannot be found on the Internet or any dictionary but is well-defined in the vocabulary of 700AD, cited in the OED (Oxford English Dictionary). Were there an OFD to recall puns and idioms of Frankish origins.

Lief is an excellent medieval word to restore. It is the essence that precedes belief, as explained often in The Young Life. Outremer (EWT-ra-mare) meaning 'over the sea' is a period term for places reached by ship in the Mediterranean. It covers the current Middle East nations of Turkey, Syria, Lebanon, and Israel.

Damisel is my chosen spelling, sharing a hint of the poetic quality in mademoiselle. It is equivalent to maiden; the English term used when she becomes their queen.

Scholar's Riddle

In the custom of the ancients – Marie de France testifies to this – obscure portions of books can be expressed so that those who come after, might study with greater diligence to find further thought within. The *Young Life* begins with Amira meeting Spark (Eleanor). How did she get that name? How many years apart are they? They meet in what year, month, day, weekday, and hour?

Raise a Glass to Eleanor

Writing about Eleanor of Aquitaine connects one to a vast range of experts, readers, and artists that seek to recover her story from precious few accounts and artifacts. Throughout history, she has been somewhat of a blank canvas on which emerging values of current cultures are projected. My policy has been to let the unearthing of the past shock us rather than to look away. As L.P. Hartley remarked: "The past is a foreign country; they do things differently there."

In my vast reading and correspondence with experts, and I count over two hundred writings on my shelf, I have sifted through the discord of the sources. I hope to have brought you to where I have arrived, with pivotal insights into the entirely original experiences of Eleanor's multifaceted life.

Let me toast the following. My thanks to the first editing run by Sarah Esserlieu, Jennifer Esserlieu, and a grounded edit by Joanna Beaulieu. Simone Z. Endrich for later edits. Thanks to Jenice Graham Benedict for father, daughter, and equestrian points of view. Thanks to Carine Dartiguepeyrou for the bise. Special thanks to Michele Em for providing editorial opinions that ranged from angel floss to merde. She first read the screenplay, took on the novel, and in a second reading, helped keep the era intact. Thanks to Patricia Ancona on medieval clothing of the twelfth century. Kathryn Johnson for notes. Cindy Taylor and Siri Formsgaard for the Mino with my name on it; the buttons wore off capturing ideas. I am indebted to encouragement by historian Elizabeth A.R. Brown; troubadour translator: Leonardo Malcovati of trobar.org. Speaking your writing aloud is a writer's tip, but hearing others read your story out loud is a precious gift. Thanks to opera singer Courtney Huffman whose narrations rounded the music of stories and announcer Robert Crowley for a fine male voice that brought balance.

Open a second bottle for Marilyn Yalom for her inspiring *How the French Invented Love*, validating the 12th-century shift to romantic culture. Eleanor is a chapter one figure. Marilyn was kind to read and provide many erudite remarks about jewelry, marriage rites, and pronunciation to reify the Age of Eleanor.

Principal Characters and Page of Appearance

Character names differ from the historic panoply. Although she was born Alienor, I've also given Eleanor the names she accepted from friends and cultures throughout the series.

Jofree de Rancon, Lord of Taillebourg, is spelled Jofree, not Geoffrey, to favor the greater Geoffrey, the Duke of Anjou, who will figure mostly in Eleanor's later life. He was a Prince and troubadour (trobar) who sang in the vernacular Occitan language, never in Latin.

Initially Fonte Ebraudi in Latin, I use the vernacular Fontevrault, which I prefer to Fontevraud, the French government modernization. I use the aggressive medieval consonants as in Chanson de Rollant, not Roland.

Louis VII. 'Louis Sept' sounds proper, better than 'Louis the Seventh.' Three short syllables rather than five that lumber. This is a choice of ear for his character. Louis Sept is voiced as LoowEE SET (Louisette); the 'p' is silent. In Latin church settings, he is called Ludovicus.

Page numbers refer to the print edition of 312 pages.

Adam Suger (suJAY): abbot of saint-denis, p264

Aenor of Châtellerault: duchess, mother of eleanor, p36

Aigret, Little William: brother of eleanor, p34

Alberic: jongleur, p61

Amira Neas: first maid, counselor, and secretary, p11

Armstrong of Alsace, Lance Du Lac: chevalier, p162

Arno Allant: chevalier, eleanor's bodyguard when ruling france, p18

Berry and Guisana: disciples at fontevrault, p223

Bleddri: jongleur, p59

Calbi Lebeau: chevalier, cathar priest, p18

Cercamon: troubadour, p116

Daena Hanah: slave from england, life partner of calbi, p139

Dangerossa: grandmother of eleanor, p44

Edeva Franklin: franklin, farmer, p133

Eleanor, Alienor, Spark, Helienordis, Al'nor, Elle: princess, duchess, queen, p16

Ellen: steward to eleanor, magistrate of poitiers, p43

Envoy of Paris: diplomat of king louis, p252

Genet Carrelle: teacher of presences, p125

Helena Neas: orphanage helper, mother of amira, p11

—◦◦◦—

What we call France and England did not exist in the twelfth century. Eleanor and her family ruled those regions as if they were the same place. By her life's end, she has placed her progeny in the thrones of what would become Spain, Italy, Germany, France, and England. Eleanor attained one of the broadest views of the world, bringing Europe into the thirteenth century.

Author

Mark Richard Beaulieu is author of the six-book series called the Eleanor Code. He is an expert on the 12th-century world of Eleanor of Aquitaine. Mark is known as an accomplished author, collected painter, award-winning photographer, and innovative software technologist. Mark is on a first name basis with Eleanor and her staff, cooking for her from time to time. Mr. Beaulieu trained as a studio artist and holds a Master of Fine Arts from the University of California at Davis, and a Bachelor of Fine Arts from Trinity University in San Antonio, Texas. He grew up in Heidelberg, New York City, Texas, and California where he lives in Escondido with his wife and pets, watching their children come into the new word.

The Young Life is his first book in the six-part Eleanor Code series.

Challenge can be a book required to be read. Forced to take Medieval Studies at the University of Texas at Austin in 1971, I picked up a thin red volume translating Andreas Capellanus "Art of Courtly Love," written and reedited between 1170 and 1190. The subject has concerned me ever since. ~mrb Escondido, California, Spring 2012.

The six books of the Eleanor Code series, with her primary identities:
1: Eleanor of Aquitaine - The Young Life · Alienor 1124–1137
2: Eleanor of Aquitaine - The Journey East · Helienordis 1138–1148
3: Eleanor of Aquitaine - The Voyage West · Al'nor 1148–1151
4: Eleanor of Aquitaine - The Generation · Elanor 1151–1167
5: Eleanor of Aquitaine - Love + Rebellion · Elle 1168–1173
6: Eleanor of Aquitaine - The Legacy · Eleanor 1173–1204

The spine colors are yellow, gold, blue, green, scarlet, purple.
A select bibliography of works and other Eleanoria can be found at:
www.eleanorofaquitaine.net

Made in the USA
Monee, IL
12 November 2020